Heartbeat after heartbeat went by as Salim's eyes darted back and forth, but the expected attack failed to manifest. The room was silent, save for his own heavy breathing. Then the blood pounding in his ears calmed, and he heard a new sound—a low, dry whimpering. Sword at the ready, he stepped forward and kicked the crackling shroud farther into the room.

The third ghoul was curled up in the back of the burial chamber, hunched over into a fetal position in order to pull itself as far as it could into an empty wall niche. It clutched its knees and moaned again as Salim advanced.

"Please," it whined. Coming from the twisted form, the voice was shockingly human. It strained to shape the words with its grotesquely overlong tongue. "Please don't kill. I'll go. No more hunting. No more brothers. Just graves. Please."

In its fear, the ghoul came closest to resembling the man it had once been. Had the creature's previous incarnation made a similar plea, as farmer to ghoul? Salim said nothing, but the ghoul nodded anyway. Chin to knee, it curled tighter and closed its eyes.

"Hungry," it whispered. From behind bruised-black eyelids, a tear welled and slid down the creature's face. "So hungry."

This time Salim did respond.

"I understand," he said.

Then, with both hands, he lifted his sword and brought it down.

The Pathfinder Tales Library

Prince of Wolves by Dave Gross
Winter Witch by Elaine Cunningham
Plague of Shadows by Howard Andrew Jones
The Worldwound Gambit by Robin D. Laws
Master of Devils by Dave Gross
Death's Heretic by James L. Sutter
Song of the Serpent by Hugh Matthews

Death's Heretic

James L. Sutter

paizo
PUBLISHING

Cover art by Kekai Kotaki.
Cover design by Andrew Vallas.
Map by Robert Lazzaretti.

Paizo Publishing, LLC
7120 185th Ave NE, Ste 120
Redmond, WA 98052
paizo.com

ISBN 978-1-60125-369-9 (mass market paperback)
ISBN 978-1-60125-370-5 (ebook)

Publisher's Cataloging-In-Publication Data
(Prepared by The Donohue Group, Inc.)

Sutter, James L.
  Death's Heretic / James L. Sutter.

  p. ; cm. -- (Pathfinder tales)

  Set in the world of the role-playing game, Pathfinder.
  Issued also as an ebook.
  ISBN: 978-1-60125-369-9 (mass market pbk.)

  1. Soul--Fiction. 2. Abduction--Fiction. 3. Immortalism--Fiction.
4. Imaginary places--Fiction. 5. Good and evil--Fiction. 6. Fantasy
fiction. I. Title. II. Title: Pathfinder adventure path. III. Series:
Pathfinder tales library.

PS3619.U884 D438 2011
813/.6

First printing November 2011.

Printed in the United States of America.

For the Lafond clan, who never doubted.

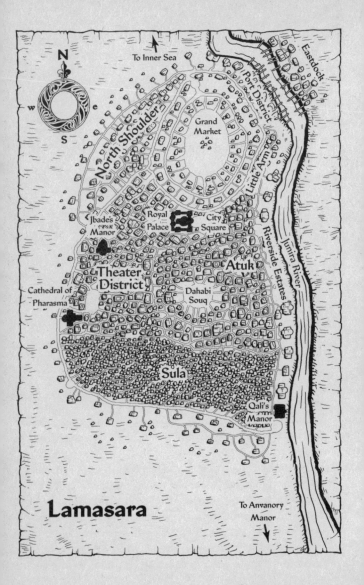

To Inner Sea

N

W E

S

North Shoulder

Grand Market

Port District

Eastdock

Little Arm

Jbade's Manor

Royal Palace

City Square

Atuk

Riverside Estates

Jumira River

Theater District

Dahabi Souq

Cathedral of Pharasma

Sula

Qali's Manor

Lamasara

To Anvanory Manor

Prologue

Death always smelled the same.

After all this time, it wasn't the stink that got to him—the reek of excrement, of putrefying flesh and organs never meant to see daylight. That was expected, easily imaginable by even the greenest killer. No, what stuck with Salim was the insufferable *sweetness* of it, the fact that behind the stomach-churning stench was the saccharine ghost of fermentation, cloying and coating the insides of his nostrils. It was impossible not to respond to it. Somewhere in the back of his brain, the part that was little more than animal, he knew that smell meant a kill, and that a kill meant success. That part of him wanted to crow, to roll in the filth until it covered him like a badge. On its own, the stink was tolerable. Combined with that sweetness, it made him want to vomit.

The undead had that smell, too. With some it was musty and old, others mixed with the heavy scent of wet earth, and still others—those that walked among the living without notice—so faint that the lightest perfume could cover it. Yet it was always there.

The ghouls had it in abundance, their dry, stretched flesh never quite sure if it wanted to heal or slough off completely. Without looking down, Salim stepped carefully over the nearest corpse and pressed up against the wall, studying the doorway.

He'd killed most of the pack, though not before they'd glutted themselves on the parishioners. It hadn't been difficult. These weren't civilized horrors like the monstrous citizens of Nemret Noktoria, but rather the newly risen dead, as naive in their own way as the rural farmers they fed upon. They were strong, and hungry, but knew nothing else. They'd never been hunted. Fear was something they inspired in others, and by the time Salim taught them otherwise, it was too late.

Still, it was the easy prey that surprised you, and there was no point in taking chances. There were still three of them beyond the door, waiting like cornered rats to rend and tear. It would only take one scratch from a poisoned finger-turned-claw to stiffen his limbs and leave him paralyzed, helpless while they fed—or, worse yet, let the infection in their bite spread through his veins like wildfire, burning out his flesh until he became one of them. No, this was no time to get cocky. Taking the ghouls might be easy, but there was no room for error. The execution had to be flawless.

The glow of his torch was barely enough to light the antechamber in which he stood, its flickers seemingly swallowed up by the black void beyond the archway. Fixing that was the first order of business. If they went for his light—and they certainly would—the burns they'd get trying to take it would be nothing compared to the disadvantage his human eyes would be in the tomb's darkness.

Salim glanced around the crypt, silent save for the crackling of burning pitch. It was humble, little more than a brick-walled pit with steps leading up to the church, but it was this village's holy of holies. Each of a dozen narrow wall niches held a cloth-wrapped form, most still thick with dust—the ghouls hadn't bothered feeding on these mummified husks when the church graveyard bore riper, more putrescent fruit. Hands folded, covered with the withered threads of what were once flowers, the honored dead might have continued their dreamless sleep undisturbed, were it not for the two ghoul corpses that fouled the gray stone floor.

They were exactly what he needed. Without a second thought, Salim moved to the nearest niche and took hold of the corpse's homespun burial shroud. A single pull sent its contents spinning to the floor, leaving Salim holding several yards of cloth, which he promptly put to the torch.

Flame caught the simple embroidery and raced up its edges. As he let the flickering tongues writhe over the sheet, Salim glanced down at its former occupant. A young man, and not recently dead by the look of him— tendons showed through withered flesh, but they still held the sack of bones in the rough shape of a man. The body's relative cohesion gave Salim an idea, and he set down the torch, wrapped the now merrily blazing cloth around the blade of his sword, then leaned down to scoop up the corpse with his other arm. With the grisly parcel clutched to his chest like a lover, he moved along the wall toward the doorway.

No time like the present. With a flick of his sword, Salim sent the burning shroud sailing into the room, the fabric flapping open to light the sepulcher. Something hissed in the darkness, and he followed the light with his other prize, swinging the corpse around the corner and into the room at shoulder height.

The ruse worked. Thinking Salim had charged in after the blazing blanket, two of the ghouls pounced, dropping from the walls and ceiling to rend the corpse's brittle flesh. In the second it took them to realize their mistake, the real Salim was among them, sword flashing.

The ghouls' leathery hide was stronger than human skin, but it still parted easily under the edge of his blade. Salim's initial thrust caught the first one in the center of its back and slid in smoothly, the flat of the blade kept parallel to the ground to avoid getting stuck between the creature's ribs. His recovery gave the second ghoul time to face him, but not enough to get its glistening claws up. Salim's swing didn't take its head clean off—his sword was light, and that sort of thing was more for storybooks and campfire tales than real battles—but it did the job, sending the creature slumping backward, head lolling to one side on a thin strand of flesh. Salim ignored it, withdrawing to a defensive posture with his back to the wall next to the archway, waiting for the third ghoul's attack.

It didn't come. Heartbeat after heartbeat went by as Salim's eyes darted back and forth, but the expected attack failed to manifest. The room was silent, save for his own heavy breathing. Then the blood pounding in his ears calmed, and he heard a new sound—a low, dry whimpering. Sword at the ready, he stepped forward and kicked the crackling shroud farther into the room.

The third ghoul was curled up in the back of the burial chamber, hunched over into a fetal position in order to pull itself as far as it could into an empty wall niche. It clutched its knees and moaned again as Salim advanced.

"Please," it whined. Coming from the twisted form, the voice was shockingly human. It strained to shape the words with its grotesquely overlong tongue. "Please don't kill. I'll go. No more hunting. No more brothers. Just graves. Please."

In its fear, the ghoul came closest to resembling the man it had once been. Had the creature's previous incarnation made a similar plea, as farmer to ghoul? Salim said nothing, but the ghoul nodded anyway. Chin to knee, it curled tighter and closed its eyes.

"Hungry," it whispered. From behind bruised-black eyelids, a tear welled and slid down the creature's face. "So hungry."

This time Salim did respond.

"I understand," he said.

Then, with both hands, he lifted his sword and brought it down.

In the aftermath, Salim recovered his torch and let the light of it and the blackened, sputtering shroud show him the room in all its meager glory. It was as humble as the outer chamber, but it was clear that the room had been both crypt and funereal preparation chamber. A long stone slab that was almost an altar sat to one end, surrounded by the mundane implements of embalming, while the walls held more spaces for bodies, unlit lanterns, and fine tapestries showing the glory of various gods, from stag-headed Erastil to the Lady of Graves herself. Clearly, these villagers worshiped an array of divine beings, pooling their resources into a single church.

And hedging their bets, Salim thought.

Setting his torch down on the altar, Salim moved over to the baptismal font in the corner and looked down into its shallow basin. The holy water was still clear and unsullied—either the ghouls hadn't had time to soil it properly, or one of them had accidentally been splashed and the rest had learned to keep their distance. Salim's eyes, hooded and tired, stared back at him from the water's reflection. The rest of his face—dark hair, dark skin, and thin, dark beard—all blended together into the chamber's gloom. The splashes of black ghoul blood didn't help, either. Balancing his sword along the stone where the font emerged from the wall, he leaned over and splashed his face, then began scrubbing his hands vigorously, setting clouds of black filth blooming like ink through the water.

And not just black, he realized. There was red in the water as well. He glanced quickly down at his robes. Had one of the ghouls managed a lucky scratch without him realizing it? If so, he needed to move quickly to avoid sharing their fate.

But no—he was unharmed. Looking down at the basin, he realized that the blood was welling up from beneath his fingernails, his hands slowly weeping red into the baptismal font. The realization was followed immediately by a telltale tickle on his upper lip.

Oh. Of course. Salim dipped his hands back into the icy water. From behind him came the soft flutter of wings, as of a flock of doves suddenly startled into flight.

"Hello, Salim."

"Ceyanan." Salim waited a moment, hands gripping the font's stone lip, then collected himself and turned.

The angel was floating in the chamber's center, its toes pointed like a dancer two feet above the floor. The robes that flowed around it in an undetectable breeze were gray against worm-pale skin, and combined with the black hair they made the figure look like a charcoal sketch. Its features were too perfect to be truly beautiful, like a marble statue, and androgynous enough that not even the sheer fabric revealed a gender.

More arresting than all of these were the black-feathered wings that sprang from its back. Even half-folded, they were clearly not normal appendages. More shadow than form, they gave the impression that if they spread, they would not so much unfurl as bloom, the way the ghoul's filth had expanded in the water of the font. Yet the angel's floating seemed to have little to do with them, and they remained still, the individual feathers flickering in and out of visibility. It looked around the room.

"I love what you've done with the place," Ceyanan said.

Salim ignored the apparition and instead located a clean patch of sleeve, which he used to wipe his nose, succeeding only in smearing the blood around.

"Is this really necessary?" he asked, gesturing at bloody lips. "Every time?"

The angel laughed, as innocent as a child, and spread its hands.

"Consider it a gift, Salim. What better way to know that you're still alive?"

Salim let that one pass, but the angel wasn't finished.

"Besides," it said, motioning toward the floor, "was *that* necessary?"

Salim looked down. He was almost standing on the corpse that had acted as his decoy. The young man's arms and legs, once locked tight in the stately constriction of the dead, were now sacks of shattered bone, flesh tattered by ghoul claws and the rough landing. Salim shrugged.

"He didn't object," he said, but he was still careful not to kick the corpse as he stepped over to one of the ornate tapestries and began systematically cleaning his sword. Ghoul blood had already dried along its length, crusting both the shining blade and the twisted, melted-looking hilt with filth.

"They rarely do," the angel acknowledged. "But that's neither here nor there. You know that I come bearing tidings."

"And here I thought this was a purely social visit." Salim sheathed the blade. "But please, Ceyanan, don't keep me in suspense—pray tell me what the bitch-goddess wants from me now." He turned to lock eyes with the angel. "Is there a vampiric orgy in Caliphas that I'm to break up? A mummy that needs unwrapping? Or did someone forget to dig a grave deep enough, and a coyote ran away with some bones?"

The angel frowned.

"You should learn to show proper respect," it said.

"And you should know by now that I only give it where it's due." The mocking politesse was gone now, replaced by a cool, smooth anger. "If your lady wants to win my love, she's got a long road ahead of her."

The angel waved its hand as if shooing a fly, refusing to be baited. It was an old game.

"Have it your way," it said. "You have the opportunity to work great justice in this world, but you're welcome to see it as an order if it pleases you."

Salim waited.

Ceyanan sighed. "No undead this time. Rather the opposite, actually—something uniquely suited to your skills. A kidnapping."

"Kidnapping?" Despite his resentment, Salim couldn't quite keep the curiosity out of his voice.

"That's hardly my usual fare. Or yours, for that matter. How do I factor in?"

"In this case, the victim is already dead."

The angel paused a moment to see if Salim would say anything. He didn't.

"The merchant in question," Ceyanan continued, "was the target of a routine assassination—nothing special there. But after his death, his soul was stolen from the Boneyard before it could pass on to its final reward. Not destroyed—stolen. The local clerics have been unable to raise the body, and now the kidnappers are offering to sell back the man's spirit. Naturally, the church is more than a little upset. We've already got the local clergy working on the problem, but we'd like you to step in and handle things. You might consider it a nice change of pace." The angel's hand swung to encompass the crypt and the already decaying ghouls.

"Makes sense," Salim said. "Letting a soul go missing hardly reflects well on the church. But why me? And why don't they just pay the ransom and be done?"

"The situation is in Thuvia."

Thuvia. The name hit Salim like a blow. That was too close. Far too close. But if the kidnapping were in Thuvia—

"The sun orchid elixir," he said.

"Precisely." The angel looked pleased.

"Stealing a soul and selling it back for a shot at immortality. No wonder the Gray Lady's pissed."

"Now you understand," Ceyanan said. "You'll depart immediately."

Salim gritted his teeth. "You know I don't like being that close."

"As you so eloquently pointed out, winning your affection is not my first priority. Your familiarity with the region and its customs will make you that much more efficient. And you might even enjoy your time there."

"Not that I have a choice."

The angel smiled down at him again.

"You did, once."

Salim opened his mouth to respond, but the angel had already grown transparent, its voice a whisper that receded into the distance.

"Enjoy the desert, Salim."

Chapter One
A Death in the Family

Salim stepped off the deck of the barge and into a land of perpetual summer.

Not that it hadn't been hot on the ship—it was warm in Ostenso as well, the ships' boards searing the sailors' callused feet. It had been the same on the Osirian river barge, pulled upstream by a team of oxen, though the wealthy Osirians were loath to go without creature comforts, and had their own ways of dealing with the elements. Yet here, on the end of the sweltering pier, Salim was confronted once more by the dry, baking heat that comes only from the desert. Not even the spray from the river could completely eliminate the fine, particulate grit that permeated the air. Alkaline salts weathered the wood of the dock and made it crack and splinter, and dust too fine to be seen coated his clothes immediately, making the fabric smooth and stiff, as if it had been starched. The sun beat down, and the air clawed at his throat as the deckhands behind him cursed each other and began off-loading oversized barrels of trade goods.

Salim loved it. Moving down the pier, past fishing dories and slender single-masted pleasure craft, he realized for the first time in years how much he had missed it—the cleansing heat of the sun, the beads of sweat in his hair. Man is made for the desert, they said here, for what is man but dust and water? In the end, everyone returns to those. Or almost everyone.

Past the edge of the dock, Lamasara spread out before him. Though the reeds along the river's bank immediately began to give way to the dust and hardpan of desiccated and well-trodden earth, the city that sprouted there was as bright as any garden. Just past the boards and cart roads of the waterfront, the city opened itself in a barrage of color and sound. Awnings dyed every hue of the rainbow shaded market stalls in which hawkers pressed their wares on passersby at the top of their lungs. Irritable camels stomped and spat, and urchins ran riot through the streets, thieving what they could from greengrocers and wine merchants. And everywhere—everywhere—there was music. Sitars and tambourines and low horns, and a thousand others besides, blending in with the crowd until it was impossible to tell the rumble of the drummers from the breathing of the city itself.

Salim stepped quickly across the road and let the market envelop him. With his purse tucked securely inside his dark robes, and his sword conspicuous enough to earn him a wide berth from the pickpockets, he strode confidently, taking it all in. There was a reason they called Lamasara the jewel of the desert. Here was Thuvia's artistic heart in full flutter, the fabulous wares and performances of which even the pale northerners of Avistan had tales. He moved past an ascetic lying on a bed of nails—the trick simple physics, not even worth a second glance—and a parade of scantily clad dancers before he began to reach the real attractions. Jugglers spinning dozens of knives, some while blindfolded. Drummers frantically pounding out a rhythm while a child-sized rat creature danced awkwardly from side to side on its hind legs at the command of its master. There was even a beautiful fire-eater whose limbs were tattooed with flames, distinguished from the others not so much by her beauty as by the fact that she managed to light a candle through a small piercing where throat met collarbone. This last he stopped to watch for a moment, meeting her gaze and nodding approval as she mutely acknowledged the applause and collected coins. Then he turned and moved to the nearest stall.

"Greetings, honored one! May the sun smile upon you." The man was a poultry merchant, and the tiny stall stank of the crowded cages.

"And you as well," Salim returned, slipping back into the old accent with barely a thought. "I need directions."

"Ah!" The merchant clapped his hands. "You *think* you need directions, my friend. But what you actually need is a chicken!"

So fast that he hardly seemed to move, the man suddenly held one of his half-plucked charges, beady eyes staring at Salim over the top of the merchant's meaty fingers.

"Not today, friend," Salim replied. "Only directions." He held up a coin.

"Oh no, my friend, no!" The chicken merchant made a shooing motion, the dazed bird bobbing up and down in his hand. "There's no way I could take a good man's money for something as simple as directions. The Dawnflower would burn my eyes for such lack of charity. No, I cannot accept your money. But neither can I let a good man go undernourished, as you so clearly are. See how your bones hang loose beneath your clothes, and your skin grows waxy and pale as an Avistani! It would be next to murder, honored one, and I am an honest man."

The patter was familiar, so different in tone from the blatant northern merchants, but Salim couldn't afford to spend time haggling properly. Instead, he turned to one of the street children lounging nearby and whistled sharply, motioning him over. The child came, though not within reach. Salim jerked his head toward the merchant's cages.

"You want a chicken?"

The child nodded.

"Where can I find the temple of Pharasma?"

"Southwest of the square," the child answered promptly, pointing down the main thoroughfare. Salim flicked his eyes sideways at the merchant, who nodded.

"My thanks," he said, and flipped the child the coin. The boy caught it eagerly, and immediately began haranguing the merchant. Salim strode away without looking back. It was as it should be. Children had all the time in the world to bargain, more than even the merchant. In the end, the boy would get his chicken, and for a fair price.

Past the town square, the swirl and noise of the bazaar gave way to more permanent structures. Here were the nicer shops, the ones whose owners could afford to choose their positions and let business come to them, as well as the theaters and music halls for which Lamasara was famous. Even at this early hour, open doors let the sounds of rehearsals and matinee performances drift out into the street, both advertisement and enticement. Come nightfall, the city would be ablaze with lanterns of every color.

The cathedral of Pharasma, Lady of Graves, stood toward the outer edge of the district, where the close-packed commercial buildings began to space out and give way to people's homes and the desert proper. It rose up stark and black against the sky, its dark walls in startling contrast to the ocher mud brick of the buildings around it. Here were the same high, gothic spires and sharply peaked roofs that would have been at home in the streets of Egorian or Oppara. Clearly the priests in Lamasara had been heavily influenced by their northern comrades, rather than the lighter, airier practices of the south. The artificially darkened stone undoubtedly absorbed the sun's heat and trapped it, turning the place into an oven on the hottest days, but still he saw few concessions toward local building styles. The goddess of death, birth, and prophecy was not one for concessions, and clearly her architects in Lamasara were of the same mind.

He moved up a wide cascade of stairs toward two enormous doors of blackened iron, swung halfway open to catch the breeze. He approached the gap and was met by a slightly portly young man with hands folded into the sleeves of his cassock.

"Blessings," the man said politely, inclining his head. "How may the church be of service?" The man's black garments were perfectly arranged, but his youth and the careful, intentional way in which he affected the flat tones of a Pharasmin marked him as an acolyte rather than a full priest. He gazed at Salim with what he probably hoped was unsettling directness.

"My name is Salim Ghadafar," Salim responded. "I'm here to see the high priest."

Clearly he was expected. The acolyte's thin veneer of detachment melted away, and he seemed to shrink inside his robes. He quickly stepped aside.

"Certainly, honored one," he said, bowing in earnest now and motioning toward the doors. "Please, enter."

Salim stepped through the doors, and the acolyte followed. Inside, the temple's receiving chamber was vast, stretching perhaps fifty feet or more to an arched ceiling and stained-glass windows showing scenes of judgment and redemption. Pillars of gray marble rose up at strategic points around the room, and the matching tile of the floor was spotless, ringing with the sound of footsteps. Acolytes and priests in cassocks identical to that of Salim's doorman moved quietly and purposefully around the room, conferring with each other or efficiently carrying out the business of the church. Salim strode forward across the massive chamber, half leading his guide.

As they made their way across the tiles, he heard a number of the room's other residents fall silent, followed shortly by a low buzz as clerics nudged each other and acolytes put their heads together, gesturing surreptitiously. Their whispers were too low for him to follow, but he could imagine their content easily enough.

They reached the far side of the public chamber and came to the archway Salim had expected. Here he let his guide take over, leading him through the maze of hallways and smaller chambers. Salim probably could have navigated them unaided, but there was no need, and here the church's layout would begin to vary to cater to the needs of the locals.

The building was a labyrinthine structure, closer to an abbey or monastery than a simple church. Dormitories and kitchens for the resident brothers and sisters mixed freely with the embalming chambers and other facilities integral to the church's function. Salim estimated that thirty or forty clergy and seminarians must make their homes here, with more undoubtedly living outside its walls, mingling with Lamasara's faithful and tending to their needs.

They came to a wide stone stairwell that spiraled both up and down. The latter, Salim knew, would lead to the extensive catacombs beneath the church, in which generations of Lamasara's worthies would be interred. But instead of paying them a visit, the acolyte led Salim to the right, up the stairs that rose in a freestanding wave toward the ceiling. The youth took a step up, then stopped and glanced back at Salim anxiously.

"Apologies, honored one, but I have made an assumption. I presumed you meant High Priest Khoyar, as it was he who set me waiting for you. If you wish to see the masters of birth or prophecy, I can take you to their towers instead."

"The one who sent you will be fine," Salim said, and motioned for the acolyte to continue on. In theory, every church of Pharasma was run by a triumvirate of priests representing the goddess's threefold concerns—birth, death, and prophecy. That was in theory, and it held in some of the bigger cities. In practice, many churches had one priest—often the priest concerned with death, the goddess's most public face—who rose above his or her fellows, becoming the de facto leader of the church as a whole. As it sounded like this Khoyar had.

After passing through two more floors with yet more living quarters and studies, the stairs rose in earnest, becoming a tight spiral encased in a rounded tower. As the two men ascended, narrow arrow-slit windows gave Salim increasingly majestic views. From one side, he could see out over the cathedral's roof to the jumbled buildings of Lamasara as they spread out organically from the river's edge. Then the stairs would lead him around a hundred and eighty degrees, and he would be looking out over the outlying farms and pastures that fed the city, all the way to where the sparse plant life gave out completely and the river's legacy was subsumed by the endless dunes of the desert.

At last they reached the top, where the stairs became a small landing in front of a wooden door covered in ornate whorls of wrought iron. The acolyte knocked.

"Enter," a voice called. The acolyte pressed the latch and swung the door inward.

Salim was blasted by light. Beyond the doorway, the half-lit winding of the stairway was replaced by the full fury of the desert sun pouring in through rows of tall windows in the southern and eastern walls. Here was the view that Salim had caught snatches of through the arrow loops, now laid bare before him: a sinuous line of green weaving through the city and then running away through the trackless sands until both blended with distant clouds and were lost. The rest of the room was made up as a tastefully wealthy reception chamber, with a few low couches and freestanding sculptures representing the Boneyard and the Lady of Graves seated on her throne. It was a small room, perhaps half the width of the tower, and a doorway hung with a beaded curtain likely led to a sleeping chamber in the other half. Salim took all this in with a glance, then returned his attention to the distant horizon.

"I see you appreciate the view."

The man who came through the curtain was tall and lean, perhaps in his late forties. Though his cassock was of the same cut as the acolyte's, hanging almost to the floor, it was clear that here was no simple dyed wool or linen, but rather black silk of the highest caliber. The piping on it was silver thread, and matched both the spiral-shaped holy symbol that hung from a chain around his neck and a large silver ring on his left hand. Atop his dark hair sat a small, boxlike hat.

"How could I not?" Salim responded, and the man smiled. His thin, clean-shaven face was strong and proud, with the hooked Thuvian nose and darkly tanned skin, yet something in the way he held his lips—thin and tight—kept him from being truly handsome, giving him a somewhat effete, officious air.

"Another child of the desert. As it should be." The priest put his palms together and bowed at the waist, the forty-five-degree angle appropriate when greeting an equal—an honor, given the man's station. "I am High Priest Khoyar Roshan, steward of Death and shepherd of Lamasara's faithful. And you are Salim."

Salim inclined his head in acknowledgment, yet did not return the bow. The high priest's smile tightened, and he straightened again.

"I was told you have a problem," Salim said.

"That much is true." Khoyar moved toward one of the couches. When Salim made no motion to follow, the priest remained standing. "The situation is most unusual, though I don't know that it requires such an honor as your traveling halfway across the world."

"In my experience," Salim said, "our opinions count for little where the gods are concerned."

Khoyar's smile quirked and disappeared.

"Yes. Well." He waved away Salim's guide, who immediately disappeared down the stairs at a run, then started toward them himself. "I would offer you the church's hospitality," he continued, his voice cooled to the familiar Pharasmin flatness, "but I imagine that after such a long voyage you're eager to be about your business."

"Always," Salim replied.

"Then please, come," Khoyar said, and led Salim back down the twisting stairs.

Another man might have wondered why the high priest had brought him all the way up to his solarium, only to lead him back down again, but Salim had too much experience with church bureaucrats like Khoyar for that. The symbolism was petty but effective—by making Salim climb up to him for no good reason, Khoyar had established his position of dominance. By countering with calculated rudeness, Salim had reminded the high priest that he existed outside the normal church hierarchy. They were even.

"The situation was brought to my attention nine days ago," Khoyar said as they made their way down the circling stairs. "The victim, Faldus Anvanory, is a minor Taldan noble and merchant of some means, come to Lamasara several years ago in search of eternal youth, like all the others." He made a gesture of dismissal. "Unlike most, however, he managed to find it. He was invited to the most recent auction by Queen Zamere herself, and when the bids were tallied, he found that he'd won a single dose of the sun orchid elixir."

"And for just a king's ransom," Salim put in. Sun orchid elixir—the rare concoction that was such an integral part of Thuvia's reputation among foreigners—didn't really grant eternal youth, just a temporary rewinding of the clock. Most buyers could expect maybe fifty more years from a single vial. But fifty years was a long time to a human, and more than enough time to invest and save up for a second dose.

"Quite," Khoyar said. "Yet before the elixir could be delivered, Anvanory's brutalized corpse was found alone in his study. Not entirely surprising—these things happen, and the prospect of potentially eternal life tends to anger one's enemies. As it happens, Anvanory foresaw that possibility as well, and had already made arrangements with the church in case of just such an occurrence. It wasn't until we tried to resurrect him that the mystery revealed itself in earnest."

They reached the topmost of the cathedral's floors, which Salim had passed through on his way up the staircase, and Khoyar paused on the landing for effect. Salim waited.

"The soul," Khoyar intoned, "was gone."

Salim nodded.

"We knew, of course, that a soul can be destroyed." Khoyar was getting into the story now, clearly enjoying its telling. "It's expensive, but there are criminal groups who know how to keep a witness silenced even beyond the bounds of death. Yet our communion with the goddess made it clear that the truth was stranger yet: Faldus Anvanory may have been killed on the Material Plane, but his soul did not cease with his breath. It passed on through the veil, joining the River of Souls and progressing all the way to the Boneyard. And there it went missing."

"Missing?" Even though he already knew the basics of the story, Salim couldn't keep the incredulity entirely out of his voice. Though there were a few entities—hags and the like—that might dare to raid the River of Souls on its way to Pharasma's Boneyard, the beings who shepherded souls once they arrived in Death's realm were nothing if not precise.

"Missing," Khoyar confirmed emphatically. They started down a long and empty hallway, interrupted at irregular intervals by doors set into the walls. "It was around this time that the family was contacted by the assassins—or rather, the kidnappers. The scroll appeared on the doorstep of their estate, possibly delivered by magic, though nothing we were able to trace. The offer is simple: Hand over the sun orchid elixir, and the kidnappers will release Faldus's soul once more, allowing him to be resurrected. Fail to do so, and the Taldan lord will be denied eternity, both in this world and the next."

"And how are they to deliver the ransom?" Salim asked.

"A drop-off in the Ethereal Plane, of all places." Khoyar looked solemn. "As if we needed further proof of their abilities. Not only can they steal a soul from the Boneyard, but they expect to be able to safely retrieve their payment from the mists of that half-seen realm. Naturally, I offered to make the delivery, should Lord Anvanory's heir elect to capitulate."

"Of course. How did he react?"

"She. And furiously, as might be expected. His daughter came straight to us for consultation. She was torn between rage at the kidnappers and duty to her father, but she elected to wait and see what came of our investigation—what's now your investigation. What's more, she's thrown the full wealth of the Anvanory family behind your efforts, generously covering any costs the church may incur in the process. The elixir itself is being held under heavy guard at the royal palace until a decision's been made regarding its recipient."

Salim mulled this over. "You've already interrogated the house staff, I presume?"

"As well as everyone who visited the manor in the two days prior. Both magically and via more conventional methods, thanks to the Lamasaran Guard."

"And you've attempted subsequent divinations?"

"Certainly." Khoyar spread his hands. "And not just the Church of Pharasma, either. The Anvanory estate has funded divinations from all the major temples in the city—the bankers of Abadar, the priests of the Dawnflower—with similar results. It's clear that Faldus's soul made it to the Boneyard, but both the murder itself and what happened after his soul reached the Outer Planes is hidden, as if the whole affair were being shielded from divine view."

The high priest paused to let that sink in. Between the kidnapping, the rendezvous in the Ethereal Plane, and the apparent ability to hide the whole matter from several normally omniscient deities, it was clear that whomever they were dealing with was extremely powerful. And extremely dangerous.

"Understood," Salim said. "Yet we may still have a chance. It's unlikely that after all this work, the kidnapper's going to simply throw away the soul and move on if we delay. Given time, we may uncover something, or the kidnapper may make contact again and give away his hand."

Khoyar nodded. Touching Salim's shoulder, he stopped them in front of another pair of closed wooden doors set into the wall of the hallway.

"Agreed," he said. "But there's one other complication."

"What?"

In reply, the high priest pushed open the doors. Inside was one of the church's many audience chambers, smaller and even better upholstered than Khoyar's tower-top solar, hung thick with gold and other trappings that—though in theory meaningless to the members of the church—no doubt played a role in convincing the economic elite to consign their dead to the church for burial.

In the center of the room stood a woman. She was well out of girlhood, but not so far from it that the smooth lines of youth didn't still cling to her cheeks and brow. Her long hair, pulled back with a tortoiseshell clip, was as dark as any Garundi's, but in contrast to Khoyar and Salim, the features beneath it were as pale as snow. Blue eyes stared out at them with the fierceness of a hawk.

"Salim Ghadafar," Khoyar said, making another little bow, "may I present you to Neila Anvanory, daughter of Faldus Anvanory and sole heir to all the Anvanory holdings."

Salim bowed himself this time, and was startled when the young woman stepped forward and offered her hand. He took it and shook, noting her firm grip.

"A pleasure," she said, and her voice was no aristocratic simper, but rather a dulcet whipcrack of command—a voice used to overseeing servants. "I'm told you'll be able to handle this matter quickly."

"I can only promise my best," Salim replied.

"I ask for no more," she said, yet her tone said that his best had better be enough.

Salim mentally stepped back and evaluated the woman. Her clothing and jewelry, from the large gold hoops in her ears to the elegant cut of her burgundy dress, screamed of wealth, yet the solid, flat-bottomed shoes and leather purse belted around her waist bespoke a willingness to put sense above fashion. Practical, then—a noblewoman alone in a strange land save for her father, forced to regularly make arrangements for herself, albeit with the aid of a sizable fortune.

And how must he appear to her? Salim was suddenly aware of the comparatively filthy state of his robes, the white dust of the desert bleaching their long black folds gray. He had shaved on the barge, yet already stubble was filling in the narrow lines of his beard, and his mop of black hair hung tousled down behind his ears, bearing its own desert highlights. Only the hilt of his sword, belted over the robes with a wide leather strap, remained clean, its twisted and gleaming brass kept clear of dust by his constant and unconscious touch.

Yet she had shaken his hand, rather than bowing or curtsying as many noblewomen would have. That sort of directness was worth something. This was either going to be good, or trouble.

"Well?" she asked after a moment, crossing her arms beneath her breasts. "Let's begin."

"Of course, Lady," Salim said. "I will commence my investigations at once, as soon as Khoyar has finished briefing me."

Neila shifted to look pointedly at Khoyar. The high priest smiled, this time with sincere pleasure, and turned to Salim.

"As Lady Anvanory is intensely interested in resolving this problem as quickly as possible," he said, "as well as funding all our efforts to recover her father's spirit, she will be accompanying you in your efforts."

Definitely trouble, Salim decided.

"Your concern for your father is commendable," he said slowly. "Yet I'm afraid that will not be possible."

Lady Anvanory's eyes flashed dangerously. "I assure you, it is."

"No, it's not." Salim stepped forward, moving until he was looking down at the noblewoman from his full six feet.

"It's impossible, Lady, because it represents a conflict of interest. You see, I've already begun my work. And having looked carefully at the situation, it seems that the person who stands to benefit most from Faldus Anvanory's death would be the person to whom the sun orchid elixir would naturally—and legally—pass. I also know that the most efficient murderer is the one the victim trusts implicitly, and that bizarre situations often conceal the simplest of answers."

Neila Anvanory recoiled as if she had been slapped. Jaw tight and face beginning to flush, she moved forward as well, but Khoyar dexterously inserted himself between them before she could reach Salim.

"My apologies for not briefing you fully, Salim, but I appear to have left out some key information. Lady Anvanory is *not* a suspect in this matter. Though our divinations have been hazy on the location of her father's spirit, they have been exceedingly clear on that fact, and her innocence has been verified by a battery of tests from Lamasara's governing officials. I assure you, she is merely concerned for her father's wellbeing. And besides—" he looked apologetically at Neila "—the ransom aspect doesn't make any sense for her. It would be a ridiculous and totally unnecessary expenditure of wealth, if she could even find accomplices with this level of magical ability. She'd be far better off having her father simply disappear, not killed where he can be resurrected. It doesn't add up."

Behind Khoyar, Neila's pretty face was still flushed red with anger, but now her eyes were wet as well.

The high priest had a point. Pigheadedness and aristocratic entitlement aside, she was still a girl who had lost her father. There was no need to press the issue.

"Of course," Salim said, stepping backward. "My apologies, but thoroughness is imperative in matters like this."

"Of course," Neila echoed. Salim could feel her hot eyes scouring the skin from his bones.

"Lady Anvanory will be accompanying you," Khoyar continued, his tone leaving no room for argument. "You may have been called in because the church wants answers, but Lady Anvanory is underwriting the church's services to whatever extent necessary, which in this case includes you. And it's her right as both daughter and the person who will have to answer the kidnappers."

Salim sighed internally. So be it.

"Very well," he said. "Then unless there's anything else I've not yet been apprised of, I suggest we begin with the primary witness."

"And who might that be?" Neila snapped.

Salim smiled at her.

"Why, Faldus Anvanory himself."

Chapter Two
Stories from a Corpse

Despite the heat of the day outside, the air grew rapidly chill as the three figures descended into the catacombs beneath the church. Once below ground level, the massive staircase Salim had ascended and descended earlier maintained its spiral—it was Pharasma's symbol, after all—but the stairs themselves narrowed and ceased to be marble art pieces, instead becoming functional slabs of gray stone. The descenders spread out into a line—Khoyar in front, lighting their way with a small magical globe that floated just over his shoulder, Salim in the middle, and Neila bringing up the rear. The prospect of viewing her father's corpse had taken the heat out of the noblewoman's cheeks, but she moved grimly onward without a word. Salim noted it. She had steel, this one.

After a half-dozen complete turns, corkscrewing down into the bedrock, they came to the first of the catacombs, a low-ceilinged chamber of stone that split into several passages. Though the staircase continued to spiral down, undoubtedly to deeper layers, Khoyar stepped off and led them down one of the hallways. The walls here were tiled in grim mosaics of black and gray, but Salim suspected that if he were to chip away their facings the walls would be natural stone. They were well below the level of the soil by now.

Khoyar turned and entered a small room with several slabs, not dissimilar from the one in which Salim had slain the ghouls. Yet where that chamber had been a combination mortuary and sepulcher, the faithful of the Lady of Graves had no need to economize. The temple complex both above and below would have several embalming facilities, plus a dizzying number of tombs ranging from simple stacked burial niches to elegant repositories patterned after the Osirian pharaohs, complete with anti-looting traps only the Pharasmins knew about. This room was merely a storage chamber, the cold helping to keep the bodies fresh while they awaited interment. It had the old-iron smell of a meat locker.

At present, the stones were empty, save one. A form wrapped in a gray linen shroud rested on the center table.

Neila stopped at the door, breath coming fast, and Khoyar touched her shoulder briefly in reassurance, then stepped over to the table and drew back the shroud.

Faldus Anvanory was a thin man in late middle age, his limp hair the same gray as the stone. A massive handlebar mustache dominated his gentle face, counterbalanced by a pointed beard on his chin. His cheeks were streaked with brown trails of blood. Khoyar looked to Neila, and she nodded.

He removed the shroud completely, and the wreck of Faldus's body was revealed. He still wore the clothes he'd died in, an outfit of bright blue and gray cut in the Taldan fashion, with ruffs at the shoulders and dark leggings. Those clothes were dark now, crusted with thick, bloody stains and hanging loose in places. Neila turned away, and Salim stepped close to examine the body.

Faldus had not died easy. That much was clear. Salim had expected something professional—a slit throat, an arrow in the back. Faldus looked like he'd been mauled. As Salim leaned closer, the impression strengthened. Long furrows rent the flesh and left fabric hanging, and one arm had been nearly severed. Between mustache and beard, lines of mangled flesh extended his mouth all the way back to his ears. Conscious of Neila's eyes on his back, Salim ran his fingers up the man's neck and beneath his chin, feeling the ragged line there.

"Removed?" he asked.

"The whole jaw," Khoyar confirmed. "Servants found it in a trash heap several estates to the west. My priests reattached it just enough to be functional."

Salim nodded. Without a jaw, the magic wouldn't work, and any serious assassin or career criminal understood the value of a corpse that stayed mute. He stepped back.

"Let's have a chat," he said.

Khoyar looked once more at Neila, who was still standing by the door. She had remarkable control of her emotions, but behind the sculpted face, she was clearly grieving.

"Is this truly necessary?" Khoyar asked. "My priests already interrogated the body thoroughly when it first came in, and they were unable to learn anything of use."

"I wasn't here then," Salim pointed out. "That was over a week ago?"

Khoyar nodded.

"Then he's ripe for another round. Cast the spell."

Sighing, Khoyar stepped forward and leaned over the body. Taking his spiraled holy symbol in his hand, he pressed it to the corpse's forehead, then drew the silver amulet slowly down the body, muttering liturgical chants. Giving Khoyar room to work, Salim stepped backward until he stood next to Neila. She said nothing to acknowledge him, merely kept her eyes on Khoyar's ministrations, and they stood together in awkward silence for several minutes.

At last Khoyar finished and stepped away, letting the holy symbol fall back against his chest.

"Arise, shell of Faldus," he intoned. "Wake and tell us of the memory of life, that we may honor you with justice."

For a moment there was nothing, and then a rattle began deep in the corpse's chest, becoming a sigh that rasped through dusty lips.

"I hear," it breathed, barely audible. Its eyes flicked open, and it bent at the waist until it sat upright, facing them.

"Father!" Neila cried, and started to move forward, but Salim's outflung arm barred her way.

"That's not your father," he said, voice soft. "Just his corpse. Don't confuse the two. His spirit is still gone, but his bones may yet hold some key to its whereabouts."

Neila looked back and forth incredulously from Salim to her father's corpse, then stepped back so that his arm was no longer against her chest, but she didn't try to approach the slab again. Salim moved forward.

"Welcome, shell of Faldus," he said, bowing. "We have questions for you."

There was a pause.

"Speak."

Salim glanced at Khoyar, and the man motioned for him to continue. Their questions would be limited, and Salim carefully considered his phrasing before beginning.

"What do you remember of your murder?"

The corpse turned its head as if looking at Salim, but its glassy eyes didn't bother to focus.

"I was in my study," it said, voice still raw but beginning to take on a ghost of a Taldan accent. "Facing the door. Something struck me from behind, stabbing and tearing. My head hit the desk, and everything went dark."

"What do you know of your attacker, other than that it didn't come through the door?" It was a wasteful question—too redundant—but Salim had to be sure the corpse wasn't unintentionally holding something back due to his phrasing.

"Nothing."

Well, that settled that. Salim thought hard about his next question, making sure it couldn't be answered with a simple yes or no. The key was always to keep the corpse talking.

"Whom would you suspect of ordering your killing?"

The corpse's answer was immediate. "The Harlot and the Jackal."

Salim turned to Khoyar. "And what the hell does *that* mean?"

"I know," Neila said, speaking up. "The Harlot and the Jackal were father's primary competitors for the elixir—or rather, his nicknames for them. Lady Leantina Issa Jbade and the merchant Akhom Qali."

"I thought there were always six vials at an auction," Salim said. He didn't know much about the process, nor care, but everyone had heard stories of the sun orchid elixir.

"There are, but father couldn't afford to go up against the wealthiest bidders. They were guaranteed to win—everything we had was banked on trying for the sixth vial. The same was true of Jbade and Qali—Father had business deals with both of them, and got along with them as well as could be expected. But he didn't trust either."

Salim nodded his thanks. That made sense. He looked back to Khoyar.

"How many more?" he asked.

The high priest held up a finger.

One question left. He had best make it count, or they wouldn't be able to try again for another week—corpses could only be prevailed upon so often, or the spell would lose its potency. Salim thought hard. The silence stretched out, and finally he asked, "Aside from Jbade and Qali, who has reason to want to see you dead?"

In response, the corpse's lips twitched. With careful slowness, their edges curved upward, expanding into a smile that stretched until the delicate stitching at either end of the mouth tore free, splitting its cheeks and showing molars in a rictus grimace.

"Everyone," it said.

Then the magic left it, and the corpse fell back on the stone table like a puppet with its strings cut. Khoyar leaned forward and closed the body's staring eyes.

"That could have been more helpful," Salim muttered, keeping it low out of respect for Neila. Then, louder: "Thank you, Faldus." He turned to the noblewoman, who was looking sadly at her father's corpse once more.

"I'm going to need to see the study where he was killed," he said, "as well as speak to the household staff, and to you in particular."

"Yes."

"My priests will be happy to assist you in any way you require," Khoyar put in. "But unless you desire to examine the body further—and I assure you that the city's reports on that matter are thorough, and will be provided to you straightaway—I suggest that we ascend once more, and leave the dust of Faldus Anvanory to what peace it's been granted."

Salim nodded and turned to follow the high priest to the door. Behind them, Neila stepped forward and touched the corpse's lifeless hand.

"Goodbye, Father," she whispered.

Up above, in the great cathedral's columned reception hall, Khoyar summoned an acolyte who stood ready with a sheaf of papers. This he handed to Salim.

"Here are copies of the Lamasaran Guard's findings," he said. "When you return, there will be a room prepared for you here, should you desire it. Furthermore, Brother Hasam will stand ready to act as runner, guide, or anything else you need."

The young acolyte beamed anxiously, and Salim recognized him as the man who had guided him up into Khoyar's tower earlier.

"My thanks," Salim said, bowing slightly to Hasam. The acolyte's chest puffed out. "I suspect, however, that my investigations will leave me little time for sleep, and it may well be several nights until I return."

"As you wish," Khoyar said. "Your comings and goings are your own."

If only, Salim thought, but there was little point in antagonizing the high priest now that they understood each other. He bowed properly this time and turned to Neila.

"If you would show me to your estate, Lady?"

"It would be my pleasure," Neila replied, and despite the show she'd just witnessed with the meat husk that used to house her father, her voice was smooth and calm. "Please, come with me." She turned toward the cathedral's doors and Salim followed, stowing the papers in an inner pocket of his robe.

Outside, the afternoon sun beat down in full strength, and the air hung heavy and dry. The sudden contrast hit him like the blast of a furnace, and made him suspect that the cathedral's relative comfort had more to do with magic than simply the shade of the high walls.

The thought disgusted him. The priests could have accomplished the same end simply by incorporating some of the local, open-air building styles. That people would indebt themselves to a god in exchange for magic, just to waste that power on minor tricks and comforts . . .

At the bottom of the stairs, a carriage had been pulled around. It was constructed in the Taldan style rather than that of the local rickshaws, completely enclosed and pulled by two magnificent horses. The scrollwork on the sides was highlighted with gold that glittered in the sun, blazing from the carriage's near-white wood. Its wheels were the large, thin cart wheels of a vehicle designed for cobblestone streets, rather than the shifting sands of a desert road, but Salim supposed the Anvanorys rarely had cause to venture off the best-maintained thoroughfares.

The cart's driver, on the other hand, was a local. His deeply lined face was as brown as the twisted scrub trees that bore leaves only after the flash floods, and his body was swathed in loose robes of a sensible off-white. His head was garbed in a similarly colored keffiyeh that fell down in back to shade his neck. As Neila and Salim descended the steps, he leaped down from his perch and opened the carriage door for them.

"Thank you, Olar," Neila said, and stepped lightly up into the raised carriage. Salim followed, and the servant shut the door.

Inside, the carriage was upholstered in lush purple, with bench seats both front and back. Windows of stretched fabric instead of glass allowed a small amount of airflow while still keeping out the worst of the dust, and the light passing through it lit the interior with a soft red glow, like sun seeping through closed eyelids on a bright day. Neila took the backward-facing seat toward the carriage's front, and Salim the other. She reached up and slid open a narrow, rectangular window in the front wall, then rapped once on the ceiling.

"Home," she called, and the servant said something back in acknowledgment, his words cut off as she slid the window closed. There was the crack of a whip, and the carriage swayed as it began to move down the road. Neila settled back into her seat and crossed her legs.

"So," she said. "Where do we begin?"

Salim studied the woman—though now he thought she was more of a girl, really—sitting before him. Now that she was away from the church—and presumably the remains of her father, which would be enough to unsettle anyone—she seemed to relax significantly. Where before she had seemed pretty in a sharp, aggressive fashion, like a bird of prey ready to strike, she now had the air of a proper aristocrat, smooth and soft. Her cheekbones were high, and the fabric of her dress, though cut modestly enough so as not to invite scandal or unappreciated attention, still swelled pleasantly with the curve of her breasts. Yet the hands that folded now on the covered point of her knee were strong and not overly manicured or jeweled, the mark of a woman not afraid to do things herself when necessary. Here was someone who could play both roles with equal ease: the retiring daughter of an affluent noble, or the commanding and iron-hard lady of the house, in charge of managing estate affairs and doling out punishment to the domestic staff. Both images probably served her well in this foreign land, so different from the one she had been born into.

"Perhaps you could start by telling me how you and your father came to be in Thuvia."

Neila nodded.

"I was born in Yanmass," she said, taking up the rhythm of someone with a long story waiting in the wings. "My mother died of fever shortly after my birth—as far back as I can remember, it's always been just me and my father. Father was a successful speculator and caravan organizer, and as I got older, he grew even more successful. Yanmass is a primary hub for caravans coming out of Casmaron, and father was a master of the market. In addition to financing his own expeditions, he would walk through the markets and talk with the drovers, get a sense of what would fetch the highest price next season, and buy it all. We had a great house overlooking the river.

"Though we were very rich, father was never quite content. He never took another wife, and while he was generally a happy, laughing man, he was prone to bouts of melancholy. No matter how well his business did, he could never come to terms with the fact that he was growing older. It had always been just the two of us, and the idea of leaving me alone one day filled him with grief. He said he wanted to be there to watch his grandchildren grow up." She raised an eyebrow to indicate what she thought of that particular sentiment.

"For years he dwelled on the issue, taking less and less pleasure in his surroundings. And then one day something changed. Where he had been growing steadily dourer, he was suddenly his old self, but with a newfound and unprecedented zest for his work. He threw himself into it, staying up long into the night poring over manifests and reports from the Empire of Kelesh. Our fortunes grew accordingly. And then, after a year of this, he came to me and told me to pack my things. We were going to be taking a journey. A very long one.

"I threw a fit, of course—I was a child of Taldor, and hardly used to being put upon in any fashion. Yet for once, all my tears did little to persuade him. We sold off most of our holdings, boarded up the manor, and set sail down the river to Cassomir, and from there onto the sea. It was as we were leaving the Cassomiri harbor that he finally told me where we were going, and why."

"The sun orchid elixir," Salim said.

Neila nodded.

"And what did you think of that?"

She spread her hands. "Everyone's heard the legends, but it's another thing entirely to actually pursue them. To halt aging—it's a universal dream, is it not?"

"Almost," Salim said. "But go on."

"Father's plan was simple—using the funds that he'd acquired over a lifetime, he would set us up here for however long it took to ingratiate ourselves and be offered an invitation to bid. Once he'd acquired the elixir, he would drink it, and immediately set to work earning the funds to purchase me one."

"And that's what you wanted as well?"

She shrugged. "I suppose. Death isn't something I dwell on overmuch. Or at least, it wasn't. But I have no desire to die."

Salim leaned back in his own seat and steepled his hands. "Tell me about your arrival."

She gazed at the cloth window, across which flickered the occasional shadow as they passed buildings which temporarily blotted out the sun. The sudden flashes of shade stroked her face in an unknowable rhythm.

"It was . . . different. Completely unlike Yanmass. The heat was unbearable, and the green that I had grown up with was only a narrow band along the river banks. The people were strange, and often lapsed into languages that were meaningless to us. Yet the fundamental principles were the same. Commerce never changes, as Father was fond of saying, and he was able to purchase an estate along the river so that it might feel more like home. That was three years ago.

"Needless to say, we've both adjusted. I enjoy the chaos of the markets, and the respect Garundi men pay their women, even if most of them don't know what to make of a foreign one who speaks like a man." The corner of her mouth twisted in a little smile. "At least here there's no stream of perfumed dandies who expect the ladies to be colorful songbirds, kept solely for display. For all their modesty, Thuvian women are masters of their domain."

"So you adapted quickly, then."

She laughed, a genuine peal of amusement.

"Not in the least," she said. "Father refused to trim his beard or wear a hat for the first six months, and was sunburned terribly. I spoke nothing but Taldane, and regularly paid twice what I should for everything we needed. The locals looked at us like we were half-orcs, and our interactions with them were a constant stream of faux pas and miscommunications. Yet we learned, and so did they. Our servants now are every bit as competent and dependable as those we left behind in Taldor. And though Father is a shrewd businessman, the merchants here appreciate a worthy adversary, and he quickly worked his way into the city's higher social echelons. They all knew why he was here, but they're used to it, and don't mind. For every winner of the sun orchid auction who has the capital—and arrogance—to simply show up and demand an invitation, there's another like father who seeks to ingratiate himself first. He was good at it."

Salim scratched at his chin. "So he had a lot of friends."

"I wouldn't go that far." She cocked her head. "Father was a driven man, and didn't have a lot of time for friends. I would say that they respected him, and he them."

"What about this Harlot, and the Jackal?"

Neila's lips made a moue of distaste.

"I didn't know either of them particularly well, but Father did. They're foreigners like us, though not from so far away. All the elixir hopefuls know each other. Keeping an eye on the competition."

"But you didn't like them."

A slight shake of her head. "Akhom—the Jackal—is personable, but it's hollow as a blown egg. And Jbade . . . well, let's simply say her nickname is accurate. Not the sort of woman I'd want around my father."

Interesting. Salim wondered just how close Faldus and this Jbade woman had been, and if there might be a certain amount of jealousy there.

"Do you think one of them could have killed your father?"

She looked away, toward the patterns of light on the window, and then met his eyes abruptly.

"Yes," she said, and her face was stone. "I think either of them could have ordered it. Or someone else entirely—someone father might not even have known. In winning the auction, father made us targets for every desperate lowlife in this city."

It was true. The prospect of immortality, even one that had to be regularly renewed, was an unimaginable draw. The elixir itself, Salim knew, was produced in a secret redoubt somewhere in the desert. Each year, a blind and mute servant emerged from the temple-fortress with six vials of the elixir, produced from the exceedingly rare flowers of the sun orchid. Those vials were then transported to one of the five major cities of Thuvia by any number of careful and mysterious means. Sometimes it was armed caravans, sometimes teleportation, always following different paths to help avoid thieves and bandits. The right to sell the elixir rotated between cities every year, and those invited to participate in the auction were allowed a single sealed bid, with all proceeds—win or lose—going to the city government.

The elixir was the promise of eternal youth. It was quite literally priceless. And it had cost this girl her father.

"That's why your father made the arrangement with the Church of Pharasma, for them to resurrect him in the event of his murder."

Neila shook her head. "My idea. Father was too excited to worry overmuch about such things, but he saw the logic of it when I explained it."

"Was your father a member of the faith?"

"Father?" she asked. "Not at all. He worshiped Abadar the merchant god, though primarily as an aspect of his business dealings. He would have made the arrangement with their banker-priests, but of course their rates were higher."

"And you?" Salim pressed. Neila eyed him levelly.

"I've never bothered much with gods," she said, watching for his reaction.

"Good."

Her eyes widened in surprise. She looked about to say something, but then the gentle rocking of the carriage ceased, and Salim heard the muted thump as the driver hopped down from his perch. Neila looked to the door as it swung open.

"We're here," she said, and gestured for him to go first. He slid out of his seat and stepped down from the carriage, long legs not bothering with the hanging wooden running board.

He was no longer in Thuvia. The structure that sat at the end of the circular, crushed-stone drive was built in the style of a southern Taldan plantation house, white-sided and fronted by a half-rounded, columned portico. Yet it was not the architectural style of Anvanory Manor that made Salim feel suddenly disoriented. It was the color.

Where the rest of Lamasara's landscape had been painted in shades of yellow, red, and ochre, the Anvanory estate was green. Full-size fruit trees surrounded and half-screened the house from the rest of the grounds. Beyond them were fields thick with ripening crops, irrigated by long and meandering canals. To the east, the waters of the river were just barely visible, lazily swirling past the entrances to the canals and bringing life to the fields. And to the south, demarcating the edges of the Anvanorys' fields, was the telltale green smudge of a full-fledged forest, following the meandering river up toward its headwaters.

"Unbelievable," Salim breathed. There couldn't be more than a few stands of trees that large within a hundred miles.

"Stunning, isn't it?" Neila stepped down lightly from the carriage behind him, ignoring the driver's proffered hand. "It cost Father a fortune to acquire such a large swath of riverfront, but he insisted that it was imperative for us to be reminded where we come from. So he had this house built, and the surrounding land cleared as a plantation. It's proven rather productive—it turns out that farming has done as well by us as mercantilism, albeit on a smaller scale." Lady Anvanory moved past Salim and up two smooth stone stairs, into the shaded entryway. "Please, come in."

Salim followed. Inside, the strange feeling of having been somehow transported back to Taldor was only amplified. Though the walls were primarily of the same adobe as the rest of the city, rather than absurdly expensive wood, the style was all wrong—in place of clean Thuvian lines, every surface was hung with framed portraits and curtains, the floor of marble instead of baked tile. Two grand staircases curved up from the high-ceilinged entryway to a recessed balcony that was the main hallway of the second floor. Were it not for the brown skins and loose robes of the servants, Salim would not have been able to say for certain that he was still in the desert.

One of those servants approached now and bowed low, his demeanor and the small coat of arms stitched to the breast of his robes marking him as the majordomo.

"Developments?" Neila asked, without greeting the man. The word was sharp and quick, but out of efficiency, not anger.

"None regarding the master, Great Lady," the man said, remaining bent at the waist as if he were addressing her feet. "There was another incident in the southwestern field, but the men are fine, and the harvest continues on schedule."

"Good," she said, then turned to Salim. "Are you thirsty?"

Salim wasn't, particularly, but something about the way she looked at him held significance. Suddenly he realized that she was, in her own way, presenting her version of the water ritual between host and visitor. The thought of it coming from this white-faced Taldan girl was amusing, but he held up his end.

"Your hospitality honors me, as it does your ancestors," he replied formally. She nodded in approval.

"Have drinks sent up to the study, Amir" she said, "but don't let anyone enter it."

Still not meeting her eyes, the servant nodded, then stepped back a pace before straightening and moving briskly down one of two long hallways that appeared to run most of the length of the house.

"Come," she said to Salim, motioning for him to follow her down the hall the servant hadn't taken. "I suspect you'll need to know the layout of the house before you'll be able to tell me anything about the assassins." Salim murmured his agreement.

Anvanory Manor was an enormous, sprawling maze of rooms, made even more grandiose by the fact that it existed solely to house a man and his daughter—plus their extensive retinue of servants. They passed through the so-called front rooms—the grand dining room with chandelier and a table fit to seat twenty or more, several sitting rooms and parlors, a den that smelled thickly of old pipe smoke and bore the leering, mounted heads of half a dozen game animals—and on into the servants' quarters.

Where the other rooms had been perfect, precise, and lifeless, held in state like a well-preserved corpse, these new chambers were ablaze with life and activity. Cooks in the kitchen bawled orders to maids, who in turn shooed children away from new loaves of bread before any could go missing. Steam and smoke filled the air with the aroma of garlic, cumin, and turmeric. Out the back doors, washerwomen sang in rhythm with the rasp of fabric on the washboards, their beautifully discordant harmonies reminding Salim of the cries of wading birds in the river. Beyond them were the open-air sleeping porches that housed the field workers and their families, with their canvas sides that could be closed in case of sandstorms or the periodic downpours that brought life to the desert. Neila led Salim on a circuit of all of this, then up the entryway stairs to the second floor.

"Your home is remarkable," Salim said, with no exaggeration. "Yet it's hardly defensible, with such an open layout. Surely you both realized this."

"We don't need a fortress," Neila replied. "Or at least, we didn't think we needed one. Our safety comes from our station, and the loyalty of our staff. Certainly, any one of them could make off with enough of our belongings to equal a year's wage. But when that year was up, he'd be out of a job, and those who remained would still have food to eat. No, we pay our staff well, and in return they serve us faithfully. We represent their livelihood, and their families live here alongside us. Our home is theirs, and they protect it as such."

Salim nodded. It was a good policy, under normal conditions. But when something like the sun orchid elixir was involved, nothing was normal.

"Your man spoke earlier of an incident," he prompted.

Neila waved her hand, dismissing the idea as she would a servant. "An irritant," she said. "Before we arrived, no one had owned these woods for generations—a hunting preserve for the queen and her family, but one they were more than willing to sell to Father for the correct price. Ever since we cleared part of the land to construct this house and the fields— recouping much from the timber sales—the fey of the wood have been restless. Clearly they thought of the land as theirs, and they've been slow to adjust. Our field hands are harassed with some regularity by the sprites, with tools gone missing and the occasional direct confrontation, but the men are used to it and the fey are slowly learning to accept our presence."

"I see."

At last they came to a heavy door of nut-brown wood, the first such portal that Salim had seen closed in this aristocratic wonder. Beside it, a halfling servant stood at attention with a salver, upon which rested two crystal champagne flutes. He bowed gracefully, without the liquid so much as trembling in the glasses, and held them out to the two humans. Neila took them both and handed one to Salim.

"Thank you," he said, and drank. The water inside was cold enough to make his teeth hurt, the product of either magic or a well-insulated cellar. Neila flicked her fingers, and the servant straightened and left them, his child-sized steps completely silent on the piled carpet of the second story. Neila produced a key ring from the purse on her belt and unlocked the door, then pushed it open.

"This was my father's study," she said.

The room was lit by sun pouring in through an enormous, arched window that stretched across one wall from the floor to the ceiling fifteen feet above. In front of it sat a wide wooden desk, facing not the amazing view of the river but rather the door to the study. Bookshelves lined the walls, holding both leather-bound tomes and an assortment of curios, from expensive trinkets and carvings in the local style to bottled Taldan warships and racks of fine fencing swords. The carpet was a midnight blue as dark as the sea, and almost as yielding as Salim waded through it, taking in every detail.

"He was found at his desk?" he asked.

"Yes." She stepped lightly around him and led him behind the imposing wooden structure in a wide arc. She had the good sense to keep her distance from it as she did so, avoiding the darker splotches on the carpet that Salim recognized easily. Bloodstains.

"Who's been here since you found him?"

She moved so that she could look out the window, rather than at the desk. "Only the guards and the church," she said. "The former did a cursory investigation, but didn't bother overmuch, given the arrangement we had with the Church of Pharasma. When the priests came, they removed the body, and the servants cleaned as much as they could—we didn't think we'd need to look for clues, once Father was resurrected. But otherwise it's all as it was."

Salim leaned against a corner of the desk. "Why don't you tell me everything, starting with when he was first discovered."

She took a deep breath and turned back around.

"Father was elated, of course. It was his dream—winning the auction. He hadn't expected that they'd hold the elixir at the queen's palace until the deeds to the pledged property could be verified and transferred, but a few days hardly seemed to matter. Time was about to become meaningless. He came up to his study to smoke, as he often did in the evenings."

She closed her eyes. "No one heard a cry. It wasn't until it had gotten quite late that I came to check on him. The door was closed. I knocked, but . . ."

She paused, and he waited silently for her to continue.

"He was slumped facedown on the desk. There was blood everywhere. I screamed, and servants came running. They summoned the guard, and I sent a runner to notify the church. We knew there was danger, but we hadn't . . . we hadn't really thought . . ." She took another deep, shuddering breath.

Salim gave her a moment, then prompted her again. "So the guard came."

She opened her eyes and met his. "Yes. As I've said, they didn't stay long. You have copies of their report. The clerics came next, but they were primarily interested in transporting his body to the church for resurrection."

He nodded. "And when did they inform you that something was wrong?" He realized as he said it that it was a strange way to refer to a murder—presumably something had gone terribly wrong long before the resurrection attempt, but she took his meaning.

"The next morning. Father had paid them well, and they performed the resurrection promptly—or at least attempted to. When their efforts failed, they began casting divinations to determine the source of the problem. But by that time the scroll had already appeared on our doorstep."

"The ransom note. May I see it?"

She shook her head. "It appeared on our porch from out of nowhere—no one saw it arrive. Olar, the carriage driver, brought it straight to me. It felt solid enough when I unrolled it, but as I read it the paper began to dissipate like smoke, until it disappeared. I only know what it said—that Father's soul was being held between worlds, and that if I wanted him to return, I must have the sun orchid elixir delivered to a point on the Ethereal Plane coterminous with the southeastern corner of our property—whatever that means."

Salim nodded. He'd expected as much. Any kidnapper who could steal a soul from the Boneyard and shift between this world and the eerie half-reality of the Ethereal Plane wasn't going to simply leave a ransom note around to be traced back to him.

"At that point, the guard became interested again, and thoroughly questioned both me and the house staff, but stepped back once it became clear that the Church of Pharasma was even more interested in solving the situation, as a matter of professional pride. I've been using our remaining funds to support their efforts ever since."

"And weighing whether or not to pay the ransom."

Neila's eyes had been drifting back to the window while she spoke, but now they jerked back to him.

"I love my father!" she snapped. "There's no decision to be made. I've been told by the Pharasmins that I can expect answers. If you prove unable to offer them, then I will have Khoyar deliver the elixir. I will not allow your church's failure to kill my father." Her eyes were red now, and the tendons stood out on her neck. "Unless you have further questions for me, Mr. Ghadafar, the servants could use my attention. Take as much time here as you need."

She waited a moment, eyes daring him, but he inclined his head. She departed, shutting the study door firmly behind her.

Salim looked at the closed door and sighed. The woman's emotions were going to make this more difficult than it already was.

Kneeling down, Salim examined the desk and the bloodstained carpet. As with the corpse, the wood of the desk had several sets of parallel scrapes and notches, like claw marks.

While Salim was no expert in assassination—by the time he was brought in to solve a problem, people usually had a pretty good idea of what they were up against, and few undead attacks could be called subtle—he wasn't particularly surprised. Magically summoned monsters were quick, powerful, and convenient. Not only did they disappear once the spells that called them into being ended, but the real killer could strike from a distance. If the caster who had taken out Faldus Anvanory were good enough, he could have stood in the yard and summoned the monster directly into the study through the window. Faldus, whose desk faced the door—no doubt because he didn't like being surprised by people—wouldn't even see it coming.

Which, as it turned out, he hadn't. Something had appeared behind him, torn him to ribbons, and then disappeared.

Salim held his own hand up to one of the claw marks for comparison.

Something big.

He continued to search the carpet and desk for a moment, looking for anything else that might give him a clue as to the beast's nature, but found nothing. Glancing out the window, he confirmed what he'd suspected—a wide lawn stretching down toward the river. A killer could have stood out there—or floated, or sent his familiar, or ridden a griffon for all Salim knew—and been effectively invisible in the darkness to anyone inside the well-lit manor house.

One by one, Salim opened up the drawers in the desk, doing his best not to disturb the contents as he rifled through them. Stacks of well-thumbed caravan manifests, transaction summaries, and figures sheets painted a picture of Faldus Anvanory much in accordance with the one his daughter had presented: a man driven to commerce as if the Lady of Graves herself were on his heels. Which, of course, she was.

The bottommost drawer was locked, which was unsurprising—trust in one's household staff was a virtue, but too much was foolish. Besides, three years in Thuvia didn't make the Anvanorys Thuvian, and they probably still expected a certain amount of petty theft from their help.

Salim didn't particularly feel like chasing after Neila and asking for the key, but then the gleaming brass face of the keyhole caught his eye. On a hunch, he opened all the other drawers and felt around inside them, this time ignoring their contents in favor of the wood. In the second-highest one, he found what he was looking for. He depressed the catch and pulled on the locked drawer. It slid smoothly open, revealing the real locking mechanism: a carefully geared set of rods controlled by the catch. The keyhole on the front was real enough, but attached to nothing. Only the perfect smoothness of its faceplate, which should have been at least mildly scratched by the key after years of regular use, had given it away.

Inside was yet another stack of papers, but these were of a different sort—deeds and statements of ownership, all signed and witnessed with the key-shaped wax seal of the Bank of Abadar. Doubtlessly this drawer had been much fuller just a few weeks ago, yet there were still enough paper holdings here to keep the manor comfortably appointed for a hundred years.

On top of all the papers sat a small painting, just a few inches to a side and bound in a frame of carved and lacquered wood. Salim withdrew it carefully.

Upon first glance, he thought it was a portrait of Neila, so similar were the two women's faces. Then he realized that the woman in the painting must be several years older, her face slightly less rounded. Unlike most aristocratic portraits, where everyone looked awkwardly dour, as if suffering from intestinal flux, this woman had been captured at play, relaxing beneath a garden window with a book. The green and gold light from beyond painted her cheeks, and her eyes were bright, as if she'd just looked up from the story.

The senior Lady Anvanory, no doubt. Salim slid the painting back on top of the documents and closed the drawer.

Seating himself in the chair where Faldus had been dispatched, Salim took Khoyar's papers from his inner pocket and spread them over the beautifully finished wood of the desk. The summaries, written in the elegant hand of a Pharasmin priest—no doubt far neater than the barely literate scrawl of the guard's original reports—had little to offer. One sheet was a summary of the guard's conclusions, which mirrored Salim's own: Faldus had clearly been mauled from behind by some sort of large beast which left no trace of itself—likely a magically summoned creature. It probably hadn't entered through the doorway, or he would have seen it. The second sheet was a record of the various magical interrogations made by both the Church of Pharasma and a banker of Abadar acting on behalf of the city guard. The transcriptions of their interview with Faldus's corpse offered nothing that Salim hadn't already uncovered from his own interrogation, though he noted that the guards showed remarkably little interest in questioning either Akhom Qali or Lady Jbade without more evidence than the unsubstantiated accusations of a corpse. Below the transcript was an official statement of the Lamasaran Guard's opinion that Neila Anvanory herself was no longer under suspicion, having cleared several magical tests investigating both her aura and the veracity of her sworn testimony.

Salim wasn't surprised. Though Neila was the obvious first suspect, he was a fair judge of character himself, and everything in the woman's demeanor said that she was what she seemed to be: a young noblewoman grieving for her father. That had been clear almost from the beginning, and even if it hadn't, there were a dozen ways Neila could have done away with her father and received the elixir with little question—the current situation was one of the few ways in which she *wouldn't* necessarily end up with the elixir. But innocence didn't mean she was going to be easy to work with, especially if she insisted on dogging his footsteps.

Salim looked up from his musings and realized that the light in the room had faded significantly since Neila had brought him in here. Already the knickknacks on the bookshelves were half cast in shadow.

He looked down at the papers. If there was something more to be gained here, he wasn't seeing it. He'd need to take a more active role in the investigation. Sweeping up the documents, he tucked them back into his robes and exited the study.

He found Neila downstairs in the dining room once more, giving instructions to one of the cooks. The servant eyed Salim warily, then bowed to her mistress and retreated through a free-swinging door to the steam and chaos of the kitchen. Neila turned and greeted him levelly.

"Did you learn anything?" She was perfectly composed again, with that crystalline Taldan courtesy that sparkled as it cut.

"Only how little we know," Salim replied, attempting to keep his voice light. Nobles in general irritated him, but this one had reason enough to be volatile. She picked up on his manner and seemed to take it for contrition. Her voice thawed slightly.

"What will you do next, then?"

He waved a hand toward the door. "Work with what we have—specifically, with Faldus's own suspicions. The city guard may have been understandably reluctant to question other local powers without direct evidence, but I have no such compunctions."

Neila's eyes were hard and bright. "The Harlot and the Jackal."

"Precisely."

She smiled, and for a moment he almost thought she'd rub her hands together in anticipation. Inaction clearly pained her. "A fine idea," she said. "When do we leave?"

Salim sighed.

"It's already evening, and I hardly think either of them would welcome guests this late. I'll pay my respects to both of them tomorrow."

Neila caught the pronoun and stared at him hard, brow furrowed. When he made no move to correct it, she drew herself up slowly and pulled her shoulders back, spine straight as any soldier on parade.

"Mr. Ghadafar," she said, "I thought we had an understanding. I see now that I am mistaken. Perhaps it would be best to inform the church that I will not be needing your assistance."

She had an iron will, this one, yet the sheer stupidity of her insistence kept Salim from appreciating it. When he answered, he let his own control lapse far enough to show a flicker of irritation.

"With all due respect, Lady Anvanory," he said, his tone making it clear exactly how little that was, "you've just proven how much you do. Or do you really think that, should either Akhom Qali or Lady Jbade have murdered your father, *you* would be the best person to interrogate them?" As in their initial meeting, he took a step toward her, forcing her to look up to meet his eyes.

"Whoever planned this extortion," he said, "has gone to considerable lengths to cover his trail, using a caliber of magic that would put most wizards to shame. Both Jbade and Qali are undoubtedly expecting me, or someone like me, to contact them. The chance of the killer slipping and revealing something in conversation is, by my calculation, roughly the same as the next rain turning Thuvia into a jungle. Yet I'm willing to try."

Another step forward. "Tell me, Lady, what cleverness have you concocted that will make either of them reveal their hand in front of their victim's daughter?"

He was no more than two feet from her. She stood her ground, but instead of anger, those high cheeks now flushed with embarrassment. She met his gaze for a long moment. Then she pivoted back and to the side, arm swinging toward the dining table in an after-you gesture.

"You practice a strange form of courtesy, Mr. Ghadafar. Yet you are undoubtedly correct. I will remain here and eagerly await your reports. In the meantime, I would of course offer you the hospitality of the manor, but I'm sure you're eager to get back to the church."

Despite Salim's irritation, the absurdity of the statement got the better of him. Suddenly the whole situation seemed ludicrous. He stepped past her to the dining room table, pulled out one of the ornate chairs there, and collapsed into it, one leg hanging over the arm.

"Miss Anvanory," he said wearily, "if that church caught fire tomorrow, I could not be happier."

The startled look on the woman's face, mouth open and arm still outstretched slightly toward the table, was priceless. Salim realized he was grinning.

"You are a strange sort of priest," Neila said at last, and Salim couldn't restrain a cough of laughter.

"I assure you, Lady, I am no priest."

Her face darkened toward anger, fearing he was playing her for a fool, and he motioned toward one of the other chairs in an echo of her own gesture.

"Sit."

If she took issue with his command, curiosity kept her from protesting. She sat primly, knees together and hands folded. Salim removed his leg from the chair arm and turned toward her.

"Khoyar told you that I serve Pharasma, and that's true. But I am not a priest, nor a member of the church. Rather, I exist both within and without it—I serve the dark goddess, but bow to none of the carrion crows who worship her."

Neila studied him cautiously. "So you're a paladin, then? A holy warrior?"

Salim laughed again.

"Don't confuse fidelity with piety, Lady. There's little love lost between me and the goddess. Suffice it to say that she finds me useful. And I obey." The last word came out with more bite than he would normally have allowed, and Neila leaned away slightly, continuing to stare at him.

"I see," she said, slowly. "Well, Mr. Ghadafar, it seems that I may have made a number of assumptions." She gestured to the table. "If you would care to stay here for the duration of your investigations, you are welcome. I'll have a servant make up a room for you."

"My thanks, Lady." The response was automatic, but as he spoke, Salim suddenly felt—not ashamed, exactly, but disconcerted. This girl was so composed, so commanding in her presence and speech, that it instantly kindled his revulsion for the church and all the other bureaucrats and petty dictators that operated with a similar arrogance. Yet his anger was with Khoyar, and Ceyanan, and the grave-loving bitch-goddess herself. Not this hard-eyed young woman who was doing everything in her power to track down her father's killer.

Including dealing with an uncouth swordsman and the mountain-sized chip on his shoulder. Salim stuck out a hand.

"Salim," he said.

The noblewoman stared at it. He left it out, watching as understanding dawned. She took it and shook.

"Neila," she said. "Pleased to meet you."

Chapter Three
The Jackal's Den

Salim awoke early the next morning, just as the sun was beginning to peer over the horizon, painting the walls of the bedchamber a brilliant orange. Rolling fully clothed off the bed—as he'd suspected, the blankets had been completely unnecessary—he ran rough fingers through his shaggy hair and adjusted the hilt of his sword, then opened the door and slipped out into the hall.

Downstairs, the manor was already humming with activity. Pots and platters rattled in the kitchen as the servants prepared breakfast for their lady (who no doubt wouldn't wake for several hours yet—the privilege of nobility). Through open windows came the distant sounds of men singing in the fields, their low voices a chanted counterpoint to the washerwomen's wailing songs of the previous evening.

Salim passed through the kitchen where the fat cook and her apprentices were doing their best to carefully time the food's readiness with their mistress's unpredictable waking. They jumped when he entered, but he put a finger to his lips and grabbed two fresh circles of flatbread from a tray, secreting them in a pocket along with a handful of dates. The fat cook scowled at him as if she would have liked to say something, but didn't dare call a guest to task. Salim winked at her and passed through the door that led out into the yard.

Outside, the day was coming alive. Insects buzzed in a rasping chorus that filled the rolling green grounds between the house and the river. With the sun just up, the day was still pleasantly cool, and the entire world smelled of growth and life.

Salim looked up at the windows of the second story, noting the tall one which was Faldus's study. Only a northerner could sleep through the morning. In a desert nation like Thuvia, as in Rahadoum and Osirion, it was often said that life took place at dawn and dusk. It was true in several senses—literally, the boiling heat of the day made work in the full sun oppressively hard, if not outright dangerous. In the more metaphorical sense, that threefold division represented the majority of life, the hard work of adulthood separating the unfettered games of childhood and the deserved rest of old age.

One of the footmen approached him. It was the man who had driven the carriage the day before—Olar, his name had been.

"Good morning, honored master," the servant called, formal but friendly. Salim returned the greeting.

"The mistress has placed the carriage at your disposal. Shall I bring it around and meet you in the drive?"

Salim shook his head. That carriage would stand out anywhere he went in Lamasara, and while he didn't expect to take either Qali or Jbade by surprise, there was no reason to show up announcing his affiliations.

"Do you have anything a little less conspicuous?"

The driver looked thoughtful, then shrugged.

"There's a farm wagon almost finished being loaded for town. It can be ready in a few minutes."

"Perfect," Salim said. "Do you know where I can find the estates of either Akhom Qali or Lady Jbade?"

The man first looked startled, then gave Salim a predatory smile.

"I do indeed. I can take you there in the wagon—both live near the marketplace, and Qali is between us and it." He lowered his voice. "You think they were behind the master's death?"

"I think they had a motive," Salim said, his voice reproachful. "But that proves nothing. It would be best not to make conjectures, or to speak about the matter at all."

"Of course, of course." But the grim smile remained. Faldus must have been a good man to work for, Salim reflected.

A few minutes later, the wagon was finished being loaded with sacks of grain and corn, plus a small mound of melons. Salim sat up front on the high driver's seat next to Olar, who held the reins. Instead of the carriage's white horses, a larger and more practical team of yoked oxen pulled the broad-wheeled cart. Olar flicked them each lightly with the whip, and the great moon-eyed beasts lumbered forward without complaint, pulling the cart down a dusty set of ruts that paralleled the manor's white stone drive until it reached the road.

On the outskirts of Lamasara, where they currently were, the residences grew steadily thinner and more spread out as they radiated away from the city proper—with one exception. Along the riverbanks, where annual flooding kept the soil rich and abundant water allowed canals and easy hand irrigation with the cranelike mechanisms called shadufs, wealthy farmers and nobles vied for space, creating lucrative plantations and estates. Anvanory Manor was toward the southernmost end of that long line of greenery stretching out from the city.

Olar was quiet as he drove, taking the eminently practical approach of the longtime servant who has learned that it's best not to address one's employer unless directly engaged in conversation. Normally that would have suited Salim fine, as he was going to need all his wits about him in the coming engagements. Yet he also had no interest in going into them at a disadvantage. Neila had given him a brief overview of both aristocrats before he'd retired for the night, but servants talked, even between households, and serving men and women regularly knew more than their masters presumed.

"Tell me what you know about Akhom Qali and Lady Jbade," Salim said.

Olar nodded as if he'd been expecting the question. "About Qali, I know only as much as everyone else," he said. "An Osirian come to Lamasara several years ago to better monitor his caravans. A brilliant man, it's said, but not someone you want to cross. More than that, I cannot say."

"And Jbade?"

Olar grinned.

"Every man in Lamasara knows the Queen of Spice. Some might try to deny it, but only in their wives' hearing. Among other men, they say that a pretty girl puts an ache in your heart, but Lady Jbade strikes lower. I saw her dance once as a boy, when I snuck away from the market with my father's purse." He sighed. "I learned more watching her on stage than I have in twenty years of marriage."

Salim did the math. "She must be retired by now."

Olar shook his head. "Not at all. Or rather, yes but no." He raised a finger toward his ear. "They say her mother was the most beautiful elf in Kyonin, overcome with lust for a simple herdsman as her retinue passed through Qadira. The result was Jbade. When she was in her prime, her dancing would make a Calistrian temple-whore blush. Half the nobles in Lamasara have attempted to claim her, but she owns the most popular theaters in the city, as well as the best brothels. If she dances anymore, it's not because she has to. Nor for us to see."

Olar drifted off, likely thinking of his formative encounter with the woman Faldus had called the Harlot. Salim let him. They rode on in silence for a while longer. When the farm manors began to be absorbed and replaced by the more urban establishments signifying the beginning of Lamasara's recognized districts, Olar stopped the cart.

"Akhom Qali's dwelling is two streets down," he said, nodding toward the stretch of city between them and the river. "Lady Jbade resides in the theater district, just up the hill from a place called the Firelark. Anyone in that area should be able to direct you to it. Shall I wait for you in the market?"

Salim thought about it. They'd come a fair distance in the cart—not unwalkable, but also not a trip he'd relish making in the full heat of the sun.

"If it's not going to inconvenience the manor," he said. After a second, he added, "Or you."

The driver smiled again.

"No worries, Excellency. They'll be fine without me for a few hours, and I'm sure I can find ways to entertain myself in the market."

After his story about Jbade, Salim reckoned the man could. At Salim's nod, Olar slapped the reins and rolled onward down the road. Salim watched him go, then turned and made his way through the warren of mud brick buildings in the direction the driver had indicated. He had time to wonder momentarily if he should have asked for a description of Akhom's property, and then he emerged from an alley onto a wide street, where the point was rendered moot.

There could be no mistaking Akhom Qali's estate. Long, brown walls six feet high extended the length of a city block, topped with shocking greenery that hung out over the street as if trying to escape. A gate of iron bars stood in the wall directly across from Salim, and beyond it he could see the shining gold-painted roof of a house rising above the trees, capped by a dome fit for a capital building.

Salim shook his head wonderingly and crossed the street toward the gate. The amazing excesses of these moneyed nobles, to waste gallons of precious water on ornamental greenery when the rest of their countrymen dug mud from wells in the sand, and nations like Rahadoum struggled to keep from being totally subsumed by the desert.

Behind the gate sat a guard, using a waist-high clay pillar as a stool. He straightened and half-bowed politely as Salim approached.

"I wish to speak to Akhom Qali," Salim said, attempting to put a little aristocratic expectation in his own voice.

"Of course," the guard said. From his tone, it was clear that the statement meant only *of course you do*, not any indication that he intended to open the gate. The guard wore a white turban, and his flowing robes couldn't hide a frame that was at least half again as large as Salim's. "And whom may I tell the master is calling?"

Salim had already evaluated several possible answers on the ride into town. "Tell him an emissary from High Priest Khoyar Roshan of the Church of Pharasma is here to see him."

"Certainly." The guard snapped his fingers, and a boy of perhaps twelve that Salim had completely failed to notice emerged from the screen of trees. Another twitch of the guard's wrist sent the youth sprinting up the path to the house. The guard made no motion toward small talk while they waited, and Salim was content with silence. After a short time, the child returned, out of breath but holding up two fingers as he ran. The guard noted the gesture and unlocked the gate.

"Master Qali will see you," he said. "Please follow the boy." Salim did as he was instructed, and the wrought-iron bars closed behind him with a clang.

The garden path twisted between tight-packed trees to hide its destination from the gate. Within twenty steps, the guard and the street were invisible, lost in the tunnel of vegetation. The stones of the path were smooth and gray, so perfectly laid and fitted that it was as if Salim were walking across a tile floor, despite the fact that no two stones were the same size or shape. After several more serpentine turns the trees gave way to a flagstone porch that was almost a plaza. The sprawling house that stood beyond it was long and low, and above the center grew the great minaret he'd seen from the street, its faintly lined sides not just painted but gleaming with the luster of bright bronze—perhaps even gold plating. Below it, two steps led up from the plaza to wide wooden doors built in the breezy Thuvian style and covered by curtains. The doors hung open invitingly.

The child led him up the steps and into a room furnished in smooth stone and painted in cool, soothing shades of green. A servant in a formal suit approaching livery stood waiting just beyond the lintel, hands clasped in front of him. He said nothing as the child deposited Salim and then disappeared back into the bushes.

There was no preamble. "This way," the chamberlain said, and led him down a long hallway, their footsteps echoing against the stones. Bright windows lit the passageway at intervals, and brought with them a cool breeze that seemed to follow the men down the hall. At last they came to another set of the big double doors, and the servant stood next to them at attention, silently indicating that Salim should enter.

Salim had expected a study or sitting room, perhaps a dining chamber. Even a great hall or throne room, if Akhom Qali was the arrogant sort.

What he hadn't expected was another garden. Beyond the doors, several steps descended into a square, recessed courtyard that was half patio and half jungle. Trees and bushes, both potted and growing out of recessed ports in the flagstones, were everywhere, turning the stone of the courtyard into innumerable little whirling paths. Roofs to all four sides made it clear that they were not merely in a walled garden, but rather somewhere in the middle of Qali's grand house itself. Above, a square swatch of sky was blue and completely unobstructed, even the great dome rendered invisible by the recessed well of the courtyard.

"Don't just stand there. Come, come!"

Akhom Qali was a short man, almost as round as he was tall, yet his fat was the sort that seems to shine with health, like a plump baby. His hair was white, and a full beard extended halfway down his pudgy chest, matching his loose white blouse and pants embroidered heavily with crimson. He half-reclined in an iron-and-fabric chair in the center of the cortile. A second chair sat opposite him. He motioned toward it.

Salim picked his way down the stairs and through the maze of plants until he reached Qali's patio. The merchant gestured again, and Salim sat.

"Impressive, isn't it?" The wave of Qali's bearded chin indicated the whole of the enclosed garden, and perhaps the rest of the manor.

"Extremely," Salim replied honestly.

"It's nothing to match the pleasure domes under Ulunat, the great beetle of Sothis, but I do what I can."

Salim nodded. He'd known neither of Faldus's competitors would be local, as the Thuvian government flatly refused to sell the immortality elixir to anyone living permanently within its borders. So Akhom was an Osirian, one of the decadent easterners who'd built the great pyramids and then done little since, save slowly sell off their heritage to foreign exporters and treasure hunters. It was a shameful strategy, but if Akhom's accommodations were any indication, it was also quite lucrative.

"You hail from Sothis originally, then?" he asked politely.

"Of course. As you do from Rahadoum."

Salim startled, and was unable to keep it off his face. Akhom's eyes twinkled.

"Your accent," the merchant said, conversationally. He gave a wide grin, full of humor. "I'd guess somewhere near Manaket originally, but you spent significant time in Azir. Am I close?"

Too close. "My mother was from Manaket. Your ear for dialects is astonishing."

"Not nearly so astonishing as finding one of the Godless wearing Pharasmin black," Akhom countered. "Tell me, how does a citizen of the only atheist nation on an otherwise gods-fearing globe come to be delivering messages for the church of Pharasma in Lamasara?"

Salim realized he had stopped breathing and struggled to consciously relax his muscles. Akhom was good—very good. Either he'd been briefed ahead of time, or he had a remarkable capacity for deduction. Possibly both. Whatever the case, there was no question that Salim was at a significant disadvantage, and Akhom had just made it clear that he knew it. Thirty seconds in the garden, and Salim was already on the defensive. Not a good sign. Salim took a breath and started over.

"That's a long story," he demurred, "and not nearly so interesting as you might suspect. Perhaps we should begin at the beginning. My name is Salim Ghadafar. Though I am here on behalf of the Church of Pharasma, I am neither a priest nor one of the devout, merely working in conjunction with them."

At this point, there was no harm in admitting any of that. The more he thought about it, the safer it seemed to presume that Akhom had been informed of at least the basics. As such, he might as well state them himself. Akhom had successfully put Salim off his game, and this bit of explanation was an acknowledgment of the point—a professional courtesy. Akhom's nod of recognition as Salim spoke confirmed his suspicions.

"I am Akhom Qali," the bearded man replied, "and I am a commodities trader operating all across the northern coast of Garund, from my home in Sothis all the way to yours—and here again I make my impolite assumptions—in the Kingdom of Man, running caravans along the Path of Salt. For the last several years I have resided here in Lamasara, waiting for the right time to bid on the sun orchid elixir." He picked up a teacup which had been sitting next to the leg of the chair and saluted Salim with it. "Which of course you already know. Tea?"

"Certainly. Thank you."

Akhom snapped his fingers, and another guard dressed like the one at the gate stepped out of a cluster of trees not twenty feet to Salim's left. Though this one was slimmer than the gatekeeper, there should still have been no way for Salim to miss him at this distance, not when he'd spent most of his lifetime noticing such things as a matter of survival.

"Tea for Mr. Ghadafar, please, Farik."

The servant bowed deeply and then disappeared into the house proper through another doorway.

Then they were alone again—or at least, so far as Salim could tell. He doubted that a man as wealthy as Akhom Qali would take tea with a stranger unprotected.

Unprotected, hell—the merchant had just proven that he could outmaneuver Salim twice in the time it had taken him to sit down. If either of them was in danger here, it wasn't Qali.

Akhom, for his part, hadn't moved since the servant exited. He continued to observe Salim over the top of his teacup. Though his smile was genial enough, like an indulgent grandfather watching the antics of his progeny, the deep-set eyes above it were cold and calculating. After a moment, he spoke.

"I must apologize," he said, voice still light. "I have a terrible distaste for games, and yet I fear that I have engaged in them twice already. Perhaps we may speak plainly, as befits gentlemen of the desert?"

Salim nodded slowly. Akhom set down his teacup.

"You are Salim Ghadafar," he said, taking on the tone of a teacher reciting facts. "Sometimes called the Priest Who's Not a Priest. You work as a free agent at the Pharasmins' behest, ferreting out undead abominations and those who would seek to extend their lives via that heresy, especially those who prey on innocents. You are good at your job—good enough that though none had met you in person, several of the priests in the Lamasaran diocese had heard of you before you ever arrived. And you're here now, in my garden, to investigate the death of Faldus Anvanory."

Again, Salim could only nod. "You are remarkably well informed."

Akhom acknowledged the compliment with a little sideways bob of his head. "It pays for one in my line of work to be so. For you see, while I do a fabulous business in caravan management, as did the departed Faldus Anvanory, it is not my only calling. I'm also what you might call a career criminal."

Still the man's tone was conversational. Salim felt as if he'd just jumped off a pier into the ocean—that moment when the water first closes over one's head.

"Why are you telling me this?" Salim did his best to match Qali's casual tone.

Qali's answer was immediate. "Because I'm confident that, not only are you completely unaffiliated with the Lamasaran authorities, but even if you did make it your mission to uncover some wrongdoing on my part, your beard would be as white as mine before you found any evidence beyond this conversation. Ah, thank you, Farik."

The servant reappeared, setting down a little table on which rested two blood oranges and a steaming cup of tea for Salim. The servant salaamed and backed off twenty feet toward the wall, but made no attempt to regain his former hiding place.

"None of that is the real reason, however," Qali continued. "The real reason I'm telling you this is that I believe my extralegal affairs to be the simplest and most accessible proof that I had nothing to do with Faldus Anvanory's death."

"And how is that?" Salim asked, reaching for the tea. It was possible Akhom had poisoned it, of course, but at this point Salim was so obviously at the other man's mercy that it hardly mattered. He sipped. It was delicious, as strong as black coffee but with the traditional Osirian cinnamon.

"Simple!" Akhom seemed delighted that Salim was such a willing participant in his little scene. "Though I haven't been approached officially, I've heard through various channels that Faldus was murdered in his home, and that his soul is now somehow being held for ransom, with the price being the sun orchid elixir. Furthermore, it appears that the Church of Pharasma has been drawn into the matter due to the priests having accepted a rather large sum for a resurrection in the event of Faldus's demise, as well as out of general professional pride. Souls going missing is hardly good publicity for the goddess of death, let alone her servants. Is this all more or less correct?"

Salim indicated that it was.

"The irony there is delightful, of course," the merchant said, his tone almost apologetic. "That a church devoted to the cycle of birth and death would be devoting so much energy to helping a dead Taldan extend his life . . . but I'm sure you already appreciate that."

Salim did, but his caution was slowly giving way to irritation at the man's pedantry. "I believe you were about to explain how your knowledge of the situation and your criminal ties place you above suspicion?"

Akhom patted the air in a don't-be-hasty motion. "I'm getting to that. Be patient."

"Now, just as I did not press regarding your atheistic Rahadoumi heritage, I'm sure you'll understand and extend me the same courtesy if I don't go into my illicit holdings and dealings in depth. Suffice it to say that I have a great number of connections, both here and abroad, that are capable and confidential when it comes to making things disappear. That applies to money, artifacts, unfavorable documents—and people, I regret to say." He looked to Salim's sword, resting at his hip in a prime drawing position. "Judging by the way you adjust that without thinking when sitting down, I'm sure you're also well acquainted with that occasional necessity."

Salim ignored the comment. "I'm still not following you."

Akhom looked disappointed.

"Perhaps a demonstration would be more enlightening." The merchant reached for one of the oranges and studied it for a moment, holding it out to allow Salim to do the same. Then he held it up in the air above his head.

"Farik!" he called. "This orange offends me."

The movement was too fast for Salim to follow. One second Akhom was sitting there holding up the orange, and the second both he and Salim were being showered with an explosion of juice and pulp, followed by the clatter of a blade striking stone on the opposite side of the courtyard, where Salim had entered. Akhom calmly lowered his arm so that Salim could see the perfect half-sphere of orange, bisected neatly and horizontally by the servant's throwing knife. Salim glanced at Farik, who had already returned to his posture of bored attention.

"This was an orange," Akhom said. "A man is a far easier target, and the desert has no shortage of shallow graves, nor of men willing to keep a prisoner alive and hidden to prevent resurrection. I am a criminal, it's true, but I am an honest one, as I believe I have proved. And first and foremost, I am a businessman."

He looked deep into Salim's eyes. "I will not say that Faldus Anvanory was a friend, but he was affable, chasing after the elixir with the simple enthusiasm of a dog after a stick. If I had wished to remove him from the situation, I could have done so at any point before the auction and been virtually assured of winning the elixir. If I lost and decided I was unhappy with that situation, I could have sent any number of thieves into his house after it, or simply had both him and his daughter killed before it could be delivered so that it would be auctioned again. As it is, I played a dangerous game of low-bid, and I lost."

He folded his arms across his chest, still holding the dripping orange.

"I will accept the next five years as a lesson," he said. "And then I will bid again. And next time I will win." He looked hard at Salim, and there was not the slightest trace of uncertainty in his declaration.

"Now do you see?" the older man asked.

"I see," Salim said. And he did.

Akhom smiled again, and this time there was no question why Faldus had referred to him as the Jackal.

"Now then," the merchant said, raising the bleeding half of the orange and offering it to Salim. "Fruit?"

Chapter Four
The Queen of Spice

Salim left Akhom Qali's mansion several hours later. Their business concluded, the merchant had insisted that Salim stay and visit with him, exchanging stories of their travels in Avistan and farther abroad, his enthusiasm for Salim's company seemingly genuine. Despite the man's flagrant—and, Salim had to admit, deserved—arrogance regarding his own cunning and intellect, Qali proved a surprisingly pleasant conversationalist, and Salim had found himself enjoying the diversion. It was true that the merchant could be both patronizing and greasily unctuous, as Neila had implied, but neither were qualities he hadn't dealt with dozens of times among priests and nobility.

It was all staged, of course. Akhom's pageant had clearly been orchestrated from start to finish, all the way down to the show with the oranges. He'd known Salim or someone like him would come sniffing around, and had no doubt been as well briefed about Salim by the time he arrived as High Priest Khoyar himself. But even knowing every word had been carefully scripted in advance didn't make Akhom's argument any less convincing. In this case, Akhom's obvious means—both financial and criminal—effectively eliminated his motive, at least where the elaborate kidnapping plot was concerned.

Which meant that it was now midafternoon, and Salim was already zero for one. If Lady Jbade was anything like her competitor, Salim might as well head back to the port right now and see if the Osirian river barge was still taking passengers for its return trip. It wasn't often that Salim was outclassed that easily. Once a day was plenty.

But enough of that. If Akhom wasn't guilty, then by some lines of reasoning it made it that much more likely that Lady Jbade was, and the first order of business in any puzzle was disproving the most likely solutions. Even if he uncovered nothing today, he would have learned something.

Following Olar's instructions, Salim began to walk northwest through the city toward the theater district he had skirted the day before. Though he did his best to circumvent the chaos of the open market—a bustle that had once been so familiar as to be completely inaudible—it still spilled out onto street corners, hawkers enthusing and beggar children dogging his heels with cries of "One copper, Honored One! One copper!" Were he a more obvious foreigner, they would have mobbed him until he couldn't move. As it was, the way he walked and the ease with which he at once acknowledged and ignored them bespoke his familiarity, and they stayed out of cuffing range, eventually abandoning him for easier prey.

After a time, the shops and homes gave way once more to the glitter of unlit lanterns and the cries of barkers that signified the beginning of the theater district proper. Some of the venues were smaller than a simple dwelling, just mud boxes with four walls and men to accept the coppers that purchased admission. Some didn't even have that much, but were rather canvas-walled tents, or woven stockades through which passersby could discern the faint shapes of sinuous forms dancing to tambours and castanets—a calculated preview that was even more effective for what it gave away free. The shows the barkers espoused ran the gamut from traditional mummers' pageants and dancing troupes to erotic shadow plays and unnatural couplings that would make a Calistrian blanch. These delights were proclaimed loud and long for the benefit of anyone who cared to listen, and Salim saw many young boys leaning near the entrances to the more exotic venues, possessing neither the funds nor the age to get them inside but being educated all the same.

As Salim continued along his course, the buildings got steadily larger and grander, becoming proper multistory theaters and performance halls. Though some still advertised illicit fare—as with much of the world, sex often prevailed where talent was scarce—these were as opulent as the strait-laced establishments, becoming true cabarets and brothels rather than back-room rutting halls. The young starlets who hung out of windows displaying their wares were as brown as sun-baked earth, dark hair loose or braided, and eyes dusted with kohl or aquamarine. Most were beautiful, in the smooth-skinned Thuvian fashion, and many danced to better highlight their natural blessings. Some sang in threes and fours, their gentle voices blending into a siren song that flowed out into the streets like cool water. Among traders along the Path of Salt, it was said that if a Lamasaran girl's body couldn't satisfy you, her voice would.

Salim ignored their calls and shimmies and continued down the street, allowing the determination in his stride to cut a path as straight as any sword. When he reached the theater Olar had specified—an arched affair with a fresco of several tiny, phoenixlike birds—he turned and began up a slightly smaller avenue which did something few others in Lamasara did: it climbed. The slope wasn't much, but in a town that was almost completely flat, the difference was immediately noticeable.

It was a trick as old as the desert itself—simply pile earth and rubble over collapsed structures and build on top of them rather than clearing them away—but the view still increased the property's value accordingly. By the time Salim was most of the way up the artificial hill, he was able to look out over several of the theaters' rooftops and see the rest of the city, picking out a few other such mottes, as well as landmarks like the royal palace and the Pharasmin cathedral.

At the top of the hillock stood a building every bit as fabulous as Qali's compound or Anvanory Manor. This one eschewed Qali's featureless mud brick walls and abundant greenery in favor of a many-storied construction and small, artfully landscaped gardens of stones and native succulents. The walls were painted in brilliant desert colors, from sand yellow to the red of the sunset, yet these features paled in comparison to the decorations that lined the wide front porch.

The decorations were women. Women of all shapes and colors, from a black-skinned Zenj Mwangi woman with the proud shoulders of a jungle warrior to an impish Vudrani in saffron silks, and even a purple-haired gnome whose plum-colored nipples were visible shadows through the gauzy white wrap she wore. Short and tall, willow-thin or well upholstered, there was no question that each was striking in her own way. A full dozen of these women lounged in chairs or perched on benches, laughing and playing games with colored stones or quietly conversing with each other. Several looked up as Salim approached, and by the time he stopped at the edge of their tiled patio, all were studying him, demurely through lowered lashes or with brazen and appraising stares. One of them, a slim girl who appeared a native of the north coast, stood and sashayed forward to greet him.

"Welcome, Lord," she purred. "See anything you like?"

Her smile was inviting—not just the doxy's trade sign, but something with a touch of genuine friendliness— and Salim warmed to it involuntarily.

"Several things," he said, returning her smile with a small one of his own.

The other women paused in what they were doing and either sat up straighter or leaned more languorously, depending on individual strategy. The lead girl waved an arm to encompass them all.

"Any or all, my lord. A dancer or three to envelop you in the Naiad's Veils. The most passionate love stories of history and legend brought to life at your feet, or in your lap. A nightingale to sing you to sleep—eventually. Any or all."

Salim shook his head and made a show of regret that was not completely feigned.

"My apologies, most talented mistresses, but I'm afraid I cannot indulge. I seek specific company."

"Oh?" The spokeswoman arched an eyebrow. "Fair enough. Who is it that you desire? Someone you saw in a performance, perhaps?"

"I need to speak with Lady Jbade."

At once, the women's demeanor changed. Gone was the lolling cathouse frivolity, the careful air of sensuality. All around him, bared flesh tensed and leaned forward, subtly straining to catch his words. The lead woman smiled again, but this time it was harder, and with a touch of pity.

"Go home, priest," she said, not unkindly. "You're a reasonably attractive man, but you have neither the funds nor the status to engage the lady's interest, and she's not one to suffer proselytizing. Put her from your mind, and you'll be much happier. Better yet, allow one of us to aid you in forgetting."

Again, Salim shook his head.

"I have business with the lady. Of a different sort."

The woman looked at him critically for a long moment, arms crossed pugnaciously over high breasts, then nodded. At her motion, the women behind her relaxed and lost interest, returning to their games and posturing. Salim got the feeling that, had he tried to force his way into the manor, he wouldn't have made it more than a few steps.

"Come with me," the spokeswoman said, and led him across the porch and into the building itself.

Lady Jbade's manor was as different from Qali's or the Anvanorys' as night from day. Where the other two had been residences—albeit extraordinary ones, their daily routines fueled by entire villages of servants— this place looked like a combination theater and brothel. The grand entryway was hung thick with silks and tapestries, the walls beyond sporting murals and mosaics of tiny, colored pieces of glass blown from desert sands. Several more women lounged on low couches or leaned over the upstairs balcony, seemingly with no other purpose than to be seen.

The spokeswoman led, and Salim followed. In lieu of doorways, most of the chambers that extended off of the house's hallways bore curtains of diaphanous cloth or beads that could be drawn across the opening. Some had been left open, and through these Salim saw women dancing slowly and sensually for men with expensive clothes and wide grins. Some of these women wore elaborate costumes, others cascades of tiny bells that provided their own accompanying music. Still others wore nothing at all. And these were just the doors that were left open. Of the rooms they passed, twice that number had the curtains drawn, and from behind these came laughter, moans, and the occasional shriek.

Salim and the woman ascended three flights of stairs, at last coming out into an antechamber that Salim judged to be on the topmost story. Before them was yet another of the cascading thread-curtains, but this one was embroidered with an ornate tessellation of flowers and dragons, shining with thread of gold. To either side stood two oiled and muscular men wearing loincloths and holding short halberds whose delicately curved blades looked sharp enough to shave with.

"Wait here," the woman said, and disappeared through the thousand tendrils of the dragon-flowers. Salim stood as he was bid, studying the two guards. From the pale blue eye shadow and a smoothness to their features that was at odds with their well-sculpted muscles, he guessed that they were eunuchs. The way neither had so much as glanced at his guide as she swayed through the curtain lent weight to the theory, though perhaps that was simply a side effect of working in a whorehouse. After a moment the woman reappeared.

"The lady will see you," she said, beckoning him with a finger.

Salim passed through the curtain and into a sultan's harem. Though the rest of the building had been decorated with couches and wall hangings, this room was upholstered so heavily that there wasn't a hard angle to be seen. It was impossible to tell how high the ceiling extended, for twelve feet up, a web of hundreds of silk streamers strung between the walls created a layered canopy of soft colors, through which unseen lights cast a warm glow. Pillows and mats covered the floor shin-deep, crisscrossed by narrow paths of fabric stretched taut a few inches above the floor, pleasantly conforming to the foot that trod it. All of it—every pillow, hanging, and pathway—seemed specifically positioned to draw the eye toward the enormous canopied bed and its sole occupant.

Lady Leantina Issa Jbade was much as Salim had imagined her, but that in no way diminished the impact of her appearance. Lounging on the mattress like a cat, she wore a long gown of iridescent green which clung flatteringly to her slim waist and rounded hips, a long slit exposing a smooth expanse of leg all the way up to the outside of her thigh. Her arms were bare and bronze, and Salim would have put her as roughly thirty years old if her face didn't display the delicate, porcelain features of the elf-blooded. Slightly pointed ears poking through the sheer black waterfall of her hair confirmed the fact, as did slanted eyes with oversized emerald irises.

At the moment, those eyes were ignoring his arrival, focused instead on something taking place around the corner in an alcove facing the bed. Her expression was one of polite boredom, and after a moment of waiting, Salim took a risk and stepped forward, craning his neck to see what she was watching—and then quickly withdrew, face flushing.

What he'd thought was an alcove was in fact a whole side-chamber. Unlike the rest of the room, this area was bare stone, raised up a foot from the cushioned floor and positioned to act as a stage, with the bed its sole audience.

On the stage were no fewer than five women, locked in the most intricate and intimate coupling Salim had ever witnessed. All wore costumes that highlighted rather than concealed their nudity, and smooth flesh gleamed and glistened in the lamplight. Several were contorted as only trained dancers could manage, and one wore nothing but a bizarre harlequin cap, standing over her worshipful lovers on high stilts strapped to her ankles. Though Salim caught only a glimpse of the proceedings before withdrawing his head and staring fixedly at an empty point in space above the lady's bed, he could still hear the moist sounds of sliding skin and the heavy breathing of the women's exertions.

At last Lady Jbade nodded and snapped her fingers. Instantly the sounds changed, the murmurs and panting shifting to the padding of bare feet and low voices.

"Good," Jbade called, her tone encouraging. "Excellent work, ladies. Carisse, your leg is still too low, and you're not getting full extension. I trust I won't have to tell you again."

There were soft murmurs, and then the women were filing past Salim and out the door, still wearing their fanciful costumes and carrying the stilts. As the last woman passed, Salim did a double-take. It was the fire-eater from the marketplace the day before, the one with the remarkable trick of lighting a candle through the piercing in her throat. He now saw that those flame tattoos didn't just cover her arms—they swirled up over her bare bosom and down across the taut expanse of her stomach until they disappeared from view.

The woman caught him staring and glared. She lifted her chin as she passed, like a boxer inviting an opponent to take his best shot, clearly asking who he was to judge her. Then she was past him and the curtain was falling closed.

"Pay no attention to her."

Salim refocused on the woman on the bed, who had turned to regard him with those cool eyes.

"Carisse is new, and has not yet adjusted completely. Many of them are like that when they first make the transition."

"And what transition is that?" Salim stood with hands folded neatly in front of him. Jbade's eyes flicked downward, took in his not-entirely-coincidental posture, and gave him a knowing smile.

"The transition from amateur to professional," she said, and waved a manicured hand toward a deep green couch set against the wall a few feet from the bed. "Please, sit."

Salim did so, the height of the couch bringing him down so that his eyes were now level with hers without her having to sit up.

"I'm not sure I understand," he said.

Jbade waved a hand dismissively. "Talent is everywhere in Lamasara. Throw a stone and you'll bruise a dancer or a singer. Most will never make it beyond a street corner in the marketplace, let alone into the top cabarets. Yet there are a few with potential, and I try to take those under my wing, help them make a name for themselves."

Salim thought of Carisse eating fire in the market, and compared it with the act he'd just witnessed.

"And adding your own unique flavor, I see."

Jbade's smile was sultry.

"I offer them a chance to improve their routines and perform in reputable venues. And in return, they agree to help me entertain my many friends to the fullest of their abilities."

So that was her game. No wonder the women out front and in the curtained rooms had seemed so studied in their movements. Though he had never been much for art, Salim understood that patronage—more commonly known as "sleeping your way to the top"— was common in the performance circles of many cities. In Lamasara, Lady Jbade appeared to have codified it, trading top billing for the performers' willingness to prostitute themselves to their fans, with Jbade acting as their madame.

Jbade saw the calculating look in his eyes and leaned forward slightly to study him.

"I do not believe we've been introduced," she said. "It's not uncommon for men I've never met to come looking for me, but it *is* rare for Lhael to admit one of them without so much as asking his name. You must have made quite an impression."

Salim bowed his head. "My name is Salim Ghadafar, and I come on business of the Church of Pharasma, at the request of High Priest Khoyar Roshan."

"Ah, Khoyar." She gave another of her little smiles. "I'm surprised he would send a messenger rather than take the opportunity to come himself."

"Undoubtedly he would prefer to," Salim said, "but this is not a social call. The church is curious about the death of Faldus Anvanory, whom I believe you know."

Though Jbade's calculated sprawl didn't change, her delicate features locked into hard lines.

"Indeed," she said. "I knew him well, and was greatly saddened to hear of his death, so close to the fulfillment of his goal."

She sat up then, the neckline of her dress shifting lower to barely maintain its hold on her small but perfectly formed breasts.

"Please," she said, "call me Leantina. I suspect you have many questions."

He did. Where Qali had immediately gone on the attack, keeping Salim off guard with his own questions and observations, Leantina Jbade took the opposite tack, making a show of relaxedly answering all the questions he put to her with complete openness and honesty.

Jbade was indeed a bastard child of the elf nation Kyonin, though Salim didn't ask about the story Olar had told him. Relegated to the port city of Erages and denied full citizenship in her country of origin due to the human blood in her veins, she quickly developed a grudge against her elven kin. Though she matured into an unparalleled beauty, even among those who shared her benevolent breeding, she seethed with resentment, knowing that hers was a perfection that would fade with comparative speed while the true elves remained almost ageless. Furious, she took sail on a ship headed down the Sellen and left her patronizing kin behind, paying for her passage in the universal coin. It was this first transaction, with a gruff but kind river captain, that set her on her course.

From the dance halls of Cassomir to the highest courts of Absalom, beautiful Jbade practiced her art, amassing a sizable fortune as both a high-profile dancer and a courtesan and sometimes wife to a number of powerful and aged nobles. When the last of these died, she liquidated her assets and set sail for Lamasara and the fabled sun orchid elixir, with which she could at last achieve what even her pureblooded cousins could not—eternal youth.

"And here I am!" she said, spreading her arms wide in a carefree gesture no doubt rehearsed thoroughly for its effect on her bosom.

"Yet without the elixir," Salim noted.

She cocked her head to the side, birdlike, as if surprised at his utter lack of tact.

"A small matter," she said lightly.

"Yet one capable of consuming a woman's life," Salim pressed. "Or a man's."

She dropped her arms, and the glint in her eyes was no longer salacious.

"Look around you, Salim. Do you see signs of poverty?"

He humored her, and was forced to shake his head. The bedchamber was as extravagant as any he'd encountered.

"Now what about me?" she asked, leaning forward to expose the rounded tops of her breasts. "Have I withered?"

Again, the answer was clearly negative.

"In that case," she said, and her manner was suddenly businesslike. "Understand something, Salim. My bid for the elixir has already been paid, yet everything you see remains in my possession. And even if it didn't, I would retain the youth and beauty that won them in the first place—which, thanks to my bastard heritage, I'll retain long after you're too old to care about either, save in the academic sense."

She stood up, and her long, slim legs moved smoothly beneath the shimmering dress. She turned in a slow circle, displaying the garment's scooped back, and her toes were light and pointed as a fairy alighting on a flower. When she faced him once more, she extended a delicate hand. He took it, and she pulled him upright with surprising strength. Standing, he was surprised to find that she was almost as tall as he was.

"If the church has sent you to look into Faldus's death," Leantina continued, trailing an arm across his chest as she moved in a measured circle around him, "it must believe you a great judge of character, someone capable of discerning motives and detecting half-truths. As it turns out, I hope they're right, so that there can be no doubt." She completed her circuit and looked him in the eye.

"I did not kill Faldus Anvanory," she said plainly, "nor did I in any way orchestrate his death. I lost the auction, and that was no small setback, but it was not worth killing a man and jeopardizing everything I've built. In five years, or fifty, I will bid again. That difference is great to someone like Qali or Anvanory, but little to me. There will be other opportunities."

She studied Salim as he stood at attention, observing her, then laughed and cupped his chin.

"You no doubt have a terrible impression of me from Faldus's slip of a daughter," she said, "but I assure you, Faldus and I were not enemies. Far from it. We were . . . close." The hand dropped to caress his arm, squeezing the bicep lightly, as if Salim were a sack of lemons hanging in a fruit vendor's stall.

"I think she feared I'd marry her father and take her place in the household, but of course there was never any danger of that. Faldus was wealthy, but such things mean little when the queen herself competes for my attentions." Her fingers were soft, butterfly-touches. "I am a self-made woman, Salim, and I will acquire the elixir on my own terms."

She stepped backward, away from him, and straightened her shoulders. "If you're a priest," she said, looking to his robes, "you no doubt have magical means of verifying what I've said. If so, please use them. I invite you."

But Salim had seen enough. "I don't think that will be necessary," he said. "The truth of your words lies as bare as your beauty."

Her eyes widened slightly, and she moved forward until she was almost touching him, the heat of her body radiating through the space between them to warm his stomach.

"So he has manners after all," she murmured. The hand returned to his bicep, and she looked up at him with new consideration. "It's a rare man who can resist a direct invitation." Her voice was smoky.

He smiled. "If that is the case," he said, daring to put a hand on the warm skin of her arm, "then I have distinguished myself twice today."

Then he stepped backward out of her grasp, bowed once from the waist, and exited the room.

Chapter Five
Death's Reward

Salim ate a late lunch in the market, buying several slabs of fried goat meat from a man whose stand was no more than a hanging rack of skinned goats and a semicircular iron basin hung precariously over a fire, into which he dropped fresh cuts of flesh and swirled them in palm oil with a bent skewer. These he deftly speared and deposited in folded palm leaves containing mashed garlic and salt. Salim ate them carefully with his fingers while walking through the stalls, thinking less about the array of wares in front of him than what he'd learned so far.

After he'd wasted as much time as he dared, he turned back toward the theater district. This time, however, he didn't climb the hill to Lady Jbade's seductive manse, but rather continued onward to the city's edge and the great cathedral of the Lady of Graves.

In truth, he had little desire to return—simply being inside a church irritated him, its overbearing presence like a constant and irritating whine in the background—but there was always the possibility that Khoyar had fresh information. Salim climbed the steps unchallenged and entered through the big iron doors.

Inside, the grand chamber which had been bustling the previous day was almost completely empty, save for an older priest in a corner who was speaking quietly to a grieving couple, the woman's face and hair streaked with mourning ash.

"Master Ghadafar!"

Salim turned to find the young acolyte he'd been assigned the day before springing up from a short, three-legged stool placed against the wall in the shadow of the big doors.

"Hello, Hasam."

The boy beamed at being remembered. "I've been waiting for you."

Salim looked at the stool. "Waiting here? Why?"

"In case you returned and needed anything, as the high priest instructed."

Salim nodded. Then a second thought occurred to him.

"How long?" he asked.

Hasam looked quizzical. "Since you left," he replied. His cow-eyed sincerity reminded Salim again that the Pharasmins didn't do anything in half measures. If he had to hazard a guess, he'd bet that the boy had slept on that stool. Senseless.

"Where's Khoyar?" he asked, but his guide was already in motion.

"This way," Hasam said, leading Salim through the same doors they'd passed through the first time, but this time turning left down a wide corridor that was lit by more of the narrow windows, eventually coming to a straight flight of stone steps leading down. "High Priest Khoyar is conducting the ninth-hour service in the Chapel of Lights."

At the bottom of the steps they turned a corner and passed through a set of wooden doors hung thick with a curtain of midnight-blue cloth. Then they were in a small chapel.

Unlike the grand entry hall, this room had none of the great windows. Instead, the walls and ceiling were smooth blocks of bare, gray stone, whose looming weight combined with tightly packed stone pews to create an immediate sense of claustrophobia. Overall, the effect was that of having been interred inside a mausoleum. Which, Salim supposed, was the whole point.

The only light in the room came from dozens of candles—short wax tapers hung from the walls and ceiling in iron sconces, their random patterns making gently flickering star fields above them. Perhaps thirty men in black cassocks and robes similar to Salim's own crowded the narrow pews. They too held candles. Salim and Hasam took up positions near the back wall, so as not to disturb the worshipers.

Khoyar stood at a raised podium near the far wall. The altar's twisting stone narrowed to incredible thinness in the middle, only to flare out again at chest height—an artist's rendition of Pharasma's Spire, the great pillar of the planes which supported the Boneyard, and to which all souls went to be judged. Khoyar had his own candle sitting on the podium-altar's flat surface, and in one hand he held a hollow half-sphere of glass or crystal, like a wine goblet without its stem.

"So do we wander in this world," Khoyar intoned, "bereft of all but the warp and weft of the goddess's threads to guide us. Yet whether we seek to follow our course or break from it, it matters not, for in time all things are drawn back to the pattern set forth by the Lady's hand."

Inverting the glass, he placed it over the candle. As he spoke, the flame slowly dimmed, guttering as it consumed all the air in the globe.

"In the end, all become as one. Princes and beggars, thieves and saints—all of us will face our last moments alone, stripped of ambition, of doubt. But in that final breath, as in the first one taken by a newborn, we are all the same. We are our mortality—nothing more, nothing less. All go naked before the Lady, and all shall be judged."

The candle flame was now down to a single glowing coal at the end of its wick.

"Yet death is not an end," Khoyar continued. "Nor is it loss. For in the perfection of death, that single moment of unification, we are reborn. As the universe first burst forth into being, so do we burst forth from our bodies, to be judged in Pharasma's great court and begin new lives among the stars, in the unimaginable vistas of the metaphysical planes, or in the gasping cry of the birth-wet child. This is the reward of death. This is its gift."

With a flourish, Khoyar removed the glass, and the wick that had been about to wink out for good flared high in the backdraft of fresh air, suddenly brilliant.

"In death," Khoyar concluded, "life finds its meaning. And for this, we give thanks."

"We give thanks!" the congregation echoed, and Salim tensed at the sudden burst of sound. Then the reverie was broken, and the men were filing out past him and Hasam, speaking to each other in low tones.

Hasam approached the altar, and Salim followed. Khoyar looked up and spotted them.

"Salim," he said, his tone welcoming. "When you did not return last night, I was unsure when we'd see you next."

"Lady Anvanory offered me her hospitality, and I elected to spend the night there."

"I see," Khoyar said, and the corner of his lip twitched with the ghost of a smile. "I'm glad you found her so . . . accommodating."

Salim didn't appreciate the insinuation. "It seemed prudent to remain near the scene of the murder," he said, then changed the subject. "That was a nice speech there." He nodded toward the altar.

Khoyar bowed his head modestly. "My thanks. I have always been particularly fond of the Interment of the Lights."

"Of course," Salim continued, "you left out a few things. The devils that turn you into howling larvae, or the screaming demons that rend you into ribbons of steaming flesh for all time. But I suppose every religion varnishes a few truths, no?"

Khoyar's head snapped up, and his face was hard and disapproving. "Pharasma's judgment comes to every man, but such things are not spoken of lightly."

"Of course," Salim pressed. "But then, have you seen them? Have you looked out with your own eyes and seen the pits where fallen souls lie unreborn and unforgiven, forming the very stones of fiendish palaces?"

"I have not," Khoyar said stiffly. "Nor do I ever expect to. What about you, Salim? Where do you expect to go when you die?"

Salim laughed.

"I'll go wherever Pharasma sends me, including into the ground to rot. Why should death be any different?"

The two men were glaring at each other in earnest now. After an awkward moment, Khoyar realized he was being baited and got control of himself.

"What have you learned about Anvanory?"

Salim found himself reluctant to report anything to the puffed-up theocrat, but took a deep breath and launched into a concise version of his encounters with both Qali and Jbade. When he had finished, Khoyar nodded.

"That is unfortunate," he said, "for it seems our time is running short. Another message from the kidnappers appeared this morning."

"*What?*" Only careful control kept the words from becoming a shout. "Why wasn't I informed?"

Khoyar shrugged dismissively. "We were preparing to dispatch a runner, but we thought you might appear at any moment, and it's a significant distance to the Anvanory estate."

Salim ignored the excuse. "How was the message delivered?"

"The same method as last time—the disappearing scroll. Yet this time it appeared in the cathedral's catacombs, on the body of Faldus Anvanory himself. One of the sisters discovered it in the course of her morning duties, and knew better than to touch it. She summoned me, and I was able to dictate its words to a scribe before it disintegrated. Unfortunately I was not able to trace any of the magics involved in its sending, save to identify that they were extremely powerful."

"And?" Salim prompted. "What did it say?"

Khoyar shook his head in disappointment. "Very little, I'm afraid. It appears that the kidnappers have grown tired of waiting. Lady Anvanory has seventy-two hours to make her decision and complete the transaction with the Lamasaran officials, after which the soul will be destroyed if the elixir is not in place. I trust you will inform the young woman of this unfortunate development."

Salim nodded distractedly. Three days. There was nowhere near enough time. He hadn't even begun to unravel the kidnappers' identity, let alone figure out a plan for retrieving the soul. The idea that he'd traveled this far on a fool's errand was becoming a very real possibility.

Suddenly he wanted nothing more than to be out of this church, and out of the presence of smug merchants who made their bread selling intangibles and false hopes.

"It seems I had better get back to work, then," Salim said. "I trust that you'll not wait to send a runner next time, if further information comes to light?"

"Of course," Khoyar said.

"Good." Without further comment, Salim turned and headed for the exit.

"Actually," Khoyar's voice rang out behind him, "there is one more thing."

"Yes?" Salim turned impatiently, one hand already drawing back the dark curtains of the doorway.

Khoyar smirked and drew the spiral of Pharasma in the air between them.

"May the goddess's blessing go with you."

Chapter Six
Flames in the Night

Salim found the Anvanory cart on the border between the theater district and the marketplace. Olar was sitting on the cart's high seat as if he'd been there the whole time, but his sunny expression and the looks he kept casting toward a plump prostitute leaning out a third-story window made Salim suspect otherwise. He wondered if the woman was one of Lady Jbade's.

The ride back to the manor was uneventful, and this time Salim let Olar keep his silence. In truth, he was in no mood for chatter. Though it was far from over, the day had been both a success and a failure.

As inelegant as the interviews had been—and as he'd suspected, too much time questioning frightened peasants and tracking walking corpses had let his interrogation techniques atrophy significantly—they'd told him enough. Despite Faldus Anvanory's natural suspicions, neither the Harlot nor the Jackal seemed to have sufficient motive to go to such great lengths to acquire the elixir, when they could simply bid again next time around.

What's more, both of them had been telling the truth. Salim had always been adept at spotting the tiny visual clues that told you someone was lying—the dilated pupils and elevation in pitch, as well as the more obvious body language. Since falling under Ceyanan's direction, those abilities had only sharpened. He'd watched both Jbade and Qali carefully, and neither had so much as broken eye contact. They hadn't killed Faldus Anvanory.

Which was good news, he supposed. Yet it also meant that the only obvious leads had dried up and blown away like chaff under the millstone. They were back at square one.

The cart pulled up in front of Anvanory Manor at last, coming in through the long drive this time rather than the field access track. Salim hopped down. The servants didn't exactly swirl around him the way they had when he'd entered with Neila, but one of the young chambermaids immediately fell in step beside him, leading him up the wide, curving stairs and through the house with a firm but deferential manner, staying close to his side so that an onlooker would have had trouble telling who was directing whom. At the open entrance to the solarium, she stopped and took up a practiced position just outside the archway. Salim entered.

Neila was standing in the center of a room bathed in the rich light of evening. One whole wall was nothing but windows that stretched to the high ceiling, and that bank of glass protruded outward in a sweeping curve. Halfway across the room, where the arc of the windows began, the floor dropped down two feet, creating a cozy nook with almost a hundred and eighty degrees of view. Two comfortable-looking armchairs were positioned there, along with an end table and small lamp for reading after dark, but Neila eschewed all of this in favor of pacing back and forth across the top of the stairs. A small book with a cloth bookmark lay forgotten in her hand. She turned as Salim entered, and her face lit up with relief.

"You're back!" she said, and then looked startled as her overly loud words echoed back at her from the glowing windows. She visibly reined herself back to a proper volume and manner.

"Please," she said, gesturing toward the chairs with the book. "Sit. Make yourself comfortable and tell me everything you've learned."

Salim did as he was bid, descending the two carpeted steps and seating himself in one of the chairs, which he was pleased to note was upholstered in cloth rather than the common Taldan leather, which would have held the sun's warmth and seared his skin like meat on a griddle. Neila took the other one, turning it to face him directly across the space of a few feet, and sat with her knees together and balled fists resting on them. She leaned forward anxiously.

"I beg pardon for rushing you, but I'm used to handling any matters of import myself, and I'm afraid it's made me terribly impatient. While I understand completely why you needed to go alone to interrogate Qali and Jbade, the waiting was . . . maddening." She gave him a self-effacing smile, and he returned it honestly.

"No apologies necessary," he said, then took the hint and launched into an efficient but thorough description of the day's events, beginning with Khoyar's unfortunate message from the kidnappers. Neila's jaw clenched, but she withheld comment, motioning for him to continue. When he finished telling her about Qali's performance, she nodded.

"That sounds like him," she said. "Never precisely rude, but thoroughly impressed with himself, and always making certain that everyone else is appropriately aware of his brilliance. I'm surprised that he was so candid about his criminal dealings, but he's right—the word of an outsider would carry little weight with the Lamasaran authorities, and the Church of Pharasma has nothing to gain from pursuing him." She wrinkled her nose in disgust. "I still don't like him, nor trust him in the slightest, but I think you're right—if he's as dangerous as he claims, he could have had us killed the moment it became clear we would be challenging him, and he doesn't appear to be hurting for the funds to try again. What about the Harlot?"

This time Salim gave a slightly abridged version of events. Though he'd seen few scenes in the past to rival the erotic tableau in Jbade's bedroom, he was hardly interested in discussing such things with this young aristocrat. Aside from that minor detail, he gave a faithful account of his dealings with the half-elven madame. Yet while he'd thought his delivery perfectly calm and smooth, Neila's sharp eyes must have caught some twitch, or else she was simply suspicious of all men where Jbade was involved, because once he was finished she lowered one eyebrow and peered at him intently.

"And that's everything?" she pressed, voice sharp.

"More or less," Salim replied.

Reaching forward, she plucked delicately at the shoulder of his robe, then held up two long, black hairs. "And these?" she asked lightly. "Were these part of the more? Or perhaps the less?"

The look she gave him, holding up the strands of hair like a fishwife confronting her philandering husband, was too much. Salim leaned back in his chair and laughed.

"So you did let her seduce you!" Neila glared at him. "I should have known better than to send a man to deal with that doxy. How am I supposed to trust any of your conclusions if you're out sampling her wares?"

Salim's laughter died to a chuckle, and after a moment he took control of himself and leaned forward. He was still smiling, but when he spoke his voice was perfectly calm.

"Your protectiveness regarding my honor is admirable, Lady," he said, "but unnecessary."

"Oh?" she spat. "And why should I believe that?"

Salim looked her in the eye. "Because I haven't touched a woman since my wife died."

"Oh." This time the word was involuntary. There was a pause, and Neila rocked back in her chair, suddenly embarrassed. "I'm sorry."

Salim waved a hand. "That was a long time ago, and neither here nor there. The important thing is that Lady Jbade's physical charms are not a factor in my judgment, but her story is. And it's my assessment that, whether or not you approve of her profession or whatever relationship she may have had with your father"—Neila's eyes flashed at that—"I don't believe she's responsible for his death. Both she and Qali seem to be telling the truth."

Again, Neila's face screwed into an expression of distaste. They sat in silence for a few moments, both deep in thought, and then Neila pulled herself up straight, shoulders set.

"Very well, then," she said. "It seems this avenue of inquiry has run its course. In lieu of another obvious lead, it—"

But whatever she was about to say was cut off by a sudden explosion of shattering glass, the shards of which rained down on both of them like tinkling hail. A flaming shape the size of Salim's fist sailed over their heads and slammed into the wall near the door, dropping to the floor and immediately lighting the reed paper of an Osirian wall-scroll, which caught fire with a soft whumph. In an instant, Salim was out of his chair and stamping out the blaze, tearing the expensive wall hanging in half and throwing it to the floor before the flames could climb too high for him to reach.

"What is it?" Neila cried, coming up behind him. Her voice was not quite a shriek, but she would have been justified had it been. When the flare-up was safely extinguished, Salim leaned down and used a handful of crumpled art to carefully pick up the still-steaming lump. He studied it from several angles, then lifted it and carefully sniffed its surface.

It was an ordinary river stone, smooth and ellipsoidal, around which someone had carefully packed sticky pitch and resin, nearly doubling its size. He looked back toward the bank of windows, which now had a jagged hole in its top left corner.

There were more sounds of shattering glass, coming from other areas of the house. Through the muffling of the walls, Salim heard the screams of servants. Ignoring Neila's question, he moved quickly back to the windows.

Yes, there they were—out in the fields nearest the house, where the wheat and corn were already shadowed by a sprawling wing of the manor, shapes were moving. As he watched, a man-sized shadow emerged from the corn and whirled something around its head—a sling, clearly—then snapped its arm. Another guttering ball of flaming pitch sailed toward the house and found its mark in the chime of crashing glass.

"Salim?" Neila asked again, and this time her voice was fearful.

Salim turned back to her, and realized that he'd drawn his sword. The long, thin blade caught the light, and the melted bronze blob of the hilt and quillons conformed to his hand as if they'd been made for him. Which, of course, they had.

"Come on," he said, and grabbed her wrist as he dashed out of the room.

Out on the balcony above the grand entryway, the house was in chaos. Servants ran to and fro, women screaming and herding children, men carrying buckets of water or makeshift cudgels. No two seemed to be running in the same direction.

"You!" Salim called to one man carrying a long taper-pole for lighting chandelier candles. "They're out back, in the eastern fields. Grab three others and follow me." Without waiting to see if the man would obey, Salim turned and raced through the grand dining room, then through the chaos of the kitchen and out the back door, still dragging Neila behind him.

Outside, he immediately saw that the incendiaries were doing their work. Already, the telltale flickers shone from several broken windows, and the screaming of men and beasts from the stables suggested that someone had made the wise decision to lob a flame into the stores of dry hay and feed. Salim paid little attention to the grooms and serving women who were frantically running back and forth from the well to the house, carrying what water they could in what vessels they could find, from pots and pans to drenched bed sheets. Instead, Salim let go of Neila's wrist.

"Stay back and help organize the fire fighters," he said. Then he turned toward the fields and their attackers.

At first it was hard to tell what they were fighting. The shapes of the Anvanorys' servants were clear enough, despite the long shadows of twilight, but the rest seemed strangely twisted and disappeared easily into the waving stalks of the fields. It wasn't until one of the shapes detached from the mob and flew forward, almost buzzing Salim's shoulder, that he understood.

"Fey!" he called to everyone within earshot. "They're fey!"

The shape that had flown past him was no larger than a child, but it rolled and dived with the speed and agility of a swallow, sending tiny arrows into the hubbub. Where the darts struck, servants dropped as if poleaxed. As Salim watched, the shape whirred its insectile wings and darted into a broken window. It emerged a moment later, followed by a flash and the crackling of flames.

Without a bow of his own, there was nothing Salim could do. Ignoring the firebrand for the time being, Salim put his head down and charged toward the fields, sword held lightly in front of him.

A group of field workers and a few grooms were already there, making a rough battle line along the cart track which separated the bounty of the fields from the well-manicured lawn of the manor grounds proper. They shouted and swung heavy scythes and blunt hoes with deadly force, yet the shapes which darted among them were far faster and more nimble.

Salim got close enough to see several of the farmhands harrying a thin, willowy woman with skin like old bark.

A dryad, he realized. Beneath his iron calm, a part of him marveled. The tree spirits rarely traveled more than a few hundred yards from their bonded trees—to do so physically sickened them. Yet here this one was, with the river forest just a line on the horizon, attacking at a disadvantage.

Indeed, despite the wicked spear in her hands, the wood-woman seemed hard-pressed by the farmers' crude rush. She fell back steadily into the waves of grain, her steps faltering, and they followed her eagerly, howling their approval.

As the last man crossed from the road into the field, however, the dryad suddenly stood tall and raised her hands. As the field workers watched in horror, the ripple of the breeze on the wheat inexplicably changed direction, flowing toward them. Several cried out and turned to run, but the same shafts of grain they'd spent months cultivating now bent to ensnare them, threading a thousand knots around their limbs and pulling them down. Those who tripped and fell were covered over in an instant, and then the dryad stepped forward with spear raised to harvest the reapers.

The telltale drone of an enormous insect warned Salim, and he threw himself to the side just in time to see one of the tiny pixie arrows thud softly into the ground where he'd stood. Without thinking, he spun, bringing the blade of his sword up and around in a wide slash.

Caught by surprise, the pixie's momentum carried it straight into the blade, which caught it at its collarbone and sheared off an arm and a wing, spraying Salim with a fine mist of blood. The little fey didn't even have time to scream as it completed its trajectory and thumped down into the dust of the road, rolling to a stop, its gossamer wings crusted with bloody dirt.

Damn. Salim was used to killing undead—he wouldn't say he liked it, exactly, but it did hold a certain satisfaction. Yet those things were already dead. They'd had their chance, and only a twisted mockery of natural laws or the meddling of capricious spellcasters had brought them back into a semblance of life. Pixies, on the other hand, were creatures of the natural world. Salim had met a few in his travels. They were cocky and juvenile, yes, and generally a pain in the ass, but not evil. He hadn't even known why this one was fighting.

But there would be time for recriminations later, if he survived, and if he didn't, one more stain on his conscience wouldn't matter either way. He turned back to the farmers who'd unwisely advanced into the field after the tree spirit.

The dryad was down on one knee, weeping silently, and the wound in her side would have looked like a gouge in a tree trunk if it weren't for the saplike ichor flowing out of it. Several of the farmers were breaking free of the wheat now, and the broad-shouldered young man who'd been the first to escape raised up the long-handled scythe for a second blow.

Salim turned away. This was madness. There was no hope of organizing the manor's servants, nor any clear commanders of the various fey. They were simply throwing themselves at the manor like moths against a lantern and, if the dryad and pixie were any indication, with similar results. Why?

Over the shouts and screams of men and fey, trilling higher than the flames now crackling in earnest at various points around the grounds, Salim heard a sound he hadn't noticed before. A thin, reedy piping, as if someone were playing a jig to accompany a barroom brawl in a mummers' play. It seemed to be coming from the south, and without stopping to think, Salim began running in that direction, keeping his body low and using the fields for cover where possible.

The piping was getting louder. Near the southernmost edge of the manor proper, a crew of several men bearing actual swords—no doubt harvested from the various coats of arms and antiques adorning Faldus Anvanory's den and study—came running around the walls of the house. One of them saw Salim and called to him, looking for information.

A figure stepped out of the rows of corn. Even through the loose fabric that wrapped it like a sarong, Salim could see that the creature's body was that of a woman more stunning than any in Lady Jbade's retinue. Salim had seen beautiful women before, but this one tugged at his groin in a manner all out of proportion with her physical shape. Even facing away from him, toward the onrushing men, the curve of her back and hip were enough to set Salim's skin on fire with a desire to touch them, to skin himself alive just so that he might press himself that much closer to her.

"Nymph!" he screamed, voice hoarse with lust. "Don't look!"

But it was too late. With a graceful pull of one delicate hand, the knots of the wrap slipped free, and the nymph drew its garment off and away.

The effect was immediate. As one, the charging men stumbled and fell to their knees, screaming and clawing at their eyes. Salim saw trickles of blood running through the lead man's fingers.

Even with his eyes averted, Salim saw spots like those that came from staring overlong at the sun, and his peripheral vision was blasted away to nothing by the aesthetic radiance of the nymph's nude backside. She started to turn toward him, and Salim closed his eyes tight, fixing the creature's location firmly in his mind.

It worked. Salim closed the last several yards at a sprint and collided with warm, naked flesh. They tumbled to the ground, one of his hands tangling itself in the impossibly fine strands of the creature's hair.

The nymph screamed and snarled at him like a wild beast, nails cutting furrows in his cheeks, and he raised his sword. A sudden image of the crippled pixie flashed through his mind, and at the last second he shifted his grip, bringing the sword's pommel down with all his strength on top of the creature's head. The writhing form jerked and then lay still. Salim sat up and waited until he was certain it was safe, then opened his eyes.

He was kneeling over the naked body of the nymph, her eyes closed. The top of her head, where his fingers were still snarled in hair like threaded moonbeams, was marred with a splotch of blood. He looked lower. Beneath him, the nymphs breasts—still inhumanly perfect, but no longer painful in their beauty—rose and fell softly with the steady rhythm of unconsciousness.

Good. Salim stood once more and looked to the men who had caught the full brunt of the nymph's fury. Several had stood up and were moving cautiously with arms outstretched, calling out to each other in fear and confusion. Others lay sideways on the grass, knees curled up against their chest in fetal positions.

"Stay where you are," Salim commanded them. "You'll only hurt yourselves by moving. Help will come soon." Then he was off once more, heading south past the end of the manor.

The pipes were growing louder now. Salim heard screams and saw the bobbing lights of lanterns. Another few steps and he realized that they were bobbing his way. The air began to fill with the sound of heavy footsteps.

Then Salim was among them: screaming farmhands from the far fields, running flat out with no regard for strategy or the gardening implements that might have been used as weapons, only a desperate need to flee. They stared at him with eyes that seemed to register nothing. Some were babbling as they passed him, trails of snot and drool streaking from their noses and mouths.

Behind them came a capering man, bounding along on legs that bent backward. Below his bare chest, the strangely misshapen legs were furred brown like a goat, and a pair of horns curled up from his forehead. The pipes stopped for a second, and he threw back his head and howled with laughter.

"Run, you bastards! Yes! Run for your manor, and burn like you burned our forest!"

Then his eyes caught sight of Salim. Grinning wickedly, he lifted an eyebrow in invitation, then put the set of hornpipes to his lips and blew.

The note sent a tremor through Salim's body. It was only a single note, yet in that brief burst of sound he heard all the terrors of the ancient world, the things that lurk just out of sight beyond the dying campfire, waiting with claws that rend and jaws that bite. He felt his stomach tighten and his muscles turn briefly to water, and something deep in the back of his brain, almost an involuntary reflex, screamed for him to turn and run. To run, and to never stop running, churning the ground under his feet until his legs were raw, bloody nubbins and all he could do was crawl. In one breath, he felt all this.

And then, just as quickly as it came, it was gone. Salim's will returned, and the bowel-loosening fear that held the others in their grip was no more, rolling on past him like a cresting wave. He bore down on the satyr, and saw recognition dawn.

"Oh shit," the creature said. Then he dropped his pipes, letting them hang from a leather thong around his neck, and sprinted away from Salim, south into the waving fields.

"Salim!"

Salim half-turned, not breaking stride. Neila was racing toward him, shoeless, skirts held up around her flying knees with one hand, the other clutching a dirty ox goad.

"Stay here!" he called, and charged into the fields. Behind him, he heard the crashing of brush as she ignored him and followed in his wake.

The fields were low here, and it was easy to follow the satyr, both by the frantically bouncing shape ahead of him and the careless swath the fey cut through the crops. Their path was straight, and the satyr's goal obvious: to reach the edge of the cultivated fields and the start of the southern wood, where his familiarity with the terrain would give him a distinct advantage over his pursuers. Salim put everything he had into running, ignoring the cries and unladylike curses that came from behind him. Slowly but surely, he began to close the gap.

But not quickly enough. With a shout of triumph, the satyr hit the edge of the woods and bounded into it like a deer, cloven hooves launching him over tree roots and under overhanging branches with uncanny speed.

Salim stopped at the sharply defined edge of the forest. Beyond, massive trees spread leafy branches of the sort rarely seen in arid Thuvia, blotting out the last rays of the day. Already the satyr's stubby deer tail was flicking its way into the shadows beneath the canopy.

Salim had taken the race as far as he could, and he'd lost. There simply wasn't strength enough in his legs to catch the satyr in his own terrain. It was impossible. He bent over and placed his hands on his knees, breathing hard.

Alright, you worm-eaten bitch, he thought. *You win. It's your turn.*

As quickly as the words were formed—Salim hated to think of them as a prayer—they vanished, leaving his brain full of the fluttering flaps of dark, heavy wings. In their wake, a new vitality took hold of his legs like a terrier shaking a rat, jolting him upright. The energy flooded up through his veins, setting his thighs and belly afire and coming to rest in his lungs like a hot stone, radiating power and heat.

With a roar, he launched himself into the forest.

Tree boles whipped to either side of him, their branches beating at his face and chest as he rocketed past. Roots reached out to trip him, but his legs were no longer his own, and they moved with an otherworldly grace, each step smooth and gliding. His knees still churned at the same pace, but now each stride was lengthened impossibly, his body sailing forward without effort as each footfall shoved him away from the earth and left him hanging suspended in the air. It was like running in a dream, the exhilaration dampened only by the deific taint that Salim felt like oil clinging to the inside of his skin.

Ahead of him, the retreating shape of the satyr was just barely visible. Salim's quarry ran like the forest creature he was, darting from side to side erratically in an effort to keep his pursuer off balance. For long breaths the satyr would turn and be lost among the trees, only to reappear again as Salim's legs carried him along the same uncanny path.

The satyr dodged between two thick-trunked behemoths, making for the safety of a thick patch of briars. Salim changed course to follow.

The world rocked and turned sideways. Pain exploded in Salim's chest as he fell backward onto the loam and roots of the forest floor, his legs still jerking ineffectually. Between the trees, the satyr dropped lightly down from the branch where he'd swung out from behind the tree to plant both hooves in Salim's chest, the powerful goat legs crushing the wind out of him in a tremendous kick. The satyr smiled and drew his belt knife.

Salim looked around frantically for his sword, and found it lying several feet to his right, where it had dropped when he took his short and unpleasant flight backward.

The satyr saw his glance. Their eyes locked, and then they leaped for it as one.

The satyr got there first, by virtue of not bothering to try and retrieve it. Instead, he simply kicked it away into the bushes with a quick flick of his hoof. That motion in turn took him just long enough for Salim to get a grip on his furred hindquarters and pull, dragging the fey down on top of him.

They fought like beasts, without words or strategy, rolling and kicking up furrows in the deep loam. Salim got his teeth into the satyr's haunch and tore at it, the rancid fur and flesh still managing to remind him of the fried goat meat he'd had for lunch earlier. The satyr screamed and drove hard with the contested knife, its blade cutting a blaze of pain down the outside of Salim's hip. Salim twisted the satyr's wrist, and the knife fell away as well. Then it was just them, thumbs jabbing for eyes and throats, hands slamming skulls against tree roots until the whole world started to explode and turn colors.

Rolling on top, and with his opponent's arms finally pinned, Salim leaned back to get a better view of the situation. The satyr saw his chance. Lips pulled back in a snarl that revealed teeth both human and canine, he ducked his head to bring the sharp points of his horns in line with Salim's face, then lunged upward.

Letting go of the satyr's arms, Salim grabbed the horns with both hands and torqued them cruelly sideways, lifting himself with his knees so that the satyr had to spin beneath him or let his neck be snapped. Then, with the satyr's arms pinioned safely against the ground once more—this time by his knees—Salim guided the satyr's face forward as if pushing a wheelbarrow, bringing it within an inch of the rough tree trunk in front of them.

"Look at this tree," Salim said, leaning down so that his lips were almost touching the satyr's tufted ear. "You fey love trees, don't you? That's good. Because if you don't quit struggling, I'm going to grind your face against the bark of this tree until it comes off. Your face, that is. Understood?"

A whimper.

"I said 'understood?'" Salim gave the satyr's head a shake.

"Okay!" the satyr cried. "Okay, I yield! Gods, let go!"

A crashing in the brush announced a new arrival. Salim looked up to see Neila picking her way over roots and deadfalls. She'd lost her ox goad somewhere along the way, and her skirts were streaked with dirt, but she otherwise looked unharmed. She saw him crouched over the satyr and gave him a tight, victorious smile.

Irritated that she'd disobeyed his command to stay behind, Salim said nothing, just nodded his head toward the sword lying half under a bush. She returned it to him, and with its point at the satyr's throat, he stood up and moved aside to allow the satyr to do the same. The fey did so, pointedly ignoring the blade nicking the soft skin beneath his neat goatee, instead brushing the leaves and dirt from his bare chest and the goatlike fur that began just below his navel.

"Who are you?" Salim asked. "And why did you attack the manor?"

The satyr laughed bitterly and spread his hands in a mockery of formal introduction.

"My name is Delini, good master," he said, "piper of the fields and lover of the deep glens, sworn enemy of all maidenheads. As for why we attacked the manor, ask that one." The bearded chin lifted to point at Neila. "She knows."

Neila drew herself upright and shot him an imperious look.

"My father purchased this land fairly and honestly."

"*From who?*" The satyr's sudden howl of anguish and frustration made both the humans jump, and a tiny trickle of blood flowed where Salim's sword point had nicked the fey's neck. The fey seemed not to notice as he gestured wildly with his arms. "From some Lamasaran noble who's never entered my forest save to hunt my beasts or rut in the deep moss?" He began beating himself on the chest with a fist, punctuating his sentences. "This is *my* forest, *my* glens, *my* groves, and those who trespass here do so by *my* gracious leave. And I'm revoking it!"

He looked down for a moment as the echo of his shout hung in the air, and when he looked up again, his big doe eyes were wet with tears.

"You burned it," he whispered, voice raw with emotion. "You burned it and planted wheat."

Salim looked back at Neila.

"I think we just found our third suspect," he said.

Neila's eyes widened.

So did the satyr's. "What?" he asked.

Salim turned back to the fey and lifted the creature's chin lightly with the sword's point.

"What do you know about the death and kidnapping of Faldus Anvanory?"

The fey looked astonished for a moment, then his face broke out in a smile that twisted his face, turning the bestial horns and hair into mere accents on an otherwise handsome man.

"Faldus is dead?" he asked, wonderingly.

Shit, Salim thought. He doesn't know. But Neila was already stepping forward, eager to believe.

"You!" she cried in triumph. "I should have known! You killed my father, and want to ransom back his soul for the sun orchid elixir!"

The satyr laughed sharply.

"The sun orchid elixir?" he asked. "Why in the name of the forest would we want that? We're fey, little princess. We'll live as long as we live, and be reborn in time from the womb of the deep wood. Immortality is a game for pretentious, short-lived humans."

"Maybe you wanted to make sure Faldus didn't live forever," Salim countered, but his heart wasn't in it. He'd already seen the truth in the fey's eyes.

Delini waved a hand dismissively.

"If Faldus got the elixir like he wanted, maybe he'd finally go back to Taldor and leave us be. No, if we wanted to kill the Anvanorys, we could have poisoned their crops or sent an invisible pixie into the manor to slit their throats. We don't need them dead, just out of our forest."

He turned to face Neila and leered, licking his lips.

"Of course," he said, grabbing his furry crotch and shaking it at her, "we could always just breed them out."

Satyrs, Salim thought, but then Neila stepped forward and with one quick motion drove her knee up into the satyr's proffered groin. Delini doubled over in pain, and Salim was just able to withdraw his sword in time to keep the satyr from spitting himself on it.

"She's got spirit," the satyr gasped, still grinning. "I like that. A spirited mare always gives the best ride."

Neila started in for a second round, but Salim put out a hand and stopped her.

"I think he's telling the truth about the kidnapping," he said. "The fey weren't involved. It doesn't make sense."

Neila looked irritated, but didn't try to go around his arm. "Very well," she said. "Then we'll simply take him back to Lamasara and turn him over to the authorities for arson and attempted murder."

"No."

Neila whirled, staring at Salim. Delini looked up with new interest as well.

"What did you say?" Her voice was the cold, furious disbelief that only a child of privilege can master.

"I said 'no,'" Salim repeated. "The fey had nothing to do with your father's death, which is all I'm interested in. Your petty land squabbles are none of my concern, or the church's."

"But he burned my house!" Her body shook with barely restrained rage.

"As you did to them, from the sound of it." Salim's voice was calm and collected. "The trees you cleared for your manor were their home, and you burned that to put in your fields. I'd call that even."

"He attacked us!" An accusatory finger.

Salim thought back to the dying dryad, the pixie he'd cut almost in half. If he recalled correctly, pixie arrows induced sleep, not death. And the nymph had only blinded with her beauty.

"They weren't fighting to kill," he said slowly. "We were. And we did." He wiped his sword tip on the hem of his robes, then sheathed it. "Leave it be."

He turned back to the satyr, who was again grinning the rakish smile that seemed to be a permanent part of his face. He was clearly enjoying the exchange.

"You're even now," Salim repeated. "Don't press it. Next time, there will be no such clemency."

Delini bobbed his head. "Of course." He turned to Neila. "And if you should ever find your noble existence feeling hollow and empty, Lady Anvanory," he said formally, "my offer remains firm, and will continue to stand." He waggled his eyebrows and swept one arm low in a courtly bow, then turned and bounded off into the bushes like the goat he resembled.

Next to Salim, Neila was making a growling sound low in her throat, narrowed eyes following the retreating satyr. She ceased when she saw Salim looking at her, but said nothing, fixing him with much the same expression. Unperturbed, Salim turned and began to retrace their footsteps north, back toward the house. After a moment, Neila joined him.

They walked in silence for a long time, and when Neila finally broke it, her voice was forcibly light and controlled, as if nothing had happened.

"How did you catch him?" she asked. "I've never seen anyone run like that in my life. You took off like an arrow from a bow—like you'd been drawn back, and then suddenly let go."

That sounded uncomfortably close to the truth. Salim shrugged and pressed forward, drawing aside a springy branch to let her pass.

"I don't want to talk about it," he said. "Come on. Truce or no truce, we don't want to be in these woods after dark. And your house is still on fire."

Chapter Seven
Leavetaking

By the time Salim and Neila returned, the fires had been successfully put out, though portions of the great house still smoldered. Without Delini's pipes to rally them and call the tune of their grisly dance, the fey had quickly faded away into the fields, leaving only their dead to fertilize the soil of the manor's grounds. Several of the farmhands, drunk on rage and victory, requested permission to pursue the attackers into their forest, but Neila didn't even look at Salim before denying them. In truth, most of the men looked relieved not to be taken up on their offers. Even in their bolstered state, they knew better than to challenge the fey in their own woods. After instructing the senior house staff to post guards and care for the wounded, Neila bid Salim goodnight, leaving him to retire to his own bed, where he quickly fell into an exhausted, dreamless sleep.

He woke the next morning to a flurry of activity, the sounds of wood and steel clinking and men calling to one another. He went to the window and pulled aside the diaphanous hanging to reveal a sun already free of the horizon. At first he was surprised to have slept so late, and then the aches of his wrestling match with Delini woke as well, and he put his arms over his head, twisting to loosen a back that was mostly bruise. No doubt his body was working overtime trying to repair the damage of fists and tree roots, blood swirling under the skin to create black and green contusions.

Outside, a team of men led by Olar was busy using hammers and chisels to scour or tear out charred patches of the house's walls, replacing them with fresh lumber and sand-colored mortar mixed in big tubs. Beyond them, armed guards—the same stable boys and footmen who had fought the previous evening, now outfitted with bows and swords—stood at regular intervals around the house, scanning fields bereft of laborers. Aside from a few rusty patches of soil, there were no signs of the dead fey.

Salim turned and made his way out of the room and down the hall. He smelled the campfire scent of smoke as soon as he opened the bedchamber's door, but it remained faint as he traversed the house. Clearly the fey's firebombing had been more symbolic than effective—no amount of cleaning short of magic could draw the smoke smell from the air and walls that quickly if there had been any real blaze. Likely the fairies had known that when they attacked, seeking to set fire to the Anvanory's expensive possessions rather than actually torching the manor. Or maybe they simply misjudged how difficult it was to set fire to a primarily clay-brick building.

He found Neila in the foyer, speaking with her majordomo. Salim waited quietly while they finished, then the servant bowed and backed away, and Neila turned to him.

"How bad?" he asked.

"Surprisingly little damage," she said. "A few of their flaming pitch balls made it through windows and cost us several tapestries and divans, and there's some superficial scarring to the wooden trim on the eastern edge of the house, but nothing a few days of work can't repair. The longest part will be sufficiently airing out those rooms . . . I've already sent a housemaid after jasmine and lavender."

Trust a noble to think of her possessions first. "And the wounded?"

Neila waved a hand in a gesture of dismissal that was already becoming familiar.

"Four blinded, three more seriously injured, all sent to the cathedral to be healed. The rest are minor cuts and scrapes."

No deaths—that was good. "And the fey?"

Neila snorted. "Their wounded crept away, but my men accounted for at least half a dozen of them. It'll be a long time before they think to take up arms against civilized folk again, truce or no truce."

"What about the corpses?"

The wave again. "The men asked for permission to string them up along the edges of the forest." She spoke lightly, looking off toward the front door where several servants were returning from town. "As a reminder and a warning."

Salim said nothing. She waited, then sighed.

"But," she said, meeting his eyes, "I told them to bury the creatures properly at the forest's edge, with as much respect as they could muster. Do you approve?"

He nodded. "You do your station credit, Lady."

She looked at him shrewdly to see if he was mocking her, but his compliment was genuine.

"In any case," she said, brushing her hands together. "The servants know their duties, and we have little enough time. We've exhausted the obvious leads, and neither the Lamasaran Guard nor the church appears to be able to offer anything better. What comes next?"

Now it was Salim's turn to sigh. Reaching into the fold of his robes, he brought out a circular amulet twice the size of his thumbnail and let it thud softly against his chest, hanging pendulous from a rawhide thong around his neck.

"This, unfortunately."

Neila leaned forward with interest, craning her neck for a better look. Against the pure, midnight black of the stone, Salim's robes looked almost gray. In the amulet's smooth-polished center, a spiral of indefinable color shimmered. From the way Neila moved her head back and forth, Salim could tell that she was having trouble fixing the iridescent spiral in place, the engraving seeming to constantly twist and lose focus.

"What is it?" she breathed.

"A doorway," he answered. "Or rather, an infinite number of doorways. A passage to the eternal vastness of the planes, and all the strangeness therein."

She looked up at him sharply. "The planes? You mean—Elysium? Nirvana?" She paused, then whispered, "Hell?"

"Among others."

"I don't understand." She was still bent forward, drawn toward the stone. He reached up and slipped it back inside his robe.

"We know that your father's soul made it as far as the Boneyard before it was taken," he said. "The church's auguries have told us that much. As we've exhausted all our avenues of inquiry on this end, the only reasonable course of action is to begin at the other, examining the place where he was last seen."

"You mean to travel to the Boneyard." Her voice was flat, bordering on disbelief. "The land of the dead."

"It wouldn't be the first time. Nor likely the last."

She said nothing. Instead, she appeared to be wrestling with some all-encompassing thought. One edge of her lower lip caught prettily between her teeth, and she crossed her arms as if hugging herself against a nonexistent chill. At last she let out a heavy breath, and her arms dropped.

"So be it," she said. "If we must, we must. Allow me twenty minutes to instruct the house staff on actions to be taken during my absence, as well as to gather the supplies we'll need."

Salim's laugh was involuntary, a bark that escaped his lips before he knew it was coming.

"You can't be serious."

Her head whipped toward him. Blue eyes glinted dangerously. "Do you see any reason for me to be joking, Mr. Ghadafar?"

Salim felt himself bristling, and did his best to hold it down. One hand went to adjust his sword, squeezing the cool bronze.

"The planes are not your back woods, Lady," he said. "Nor are its inhabitants a mob of irate forest creatures. The denizens of the Outer Sphere care nothing for rank and station, nor will they content themselves with merely burning a few of your accoutrements. I'll travel faster alone, and I'll return as soon as I know more."

She ignored him. "I'm going to put our affairs here in order," she said. "And if you aren't here waiting when I return, I'll have no choice but to contact Khoyar and let him know that you've broken the terms of our arrangement. Regardless of your position within the faith, I'm sure he can make your existence decidedly inconvenient for the remainder of your stay in Thuvia."

The heat in Salim's gut was rising, and the imperious edge to Neila's voice was like nails on slate.

"This is unnecessary," he said, choosing his words as if speaking to a willful child—which, he supposed, he was. "And dangerous. Even on the more benign planes, there are creatures that could burn out your soul simply from passing near you. Beings whose beauty would rip your sanity to shreds, or who would sell and trade your very essence like a palm date. The towers of the Abyss are built of soul-maggots, and not all of the damned sequestered in their walls deserve to be there."

Neila's face lost some of its color, but her jaw remained set. "I'm well acquainted with such stories, Mr. Ghadafar."

"They aren't just stories!" It was all Salim could do to keep from screaming. Such deliberate ignorance! "These things are real, and they'll set upon you in a second, tearing your eyes from your head and ripping the shit from your stomach with hands like scythes!" He paused for breath, arms gesticulating uselessly. "Have you ever *seen* a demon, Lady?"

"Would you like to see one now?" Her voice was quiet, choked, and her hands flexed at her sides as if they were claws that would tear his skin. With a start, Salim realized that there were tears in her eyes. His tone softened.

"Neila—" he began.

"He's my *father*." The pain in that whisper brooked no argument. "Don't you understand that?"

Salim sighed.

"Twenty minutes," she repeated.

"As you wish," he said, and seated himself on a low couch to wait.

She was ready in fifteen. From his perch in the foyer, Salim could hear the hubbub in the rest of the house as Neila's orders made their way around. Salim assumed she had withheld her actual destination from the servants—pigheaded as she was, the girl wasn't stupid—but still her retainers would hardly approve of their lady gallivanting off in the middle of such a crisis. And with a stranger, no less. Not that any of them would go so far as to question her decisions or offer their own opinions, but the concern was readily apparent in the sustained buzz of conversation that dropped in volume even as it spread. A Thuvian servant might not tell you her opinions, but only a fool failed to receive the message.

When Neila returned, her clothing had changed entirely. Gone was the long, airy dress, replaced by a simple blouse of gray silk and snug brown breeches tucked into high boot-tops. Despite the heat, she wore a heavy blue cloak with the hood pushed back over a small leather rucksack, her long black hair pinned up sensibly behind her head. What caught his notice, however, was not the clothing, but the new addition at her hip. He looked pointedly at it, then back to her face.

"Pretty," he said. "But can you use it?"

In response, Neila drew. The rapier's blade flashed, its edge cutting a mirrored arc through the air in a salute that dropped neatly into a guard position.

Her grip was weak, and the lines of her arm and leading leg left her open to a disabling knee shot, but the draw had been smooth and quick. Salim had seen worse, and not just from wealthy girls playing dress-up. At least she wouldn't accidentally stab herself. He nodded, and she sheathed the blade, clearly pleased.

"Father didn't precisely approve," she said, "but fencing is a noble art, and he understood that a lady in a foreign land shouldn't be wholly dependent on her staff for protection." Her smile faded a little. "He had this made for me in Absalom, on our way south. Said that I'd need it to keep my foreign suitors at bay."

"Clearly it works," Salim said, and her eyes narrowed, trying to tell if she was being mocked.

"Come," he said. "If you're ready, then it's time we were away. Here." He held out a hand—no courtly gesture this time. She took it without ceremony, his calloused palm gripping her wrist like a common drover. Forearms locked, he pulled her closer to him, until their sides were almost touching, cloaks mingling.

Salim reached into his robe once more and brought out the amulet, letting it again fall to his sternum. His free hand cupped it, and as it did, the unnameable colors of the spiral began to shift, drawing the eye around its curves and down into its depth with an inescapable gravity. A high-pitched whine, like the phantom tones an ear sometimes hears in a totally silent room, began to rise, countered by a faint buzzing within Salim's bones.

"Neila."

With a visible effort, she pulled her gaze from the mesmerizing stone and met his.

"Last chance. You don't have to do this."

In response, she only gripped his arm harder. Salim looked deep into those blue falcon's eyes and inclined his head slightly. In another life, this one might have earned that fancy sword the hard way.

"Very well," he said.

Then his fingers closed around the hanging stone, and the manor disappeared.

Chapter Eight
The Boneyard

The world twisted. There was no better way to describe it. One moment they were standing in the foyer of Anvanory Manor, far too close for propriety even given the girl's position as head of the household, and the next the scene around them warped and swirled, as if being drawn down a drain—perhaps into the amulet that Salim held. At the same time, Salim felt himself pulled sideways—not physically, but as if he had a fishhook lodged somewhere in the core of his being, and was being dragged by an immense angler toward a distant surface. Beside him, Neila's grip on his arm was painfully tight.

The colors and angles continued to twist and drain, and Salim braced himself. Though he knew, objectively, that the whole process was instantaneous, that instant had its own subjective length and phases to those inside it, and the next was the worst.

For a single, blinding moment, the world was perfectly blank. Not the warm black of closed eyes, or the finite dark of a windowless cell. This was an emptiness—a complete lack of definition, even that afforded by empty space. Salim's skin simultaneously burned and froze, and through the facade of silence he could hear the howling *emptiness*, a void that sucked tears from his eyes. In that second, he understood that creation, for all its horrors, could never hope to match its absence.

And then the world snapped back into place, as if it were a bowstring coming to rest.

Gone was the foyer, the marble and adobe. In its place was a vast plain of massive reddish-brown stones and soil, stretching toward the horizon beneath a dark sky of perfect silver, its blankness somehow infinitely more comforting than the one they had just left.

Neila made a noise, and Salim turned to find her trembling, hand still locked in a death grip on his wrist. She made the sound again—a chirp far back in her throat—and he realized she was fighting the urge to vomit. Peeling her fingers from his arm, he touched her back lightly.

"You get used to it," was all he could say, and then she turned and ran, holding her stomach, behind the enormous stone at their back. As she passed from view, the gagging noises were replaced by full-on retching.

And then a scream.

Shit. Salim raced around the rock after her, drawing his sword—

—and found her on hands and knees, a little puddle of bile on the ground before her. Beyond that, the focus of her panicked stare, was—nothing.

A whole lot of nothing. Just a few feet past her unladylike expulsion, the stone and dirt of the plain fell away as sharply as if it had been sliced by a giant knife, giving way to the open sky which stretched featureless out of range of Salim's vision. Lowering himself prudently to his belly, Salim crept slowly out to the edge and looked down.

The drop was impossible, in the most literal sense. Looking down the edge of the cliff, its twisting stone face marred only by dark arches and winding, broken stairs, Salim was immediately aware that the distance between them and the ground was beyond what he should have reasonably been able to see. Intellectually, he knew that the expanse of molded rock below him was infinite, yet he found that somehow he could still see the ground and the shining city that stretched out like a golden wheel at the pillar's foot. He looked back over his shoulder at Neila.

"Come see this," he said.

The girl was now crouched crablike, back pressed up against the standing stone. She shook her head, a small movement which nevertheless sent tremors through her body.

"Come on," he pressed. "You're going to face worse than a fear of heights if you insist on coming with me. Besides, you won't fall off—Pharasma's Spire doesn't let anyone go that easily. Now get over here."

Eyes still wide, Neila did so, dropping to her stomach and slithering forward until she lay next to him, face peeking over the edge.

"This is the edge of the Spire," Salim said, and thrust an arm over the cliff, gesturing at the golden filigree below them. "And that's Axis, the Eternal City. Home of absolute logic and the folks who worship it."

They stared down at it together for a moment, then Salim stood and looked back the way they had come. Again, his eyes failed to find anything but a blank, featureless plain. The Boneyard itself was nowhere in sight. He swore quietly.

"What are those?" Neila asked, somewhat recovered and now pointing down at the strange carved shapes and pathways which wound up the cliff face.

"Who knows?" Salim answered. He moved over and hunkered down beside her, precariously close to the edge.

"Pharasma's Spire is one of the Outer Planes, but it's shaped like a lump of clay that's been rolled out into a long, thin snake." He mimed stretching a chunk of clay between two closed fists. "It's infinitely tall, and very thin, yet even though the little plateau at the top is much smaller than its length, that plateau is *also* infinitely wide—a percentage of infinity is still infinity. Make sense?"

Her eyes said it didn't, but she nodded anyway.

"When most people think of the Spire," he continued, "they think of Pharasma's Boneyard, the place of judgment where all souls eventually come to be parceled out and meet their postmortem rewards. That mostly happens at the center, at Pharasma's court, which is obviously the most significant part to mortals. Yet the Spire as a place is much older than the progression of souls—maybe even older than Pharasma herself." He nodded toward the distant carvings. "I doubt if even the gods remember what those are for, or who carved them. The planes of existence aren't as simple as most priests would have you believe."

He stood again, and Neila followed, albeit crawling backward a prudent distance from the edge first.

"So we're in the afterlife?" she asked.

"In a manner of speaking." He grasped the stone around his neck. "In a more practical sense, however, we're nowhere—out at the edge of the Spire, beyond Pharasma's court or interest." He sighed. "The amulet never fails to get you to the correct plane, but *where* on that plane is questionable. Sometimes it's right where you want to be. Other times it's smack in the middle of a boiling lake. All things considered, I'd say we broke even. But now we have to roll the dice again." He held out his hand, and Neila eyed it warily.

"Do we have to?"

Salim laughed. "When I said infinite, Madam Adventurer, I meant *infinite*. The Outer Planes have landmarks, but they're also vast in a way that our minds can't truly understand. You could walk away from the cliff edge for a thousand years and still be no closer to the center than when you started, unless someone like the Dark Lady took an interest in you and decided to hurry your journey along." He waved the hand again, impatiently.

Gritting her teeth, Neila stepped forward and took it.

This time the transition seemed mercifully short. There was a brief flash of bitter cold and glimpse of a snow-covered mountaintop, and then they were back beneath the silver pseudo-sky. But now the landscape was different.

They were in a graveyard, but a graveyard like none on their world. In three directions, the endless plain of graves stretched away out of view, unbroken by any structure larger than a mausoleum. Headstones and markers of every size and shape made a thick stone carpet around their feet, many of them toppled or half-shattered by unknown forces. From out in the forest of monuments came faint whisperings which might have been the sighs of the wind playing through the stonework, save that neither of the travelers' cloaks twitched in any breeze.

Salim paid no attention to the noises, instead fixing his eyes on the fourth horizon. There the line of graves also stretched out until the markers were little more than a low gray haze, yet this time larger structures sprang up beyond them, dominated by a collection of pale, thin towers that loomed over the lesser buildings like men over ants. Above them all hung a dead gray moon, closer than any real moon should be, its face a grinning skull. Salim grunted his approval.

"Better," he said, and turned to Neila. "This way." He began walking, and without protest Neila stepped quickly to join him, staying close to his side as they picked their way carefully among the graves.

"What is this place?" she asked. She reached out with one hand and let her fingers play lightly over the top of a stone as they passed. She started to do the same for the next one, but Salim caught her hand and shook his head without bothering to face her.

"The Graveyard of Souls," he said. "The last resting place of atheists."

"Atheists!" Neila twisted her head to look around, and Salim knew that she was now seeing what her subconscious had no doubt recognized before. Unlike a normal graveyard, the stones in this endless field were marked only with names and epitaphs, none of the normal religious iconography found in such places. No keys for Abadar's followers. No Iomedaean sword-cross. Even Pharasma's spiral was missing.

"But how?" she asked after a moment. "I understand that those without a patron god are judged by Pharasma and sent onward according to their natures, but if atheists don't believe in gods and the afterlife—"

"Only a fool refuses to acknowledge the gods' existence," Salim spat. "Though there are many such here."

"Then how—"

"Belief is different than worship." Salim stopped and turned, and his voice calmed a little, though it still held an aggressive undertone.

"The gods are real, as are the planes, and anyone with enough gold or magical ability can prove it empirically." He cupped the amulet and held it out to illustrate his point. "Yet acknowledging the gods' existence and worshiping them are two different things. Most gods—and churches—rule their people through fear. Fear of mortality. Fear of outside enemies. Fear of the wrath of the capricious gods themselves. The faithful know that by worshiping a more powerful being, they can gain its protection."

He let the amulet drop.

"Yet think of this: There are many mortals who are more powerful than either of us. People who could shelter us from our enemies, or kill us at a whim if they took it in mind to do so. So I ask you: Is power alone—the power of a warlord, or a petulant king— enough to justify giving over your self-determination? Does it deserve your unqualified allegiance? Your *worship*?"

Salim stopped himself, with effort, and Neila looked at him with new consideration.

"You sound like a Rahadoumi."

Salim gave a hard chuckle.

"You are most perceptive, Lady." Then he turned and began walking again.

They traveled in silence for a time, listening to the wind that could now be made out as the susurrus of a thousand barely audible whispers.

"Is this where all Rahadoumi go where they die?" she asked at last, softly.

Salim nodded. "Most of them. Many noble men and women lie here, waiting for the day when creation ceases and their souls disperse."

"But it's so sad!" Her words slipped out in a rush. "It seems so—lonely." Neila shivered and seemed surprised at her own observation, though Salim knew that she'd only put a name to the feeling that assailed them from all sides.

"Is it?" Salim asked. "Is it so sad to hold onto your pride? To remain in control of your own fate, rather than auctioning it off to the highest bidder? There are fools in these fields, yes—those who think the gods just myths, or themselves the center of the universe. But there are also those who would rather face eternity with their heads held high than bow and serve."

When she spoke again, her voice was almost a whisper. "And you?"

Again, the hard laugh came unbidden.

"Look not for my grave here, Lady," he said, and his voice was bitter. "I sold my honor long ago. If I'm allowed to join my fathers here, it'll be because it amuses Pharasma to do so. Nothing more." Then he shook his head and moved to circumvent a white stone sarcophagus twice the size of a man. "Step lively. We've a long way yet to go."

Without sun or stars, time was an abstract concept in the vast potter's field of the atheist graveyard, and only when the muscles burned in Salim's legs and Neila began to lag behind him did the black-robed man call for a stop. Looking up, he could see that the towering structure on the horizon was much closer now, perhaps less than half again the distance they'd come. Though they were still too far to see the movements of individual creatures, the palace itself was clearly visible now, a narrow tumult of gothic spires and stone arches that stretched far into the blank silver sky. The pure white of its walls gleamed, contrasting sharply with the bleak surroundings and the dour aesthetic of the Lady of Graves' mortal worshipers.

"The Inner Court," Salim said. "And Pharasma's palace."

Neila began to seat herself on one of the headstones, thought twice about it, then finally sat down on it anyway, face set as if daring the whispering voices to object. She dropped her pack, then stretched out her legs, shapely in the traveling leathers that were just slightly too fitted to be practical. She winced.

"Will we be going there?" she asked. Her voice didn't falter, but Salim could hear the tension in it. He shook his head, and she relaxed slightly.

"The Lady of Graves has little enough interest in the affairs of individual mortals. She concerns herself with weaving the tapestry of all life—to her, we'd be less than the fibers in a single thread. It's possible we might find an audience with one of her lesser servants, but I think we're better off avoiding it altogether." He thought of Ceyanan's constant, infuriating smile. No, he wasn't eager to come crawling back to the angel this early in the game.

Neila had no argument there. Instead she pointed past him, toward the palace. "What's that?" she asked. "That line in the sky."

Salim followed her finger to the thin, glowing line that cut through the silver sky like a twisted wire, finally mingling with the horizon and disappearing as it approached the palace.

"The River of Souls," he answered.

She made an incredulous noise, and Salim looked at her with a raised eyebrow.

"I just always thought that was a metaphor," she said, and blushed slightly.

This time Salim's smile held actual humor. "I think you'll find, Lady, that there's more truth to most of the children's stories than you'd expect."

"Where do they—" she began, but she never got to complete her sentence.

From out of the almost nonexistent shadow of an ivory-walled crypt came a hurtling shape. With one long arm, it swept Neila from the headstone and carried her along in its rush, coming up short alongside a half-fallen statue of a weeping woman.

"Cold!" it screamed. "So cold!"

The thing was taller than an elf, and had the same pointed ears and thin frame. The gangly arms that pinioned Neila and covered her mouth were spider-thin, and when straightened would have stretched almost to its knees, the skin around them so thin and taut as to be almost transparent.

No, Salim correct himself—it wasn't almost transparent. It *was* transparent. Now that he looked closer, he realized that he could see through the thing's body to the headstones beyond, as if it were a window covered in a thin membrane of oilskin.

Its face, however, was the worst part. Not in the alienness of its emaciated, skull-like mask, but rather the familiarity there. Behind an expression of twisted, wracking despair, the features were mundane rather than monstrous. The face of a village fruit seller or scribe.

From behind the skeletal hand that blocked her mouth, Neila made muffled cries, hands scrabbling for her sword but held firm by the creature.

"Cold!" the creature cried again.

Salim drew his sword and moved forward slowly, careful not to make any sudden moves that might startle the creature.

"Drop her," he said. "She's not for you."

The muscles of the creature's long legs bunched, and it leaned backward as if prepared to spring away. Neila's struggles redoubled.

"Cold," the creature whined, and over the gritted teeth Salim saw a single tear well up and flow down a hollow cheek. "Dark and cold. Cold and dark."

He was close enough. Darting forward, Salim grasped the neckline of Neila's shirt with one hand, digging his fingers deep into fabric and the soft flesh beneath. With his other, he brought the sword around in a wide, stabbing arc, careful to stay clear of the girl.

The creature was faster, however, and let Neila drop in order to fling itself backward, landing crouched atop a headstone. It gave one last cry, equal parts frustration and longing, and then bounded off into the forest of graves with a speed neither of the humans could hope to match, quickly disappearing from view.

Back on her feet and flushed with rage, Neila drew her own sword. Salim prudently let go of her bodice and moved back a step. He needn't have worried—the girl's eyes were focused firmly on the retreating shape.

For an instant, Salim worried that she might chase after it, futile as it would obviously be, but then she shook herself lightly and turned back to him with a face that struggled for composure.

"And what," she asked, "was *that*?"

Salim spread his hands.

"A soul, I'd guess. One of the fools we spoke of, who can't accept the truth of the grave."

"You mean a ghost?"

"Perhaps. Such distinctions are murky here." He looked pointedly at her sword, then sheathed his own. After a moment, she did the same.

"It seems my sympathy was a bit premature," she said lightly, but her eyes still looked a little wild. She stared down at her sword hilt for a second, then back up at him.

"I don't suppose this would have had any effect on him, then. Would yours?"

Salim shrugged again.

"It depends. Steel means little to ghosts, or to a soul in the Boneyard. But there are those whose minds never grasp the transition between flesh and the Great Beyond. If he still thought it could hurt him . . ."

Neila nodded. For one more long moment, she looked back in the direction the lost soul had disappeared, then strode forward and scooped up the strap of her pack, slinging it over her shoulder.

"Given the hospitality of the locals," she said, "I think we've had quite enough of a rest for now. Don't you?"

Letting her lead the way, Salim fell in behind, and together the two continued onward toward the palace.

When the field of graves ended, it did so sharply, without any gradual reduction. One moment they were picking their way carefully through the monuments, and the next they were on flat, open ground. Though not quite as barren as the stone at the edge of the Spirelands, where they'd initially arrived, the terrain here was still little more than cracked brown earth, with small tufts of dark grass that somehow found nourishment in a world without rain or sun.

Above them, the sky raged.

During their walk toward the castle, they'd borne steadily to the right, toward the flickering thread that Salim had named the River of Souls. Now that river broke into a delta that filled the air fifty feet over their heads.

It was, Salim remarked, precisely what its name implied. Held to its course by forces beyond his ken—maybe beyond anyone's—the river drew souls from the bodies of the dying all across the myriad worlds of the Material Plane, sucking them through the reeling gray expanse of the Astral Plane and finally delivering them here, to Pharasma's Spire. They raced and rippled, a faintly luminous tide of energy that upon close inspection resolved itself into shapes and forms.

Not all of those forms were human. Far from it—everything that lived on the Material Plane eventually died, and those who bore consciousness passed into the river on their way to the next phase of existence. In that unyielding torrent were dwarves and elves, lizardfolk and the hyena-headed brutes that plagued the deserts of Katapesh. And more—uncountable creatures, both from Salim and Neila's homeworld of Golarion and from those distant realms hinted at by scholars, which people standing on Golarion's surface saw only as bright stars in the night sky. From a thousand times a thousand worlds, the dead flowed together, speeding along en masse in their race to kneel before the Lady and be judged.

And here they were splitting apart again. As the two tiny humans watched, perched a safe distance below and to the side, the river split into eight massive arms, as well as a number of smaller currents. The former spiraled out and around to either side, sometimes snaking close to the ground as they made an invisible circle with the steeples of Pharasma's palace at its center. The remaining streams kept their course, flowing straight in toward the gleaming castle and the small city of gray buildings that surrounded it. These lesser structures, which had become more visible as they approached, were no doubt still fabulously grand up close, yet continued to be overwhelmed by the majesty of the palace proper.

Salim looked up at the larger streams, squinting to make out details.

"You said your father worshiped Abadar?"

"Yes," Neila answered, somewhat uncertainly. "Though I don't know if his faith went beyond facilitating his business transactions."

"What more could a god of merchants ask?" Salim noted absently, but his gaze was still on the sky, looking from stream to stream. At last he found what he was looking for, and nodded.

"This way," he said, and began walking counterclockwise around the circle's edge, its radius so wide that their path was almost straight.

Neila followed without further prompting, and together they walked for quite some time, with Salim periodically glancing up to ensure that they were indeed following the correct branch.

"Where are they all going?" Neila asked.

He waved a hand. "Heaven, Hell, the Abyss—each of the eight aligned planes has a place in the Outer Courts, and the souls in these larger branches are the ones already sworn to a deity, or consigned by their conduct in life. They flow directly to their destined courts, where portals take them on to the appropriate planes." He pointed back the way they'd come. "The smaller streams are those souls whose fates are contested, or not yet determined. Those are the ones that go straight to the Inner Court, to be judged by Pharasma and fought over by emissaries by the various factions."

"And this is the stream for souls bound to Abadar?"

Salim nodded. "For all of Axis, actually. This is the stream of souls for whom law and reason are the highest calling. But the Master of the First Vault claims his souls from that court, so we're going the right way."

For a moment the stream they were following dipped low, almost touching the ground, and they gave it a wide berth. The new angle put them underneath a different conduit, one which was still safely above their heads. Neila looked up at it for a moment, then suddenly jerked her head back down.

"Gods!" she said. "They're *screaming*."

Salim glanced up as well, long enough to make out the horrified faces that stretched and elongated in their headlong rush toward their destination.

"Probably on their way to Hell," he said.

As if to confirm his statement, a black-winged devil with the half-nude body of a beautiful, savage woman came swooping along the outside of the river, spiraling around it as she went. She briefly regarded the two humans on the ground, flaming bow drawn taut, then clearly dismissed them, flapping lazily back the way they had come, toward the main river. Neila shuddered.

"Is she here to keep them from escaping?"

Salim shook his head. "Hardly. They can no more escape the river at this point than they could escape dying in the first place. Their choices made in life pull them onward."

"Then what's she doing here?" In the distance, the flying devil was now no more than a dot. As they watched, other specks converged from other directions, following the streams but clearly not of them.

"All the planes have their representatives here," Salim said. "Most of them stay in their specific courts, helping to shepherd souls to their proper place on the new planes. But some stay out here, patrolling the river against those creatures like hags that would attempt to steal away souls, or feed on their substance."

"Souls like my father."

"Yes."

Neila frowned and picked up the pace.

It wasn't long until the stream they followed peeled off from the others, and Salim brightened. "We're close now," he said. "Very close. We've entered the court of Axis."

"How can you tell?" Neila asked.

In response, Salim pointed to the ground at her feet. For a second, he could tell that she clearly saw nothing but the same rocky earth and clumps of grass. Then she gasped.

"It's a pattern! All of it!"

Salim nodded. All around them, the landscape had changed subtly. While the dirt was still dirt and the rocks were still rocks, the mathematics were all wrong. There were too many right angles, too many perfect curves. Symmetry and grids that, though sometimes so immense in scope that they were almost impossible to see, nevertheless gave the impression of having been placed precisely by an enormous hand, all the way down to the smallest grain of sand. Even the flow of souls above them seemed to be more regimented now, its course twisting and rippling less.

"Order," Salim said. "The plane of perfect law. Or rather, its embassy—Axis's court within the Boneyard."

They walked on, Neila continuing to marvel at the strange way in which the landscape twisted itself to form grids and matrices, like the whole thing was one of the elaborate Keleshite rugs that some wealthy

Thuvians favored. Now the stream of souls skimmed close to the ground, snaking its way in a current that rippled, not smooth-walled but wriggling and shifting course minutely as the souls within bunched and flowed. At one point, Neila, distracted by the sight of the buildings looming closer on the horizon, failed to notice a shift in the river's course, and Salim pulled her back sharply from the hands of spirits who reached out for her.

"Careful," he warned, "unless you want your soul stripped from your body and sent on before its time."

"Would it do that?" Neila looked shocked.

Salim shrugged. "Who can say? It's the River of Souls, and not meant for mortals. None of this place is. Best you remember that." Then they continued on, giving the stream a much wider berth.

Just when it seemed like neither of them could bear to walk any longer, the portals came into view.

There were several, of varying sizes. By far the largest was a massive, square-edged thing that looked like nothing so much as an enormous doorframe from which the door had been removed. Made of the same gray stone as the distant buildings, its two columns and tower-sized lintel were featureless, imposing in their bulk and absolute symmetry. Within the frame of the trilithon, the air shimmered and burned a brilliant gold, as if light hung from it in a curtain. It was into this radiant screen that the majority of the souls in the River of Law flowed and disappeared.

Yet it was not the only one. Smaller and less imposing, several other portals glowed at measured intervals around the central stones, and these culled their own spirits from the primary flow, causing a further splintering of the branch the two humans had been following. And it was just ahead of them, at the point at which the river radiated its new branches, that Salim and Neila spied figures moving about. Neila looked to Salim, her hand going to the basket hilt of her sword, but Salim merely continued toward them. When they were close, he raised a hand in greeting, and one of the figures did the same.

There were half a dozen of them, male and female, standing in a seemingly casual yet somehow precise manner. Above them, the current of souls arched briefly over their heads before touching down again, as if to grant them free access to each of the diverging streams without having to cross them.

In appearance, the figures most resembled elves, but elves of a beauty and perfection never seen even among the fair folk. Their ears were pointed, their bodies long and lithe, and their hair as straight and smooth as rays of light, yet where the elves of Salim and Neila's world were still mortal, and bore the scars and minor blemishes that are the gift and curse of life, these were something different—an ideal made flesh. All were dressed in plain but well-fitted robes and wraps of gray or white.

"Well met, traveler," the one in front said, and put out his hand. Next to him, Salim heard Neila attempt to stifle a gasp and only halfway succeed.

Where the stranger's arm bent, the substance of both arm and cloth dissolved into a shower of sparks that swirled outward. They lingered for a moment, drifting into eddies of tiny golden grains, then flowed back together as if drawn by a magnet, configuring themselves perfectly in the new position, as natural-looking as any human arm.

Salim took the hand and shook it. "Well met," he agreed. "We're here on behalf of the Lady of Graves."

The leader—or at least Salim presumed the spokesman to be such, for the others did nothing but watch—raised an eyebrow in an expression that was both skeptical and amused.

"Not directly," Salim clarified. "We seek a soul that went missing somewhere along the river's course, after he reached the Boneyard. A human called Faldus Anvanory."

All amusement vanished from the man's face, replaced by a flat, neutral expression that seemed more natural there.

"Your claim seems unlikely," he said. "Most souls stolen from the river are taken on their course through the Astral, where it's difficult to guard it sufficiently. That's where the hags and astradaemons have the greatest luck in their hunts. Not near the Outer Courts, where the eyes of half the planes and Pharasma herself are upon them."

"Yet so we've been told," Salim said. As he spoke, his voice took on the same inflection as the stranger—flat and downturned at the end, as if both men were reciting facts to themselves rather than actually conversing.

"We will check the book," the man said, and gestured to one of the women. This time the motion was greater, and the glittering specks flew out in wider spirals and eddies, allowing Salim to see the glowing motes for what they truly were—tiny, abstract symbols and runes, like those used by scholars in the discussion of mathematics and the unseen principles that bind the world.

The indicated woman reached behind her and drew forth an enormous tome, bound in clasps of glittering metal, from where it hung from her belt on a stout chain. She opened the covers, and thin, cream-colored pages whirred and flipped by themselves before finally coming to rest somewhere in the middle. She consulted it briefly.

"Faldus Anvanory," she said. "Sworn to Abadar. Received at the central branching in the Court of Axis and sent on to the portal of the First Vault." She closed the book with a snap.

"What does that mean?" Neila whispered to Salim.

"It means his soul made it this far safely," he replied. He looked up at the diverging streams, then off to where the array of portals stood, less than a mile away. He gestured toward one in particular. "Somehow the kidnappers snagged it between here and the entrance to Abadar's realm."

"Are they sure?"

This time everyone turned to stare at Neila, and their eyes were wide with surprise—even Salim's.

"We're axiomites," the woman with the book said, as if that explained everything.

"My apologies," Salim said quickly. "My companion is unfamiliar with this plane of existence."

The spokesman nodded agreeably. "Language is rarely a perfect construct." He turned to Neila. "While the inherent instability of existence and the finite capacity for understanding, combined with the influence of the observer on both events and his/her/its perception of them, make tautological proof inherently impossible, I believe that you were instead asking about the relative probability of the event in question, which is so great as to render the other possibilities statistically insignificant." He paused and looked expectantly at her.

Salim leaned over and spoke in her ear. "That means he's sure."

"Of course," she said, making a little curtsy. The axiomite nodded.

"Have you noticed anything out of the ordinary?" Salim asked the figures. "Anything which might bear on the missing soul we're searching for?"

As one, they shook their heads, the unison eerie in its perfection.

"We only learned of a soul's absence from one of the Lady of Graves's heralds—the black-winged one. Were it not for the fact that the soul's name was never recorded at the portal, we would say that it was impossible, and that it must have gone missing on the other side. But we cannot doubt the Lady's precision."

"Thank you," Salim said. "You've been most helpful." He took Neila's arm. "Come on, Neila." Bowing slightly to the axiomites, he turned and led her down the path of the stream he'd indicated.

When they were beyond hearing distance, she spoke. "What were they?"

"Axiomites," he said. "Creatures of perfect reason and logic. They live in Axis, the Eternal City. You saw it from the edge of the Spire. Those were acting as shepherds for souls entering the court, making sure they go where they're supposed to."

"Do you trust them?"

He looked over at her and smiled.

"Trust doesn't enter into it. They're axiomites— reason and balance are the tenets of their existence. If they didn't want to tell us something, they wouldn't. They're probably capable of telling lies when they need to, but for the life of me I can't imagine why they would *care*. One human life is nothing to them."

Neila opened her mouth to respond, then reconsidered. She looked to their destination. "And that's the door to Abadar's realm?"

"One of them." Salim followed her eyes and caught the glint of gold on the distant portal. It was round and circular, like a bank vault. Around its base, another group of figures that might have been axiomites stood watching the stream of soul-stuff pour through the portal. "There are other ways, of course—the First Vault of the merchant god sits in Axis proper, where it guards the first, perfect archetypes upon which everything in existence is based. The perfect sword, the perfect chair—even the perfect man and woman."

"And we're going there?"

"Only if we're unlucky." Salim stopped and put a hand out, gesturing at the ground in front of them. "We know that the soul went missing somewhere between here and there. With luck, there'll be some sort of indication of where or how the kidnapping took place. If we reach the portal and haven't found anything, we're back where we started."

"That's the plan?" Her voice was sharp. "Walk along the River of Souls and look for clues like characters in a minstrel's mystery?"

He looked at her levelly. "Do you have a better one?"

"Of course not. I just thought that, being as you had the power to bring us here in the first place, you might have something a little more elaborate planned."

Salim gave her a small smile. "Don't place too much faith in magic, Lady. In most cases, especially where the gods are involved, it's best to rely on yourself."

"And luck."

"And luck," he agreed. "Which, you must admit, we've had so far."

Her fists went to her hips in a gesture of irritation that was probably habit. Both hair and blouse were now damp with sweat, and clung to her becomingly as she glared at him. "We're in the hind-end of a fairytale graveyard, looking for a needle that may or may not be in the proverbial haystack, while the minutes until my father's soul is destroyed continue ticking away. You call that luck?"

Salim began walking forward along their path again, eyes toward the ground and hands clasped behind him. "Tell me, Neila, have you ever encountered an astradaemon?"

"Of course not!"

Another smile.

"Luck."

She stood considering that for a long moment. Then she grasped her sword hilt and hurried to catch up.

In the end, it was Neila who discovered the first one, almost tripping over it before she realized it was there.

"Salim. Look at this."

She sat down on her haunches in a most unladylike fashion and scraped away the dirt, then held up her prize.

"What is it?" she asked. "It looks like a witch's crystal ball."

So it did. Salim moved over and peered at the strange glass sphere. Clear and greenish, it was the size of a man's fist, with a surface that was almost perfectly smooth. A lattice of thin, dirty cording enclosed it like a bag.

"It's a fishing float," he said, wonderingly. His fingers traced the lines of cord, which stopped abruptly a few inches below the ball as if they'd been cut.

"A what?"

"A fishing float—a hollow ball used to hold fishermen's nets up. They use them all along the coast of the Arcadian Ocean."

"What's it doing here?"

"A damned good question." Salim stood but remained stooped over, scanning the ground. "It doesn't make any sense, but it's more than we've had so far. Help me look."

Together they began scouring the ground, spiraling outward from the point where she'd located the ball.

Salim found the next object—a strange, illustrated card of a rabbit with a broken sword, about the size of his palm. He recognized it as being part of the deck northerners called the harrow, which they used for gambling and fortune-telling. Then Neila gave a triumphant cry and held up a feather that had been half-obscured by the dirt, a brilliant pink pinion. Together they circled in wider and wider arcs, searching for nearly half an hour before deciding they'd found all that was to be found aside from the red-brown dust of this part of the Boneyard.

In all, there were half a dozen objects: the globe, the card, the feather, a scrap of unlabeled map, a tiny and rootless pine sapling that struggled to grow in the dead soil, and the broken headstock of what looked to be a mandolin. Salim laid them out in a row, and he and Neila sat looking at them in silence. Salim brought his hand to his mouth and tapped on his teeth with a thick thumbnail. At last he spoke.

"I don't understand it," he said. "None of this makes any sense."

"Could it be trash?" Neila asked.

"Trash from where? The souls?" Salim shook his head. "They carry nothing, and the axiomites who act as shepherds would have no need for any of this. Damn it, there's no one on this plane to *make* trash, let alone leave it here."

"So it must be related to the kidnapping," Neila observed.

"It's certainly the first thing we've found out of the ordinary," Salim admitted. "But what sort of person would go to all the trouble of stealing a soul out from under the nose of the Lady of Graves, only to leave a bunch of rubbish as a calling card? And how do these pieces even fit together?"

Neila sat back on her hands, jaw tense with frustration. "I'd hope you could tell me, seeing as how you're the one familiar with all this strangeness. To me, it looks like a lot of random junk."

Salim sat bolt upright.

"That's it!"

"What, junk?"

"No. It's *random*." Salim's mind raced, and all at once things began to fall into place. "Neila—ever since we entered the court, have you seen anything that's out of place? Anything that didn't, at some level, seem to follow a pattern?"

She frowned. "No. Not that I can think of."

"That's because it's the region belonging to Axis and the creatures of pure Law, who seek order in everything. To them, randomness and chaos are abominations, to be wiped out wherever possible. Yet here we see the system torn awry, senseless objects appearing out of nowhere, and the terrain itself twisted out of true. Look." He picked up a small rock and threw it back the way they'd come, about thirty feet. It landed in a little puff of dust. "Go look at that and tell me what you see."

Neila gave him a look that said she didn't appreciate him issuing orders like a schoolmaster illustrating a point, but she went anyway. When she came back, her eyes were wide.

"It's in a pattern," she said. "Lined up with the other rocks. All the sand around it, too—it lies where it fell, but it's all so . . . *perfect*."

Salim nodded, then picked up another rock and threw it down at their feet.

"And here?"

Neila bent to look, but Salim didn't bother waiting for her reply. He already knew the answer.

"It's not just the objects. This whole area's been warped. The patterns of order and logic have been broken and then some. And that kind of magic—not to mention the audacity to pull the stunt in full view of the axiomites—tells us who we're looking for. It was a protean."

Neila straightened and looked at him. When he saw that she didn't understand, he sighed.

"What do they teach nobles these days, anyway? It was a *protean*. A creature of pure chaos, from the depths of the void called the Maelstrom. They're the sworn enemies of Axis, spreading madness and anarchy wherever they go. Simply their presence in an area can distort the very fabric of reality, making it run like half-cured cheese." He kicked the little tree, knocking it out of line. "These little presents are just a hint of what it's capable of. If it showed up in your manor in Thuvia, you might never recognize the place again. Or escape with your life."

"And you think one of these is what stole my father?"

Salim nodded and smacked his hands together, one fist on top of the other. "I know it. There's no other reason for a protean to risk its life in this part of the Boneyard, and the fact that the scar of its passing hasn't healed yet means it must have been relatively recent. No, this is it. I'd bet my sword on it."

"You're already betting my father's life," Neila reminded him. "But well enough. Now what? Can you follow it?"

Salim's sense of triumph faded. He thought hard.

"No," he said. "If it were on this plane and traveling physically, I might have a shot, but I doubt both strongly. Teleportation is second nature to proteans, and there's no reason to believe it would stay nearby."

A thought occurred. Salim looked deep into Neila's eyes, and saw in their reflection a new gravity in his own.

Things were spiraling rapidly out of control. Were this girl and her father worth the risk? Maybe. And maybe not. But Salim also knew himself well enough to know that it didn't matter at this point. He might be the reluctant servant of a morbid bitch-goddess, but he kept his vows. And if this were the end of his road, perhaps he'd have earned his rest at last.

"I can't track him," he said at last. "But I may know someone who can." He held out one hand, and with the other withdrew his spiral pendant. Neila frowned.

"Do you trust me?" he asked.

In response, she stepped forward and grimly took his hand.

Chapter Nine
The Eternal City

The Eternal City of Axis shone bronze and gold in a light that came from no temperamental sun, but rather seemed to spring from the air itself above the city, banishing all but the most persistent shadows. An enormous wheel of countless spokes, both narrow and cyclopean, the city spread out over the landscape in an orderly wave of buildings, its rim a ring of greenery and crystalline sand shod with an outer wall of flawless gold. Beyond it, should a traveler climb over the wall and venture into the wilds, he would find the base of Pharasma's Spire and a lazily flowing elbow of the River Styx. Yet for all the city's careful boundaries and demarcations, it too was infinite, making such metaphysical proximity the concern of poets and theologians rather than cartographers.

It was on a wide avenue of this urban matrix that Salim and Neila appeared, shivering and reeling slightly from their transition. Neila set out a hand to steady herself and almost collided with a passerby, an old man with the face of a scholar and the body of a massive snake. She recoiled as the naga's skin slid against hers with the dry rasp of scales. The naga, for his part, pulled himself up to his full height of well over eight feet, looking down at her through wire-rimmed spectacles with an expression of casual disdain. With a noise that was more harrumph than hiss, he slithered pointedly aside and continued on in the direction he'd been heading.

All around them, a parade of even stranger creatures was passing: Four-armed men with veils and tall, conical hats. White-winged men whose skin and radiant armor were impossible to look at directly. A dark-bearded efreeti with smoldering skin and an enormous falchion at its hip, looking like something out of a Katapeshi fairy tale, eyes searching for anyone foolish enough to meet his gaze. Behind them, a pack of emaciated horrors with blank skin where their eyes should be wove silently through the throng, split jaws spread wide but apparently unconnected to any throats. Man and beast, humanoid and grotesque, the figures passed in the smooth-paved street like two meeting currents, threading into and through each other in paces and gaits as varied as their limb structures. Most walked, but there were also palanquins and rickshaws, strange one-wheeled carts and radiant discs that floated on nothing at all.

"Come on, over here." Salim grabbed Neila's arm and pulled her across the thoroughfare, up against the wall of a nearby shop. She came willingly enough, mouth hanging open a little as she strove to take in everything at once.

"Where do they all *come* from?" she asked.

"Here and there." His gesture took in the crowd as a whole. "The Plane of Axis—which is mostly one enormous city that constantly builds on top of itself—is a plane of absolute law. As far as its masters are concerned, if your actions are reasonable—or rather, reasoned—morality is more or less irrelevant. Follow the rules, and everything else is your own business. As a result, it's a nexus of trade for creatures from all across the multiverse." He paused and jerked a thumb over one shoulder. "That would probably be true even if the God of Merchants didn't make his home at one end, but the presence of the First Vault certainly doesn't hurt. According to a lot of the folks around here, commerce is the perfect example of reasoned neutrality—laws and principles that operate completely free of bias."

"But there are devils!" Neila still sounded shocked.

Sure enough, striding past them at that moment was a red-skinned man with the classic beard and features of a devil, save that curving ram horns of glistening black bone extended not just from his head, but also around from his back in a wicked tangle that stretched like a cage about to enclose him entirely. Several of these protrusions were draped with what looked like scrolls. Salim glanced over at the devil's retreating back and nodded.

"Of course. Devils are evil, but they're ultimately bound by codes and strictures that the axiomites can appreciate. That's why your standard folk tales tell of them bargaining for souls, or being trapped by wordplay—both of which, for the record, are much more likely to result in the devil tearing you apart than the stories indicate." Salim inclined his head in the direction the devil had disappeared into the crowd. "That one in particular was a phistophilus—a contract devil, responsible for helping maintain the infernal bureaucracy. They do brisk business here, both for their masters and as free agents. The Abadarans can practice all they want, but no one writes a contract like a devil. Now if a *demon* showed up here, that would be different. Those things don't respect anything, and they'd be set upon by the city's defenders before they knew what was happening."

He took her arm again. "All of which means we should be on our best and most reasonable behavior. Now let's go get our bearings."

Without giving her time for further questions, Salim threw them both back into the tumultuous flow of the street, slipping along in the wake of a cart pulled by an enormous stag beetle.

The crowd wasn't really as bizarre as he'd made it sound. While Neila was undoubtedly still overwhelmed by the array of strange faces and stranger tongues being babbled all around them, Salim knew that in truth the citizenry they passed was made up primarily of three factions.

The first, the axiomites, were the same as the shepherds they'd already met in the Boneyard, creatures who took the form of beautiful elflike men and women for the sake of convenience, but whose every movement revealed their true nature—that of pure, mathematical laws and absolutes, ideas and theorems made flesh and given sentience. Some scholars posited that they were the multiverse's attempt to understand itself. On the whole, Salim thought they were an alright lot, and certainly easy on the eyes, though in conversation they were often detached and had an annoying tendency to slip into higher realms of logic where Salim couldn't hope to follow. Few people could make Salim feel stupid on such a regular basis—but then, if you wanted to be racist about it, axiomites were only barely people.

Still, they were easier to work with than the second group, the hive people. Those oversized, ant-shaped creatures skittered through the crowd as well, their shoulders as high as his own, and Salim was careful to steer Neila around them. It wasn't so much that the bug-men were mean, so far as he understood, but rather that their mindset made that of the axiomites seem relaxed and familiar. Their law was the collectivist order of an insect hive, a matriarchy of a million individuals existing in perfect understanding of their role and duty, and who could say what one of them might decide was in the hive's best interest? Salim would just as soon not get devoured for accidentally showing disrespect, or proposing an unsanctioned idea or action.

The last group, with members seemingly stationed at every corner or marching quickly through the crowd, were the clockwork men of Axis. One of them brushed up against Neila, and she turned to gawk at the whirring gears and belts visible beneath the cracked and broken surface of the thing's stone skin and gleaming armor.

"They're *machines*!" she whispered excitedly to Salim, and he nodded without breaking stride, speaking to her from the side of his mouth.

"The most sophisticated on any plane. The axiomites built them in the early days of the war with Chaos, to hold back the madness of the proteans. They're the shock troops and the law-keepers of Axis, both here and across the multiverse."

"But why are they broken?" Neila was looking around now, frowning, and Salim knew she was seeing the inexplicable contrast between the perfect walls of the buildings they passed—the street itself as clean as a lord's dinner plate—and the disrepair of their guardians.

"I don't know," Salim answered honestly. "But it's been that way as long as I can remember. The war with the Maelstrom still rages, and it may be that the forges of the Crucible are too taxed to keep them pretty, so long as they're functional. Perhaps their scars are badges of honor, though so far as I know the machines know nothing of emotions, even pride." He frowned. "Or perhaps it's a sign that Chaos is slowly winning, in which case we're all in trouble. But it's unlikely that anything will shift the balance significantly in your lifetime."

Squeezing Neila's arm, Salim pointed up into the air, where a strange construct like a giant eye with hands and wings was flapping awkwardly down the avenue.

"Not all them are the same, either," he said. "There are a number of different types, all built for different things. That's an arbiter, one of the weaker models. They're designed to watch and report, as well as act as diplomats and emissaries across the plains."

"It's adorable!" Neila exclaimed, and Salim blinked. He cocked his head and regarded the arbiter, and for the first time saw it not as a machine, but as a creature—a fat little eyeball flapping comically to remain aloft, like a farmed duck who'd eaten too much grain.

"Yes," he admitted, after it had passed. "I suppose it is."

Now the street rose slightly and opened out into a large plaza, and here at last the crowd thinned as it dispersed into the open space. In the center of the plaza stood a high, narrow fountain. Three concentric rings of basins made a rounded ziggurat of placid water and streaming cataracts, shaped something like a tiered cake and rising from waist height at the edge to a narrow column as tall as Salim in the middle. From its center sprouted a gleaming statue of one of the man-shaped automatons, a broad-bladed sword held aloft and a ribbon of mathematical symbols draped around him like a fluttering pennant. Unlike the others they'd passed, this paragon was perfectly whole, all smooth faces and sharp-edged corners, its gray-white stone not defaced by so much as a bird dropping.

Salim vaulted up onto the fountain's rim, soft boots never wavering on the stippled stone. He reached down to help Neila up.

The girl looked at his hand once, then hopped up lightly by herself. Her crossed feet, one in front of the other, caused her knees to bow outward as she rose in a single, smooth motion, like a ballerina's plié. Her self-satisfied smile was so big and genuine that Salim couldn't help but smirk a little in return and incline his head. Without offering his hand, he took two long steps upward to stand level with the life-size statue. Neila followed, leaping across the still fountain surfaces like a water fairy.

From the statue's vantage, huge swaths of the city spread out before them. Though many of the buildings were tall—some impossibly so, by the standards of Golarion—most were flat-topped boxes no more than a few stories high, and the gaps between them combined with subtle rises and dips in elevation to let the pair see for miles across golden roofs and carefully maintained parklands. Salim stepped to the statue's narrow plinth, putting one arm around the stone man for balance. When Neila followed him to it, his other arm slipped around her waist to keep her from being edged off into the pool. Together they stared out over the gleaming vista.

"Unbelievable," she breathed. She scanned the view slowly, carefully, as if attempting to drink it all in, to commit every scattered steeple and onion-dome to memory. When she looked up at Salim, her face glowed with a childlike delight that drew her cheeks up and crinkled her eyes slightly at the edges. A faint breeze blew wisps of her black hair into her face, flickering in front of that beaming smile, and she made no effort to corral them.

"What *are* they all?" she asked.

Feeling strangely proud—as if he had anything to do with the magnificent view—Salim bent his face in close so that she could follow his gaze without his releasing one of his handholds and potentially dumping both of them into the pool.

"You see that?" he asked, pointing with his chin toward a distant block whose black and gray contrasted sharply with the majority of the bright buildings. From its hulking central bulk, towers and lesser arms radiated outward, sending trails of black smoke and white steam into the sky, where they mixed and eddied before dispersing into the air. From the way conventional buildings shrank into nothingness at its feet, Salim guessed that the structure must be ten miles across—an artificial mountain, with only the plane's perfectly clear air and peculiar horizon making it visible at this distance.

"It looks like a factory," she said.

"That's exactly what it is. That's the Adamantine Crucible, where the construct warriors are forged. Inside, smelting pits like burning lakes hold metal stronger than steel, and great machines like nothing seen on any other plane assemble Axis's guardians in a constant stream, stockpiling soldiers against the day Chaos decides to launch its next crusade against order and rationality."

"And that?" Her cheek, smooth and warm against the rough stubble of his own, pressed his head over and up. Where she gazed, what looked like a second city floated calmly above the original. Only unlike Axis, this sky-city was made entirely of colored glass, in alien geometric shapes that twisted the eye and reflected a shifting barrage of rainbow light.

"That's the Golden Lattice," he answered. "The hive city of the wasp-men. They're like the ant people in the street, but look—well, you can guess what they look like. You don't see them down here much, but inside their hive are thousands or millions of drones that exist only to serve their queen. The whole thing is built out of fibers no thicker than your hair—so thin that the light can shine through and make those colors—yet somehow they've the strength to support a whole city."

"Have you been there?"

He laughed. "Maybe a human's been there before—I wouldn't be surprised—but if so, I've never met him. I don't even know that those glass walls could support me." He used his hands to mime flapping without moving his arms from their load-bearing positions. "I don't fly so well."

He thought of something then, and mincing carefully forward, pivoted them both counterclockwise around the statue. When Neila saw what had been hidden from view by the statue's bulk, her breath caught in her throat.

"That," Salim said, again feeling that ridiculous sense of pride, "is the Threefold Pillar of the Axiomite Godmind."

The three crystalline obelisks rose glittering into the sky, their points uneven but all three far taller than any other visible structure. Up their sides—inside them, as if projected onto their surface by one of the so-called magic lanterns of the theater—twined brilliant streams of symbols like those that made up the axiomites' true forms. It was there, in the absolute center of Axis, that the children of the Plane of Law did their true work, pooling their very essences to unlock the fundamental truths of existence. Salim knew this just as he knew the space between the pillars was the throne in which that combined intelligence—the axiomite Godmind—would manifest in times of great need and confusion, though he doubted any human alive had ever seen it. Yet even without that presence, it was still a magnificent monument, its transparent shafts burning with reflected light and scrolling shapes.

Neila let out her breath in a long, contented sigh, and Salim was suddenly keenly aware of the girl's youth, her warm body pressed against his through the thin fabric of their clothes. One of her arms had fallen against his where it wrapped around her and unconsciously hugged it to her side. Looking out over her head, which fit neatly into the hollow between his chin and breastbone, Salim could smell the light, faintly sweet scent of her hair as further sections of it came loose from its tight knot and blew around them both. He pulled aside a little and looked down, seeing the strong face in profile, smile radiant as she stared off toward the gleaming pillar. It was an expression he'd never seen on her before, like a veil had been lifted.

This must be how she looked before her father's murder, Salim realized. At that moment, she turned and met his eyes, smile widening.

"It's beautiful," she said.

Salim felt warmth spread through his chest and limbs, the vague impression that an egg had cracked somewhere inside him and begun slowly draining. Under the fingers of his restraining hand, the silk of her blouse slid over taut skin, thin as a slick of oil on a pond.

That was no good. No good at all.

"We should go," he said. Before she could respond, he let go and bounded down to the pavement, wetting the hem of his robes in the process. She shot him a momentarily puzzled look, then followed with her prior grace.

They moved quickly now, Salim navigating the streets with ease and acting as a blocker for Neila, who stepped nimbly in his wake. Though they cut across several streets as the flow of traffic directed, Salim moving more by instinct than by a perfect knowledge of Axis's infinite layout, the dark-robed man was careful to always trend toward those immense lightning rods at the center of the city.

At one point, with an avenue clogged by some sort of performance or altercation—it was hard to tell with all the onlookers gathered about—Salim led them off the roadway and into a tree-lined square that was half parkland and half market district. White marble statues of Abadar stood fifteen feet tall at each corner of the space, looking over the assembly with calm benevolence and loaded crossbows, their banker's scales hanging prominently at their belts. Within, tents and stalls not so different from the crowded marketplace of Lamasara clustered in an elaborate matrix—one no doubt designed to ensure shoppers passed by the greatest number of merchants before exiting, regardless of entry point or trajectory. Between these temporary structures, which Salim knew were probably not temporary at all, thick-crowned trees with tiny green leaves and dangling, willowlike streamers added explosions of green to the mix. The overall effect was that of both carnival and pastoral beauty, which somehow managed to coexist without either diminishing the other.

Neila's face as they entered the maze of hawkers and barkers said that it was clearly working. If anything, the childlike delight that had been placed there by her first true view of Axis grew. Where before she had moved with Salim in perfect step, threading through the crowd, now she dawdled, slowing and even pausing as new sights caught her eye.

Not that there weren't things worth staring at. Every one of the stalls was a wonder a girl who'd lived her entire life on the mundane world of Golarion could only dream about. Here were floating weapons that sang as they flew to defend their bearers. Baby phoenixes—or reasonable illusions thereof—singing mournfully from cages of unmeltable alloys. Potions and baubles of every color and description, all manned by eager merchants who were every bit as strange as the wares they purveyed. Even those stalls that were objectively horrible—the hag with her jars of screaming, tortured soul larvae, or the snake-headed artist with his moving paintings of corpses performing unspeakable acts—were still amazing in their uniqueness and vibrancy.

At last Salim was forced to take Neila's hand and tug her gently along.

"Come on, Lady," he said. "I don't know how much gold's in your pouch, but there's no way it's enough for any of this lot."

Neila grinned, a little sheepishly, and allowed herself to be led.

"I shouldn't be surprised," she said. "After all that we've seen so far, you'd think I'd be used to—"

"G'day, Madame and Gent! And a good day it is, though I gather it's always a good day when you've a woman like that by your side, eh, Master?"

JAMES L. SUTTER

The strange little man who leaped out in front of them was no taller than Salim's navel, and so twisted and wizened that it was impossible to tell whether he was some species of goblin or something else entirely. His skin bore a grayish cast, and his ears pointed slightly beneath a ridiculous, muffin-shaped hat of purple felt. His only clothing was a sash of sky blue over a deep purple jacket of the same material, with bright brass buttons and gold-cord epaulets. The jacket hung down over his potbellied stomach, but still failed to conceal his bandy legs or atrophied genitals.

"We're not interested," Salim said automatically, and sidestepped to the left, intending to keep moving. With a yell, the little man threw himself in that direction, landing hard on the pavement and somersaulting to his feet in front of them.

"Of course you're not!" Muffin Hat cried, not even breathing hard from his impromptu tumbling performance. "Who could be interested by the sight of me alone? No, not even my fabulous physique could keep your interest in such a festival of delights as this!" He puffed out his chest and spread his hands wide, standing on tiptoes. Next to Salim, Neila put a hand to her mouth to hide an involuntary giggle, and the creature smiled, wiggling its long nose.

"The lady has the right of it, sir, as ever they do, so they do. I am but a humble practitioner of the showman's arts, and nothing special when compared to the sights you've no doubt seen. Were I alone, I would likely hide myself in the skirts of one of the nearby stalls until you passed, so as to not accidentally catch your eye and distract you from more worthy points of focus. Yet such is not the case, for I come not alone, and ask your brief attention not on my own behalf, but on that of my ever-so-talented and one-of-a-kind friends."

In a practiced gesture that made Salim momentarily tense—he'd seen plenty of knifemen who had that same easy grace when going for a blade—Muffin Hat reached behind his back and drew forth a crank-driven music box which hung from the blue sash. Sensing Neila's interest, Salim sighed and resigned himself to watching the little creature's performance.

"Beautiful Lady and most exquisitely tasteful Gentleman," Muffin Hat cried, hopping from foot to foot in excitement. "Allow me to present to you a sight never seen in any market or on any plane but this one—Marlott the Marvelous's Dancing Spiders and Acrobatic Arthropods!"

With a snap, Muffin Hat—who Salim now presumed was named Marlott—unhooked a latch on the bottom of his music box and let it swing open, releasing a cascade of scuttling horrors that fell to the pavement and began to stream across it in all directions. Neila screamed and shrank back, and Salim found himself going for his sword, for all the good it might do.

"No! No need to fear the performers, gentle folk, for they are the height of gentility itself. Observe!" With one hand, Marlott began turning the crank, causing the box to emit a rickety, high-pitched tune like that of a carousel.

As he did, a strange thing happened. Where a moment before the spiders, scorpions, and more disturbing creatures he'd released had skittered every which way, now they began to draw back together, forming orderly rows. As Salim watched, they began to flex their legs in time to the music, bobbing their whole bodies up and down.

"Yes! Yes!" Marlott's voice was ecstatic. "Dance, my loves!"

As one, the spiders of the front row began to hop back and forth from side to side, catching themselves on one bank of legs before throwing themselves over and balancing on the other, matching Marlott himself. Behind them, the centipedes were raising their foresections into the air and clambering over each other to create tottering arches several times their own height. Through these, scorpions rolled in an imitation of Marlott's somersault, reaching up to grasp their own tails and then rolling like wheels, one after another.

Neila actually clapped her hands in delight. "Wonderful!" she cried. "Absolutely magnificent!"

Salim had to admit it was pretty good, even given their fantastical setting. He was about to tell Marlott so when he noticed the goblinoid's eyes flick sideways past Neila, his manic grin unchanging.

It was all the signal Salim needed. He whirled around in time to see the second figure—this one no larger than Marlott, but wrapped in a dark cloak that left only a long nose visible beneath the cowl—moving up behind Neila. With one hand, it reached toward her purse. In the other, it held a curve-bladed knife smeared with black grease.

"Down!" Salim said, shoving Neila violently aside.

To her credit, the girl didn't fall. Seeing what had been creeping up behind her, her mouth made a little O of surprise, but she immediately drew her own sword.

The cloaked figure charged, ignoring Neila in favor of Salim. The attacker came in low, dagger held reversed and flat against his forearm like a true knife-fighter, not out straight where a simple twist could disarm him. The hand came up fast, in a savage slash designed to open Salim's stomach.

But his stomach wasn't there. At the last second, Salim twisted aside and arched backward, the knife whistling past his gut without so much as a scratch. It was a good thing, too—Salim couldn't be sure what the gunk on the blade was without further investigation, but he had a feeling that a scratch was all the pint-sized assassin needed. Before the little man could recover, Salim leaned forward and put a boot in his side.

The assassin fell, but not for long, hitting the pavement with his shoulder and rolling to his feet in much the same way Marlott had. He came up swinging, the knife point whistling in sideways in a savage stab aimed at Salim's kidneys. Salim swung his own blade in a downward arc like the hand of a clock, easily blocking the knife.

Or so he thought. With an agility Salim had no idea the man possessed, the assassin sprang upward, the knife's angle rising two feet mid-thrust, suddenly level with Salim's neck. Without time to raise his own sword, Salim dropped sideways and down, falling artlessly to the ground as the dagger passed close enough to ruffle the hair on his head. Not giving his target a chance to recover, the little man moved with him, raising the knife high and bringing it down—

—and then screaming as Neila's sword flashed in, spitting his wrist. The poisoned dagger fell from nervous fingers, and Salim prudently rolled to avoid it.

Neila stood with sword and arm outstretched in a textbook fencer's lunge. The rest of her hair had spilled from the knot at the nape of her neck, and now it ran wild around her face and shoulders. Though her expression was the shock of someone who's never felt the disturbing ease with which steel slides through flesh and grates against bone, her arm didn't waver. With a twist, she withdrew her rapier and returned to a formal en garde stance, as if waiting for a referee to announce the point.

The assassin, for his part, didn't waste any time. Snatching at the dagger, he turned and fled back into the stalls, disappearing behind a brightly colored awning before Salim was all the way to his feet.

Together, Salim and Neila turned toward Marlott. The little man was still grinding away at his box organ, creepy-crawlies dancing and a big grin splitting his face. Only now that grin looked more rueful than obsequious.

"It's my sincere hope, Lady and Gent, that you've enjoyed this fully interactive and death-defying performance, in which you yourselves have been the stars, and acquitted yourselves with remarkable flair. Yet I'm afraid I cannot linger—much to do, yes, much to do! 'Bugs to trade, traders to bug, then a-buggering a lassie with a pretty-pretty mug,' as the old song goes. I will, however, allow you to personally thank the performers." He quit turning the crank, and pointed toward the two humans.

"Go meet your audience, lovelies."

As one, the mass of skittering horrors swarmed toward Neila and Salim.

After the near-skewering Salim had just escaped, it wasn't much of a battle. Swords were next to useless against the bugs that, while poisonous, were still nothing more monstrous than the tiny desert scorpions one might shake out of a shoe in the morning. As it turned out, shoes were their primary weapons. Within moments, many of their attackers had been transformed into black and purple smears on the pavement, and the rest had scuttled away into the bushes and stalls, searching for more appropriate prey. Yet it was long enough—by the time they could cease their own dance of destruction and look up, the grinning Marlott was nowhere to be seen. Salim crouched down, stretching stiff muscles in his thighs.

"They meant to kill us," Neila said, tentatively.

"Yes."

"For our gold."

"Yes."

She let this sink in. Clearly, the thought that someone on this magical, unimaginable plane might kill her for the handful of coins in her purse had never crossed her mind. He watched as understanding dawned. On this plane or any other, a market was still a market.

"And we had no choice but to defend ourselves," she continued. "If I hadn't stabbed that man, he would have run you through."

Salim heard the question inherent in her statements, and answered it.

"Without a doubt. That dagger was almost certainly poisoned. One nick and you'd be on your own now."

"Right." Her features softened with obvious relief. Salim gestured at her sword.

"You should wipe that off before you sheathe it."

Neila nodded. Glancing around like a guilty child to make sure nobody was looking, she rubbed it down with a fold of canvas from a nearby awning, leaving a long red smear. Then she sheathed the sword, and together the two of them moved quickly out of the park, no longer enthralled by the wonders of the stalls or the calls of the barkers. As they passed one of the statues of Abadar, Neila paused, then looked backward over her shoulder, her expression wistful.

"Too bad about the spiders, though."

Chapter Ten
The Clever Endeavor

Later, as they were walking along yet another side street—this one far less crowded and home almost exclusively to dark-skinned humans and the gleaming, diamond-and-clockwork servitor constructs that followed them around—Neila asked a question.

"If this is the plane of ultimate law," she said, "how come those two back in the market tried to murder and rob us?"

Salim took her arm and sidestepped to allow a clockwork creature—not one of the axiomite's warrior automatons, but something altogether less sophisticated—to pass them. The waist-high machine was shaped like a Tian puzzle-box with legs, and hummed an off-key song as it ambled by, upright pipes puffing little rings of steam. A net bag of oranges was balanced precariously atop its head, the bag's mouth secured by a small pincer apparatus.

"Law and morality are different," Salim said. "Axis welcomes all who walk the ordered path, and while that makes it popular with gods like Abadar, there's room in its streets for all who follow a code. Those men who attacked us, for example. I suspect they're children of Norgorber."

"The Reaper!" Neila was aghast.

Salim nodded. "The assassin god has a sizable following in the city. It's said that the god himself resides in the strange passages beneath Axis, his realm touching all points and none. Certainly his worshipers run the undercity, and navigate the old bug tunnels like sewer rats."

"But that's terrible!" Neila pressed. "Why don't the axiomites send those warrior things—the machines—to drive them out?"

Salim raised his shoulders. "Why would they? The Reaper may not be as trustworthy as a devil, but a good assassin stays bought, and that has its own sort of code to it. Breaking a law in a consistent, regimented fashion is itself an expression of order." He stepped wide to avoid an access shaft in the street, its man-sized ladder leading down to the ant-folk's elaborate network of hive tunnels.

"Besides," he said, "sometimes assassins come in useful, even on Axis. The rules of commerce don't preclude a little trimming of the competition now and again, and axiomites tend to mind their own business as much as possible. The men who attacked us had a reasonable motive—getting into our purses—and we defended ourselves in a reasonable manner. As far as most folk around here would be concerned, everything's balanced. It might as well have never happened."

Neila nodded, but her eyes remained fixed on the wide tunnel mouth as they passed. She shivered and moved to quicken her pace, but Salim stopped suddenly and turned to face the buildings to their right.

"In any case," he said, "we're here."

Neila looked doubtfully at the plain eaves and brick facades that faced them. None of the buildings in this neighborhood had windows, and these particular doors didn't have the welcoming look of shops or inns. If Salim had to guess, he'd presume they were storage houses of some sort, or workshops for those who valued their privacy. Knowing Neila must be thinking the same thing, he stepped forward and tapped authoritatively at a small brass plaque affixed to the wall. It rang louder than it had any right to, as if Salim had struck a bell.

"What—" Neila began, then broke off as beneath and to the left of the plaque a door began to open in the wall.

It was low, the top of the opening beginning just a few feet off the ground, but it was wide enough for two people to walk abreast. In front of it, the cobbles of the sidewalk fell away in a metered cascade, creating a grand staircase leading down into the ground. In seconds, the whisper of oiled stone grew silent, and the humans were left staring down into a descending tunnel whose walls glowed with faint phosphorescence.

"After you," Salim said, and bowed.

Neila looked from him to the tunnel and back, then nodded and stepped forward. Her hand went to the hilt of her sword, but Salim reached out and touched it.

"There's no need," he said. "Or at least, there shouldn't be. Trust me."

The dubious expression returning, Neila nevertheless removed her hand and stepped quickly down the stairs, shoulders squared and chin held high. Salim fell in behind her, and then they were off the street and descending steeply into the stone tunnel, the steps rising silently back into place behind them.

The stairs terminated in a wide brick landing. Before them was an archway that looked almost like the front doorway of a tavern, save that it lacked even the modest bat-wing doors that such establishments sometimes boasted. Above it, a mosaic of tiny colored tiles stretched several feet from the arch's top to the ceiling, masterfully depicting a grinning, anthropomorphic rat counting out stacks of coins. An unfurled scroll beneath it read "The Clever Endeavor."

Inside, the drinking house was dim, lit by wrought-iron lanterns along the walls which held not the normal flickering of flame but the same steady glow of the phosphorescence in the staircase. Against the far wall was a long wooden bar, clean but worn, and behind it rack upon rack of shelves which held bottles in a wide array of sizes and colors, some of them clear, others opaque, and a few jittering lightly in their niches as if their contents were struggling to get out. A thin man of dark hair and indeterminate age leaned against the inner side of the counter with a barman's rag hung over his shoulder as naturally as if it had grown there. Though he faced the door, he didn't appear to be looking at the newcomers. Yet he didn't appear to be looking at anything else, either, simply gazing off toward the unadorned wall next to the doorway with a face that registered nothing except vague idleness.

The other patrons of the bar—though Salim thought "tenants" might be more appropriate—were practicing much the same skill, none of them doing much of anything yet somehow all managing to just miss looking at Salim and Neila. This was made all the more impressive by the fact that the bar's layout placed tables in scalloped alcoves all around the walls, leaving the center empty and giving every table, no matter how deep and dark its corner, a clear view of the door where the two humans stood.

In the Clever Endeavor, every table came with a wall to put your back to, even if it meant bulging the walls out in ways no normal architect would advise. It was that sort of bar.

Salim returned the other drinkers the favor and studiously avoided looking directly at any of them as he led Neila across the floor and toward an open table in one of several back-left corners. As they passed close to the bar, he raised a hand to his brow and twitched it down in a little two-finger salute, thumb outstretched and last two fingers furled in.

Immediately, the bartender's eyes focused on them both. "Welcome back, stranger," the barman said, with a little smile that looked at once wry and good-natured.

"Lahan." Salim met his gaze and held up two fingers again. "Something tame."

The bartender's eyes flicked to Neila and back. He nodded. "Soft as mother's milk and smooth as the teat that made it. You got it."

But Salim was already past him and pulling out a chair at the table. This he took for himself, leaving the wall bench with the view of the door for Neila, though he knew she wouldn't catch the gesture. Nobles had all sorts of manners, but never the ones that actually mattered.

Neila took the seat without commenting. Instead, she looked at him levelly, her expression calculating.

"You know him. The bartender." It was not a question.

"I used to spend some time here."

Again that focused look, as if he'd presented her with a riddle and she was determined to figure out the answer for herself. At last she said, "You believe in playing all your cards close to your chest, don't you? Regardless of what they are."

Salim thought about asking her what a young merchant's daughter in Thuvia would know about cards, but then Lahan was setting two mugs down in front of them, retreating as quickly as he'd appeared. The liquid in each was blood red and roiling with carbonation. Salim picked his up and sniffed at the vapors.

Neila eyed her own drink warily. "What is it?"

"Camel piss," Salim responded, and drank deep. Then he smacked his lips and smiled.

Salim didn't know why he'd said it, exactly, but something deep within him enjoyed the look of shock that flashed across her face at the crudity. As suddenly as it came, it was replaced by a scowl, and then she was lifting her own mug and drinking without hesitation. As she did, her expression changed to one of wonder.

"It's cherries!" she said.

"Like none you've ever had," Salim replied. "Hard cherry wine from the orchards of Axis. I don't know what causes the bubbles, but they keep your head clear. No point in you getting sloppy when there's work to be done."

She ignored the jibe. "So what exactly are we doing here?"

"Waiting."

Neila gave an exasperated sigh and clearly decided not to answer his ribbing. Instead she drank more of the wine, the mug leaving a thin line of red on the bridge of her nose. As she looked away from him, seeking something else to fix on, Salim touched her hand.

"Don't look directly at them," he said quietly. "It's not polite."

Neila grimaced as if to ask who *he* was to decide what was polite, but she still managed to affect a reasonable imitation of the bartender's vacant, unfocused gaze, as if she were merely staring off into space over Salim's shoulder.

Salim knew what she was actually looking at. He'd taken in the other patrons of the bar with a single glance as they'd entered, analyzed the faces and postures, and summarily dismissed them all as unrelated to his and Neila's business. But then, he'd seen the freak show before.

Neila hadn't, and even with the unfocused gaze, it showed on her face, the tension at the edges of her eyes and mouth as she attempted to keep from registering her amazement.

On the street, Axis's motley menagerie of residents had been astounding, but that parade of wonders swept past as fast as you could recognize them, and anything presented in such brief glances could still manage to feel unreal, your brain accepting the input but not truly processing it. Salim had seen the same thing from soldiers in battle, unfazed by the slaughter all around them simply because of the speed at which it took place. A man was there, and then he was gone, and you were still moving—at a quick enough pace, the mind didn't have time for anything more than that.

Here, however, there was time for Neila to focus and actually study individual creatures in depth. And despite the bar's relative emptiness, there was plenty to see.

Near the door, at a special table built wide and low for their kind, sat two of the hive people, the red-brown carapaces of their ant bodies reflecting the torchlight as they dug into tureens of writhing, liquor-infused grubs, mandibles clacking. Though they both bore the claws and barbed stings of the warrior caste, and on the street would be impossible to tell from any others of their kind, Salim knew they must have gone rogue some time ago, likely deserting out of an addiction to those same grubs. Otherwise they would never have found a place like the Clever Endeavor.

Farther in, several axiomites sat deep in conversation across a table strewn with charts and diagrams, fingers flashing into glowing symbols as they gestured to punctuate their arguments. Even had they been shouting rather than speaking in their low, earnest tones, it was unlikely that anyone else in the room would have been able to understand what they were discussing. Axiomite scholarship and politics—which were most often one and the same—were both esoteric to the point of indecipherable where members of other races were concerned. These particular specimens no doubt thought of themselves as revolutionaries, proponents of a theorem dismissed by the majority.

In the back-right corner, opposite Neila and Salim and shrouded deeper in darkness than was reasonable given the lit lamp just above it, squatted a d'ziriak, one of the inscrutable residents of the Plane of Shadow. A black-shelled cross between a man and a termite, it seemed to bend the light around itself while simultaneously emitting small flares of color from the sigils ranged across its torso and thorax. It drank deep, with both hands holding its oversized mug, not looking around with even the sidelong glances of the other patrons. But then, if the rumors about their telepathy were true, it didn't have to.

And there were others—humanoid, mostly, but so swaddled in cloaks and other concealing clothing that it was sometimes impossible to tell whether a bulge between the shoulders meant a rucksack or a carefully folded set of wings. That was also unsurprising. The rule against staring or expressing obvious recognition in the Clever Endeavor wasn't just a polite custom—it was key to avoiding bloodshed. With the exception of Lahan, who made a point of never using names unless it was absolutely vital, nobody came to the Clever Endeavor to make friends.

After several minutes, Neila finished her oblique survey of the room and turned back to Salim, just as he had set down his empty mug and was raising his hand to summon a second. She looked pointedly down at the dry vessel, then back up at him. This time her expression was serious.

"And is that your master plan, Mr. Ghadafar?"

Salim almost answered with another wisecrack, then decided he'd pushed her far enough for one day. He honestly wasn't sure what about her made him feel at once so protective and so eager to rile her, but he thought it might be good to remember that this was still the girl who'd been willing to travel to the very gates of Death in order to save her father. Whether or not he'd asked her to come along, she deserved to know what they were doing.

He showed his hands, palms toward her. "Alright. The answer is that we've come as far as we can on our own, and now we need help. So we're running up the flag and seeing who rallies."

An arched eyebrow. "And how do we do that?"

"We already have."

At that moment, Salim heard the solid thud of stone on wood, matched by the low creak of straining floorboards. Momentarily forgetting the rule about staring, Neila gawked open-mouthed, eyes fixed on the door. Salim didn't bother turning around, merely sat with his hands folded in front of him as the rhythmic thumping grew louder, listening as well to the telltale quieting of the other voices in the bar that told him all he needed to know. A few feet behind his chair, the heavy footfalls ceased.

"Salim." The voice was all bass, the rumble of a distant storm.

"It's been a long time, Calabast."

"Only by some definitions."

Salim turned.

Before him, tall enough for its crested helmet to almost scrape the ceiling, stood a humanoid juggernaut of stone and armor. Thick plates of golden metal gleamed in the glow of the lanterns, and through the gaps between bracers and breastplate, skirt and greaves, Salim could see thick, corded muscle that moved like flesh, but was obviously not. No skin born of a woman had ever had that glossy stone finish, chipped and scarred by countless battles, and no giant—however robust—could match the knots of adamantine filaments that twitched and whispered through a broken patch in the stone of the newcomer's right bicep.

Now those big onyx hands made fists, crossing in front of Calabast's midsection. Where they touched, a play of blue and yellow sparks crackled along the bracers, and Salim felt every hair on his body struggle to stand up.

"Please," Salim said, "be welcome. Have a seat." He pulled out the third chair at their table—a comically man-sized furnishing that would support the stoutest human, but no doubt collapse to splinters at the first touch of the automaton's bulk.

Calabast didn't laugh—the residents of Axis were already a sober lot, and Calabast was a machine—but neither did he blast Salim into tiny, steaming gobbets for wasting his time. As always, Salim took that as a good sign.

Instead, the behemoth took two more of his room-shaking steps and squatted alongside their table, between Salim and Neila. As he moved, Salim caught a glimpse of the bar's other tenants. This time they really were ignoring Salim and his friends, and with all their might. Several appeared to be trying to shrink back into the shadows, letting their hoods fall low. Not that it would do them any good, had Calabast come for them, but Salim doubted that any of them had anything to fear. The machine soldiers of Axis served many functions, but always within their distinct roles. Had one of the man-sized contract enforcement models entered, many of the customers would likely be justified in their fear. If it were one of the horse-bodied law keepers with arms like razor whips, sent to round up those who sought to evade legal punishment, Salim suspected that anyone present would make a fine catch. But Calabast—no. The fact that they hadn't already been rent limb from limb meant that these men were safe. Safer than Salim himself.

Neila made a noise like a goose being throttled. Salim tore himself from his musings long enough to catch the big-eyed stare directed toward their guest, whose massive head peered down at her from three feet away with silent, unmoving interest.

"Forgive my manners," Salim said. "Calabast, this is Neila. She's helping me solve the Dark Lady's latest issue."

Beneath the golden helmet, blank black eyes didn't blink. "Neila. May you run your full course, and end it well."

"And—and you as well," Neila managed, her voice wavering only a little.

"Don't worry," Salim said, somewhat apologetically. "Calabast is always like that. It's part of his job."

"What's that?" she managed.

"My function is to enforce the laws and cycles of mortal existence, and to correct those who seek to defy or pervert them." Though Calabast's words and tone were courtly enough, the voice was still far from human, crackling up from deep within his throat like the roar of a blast furnace.

"Oh."

"He means he hunts immortals," Salim translated. "Calabast and I have worked together in the past. As you might expect, the lords of Axis share Pharasma's desire to see the cycle of souls remain inviolate. Neither takes kindly to those mortals who would step outside that flow."

There was a moment's pause while Neila processed this, and then the panicked look returned, stronger than ever. She cast a glance at the gleaming war machine, who remained perfectly still in that unnerving way of his. "But—"

Salim had a good guess what she was about to say, and cut her off before she could. "Stealing souls from the Outer Courts is a violation of the natural order at the highest level. It's in both planes' interest for him to help us."

And keep your mouth shut about the elixir, his eyes said. He stared hard at her to make sure she understood. Since Faldus hadn't consumed the elixir yet, there was nothing to worry about. And even if they succeeded and the merchant managed to achieve his false youth, he'd still be small change compared to Calabast's normal quarry—for the next thousand years, anyway. But that didn't mean Salim was eager to muddy the waters any more than absolutely necessary.

Neila got the message. "Of course," she said, forcibly regaining some of her usual composure. "That makes sense."

"If you would present the facts," Calabast put in, "we could begin."

Salim grinned. "Always the sentimentalist, eh, Calabast? It's good to see you too."

As the armored giant listened patiently, hands still clasped in front of it, Salim gave a quick overview of the situation—or at least, as much of it as Calabast needed to know. How Neila's father had died and joined the River of Souls, only to be stolen away at the last minute by an unknown force, which now sought to ransom Faldus's soul back to his family. He left out the fact that the soul, once returned, would almost certainly opt for resurrection—a small sin in Calabast's book—and the elixir, which was rather a larger one. No point complicating things. Calabast said nothing until Salim had been silent for several moments.

"You suspect a protean." The machine's voice was flat and cold.

Salim nodded. "It makes the most sense, given the sign we found."

"Take us there."

"Now?" Salim was momentarily surprised, and then mentally chided himself for it. It really had been a long time, if Calabast's abruptness was catching him off guard.

"Delay favors the transgressor."

Salim nodded slowly, then reached inside his robe and produced the amulet. With his right hand, he gripped the deep black spiral. The other he stuck out in the center of the table.

As soon as his palm touched the wood, the back of his hand was covered and enveloped by the massive palm of the construct, his stone skin cool against Salim's. Though the touch was gentle, Salim still couldn't help but think of the five-fingered stone slab as the head of a sledgehammer, dangling above his flesh on a thin thread of silk. He'd seen what those hands could do. If Calabast decided to bring his hand down, it would crush Salim's hand the way a man crushes a moth, smashing through the table and likely continuing on through the floor. As usual, all this passed through Salim's mind in a second, after which he circumvented the issue by steadfastly refusing to think about it.

"Here?" Neila asked, reaching forward hesitantly to lay her thin, pale hand against the stone of the construct's humanoid paw.

"As good as anywhere else," Salim said. "Lahan may be particular about how you come in, but he's not picky about how you leave, provided it's not without paying. Speaking of which—" Salim turned his head toward the bar, where the bartender was putting all the actors of Lamasara's theater district to shame with his staunch refusal to acknowledge what was going on in the corner.

"Put it on our tab," Salim called.

That got the barkeep's attention.

"Hey, you can't—"

But then the colors of the stone flashed, and they were falling.

Neila stumbled as they arrived once more in the Boneyard. Though she didn't fall, she remained doubled over, holding her stomach. "Gods, how do you stand it?"

"Be thankful," Salim said, though in truth he didn't feel so great himself. "We've been lucky so far. Using the amulet is an art, not a science. We're fortunate to get here at all."

Neila made a gagging sound that could have been commentary, or something more immediate. Salim politely directed his attention elsewhere.

Ignoring them both, Calabast was already moving toward the River of Souls with his big, gear-driven strides. Salim's aim had been true—damn near miraculous, actually—and they'd come out just a few hundred feet from the disturbed area they'd discovered on their last visit. Picking his way carefully through the detritus and swirls of disrupted dust and stone, the guardian of Axis studied the ground. He stopped over the objects Salim and Neila had discovered—and which, Salim now noticed, were no longer in the neat row they'd been laid in less than two hours before—then reached down and picked up the fishing globe, turning it over in his massive hands with surprising delicacy. Salim had time for maybe two more breaths, and then Calabast spoke.

"We need to return. To Axis."

"What?!" Neila had straightened, but still had the wild-eyed look of somebody who'd just shot the rapids without a canoe, and was now being told it was time to hop back in the river.

Salim was unsurprised. He'd seen Calabast at work before. While some might see the automaton's brute size and crackling fists and presume that fighting was all he was good for, Salim knew otherwise. Tracking down those necromancers and other powerful individuals who'd spent centuries or millennia thumbing their noses at Death herself took brains even more than brawn, and underneath that helmet Calabast was sharper and quicker to make connections than Salim—with his head full of gray curds and juice—could ever hope to be.

"It was a protean." Calabast's voice was as flat as ever, with no trace of irritation at being questioned. "The warpwave scars and the objects prove it. Now that it has completed its task, the odds of the protean remaining on the same plane rather than retreating to the safety of the Maelstrom are low, even given the proteans' illogic. My ability to track it is insufficient to cross planar borders. Therefore, we require assistance."

Salim nodded. "And you have someone in mind?"

"My superiors."

That made sense. If anyone would know how to track a single protean through the chaos of the Maelstrom, it would be the servitors of the Axiomite Godmind. Salim walked over to Calabast and put his hand on the construct's arm.

"That's it?" Neila's voice was exasperated. "Two minutes here, and you're all ready to go back?"

Salim shrugged and lifted the amulet on its thong. "Calabast needed to see it for himself. Now he has, and there's no reason to stay. Unless you'd like to wait for us here while we go find the protean who stole your father? It's highly unlikely that anyone else will decide to violate the Court of Axis while we're away, so I'm sure you'll be fine by yourself until we return."

Cursing, Neila leaped forward and put her hand on Salim's. The world turned—

—and found them standing at the crystalline foot of the Threefold Pillar. Neila's head tilted back as she followed the line of the building up, up, up, and she would have overbalanced and fallen from the sudden vertigo if Salim hadn't grabbed her hand to steady her.

Up close, the pillars were even more magnificent than they had been from the humans' vantage on the fountain. The golden symbols that had gleamed and twisted their way up the three pillars so prettily from a distance were now bright brands that flared like the sun itself, forcing Salim and Neila to squint their eyes or be blinded. This near the source, the symbols didn't flow smoothly like gleaming water or motes in the eye. Instead, they rocketed up from the ground in a rush, burning brands thirty feet across that shot up the face of each spire with a puff of air and the soft *whump* of a torch being ignited.

Neila's smile was back, her twisting stomach forgotten for the time being.

"Amazing," she whispered. Her hand squeezed his, and before Salim was aware it was happening he had squeezed back, her delicate fingers smooth against his callused ones. Then the absurdity of the action struck him, and he immediately let her hand drop and turned to Calabast.

"And you think the servants of the Godmind will help us?"

Calabast's reply was suitable for a monk—or a hard-assed magistrate. Both of which, Salim knew, were fairly accurate descriptors for the metal giant.

"Those that break one law break them all," Calabast rumbled. "My superiors will undoubtedly assist us. But the Lady of Graves is still not one of us, and balance must be maintained. There may be a price, farther down the continuum."

Salim nodded. "Of course." He might be sworn to serve the goddess, but be damned if he was going to haggle on her behalf. Let his team deal with finding Neila's father. Ceyanan could foot the bill.

"You will not be allowed to accompany me. You lack sufficient authorization, and your capacity for processing would only slow us. Inside the Pillar and the Crucible, we have methods of communication that render speech ineffectual."

Salim expected some sort of objection from the girl, but Neila merely nodded.

"I will return," Calabast said. Then he turned and stomped a little ways from them along the pillar's face. From nowhere, a dark, squared-off portal appeared in the crystalline wall. Calabast entered, and then the pillar's surface was smooth and unblemished once more.

"He doesn't waste any time, does he?" Neila seemed to stand easier now that it was just the two of them again.

"I'm not sure he's capable of it," Salim replied.

Together they put their backs to the brilliant pillar and stared out over the city. Though the monolithic hump of the Adamantine Crucible—and indeed most of the cityscape they'd observed—had receded into obscurity, the gnarled and rocky line of Pharasma's Spire still stretched up in a thick line from just beyond the city's edge, soaring away into the silver blankness of the sky. They stared up at it, tracing its length as far as their eyes would dare.

"Hard to believe we were on top of that just a moment ago," Neila said.

"Yes." Salim knew that the apparent height was an illusion, and that the actual Boneyard was no nearer or farther than any of the other Outer Planes. Rather, its apparent closeness was symbolic, the human mind and the multiverse working together to try to put things into an understandable framework. But he remained quiet.

"It makes you feel like an ant." She paused, clearly thinking of the hive people in the bar. "Or something small, anyway."

Salim nodded. "That's one thing you learn traveling the planes. No matter how important you think you are, you're still just an insect among giants."

Or a pawn, he thought. Salim supposed that to many people, being a game piece sounded better than living and dying in obscurity, without ever being acknowledged by the powers that be. Salim knew better.

There was a soft whir behind them, and then a familiar thumping gait. They turned to find Calabast standing at rest, stone arms at his sides.

"The servants of the Godmind have identified the protean."

"Divinations?" Neila asked, and her voice held none of the awe it might have a week before.

"Divination is simply deduction by a more powerful mind," Calabast said. "In the end, Law always overcomes Chaos, and even the proteans have patterns." He held up the glass fishing float, which Salim hadn't noticed him take from the Boneyard. "This fits the model made for the protean named Sarusek—an imentesh."

Salim let out a breath he hadn't known he'd been holding. Imenteshes were the emissaries and ambassadors—such as they were—of the protean race. It made sense that one of them would be responsible, as they were the only ones who had dealings with other races outside the twisting, unsettled landscape of the Maelstrom. Faced alone, a single imentesh was still more than a match for him and Neila, but Salim had seen Calabast in action more than once, and he suspected that the machine warrior would have little problem defending them. Were it a keketar, now—one of the proteans' priest class could have reshaped them all to suit its incomprehensible aesthetics before they'd so much as spoken its name.

Salim decided not to think about that. They'd just have to hope the creature wasn't reporting or making its confessions—or whatever it was they did—when the group caught up to it. "Were they able to track him?"

Calabast's nod was accompanied by the quiet squeal of metal on stone. Somebody needed to oil his helmet. "He's in the Maelstrom."

It was no more than Salim had expected, but he still didn't like the idea of confronting the creature on its home turf.

"What should we expect?" That was Neila. She was looking at Salim, and some of his concern must have shown on his face.

"Everything. Nothing. That's the problem with it." Salim ran a hand through his hair. "The Maelstrom is chaos, plain and simple—the sea in which all the other planes float. Near the edges, it's not so bad, but if our kidnapper's in the depths . . ."

"The terrain is unknowable," Calabast agreed. "And rarely static. I have knowledge of the protean's present location, but not the region's present nature."

"Coordinates without a chart." Salim had spent some time around deep-water sailors off Rahadoum's western coast, on the Arcadian Ocean. Such men frequently knew where they were, thanks to the stars and their careful reckoning, but that didn't always mean they knew what they'd find just over the horizon.

"My information is already degrading," Calabast said. "Entropy does not wait. Soon our quarry will move, or the Void itself will twist and render our information obsolete."

"Then let's not waste time." Salim reached for the amulet around his neck, but Calabast raised a stone finger in negation.

"I cannot transmit my knowledge in an acceptable format," he said. "I will transport us there, but we will need your device to return." Gauntleted fists that crackled with flickering blue energy were held out, fingers splayed toward the humans. They hung there, outstretched and steady. Salim looked at them apprehensively.

"You will not be harmed, Salim son of Anand."

"Of course," Salim said, but the words were calmer than he felt.

To Salim's surprise, it was Neila who stepped forward first and took one of the construct's hands, grasping two of the massive fingers. As she did so, the lightning spread up her own arm almost as far as her shoulder. She looked at it in wonder, watching the sparks play over the pale skin without leaving a trace.

"Come, priest-hunter."

Salim looked up sharply at that. He glared at Calabast, then glanced quickly sideways at Neila, who was still enraptured by the blue light. From a human, the words might have been a simple slip of the tongue. But nothing Calabast's sort said or did was ever unintentional.

Baited by a damned machine, Salim thought.

Then he stepped forward and embraced the lightning.

Chapter Eleven
Riddles and Chaos

Taking Calabast's hand was like plunging his own into boiling water, but without the heat. Twisted and branching lines of electricity surrounded Salim's arm, as they had Neila's, and then they were suddenly climbing farther, enveloping all three of them in a glow like swampfire. Salim had a quick glimpse of Neila, eyes closed and back arched, and then he was closing his own as the tingling climbed up his neck and over his face.

There was a soundless explosion that seemed to come at once from inside his head and outside of it. There was no noise—not in a physical sense—but rather the weight of the sound pressing on his skin and reverberating in his bones. There was a sudden, terrifying instant where he thought he might be deaf—the silence of the unheard thunderclap made him think of soldiers too close to an alchemist's grenade, deafened by the concussion before the sound could even reach their brains. Then the wall of pressure lifted and eased, and he began to hear new noises, the bustle of Axis replaced by unfamiliar hoots and birdsong. He opened his eyes.

They were standing at the edge of a forest, its leaves brilliant red and yellow. Under their feet, the loam of the trees' moldering foliage gave way to the gray stone of an outcropping that thrust suddenly and steeply up from the woods below. Though they were only a short distance up the promontory, it was enough for them to look out over the treetops and see the long, sinuous line of the forest's edge, where it terminated sharply in a line of golden field, which in turn became a jagged cliff face and the rolling waves of a green sea. Bird-shaped things, some much larger than any avians Salim was used to, darted up from the forest canopy, screeching their wordless mating songs and battle cries as they chased each other through the open air and then dove back into the shelter of the trees.

At the top of the rock on which they stood—and which Salim could now see was a rise in the cliff face itself, sheer-walled and overhanging on its opposite side— stood a tower. It was perfectly cylindrical, and thick enough that despite its height it seemed to squat rather than soar. Time had taken its toll, and overshadowing the few narrow windows were yawning gaps in the stone where mortar had crumbled, sending man-sized blocks tumbling down. By far the worst damage had been to the crenelated crown, where fully half of the upper works had broken off in a jagged line, leaving the tower's top ragged and lopsided.

"This is the Maelstrom?" Neila asked. The colored forest and darting birds apparently didn't match her concept of perfect chaos.

"At the moment," Salim said. "But that doesn't hold a lot of bearing on what it'll be next. That's the problem." He looked to Calabast. "Which way?"

In response, the automaton turned and began stomping up the rise toward the tower, confirming

Salim's suspicions. Hands on sword hilts, the two humans followed.

They were no more than halfway up—a few minutes of walking—when the first of the tremors hit. It began low, a buzzing in their teeth and bones that was barely perceptible, then suddenly spiked in intensity, becoming a rapid vibration that shook the earth beneath their feet and sent both Salim and Neila reeling. After a second, Salim went down to one knee, putting a hand on the ground to steady himself, which worked well enough. Windmilling her arms like a tightrope walker about to be out of a job, Neila miraculously managed to keep her feet. The shaking went on for almost a full minute, then subsided as quickly as it came. From the forest rose a raucous cry as a host of winged creatures, red and green and topaz, burst from the canopy and swung left away from the sea, their noises quickly fading. After a moment in which both humans held their breath, waiting to see if the shaking was truly finished, Neila spoke.

"What was that? Earthquake?"

"Not quite," Salim said. "Look." He pointed out along the line of the sea cliffs, and she followed his gaze.

Far off in that direction, the sky had changed from pastel blue to a bright pink, like newborn flesh scrubbed raw. Yet that wasn't the disconcerting part. The real issue was the enormous chunk of cliff face, wide enough to contain both golden field and a few trees from the forest, which had broken loose in the shaking. Instead of falling into the sea, it was now rising, a hundred feet of solid rock sheared from its moorings and floating ponderously into the glowing air.

"Oh," Neila said.

"That's the Maelstrom for you," Salim observed.

"Come." Calabast began striding up the hill once more. "Time grows short."

The tremors hit again as they climbed, and then again, with increasing frequency. Now, however, Salim and Neila were prepared and managed to keep their balance, adopting a bandy-legged walk like sailors on the rolling deck of a ship. Calabast, for his part, seemed to have little trouble keeping his balance, no doubt due to the sheer weight of his stone and adamantine bulk.

With each shaking of the ground, new pieces of the horizon broke away, floating up into the sky or pulling apart messily like a poorly cut pie. Out of the corner of his eye, Salim saw a crack open up where the sea cliff met the waves, spreading to reveal more of that sickly pink sky beneath. Immediately the ocean around it boiled, becoming an immense whirlpool that swirled violently as it drained, the sea losing its normal waves and tearing rocks from the cliff face in its uncontrollable desire to join the water flowing in a great cataract down into the pink nothing.

Panting and stumbling, occasionally going down on all fours on the steeper slopes, the humans came at last to the tower. Up close, it was easily sixty feet high, the great gray stones covered in places by patches of moss and runners of deep green ivy that branched as it climbed. If there had been any door or gate, it had long since rotted or rusted into oblivion, and now the arch only gaped to reveal the half-light within, like a mouth in which all of the teeth have been broken. Without pausing, Calabast continued inside. Glancing once at each other—it seemed they shared the same misgivings—Salim and Neila followed.

Inside, the tower was a hollow shaft. Niches that must once have supported the crossbeams of the upper stories climbed the curved walls at regular intervals, but any beams they might have held appeared to have also rotted away without a trace. High above, the tower's top was a circle of blue turning slowly to pink, with no shreds of roof to block it. Yet due to the tower's height, the light that managed to bounce and reflect its way down to ground level was weakened significantly, giving Salim the disconcerting impression of being at the bottom of a well. Indeed, the floor where they stood was damp, the moss thick and spongy beneath their feet, bulging in places over what he hoped were fallen stones or the remains of the tower's former furnishings. But all his misgivings about the light and the detritus that might lie underfoot were pushed aside by the greater issue of the tower's resident.

The protean floated placidly in the center of the space, halfway up the tower. It was as big as Calabast but more sinuous, its lower half the body of an iridescent snake, coiling over and around itself. Above that, the bare, pale chest and shoulders of a man extended into wiry arms with hands like talons, yet the true wonder was its head: a strange, long-muzzled face which at once combined the bright feathers of a tropical bird with a fanged, reptilian maw. The creature bobbed slightly as it hung in the air, as if suspended in some sea whose eddies were felt by it alone.

Those great bird eyes snapped open as the companions entered, their blazing amber fixing all three of the newcomers in a searchlight glare.

Salim exploded. Or at least, that's what it felt like. Beneath the thin sheath of his skin, his body began to swell painfully, inflating like a pig bladder blown full of air. Bones creaked and stretched, and the long muscles of his legs and arms cramped and knotted. Tanned flesh burned and bulged as it struggled to accommodate the unprecedented growth spurt, and he suddenly had a terrifyingly clear vision of himself swelling too far and bursting like an overcooked sausage, spewing hot Salim-juices all over Calabast and Neila.

Neila. Salim struggled to turn his head but found it already fused in place by the overgrown muscles in his neck and shoulders. He heaved at his elephantine legs, accomplishing a whole thirty degrees of movement, but it was enough for his bulging eyes—quickly distorting into uselessness from the pressure of his expanding skull—to see the girl.

The young noblewoman was still the same size—no change to those slim hips, the solid shoulders—but her hands were clasped to her throat and her mouth was wide, a muffled squeal all that came of her attempt to scream around the foot-long, sickly gray-green tentacle that now protruded from her mouth like a grotesque tongue.

Above them, the floating protean began to uncoil. It hissed—a long, trilling call that was as much bird as serpent—and Salim would have sworn that its expression was one of both anger and a delight at being angered.

"Enough!" Calabast stepped forward and went to one knee, bringing his massive fists down on the mossy floor. As they struck, there was a flash that lit the tower brighter than full noon. Earth and stone flew from the point of impact in a shock wave that narrowly missed Salim and Neila. The tower shook, and a high section of the walls crumbled, fortunately raining its masonry outside rather than in, where it would likely have squashed the humans flat.

The weird growing sensation ceased. Salim fell backward onto the freshly churned dirt and moss and gasped for breath. He managed to roll his head to the left and was unsurprised to see Neila doing the same, choking and gagging. He started to crawl toward her, but she caught the motion and waved him away. She sat up awkwardly.

"We are not here to start a war, chaos worm, but we will not be toyed with." Calabast's voice was the fury of a storm. "If you would speak, we would hear. But if you harm them again, I will destroy you. You know this."

The bird-snake's coils slithered over and around themselves in a complex, never-ending knot. When it spoke, the protean's words were out loud and perfectly clear, yet there followed in their wake a sudden rush of whispers, half-heard and indecipherable, that seemed to come not from the thing's mouth, but from the dark places in Salim's own head, filling it with a low rustle.

"Warsongs are not yours to call, clock-man. War is in the meeting/in the eating. But we will talk—yes, we will speak."

Next to Salim, Neila got unsteadily to her feet. He followed suit, a deep, aching exhaustion in his muscles the only sign that they'd been so recently abused.

"You *bastard*," she spat at the creature. "You filthy *snake*."

The floating protean looked amused. "Art is wasted on the narrow-minded," it said, but its tone was agreeable, almost courtly.

Salim took a deep breath, doing his best to get a grip on the situation, and then stepped forward.

"Chaos lord," he said, striving to match the creature's own casual tone. "We know that you were responsible for the theft of a soul from the Boneyard. We have come seeking it."

The imentesh hissed again in that weird tone that sounded both pleased and dangerous. Scales the multicolored sheen of oil on water coursed over each other, their sound the rasp of leather against a barber's razor.

"We know who you are, stormsmiter/longwalker/daughter of none."

Salim paused, momentarily taken aback by the creature's description, then continued.

"Stealing a specific soul from one of the Outer Courts—let alone the court of the axiomites—is most impressive." Salim didn't have to fake an admiring tone—such a theft should have been damn near impossible. "Yet the sun orchid elixir would mean nothing to you."

"True!" the protean crowed, its voice now creating a weird, melodic counterpoint to the waves of droning whispers in Salim's head. "The little lives of mortal men are nothing to the Maelstrom's ken. We will sing the Deep Songs long after your world is dust/fire/ash, oh yes!"

Beneath Salim's feet, there was a low grinding sound and the squealing crack of shearing stone. Immediately, the inside of the tower was bathed in a pink glow that came from behind the travelers and cast their three-part shadows long across the far wall. Salim glanced back and saw that the mossy ground upon which they stood now ended at the tower's doorway. Beyond it, where moments ago they'd clambered up a rocky rise overlooking sea and fields, was only pink light.

"Stop that," Salim said, his voice steadier than he felt.

Birdlike shoulders shrugged, ruffling the long, thin feathers.

"What is ours to stop? It is the Song of the Depths/ the Will of the Speakers. It will mold as it wills from the sky/sea, and from you/us."

Before Salim could respond, Neila shoved past him, close enough to the protean that she had to crane her head almost straight up to address it. Salim noted white knuckles on her sword hilt, but she hadn't drawn. That was good.

"Who?" she shouted. "Who are you working for? Qali? Jbade? If you don't need the elixir, who does?"

The protean smiled, the lipless skin of its reptilian mouth pulling back further to reveal rows of white, triangular teeth.

"You have come far, human child, but the hand with the knife is the arm of the body—oh yes. The end recalls the beginning."

Neila screamed. It was a cry of rage and frustration so bestial that Salim almost took a step backward before he caught himself. Even the protean's pupils dilated in surprise, the feathers on the back of its neck rising like a dog's hackles.

"Speak plain!" she howled.

In response, the snake-man looked to Salim.

"That you are a priest is false, yet you are not a false priest—that honor lies elsewhere, and death's trumpeter blows quietly for himself."

Neila looked angry enough to climb the very air and throttle the riddling protean, but Salim barely noticed. His attention was fixed on the protean's eyes. Though the thing continued to speak in koans, those lamplike eyes bored into his, and behind the detached, unbalanced demeanor of the creature, he thought he saw something. Interest. A real desire for Salim to understand.

And then, suddenly, he did.

"Khoyar."

The protean's face lit up at Salim's whisper. Saurian teeth bared once more, and it twisted itself through a rapid figure eight.

"Good, longwalker! You see through the veils and hear the song!"

Neila turned toward Salim. "What's it talking about?"

Salim barely noticed her, so full was his head with newly formed theories.

"It's Khoyar. The high priest. He's the one who's extorting you."

Neila stared at him, mouth open.

"That doesn't make any sense. Why would the high priest of Pharasma blackmail me for the sun orchid elixir?"

"Because he shouldn't want it." Though Salim was reluctant to take anything the protean said at face value—the servants of entropy loved nothing more than sowing discord, and the imenteshes were the most proficient of the lot—everything was clicking into place now. "Officially, Khoyar should have nothing but scorn for those trying to extend their lives and cheat the Lady of Graves. For him to admit that he wants to as well would be the greatest heresy imaginable. Hence bidding for it himself is out of the question. He needs some way to get the elixir without anyone knowing he's involved."

Neila's eyes flashed. "Such as his offer to deliver the elixir to the kidnappers personally, in a place no one else can follow."

Salim nodded. "And the way the most recent note conveniently vanished in his possession."

Neila ruminated on this a moment, brow furrowed. "The thing I don't understand," she said, "is why he would call you in to investigate."

"He didn't. I was sent by another." Salim was already thinking back to Ceyanan's smirk as he unveiled the assignment, and to his own first conversation with Khoyar. What were the high priest's words? *I don't know that it requires such an honor.*

Behind Neila, the walls of the tower had begun to melt, gray stone flowing and running as if it were a painting splashed with thinning spirits. Time was growing short. Salim turned back to the protean.

"So Khoyar contacted you to steal the soul." A brief flash of Faldus Anvanory's body, rent and torn by the claws of some huge animal, filled his mind. Salim suspected they'd found the owner of those talons, but opted to leave that detail out for the time being. Neila was handling herself remarkably well, but there was no telling what she might do if she realized that her father's killer stood before her. Or rather, floated.

"It sees!" the protean giggled. "The river calls, and the soul must sail—none may deny its passage. But the other end—oh yes, oh yes! At the river's mouth, the claimers come, and from the pocket of the hoarder, a single coin can vanish!"

Blobs of the melting walls were floating free now. Several of them began to swirl around the protean in randomized orbits, changing color and size as if in time with the pulsing of some great, unheard heartbeat.

So Khoyar and the protean hadn't had the ability to stop the soul from joining the well-guarded river, but instead had to wait until it reached the Outer Courts and was divided up with all the souls, ready for delivery to their new masters. Including this protean, who had appeared smack in the heart of enemy territory to harvest Faldus's spirit. The plan was completely insane—but then, the proteans had always been good at making that work for them.

"What did he pay you?" Neila demanded. "My father can double it."

The laughter that broke from the protean now was no manic giggle, but a gale-force shout of amusement.

"Little monkey offers the hunter a stone!" The serpent-man swirled and corkscrewed down through the air until those burning, oversized bird's eyes were only a few feet from Neila's own, letting the magnificent length of its thick tail play out behind it. "The Void cannot be bought, soul-daughter. It sings its song/scream, and those who hear will dance."

Before Neila could do something rash, Salim grabbed her arm and pulled her backward. As he did so, he found that the motion was enough to pull them both free of the floor, sending them drifting slowly up and backward through the air. Neila's legs and hands jerked awkwardly as she attempted to correct the slow, tumbling spin that would soon turn her upside down, but Salim held on. Their new trajectory carried him up to the same height as the protean, and he met its eyes with all the composure he could muster.

"So you answered Khoyar's summons for the same reason you do everything—for the hell of it. And maybe because the idea of stirring up trouble in a church of Pharasma appealed to you."

The reptilian smile grew broader, parting the jaws to reveal a mouth without a tongue, the maw held together at the back by threads of skin and muscle which probably allowed it to unhinge for special occasions. Such as if it decided to swallow an impertinent human.

"The butterfly brings the storm, whether its wings flutter or burn."

"Sure, fine." Salim was getting tired of the thing's ceaseless riddles. And, truth be told, he was starting to get nervous. They'd made it this far, but past performance meant nothing in the Maelstrom. The longer they were here, the greater the possibility that either the protean would forget its truce and transform them into something uncomfortable, or the plane itself would unravel their essences and save its guardian the effort. "The point is: You've already turned the church upside down by stealing the soul, and thrown a bunch of lives into chaos. But that chaos is finite—it's already run its course. That is, unless you were to give the soul *back*. Then we'd be able to go back and confront the priest, and there'd be even more chaos."

It was flimsy logic, but the best Salim could do under the conditions. Already he could feel a weird slithering sensation as his skin began to ripple and twist of its own accord. He held his breath.

The protean purred, low like a big cat, and this too conveyed amusement. Was there anything the protean *didn't* find amusing, in its bizarre way?

"You sing the songs, longwalker. But the soul is elsewhere."

"Where is it?" That was Neila. Sideways and perpendicular, she now clung to Salim's robe for support. She'd lost her cloak somehow, its fabric already floating away out of reach, but above a sickly pale complexion her eyes were still fierce.

Around them, the tower split and peeled away in four chunks like segments of an orange, leaving them floating in a pink void.

"Salim, we must go." Calabast was perhaps ten feet away, his huge, armored bulk hanging incongruously in the glowing air.

"Where?" Neila's shout was hoarse.

In response, the protean slithered closer and began to swim slow loops around all three of them in the pulsing, maddening sky. In the distance, a screaming began, akin to the earlier tearing of stone but on an infinitely magnified scale. Far to Salim's left, a patch of sky turned a blue so dark it was almost black, and began to grow.

"A life, a ring, a simple thing." The protean's tone was the patient note of a parent with a particularly stupid child. "Can the hand that grasps let go/unclench/release? No and never." It looked toward the dark patch of sky, which was expanding at an astonishing rate, advancing with a hurricane howl. The protean ceased its circling and reared up, closing its eyes and tilting its head back, as if leaning into a wind from the screeching darkness.

"Salim!" This time Calabast's voice was a command, but Salim was already moving. With one hand on Neila and the other on the amulet around his throat, he kicked off of a loose coil of reptilian tail and launched himself at the clockwork man.

Behind them, the protean sighed softly as it stretched out its arms, welcoming the hurtling storm.

"You will hunt priests again, longwalker," it said. "Khoyar has your soul."

Then great arms of stone and steel encircled the two humans, and everything changed.

Chapter Twelve
The Well of Wonders

They arrived in the streets of Axis in a heap, the sudden return of gravity slamming them to the pavement. Calabast was fortunately on the bottom, his armor ringing loudly against the stone; otherwise the humans would have been crushed by his massive bulk. As soon as they landed, Neila was up on all fours and scrambling toward a nearby alley, turning the motion into a stumbling run as she struggled to make it out of sight before vomiting. She was only partially successful.

Salim got to his feet slowly. He almost reached out a hand to help Calabast up, then realized the absurdity of the action. Instead he took a respectful step backward and allowed the clockwork man to rise of his own accord. "Another close one, eh?"

The metal man made no attempt to buff out the scratches or brush off the pavement dust that clung to his armor—such efforts had undoubtedly been considered and judged pointless. "The Cerulean Void is not kind to outsiders."

"You don't say." Salim glanced sideways to check on Neila, who was still bent double in the shadows of the alley. "But at least we got our answer."

Calabast stared at him with his blank construct's eyes. "The protean was waiting for us."

It was true. And it had known more of Salim's history than he cared to admit.

"No surprise there," Salim said. "I suspect Khoyar informed it the minute we announced our intention to visit the Boneyard. Probably he thought the creature would dispatch us easily, if we even managed to find it. But you prevented that."

"No." The construct's voice was flat. "The chaos worms are not known for their prudence. I suspect that it had decided on its course of action long before you made your argument."

Salim considered that for a moment. "Interesting. Do you think it was telling the truth?"

Calabast hesitated only a second, but Salim knew that for the construct, that pause was the equivalent of mulling the question over all night. At last he said, "It is dangerous to take anything a protean says at face value. But your arguments were strong, both for the priest's betrayal and the protean's subsequent revelation. Do you believe that this high priest is responsible?"

Salim took a deep breath and looked inward to the intuition that had carried him through so many tight spots, but even as he did so he knew the answer. Yes, he believed Khoyar was responsible. In a way, it felt like he'd known ever since their first meeting—something about the man's manner had been slightly off. If Salim hadn't been so focused on his own resentment of the priesthood as a whole—and on the problem of being saddled with a young noblewoman—perhaps he would have noticed it earlier. But now that it was out in the open, it felt right.

"Yes," he said. "I do."

"Then you know as much as you can," Calabast said. "And I wish you well." He scanned the skyline, then made to turn away.

Salim felt a sudden and unexpected pang of regret. "You're not coming with us? To see this through?"

The clockwork man stopped. "I have given you all the assistance I can offer." His voice sounded even more hollow and metallic than usual. "You have traded heavily with the leaders of Axis, on both your superior's name and the protean's involvement. I have other responsibilities."

"Of course." One human trying to squeeze a few extra years out of life was hardly the caliber of transgression Calabast was designed for. Yet it would have been nice to have the metal warrior on their side. Without thinking about it, Salim stuck out his hand. "Thank you, Calabast."

The machine looked at him for a moment, then reached forward and took the tiny, fragile human hand in his own.

"May your outcome be favorable," he said.

Then he turned and began to stomp steadily down the street. When he was perhaps thirty feet away, he stopped and looked back.

"You know this cannot last." Though travelers bustled all around them, Calabast's words reached across the intervening space as clearly as if they were spoken in Salim's ear. "One day, your name will reach the top of my list, and I will come for you."

"And I'll welcome it, old friend." Salim's voice was almost a whisper, but it didn't matter. Calabast had already turned and continued his march down the avenue, the crowd parting around his enormous, armored shoulders like the wake of a boat.

Neila, still a little green around the gills but walking upright now, approached and stood at his side, watching their companion go.

"What was that all about?" she asked.

"Nothing," Salim said. "Just an old joke between soldiers." He looked down and saw that he'd unconsciously put his arm around her. He turned the gesture into a comradely pat on the shoulder. "Come on. It's getting late, and we have some shopping to do before we return."

"Shopping?" The noblewoman's voice was sharp. Now that she knew who was responsible for her father's death, she was clearly eager to return the favor.

"Trust me."

Salim led them quickly through the crowded grid of streets. Neila was quiet for a long stretch, and Salim maintained his own silence, leaving her to her thoughts, which no doubt revolved around what she'd do to Khoyar when they finally confronted the man face to face. Salim hoped that the girl's eagerness wouldn't get her into trouble.

After several turns, they rounded a corner and found the shopfront Salim had been looking for, precisely as he remembered it. He stopped Neila and motioned toward the door. Over the entrance hung a traditional, pub-style board sign showing a modest stone-and-mortar well, its mouth disgorging a brilliant rainbow festooned with strange beasts and objects, from flaming swords to stag-horned rabbits. Beneath the image, the shop's name shimmered in silvery writing that seemed not so much painted on as hanging in the air a hair's breadth in front of the sign.

"'The Well of Wonders?'" Neila looked to Salim. "What are we doing here?"

"Supplies," Salim said. "I believe Khoyar has your father's soul, but that doesn't mean he'll just hand it over when confronted. He doesn't strike me as the type who would let something that important out of his sight—the protean basically said as much, in its way—but I suspect it's been carefully warded. It might be sitting smack in the middle of his chambers at the temple, and we wouldn't be able to find it."

Neila showed her teeth. "You could make him tell."

Spoken like someone who'd never seen torture firsthand. Yes, Salim thought, maybe I could. And maybe you'd spend the rest of your life wishing you hadn't seen it. But what he said was: "Khoyar's already risked everything he has on this plan. He might be the sort to take the knowledge to the grave, and then you'd be worse off than you are now. This way is easier." Then he pushed open the door to the shop.

Inside, the room was exactly as cluttered as Salim remembered it. Shelves along the walls and freestanding tables shoved about the room in no particular pattern were piled high with random objects. Salim spotted a few swords in the mix—one of them glowing a faint and unhealthy green—and a helmet with a brush-plume of fire instead of horsehair. For the most part, however, the clutter consisted of bottles and scrolls of all shapes and sizes, as well as bizarre items of unknown function: a compasslike device that floated in the air, a bundle of burning sticks revolving slowly in a glass box, a marble statue of a crab as large as a small dog. Only the bar-style counter at the far wall was clear of debris. Next to Salim, Neila gaped at the menagerie.

"No!" The voice that greeted them was high and raspy. "No no no *no!*"

There was a muffled thump, and then a tiny man was shuffling around from behind the counter. The deep blue hair slicked sideways across his balding pate, combined with his diminutive stature, proclaimed him a gnome, yet the normally bright, oversized eyes of his kind were squinted behind rectangular spectacles, nearly disappearing into the glowering wrinkles of his face. He wore an orange vest with numerous pockets, and each had a gold chain like those occasionally used for key rings, sometimes attached to the vest itself and other times seeming only to trail between items in the pockets. He moved with a significant limp, yet he clumped around the counter with surprising speed, aided by a claw-headed walking stick. This he now raised to point at the intruders, sending a little swirl of multihued electricity crackling out from the end in a spiraling cloud.

"No!" he said again, as if his point hadn't already been made.

"Buskin!" Salim smiled and spread his arms wide. "How's business?"

The little man scowled back at him, jowls drooping comically. "Fine until you came in."

"Good, good!" Listening only to Salim's tone, one would have thought the shopkeep had greeted him with the same enthusiasm. Salim reached out and picked up an object at random—a clear bottle with a teardrop-shaped stopper, its edges sealed with lead. Inside floated a tiny, preserved creature that looked like a gnarled tuber or root or some sort, with hollow eyes and a jagged little mouth. "Listen, Buskin, we need some help."

"When don't you?" the gnome snarled, but his voice was already fading from genuine anger to mere irritation. "And put that down!"

Salim did as he was instructed, respectfully setting the bottle back down among the others, then walked over and leaned on the wooden counter. Neila followed, eyes still wide as she tried to take in the vast stores of strangeness hanging all around her. Buskin was forced to scramble back around the bar, climbing up on a specially made stool so that he could keep both of them in view.

"What is it this time?" The gnome banged his walking stick on the edge of the counter with a loud clack. "And be quick about it! I have legitimate business to be about."

Salim put on a hurt expression. "Buskin, when have I ever been anything but legitimate business?"

The gnome responded by making a rude noise. Neila was so astonished by this childish display from a businessman—and a clearly ancient one at that—that she laughed involuntarily. Her hand went instantly to her mouth, cheeks reddening, but the gnome looked over at her, and one side of his mouth quirked upward slightly.

"Serious business, Busk." All jocularity was gone now from Salim's voice. "This woman's father has been killed, and his soul kidnapped from the Boneyard. I've been tapped to get it back."

The gnome frowned. "Serious business, indeed." He made the spiral of Pharasma with the handle of his walking stick, the crystal trapped in its clawed end leaving a faint line of color in the air. "You have my sympathies, Lady. Yet I don't know that I can locate a soul."

"You don't have to," Salim said. "We already have, more or less. We know who has it, and suspect that he'll probably have it nearby, but it's undoubtedly heavily disguised. We need something that'll let us see through any illusions and wards that might be concealing it."

The shrewd shopkeeper's gleam was back in Buskin's eye. "It's never easy with you, is it?" he asked. Yet he got down off his stool anyway. "Wait here. And touch nothing!"

Salim and Neila did as they were bid, and the old gnome fell upon his stacks of items and began to rifle through them with decidedly less care than Salim had displayed, knocking over old books and jeweled daggers. One of the latter hit the ground and shot a brief burst of flame along the floorboards, which Buskin stamped out absentmindedly. At last he gave a muffled grunt of triumph and emerged from a chest of scarves and cloaks holding a glittering pendant.

Neila gasped. The emerald hanging from the chain was half the size of Salim's palm.

"Here we are, then," Buskin said. "A little cracked, and mayhap not as effective as it once was, but it'll do the job."

"What is it?" Neila asked.

"A seeing gem," Salim said. "Hold it up to your eye, and any illusions are revealed. Is that right?"

The old gnome nodded, smiling—when he smiled, he looked like a half-sized version of someone's kindly grandfather—then dropped the expression and pulled the gem back as Salim reached out his hand for it.

"What about payment?" the gnome demanded.

Neila reached for her purse, but Salim stopped her with an outstretched hand. "Don't bother. You can't afford it. And we don't have to." He turned to the gnome. "Ceyanan will pay. And we're only borrowing it, anyway—we'll send it back."

The gnome snorted. "Most likely you'll break it!"

"Then you'll get full price, won't you? Quit whining, old man. You'll come out of this laughing either way, as always."

The gnome harrumphed, but he handed the stone over nevertheless. Salim took it and tucked it away in a pocket inside the breast of his robe.

"I don't suppose you'd agree to a trade?" The gnome looked pointedly at Salim's sword. "There's still a space in my collection for the Melted Blade, if you've changed your mind."

Salim bit back a harsh reply and settled for resting his hand on the sword's disfigured hilt. "You know the deal, wizard. The day the Lady of Graves takes pity on me, you'll get the sword. Until then, you're wasting your breath."

"Bah!" The gnome spat on his own floor and waved a hand as if shooing a fly. "Get out, then! Thieves, the both of you."

"Good to see you too, Busk." But Salim was already moving toward the door, pulling Neila along in his wake. When they were both outside and the door had slammed behind them, Neila turned to him.

"You seem to know a lot of people here."

He shrugged and looked toward the street, where a palanquin was going by carried by four emaciated men that might have been dead. "It's a long story."

"I'd like to hear it, once this is over."

Salim looked back toward her. She was gazing at him steadily, and he found himself remembering how it had felt to have her next to him on the rim of the fountain, staring out over the city's skyline. Her dress was smudged with dirt and grime from the Boneyard, and the panicked floating in the protean's dissolving tower had removed any semblance of cohesion from her dark hair, which tumbled loose around her in a dark wave. Yet she still held herself straight and tall, and the look she gave Salim now was that of a child studying an insect. He suddenly felt too warm in his dark robes.

"Maybe you will," he said. "But if you're feeling ready, I think it's time to return and pay our high priest a visit."

The thought of surrendering herself to the gut-churning amulet once again was enough to break Neila's gaze and drain some of the color from her cheeks, but she made no protest. "One more time," she said.

"One more time," Salim agreed. Through her exhaustion, Neila smiled up at him and took his hand.

Salim reached for the amulet, and then they were enveloped by the hot air of the Thuvian desert.

Chapter Thirteen
The Wastelands

Only it wasn't Thuvia.

Something was very wrong. Salim had fixed his mind firmly on their destination, and had hoped they'd be deposited in the fields of Anvanory Manor, within sight of the big house. Failing that, he would have expected to appear somewhere in the surrounding deserts, or in the markets of Lamasara itself, surrounded by the smells of cooking kebabs and fragrant camel-dung fires.

Instead, they were in something like a desert, but not any desert on their world. Beneath their feet, the plain was cracked and rust-red stone, yet that was where any resemblance ended. The hills that rose in the distance didn't look like mountains so much as tumors, festering lesions that twisted their way up out of the rock in fleshy mounds, their sides coursing with dark rivulets of pus. As Salim watched, one of them heaved spastically and settled again, like some great lung or heart attempting to beat. Above them, the black sky was filled with a howling torrent of red dust.

"Where are we?" Neila's shout was muffled by the wind.

"I don't know!" Salim called back. Except that he was afraid he did. He'd ventured into the lower planes before when necessity commanded, but never without adequate preparation. This could be Hell, or the Abyss, or the wastelands of Abaddon, where the Four Horsemen ruled over flocks of shrieking daemons and waited for the chance to ride forth and devour the world. It didn't matter—all that mattered was getting them both out of there. Fast.

"I thought you were taking us home!"

"It's not exactly like driving a cart, girl!" But there was no time to argue. Salim looked down at the amulet, studying the spiral inscribed in its black stone. There was no way to tell why it had taken them here this time. Even under perfect conditions, there was always a chance that the magic would simply send them traveling sideways toward some unknown destination, and he'd already expended a great deal of energy today. And then there was the possibility that the protean's weird, distorting aura had somehow twisted the magic, but that—

Neila screamed. Salim whirled, the amulet forgotten.

Behind them, less than thirty feet away, the plain was split by a jagged chasm perhaps a hundred feet across, its long arms stretching crookedly away toward the horizons like a lightning bolt. On the far side, a cracked rock face dropped straight down out of sight, its craggy sides wetted here and there with dark trickles emerging from between the stones.

Two creatures were clambering out of the trench. They were shaped vaguely like men, but stretched out and skeletal. Through their reddish, leathery skin, which wept with a sheen of slime, Salim could see every bone and tendon of their thin frames. Their hands were long claws, but it was their heads that killed any illusion of humanity once and for all. Below dead black eyes, needle teeth slanted outward from an underslung jaw. Above them, the smooth bone of the skull swept backward and up in a single thick, pointed horn.

As quick as Salim turned to look, they were out of the crevasse and crouched at its edge, all barbed elbows and thrashing, glistening tails. One of them held a long-bladed spear easily a foot taller than Salim, manipulating it as lightly with one bony hand as if it were a stalk of grass. The other licked at its dripping talons, showing the humans its too-wide smile. The spear-wielder coughed something hawklike and grating, and the other responded with a laugh of tearing metal.

Then they moved.

The girl's instincts were good. Neila's sword was out of its sheath before Salim had finished reaching for his own, and she stepped forward again in that textbook lunge, the point of the thin rapier driving straight for the demon's heart—and then sliding off with no more effect than if she'd stabbed a brick wall. As the sword broke contact, it sizzled, the slime of the creature's body etching the blade with trails of blackened rust. The weapon might be finely crafted Taldan steel, but Salim knew all too well that no mundane edge could reliably pierce demon flesh. The creature casually batted the blade wide and reached out with one oversized claw, seizing Neila by the shoulder and dragging her forward.

Damn it, the creatures were *fast*. Salim's sword was in his hand now, hilt warm and basket curled around his knuckles, the blade's fierce desire to kill singing in his blood. Yet already the demons were toppling backward over the cliff, catching themselves easily with strong claws that dug into knife-edged stone. Each creature slung itself out over that edge with only a single hand, one demon carrying its spear, the other holding Neila loosely in the crook of its corrosive arm. The girl met Salim's eyes once, mouth open in a scream that disappeared into the howl of the wind, and then both demons and Neila were gone from view.

Salim charged.

There was no time for anything else. In his youth, his instructors had tried to teach him to fight with his head, to know with perfect certainty which strike would drive home before he began to move. It had been difficult, but in the end, he'd finally mastered that coolness, the ability to detach and become the Rahadoumi ideal—a creature of perfect reason, even in battle.

It wasn't until years later that he realized it was all bullshit. The calm was necessary—rage made you stupid—but anyone who thought too hard about a fight eventually lost the draw to someone who didn't bother. If you wanted to stay alive in his business, your best bet was to *move*, and figure out what you were doing while you were already in motion.

Brawlers fought with their hearts. Swordsmen fought with their heads.

Salim fought with his gut.

In this case, that tactic appeared to be taking him toward the cliff edge at a dead sprint. Last time he'd run this hard, chasing down the satyr, he'd called on the goddess, letting her taint run through his veins in a burst of unnatural speed. Then, he'd been using his head—just another soldier with a job to do.

Now all he could think of was Neila's flesh blistering red and black under the demon's embrace. No time for prayers, or spells, or threats. Just movement.

His right foot touched down one last time on the crumbling edge of the cliff, and then he was sailing out over the void.

Time slowed. Below him, the crevasse dropped away out of sight, descending into sharp-edged shadows and flickering pinpoints of fire that flowed in a line along the trench bottom. The scream of the wind was gone, and even his own breathing ceased. No sound left except for the blood thumping in his ears.

Beat.

Twenty feet down, the demons skittered along the wall like spiders, the top one with its spear, the lower with Neila. Just below them, the cliff face opened up into a dark-mouthed cave stretching back into the rock. At its outer edge, a sliver of stone made a shelf perhaps wide enough for two men to lie end to end. Salim leaned backward, twisting in the air.

Beat.

The wind was cold, thick syrup, crawling past his face and over his exposed eyes. Behind him, the cliff face began to slide upward even as it receded. Still rolling, Salim stretched his arms out toward the wall like a man set loose from a trapeze.

Beat.

The topmost demon looked up. Salim reached.

Exhale.

Time resumed. Salim slammed down on the back of the spear wielder, catching himself with a looped elbow around the creature's neck, the sudden transfer of momentum nearly tearing his shoulder from its socket. The unlikely pair swung inward like

235

a pendulum, driving the demon flat against the wall. Then the creature's grip failed and they were both falling.

This time there was no opportunity to maneuver. Salim and the demon hit the narrow shelf full-force and side by side, the stone an open palm that effortlessly swatted the breath from Salim's lungs.

The cave was the mouth of a tunnel, nearly circular and ribbed like the guts of an enormous worm. Though the entrance where Salim and the demon had fallen was still well lit by the sickening fire of the sky, farther in the light quickly gave way to a solid, impenetrable black. It was into this darkness that the other demon, far enough ahead to avoid their falling forms, had half-retreated, still clutching Neila easily with one arm. Both demon and girl were only half visible, their flesh blending with the shadows.

But there still wasn't time. Next to Salim, the other demon had already gotten to its feet, its ragged sinew recovering faster than the human's own tender flesh. Without a pause to catch its breath—if breath it even had—the creature brought the spear over its head in a wide arc, slamming it down into the center of Salim's chest.

Or at least, where his chest should have been. Again acting on instinct, Salim rolled hard, coming dangerously close to the cliff's edge before stopping his momentum and rising to a crouch, sword still in his hand and back set against the cave's curving wall.

The demon came on, spear held diagonally across its body, and this time Salim closed with it, kicking off the wall as he came. The spear—more like a halberd, given its size—flicked outward in a smooth motion, but Salim met it with his blade.

The shock was tremendous. By all rights, the demon's unholy edge should have sheared the thin, straight length of Salim's sword—but then the Melted Blade wasn't a normal weapon, either. Regardless, the strength of the impact nearly cost Salim his footing. He saved it by spinning with the motion, throwing his back against the spear's haft and kicking out ineffectually at the demon's legs as he went.

Now they were facing each other again, the demon's glassy eyes unreadable. It screamed, the bloody phlegm of its voice a language Salim had no desire to interpret.

He tried a feint, sweeping in high with a slice that dropped at the last moment to come in at the knees. The demon's spear blocked it easily. A stab in under its left armpit received the same treatment, and then the spear was coming back at him in a whirlwind, the demon attacking with both ends, striking everywhere at once.

Salim had fought plenty of pikemen in his time, but this was more like the desert monks who refused to fight with anything but their walking sticks. The demon was everywhere—the moment Salim caught the blade from one angle, the butt was already coming in from another.

One of those backstrokes got through his guard, the wooden shaft—which certainly came from no tree anyone in the mortal world would recognize—slamming square into his solar plexus. Salim's breath left him for the second time in less than a minute and he folded, curling over his stomach and gasping open-mouthed, to no effect. The demon screamed with pleasure, then raised its spear and brought it down in a vicious stab.

With leaping away out of the question, Salim did the only thing he could. Still doubled over, he thrust his sword up over his head and moved forward, crashing face-first into the creature's torso.

It worked. Though weakened by the lack of air, Salim's parry was enough to deflect the spear's barbed blade, sliding it harmlessly over and behind him as his nose and cheeks smashed against the creature's protruding ribcage. Instantly, his face began to burn as the creature's acid ate through his pores.

Salim wasted no time. Keeping his eyes shut against the caustic slime, he looped his free arm around the creature's emaciated waistline, embracing it even as he slid his left leg behind its right knee. Straightening, he swiveled and pulled, crushing the demon tight against him as he slid around its body. Now he stood behind it, hip to hip and arm across its stomach, as if the demon—a full head taller than him—were his dance partner and the house had turned the lanterns low. Though his eyes remained closed, the image drew a little smile.

"Song's over, darling," he said. Then, with his encircling arm locked, he brought his sword up point-first between the demon's bottom two ribs.

The creature screeched and flailed. Salim maintained his hold, not daring to withdraw his sword completely, but instead pulling it halfway out and then ramming it home again at a slightly different angle, feeling new bones grate and organs give way with each thrust. Pain flared as the demon flailed behind itself with the useless spear, then dropped it and began raking him with its claws, to greater effect. But the damage was already done. Hot blood ran over the sword's hilt, and the demon went limp in Salim's arms. He held it up for a second, like a man leading a drunken companion home from the tavern, then withdrew his sword and let the corpse drop. He opened his eyes.

The other demon was still watching him from the darkness, and through blistering tears Salim saw that Neila was still in its arms, struggling valiantly to free herself from its unnaturally firm grip.

"Come on, then," Salim said. "Next dance is yours."

The demon looked down at Neila, then thoughtfully at Salim, his right hip soaked with the steaming blood of its companion. It met his eyes for a moment, and seemed almost to shrug.

Then it whipped out its arm and threw the girl full-force into the smooth stone of the far wall.

Salim shouted, but whatever he said was covered up by the all-consuming eggshell crunch of the girl's head striking rock. The little shape in the sensible traveling clothes crumpled to the floor and was still, with no attempt made to stop the bleeding skull from meeting the stone a second time with a sickening bounce.

The demon moved, and Salim moved with it. The burning on his face and hands was forgotten, replaced by one that seemed to be coming from inside his skin. He knew, intellectually, that closing with the unarmed demon was exactly the wrong thing to do. Inside its range, it could bind up his sword, leave him at the mercy of claws and teeth, that searing acid. Better to stay wide and mobile, wear it down, then dart in quick for a finishing thrust.

His gut thought otherwise.

Salim slammed into the creature at full speed, bowling them both over backward. They landed with Salim on top, the demon's claws slashing through his robes and into the already lacerated skin of his back, bringing fresh gouts of blood. Salim ignored them. Too close for the blade or point, Salim raised his sword and brought the bronze pommel and basket down onto the demon's face with all his strength, breaking teeth and pulping the finer bone structures. Once. Twice. Three times the hammer of his arm came down. With each blow, he heard again the crunch that Neila's head had made against the wall.

At last the demon managed to get a foot between them, its hips rotating farther than those of a human, and kicked. Salim flew backward, landing on his ass on the cavern floor, and was up again in a second.

The demon was wary now. It began to circle him, hands low and extended, the claws dripping with blood—Salim's blood. Above them, the thing's face was a ragged mess, but the eyes still watched him.

Without warning, the inside of Salim's head erupted in a high-pitched scream. If there were words in that screeching, howling cacophony—and Salim suspected there were—they were unintelligible, but the voice was recognizable as the same hideous hunting call the demons had used when first rising over the cliff edge.

So they're telepathic, too, Salim thought briefly, and then the maddening torrent of words blocked out all thought. He flinched away from the onslaught, struggling to thrust it out of his mind, and for a moment his eyes closed reflexively.

It was all the opening the demon needed. With a howl of triumph that shook Salim's skull from both within and without, the demon shot across the floor, its taloned feet clicking against the stone. One clawed hand swept low and lazy, like a parent lobbing a ball to a child, then whistled upward in a savage arc meant to take off Salim's jaw and most of his throat.

Eyes still slitted against the mental assault, Salim sidestepped the uppercut with perfect precision, flowing out of the demon's path in a wave of dark robes. His sword flashed briefly as it rose—the wave's white-capped crest—and then came down once, decisively.

The screaming in his head cut off. On the floor, the demon twitched, its spine severed just above where the neck—carelessly outstretched in its eagerness for the kill—met bony shoulders.

"You think you're the first one to come up with a decent battle cry?" Salim asked. Then he kicked the thing hard in the side of the head.

For a moment his mind was lost in the same haze it always entered after battle—that calm, flat place where only continued breathing mattered, and everything else was a distant buzz. Then it woke.

Neila.

He spun and was at the girl's side in a dozen strides, kneeling next to her on the stone floor. Facedown in a pool of dark blood and darker hair, her crumpled body seemed too small to be the feisty girl he'd argued so heatedly with just that morning. The awkward angle of her limbs didn't bode well, and for a moment he was afraid to touch her.

Once, during his early days as a soldier, Salim had seen a man who'd been backed clean off a cliff during a skirmish with some rogue genies outside of Manaket. The man had still been alive when the battle ended, and strong enough to joke with his squadmates who climbed down the cliff after him. Salim would never forget the man's smile as he reached out to grasp his rescuers' hands. Nor would he forget the sound that accompanied it—a quiet clicking, like two dice striking together in a gambler's hand.

According to the medic, the soldier had been dead from the moment he landed at the foot of the cliff, and just hadn't known it yet. The spine was a delicate thing. All it took was a sliver of bone in the wrong place, and your heart stopped beating, your lungs forgot how to breathe.

Salim drove the memory out of his mind. When you had no choice left, you did what you had to, and the dice fell as they would. Slipping one hand under Neila's head and the other beneath her ribs, Salim turned her over as gently as possible.

Her face was a wreck. Surprised by the demon's throw, she hadn't been able to get her hands up to shield herself, and her head had taken the full force of the impact. A dirty, ragged gash above one eye was deep enough to show the white of bone flickering out from beneath the mud of blood and dust. Her nose had been smashed nearly flat, and the blood from these two injuries covered her face in splotches and rivulets, tracking across formerly white cheeks and split lips. Yet the worst part was her head—beneath the black locks matted with blood, the gentle dome of her skull was no longer symmetrical, the top left side reformed into a disturbingly flat angle.

For a terrifying few seconds, he thought he was too late. Laying his ear to her chest, just where the swell of her left breast began, he listened desperately for a heartbeat, yet the only drumming he could hear was that of his own blood coursing through his ears. Then he looked back toward her face, and his heart gave a sudden leap.

In the ruins of her nostrils, little bubbles of blood and mucus were forming and popping. She was still breathing.

Relief washed over Salim, his body shaking with the aftershocks of adrenaline. He felt warm wetness on his cheeks that could have been blood, but wasn't. She was still alive.

Farther down the dark tunnel, something inhuman screamed. Salim jerked reflexively in that direction, then turned just as quickly back to Neila.

Alive, but far from safe. And he'd already moved her more than was wise. It had to be here, and it had to be fast.

Still kneeling, Salim placed one hand on the girl's sternum, and the other as gently as possible on her forehead, cupping the broken brow with his callused palm. His hand was nearly big enough to cover the whole top of her head. She was so small. So fragile.

Salim bent his own head, closing his eyes against the sight of the broken girl, shutting his ears against the hunting cries. From the deepest part of himself, he called out, casting his prayers into the darkness.

Please, he began. *Please, I—*

That wasn't right. Even as he started, he could feel the hollowness of it. What was it the angel had told him, so long ago? *Prayers must be honest, Salim—that's where most men go wrong before they start.*

Very well, then. He'd give them honesty. In that still place inside his chest, Salim opened up his heart and let the rage flow, unfolding in a bright flower. A signal fire.

To hell with please, he prayed. *You don't deserve please.*

The flame that burned inside him was everywhere, consuming, turning him into a light they could see from Heaven to the Abyss.

I deserve this punishment. I earned it, I brought it upon myself, I made *my Hell, and you accepted my offer. But she's done nothing. She's just a child.*

There were soft sounds as the acid still in Salim's eyes sent hot tears out between his closed eyelids to drop onto the girl's still form.

Fix her, damn you. The hand on the girl's chest balled into a fist, but he kept the one on her brow gentle, slowly stroking her hair.

You can't have her. Not yet. Not again.

Outside, the scrabbling sounds in the cave were getting closer, but inside Salim the silence was heavy, expectant. He wanted to scream at that smug, indifferent void. Instead, he gathered everything he had, clenching his teeth and his chest until it seemed like he might implode, and put everything he had into one last unvoiced shout.

You wanted me, that voice screamed. *And you got me. Now use me.*

It was hardly the most eloquent prayer. For a moment, nothing happened. In a darkened cave, Salim knelt over the body of a girl who was quickly bubbling out her last breaths in tiny rivulets of red, while outside the eternal storms of the Abyss raged and laughed.

A stream of power slammed through Salim's body, arching his back and turning his balls to water. His teeth snapped together and clenched, biting down against the strain and the sudden taint that filled his blood, flowing up through his chest and down the conduits of his hands. It felt like holding a lightning bolt dipped in tar, and the sense of total violation—another being using his body as a damn *channel,* as if he were the bung on a freshly tapped keg—opened his eyes and made him want to scream. Through sheer force of will, he managed to hold his silence and keep his hands pressed against the still body of the girl.

The goddess of death might not be gentle, but she was effective. As Salim watched, literally unable to turn away, bones moved beneath the girl's skin. Above the rapidly knitting cut on her brow, which was even now weeping out the dust and dirt that had collected there, the injured section of her skull was inflating back into its normal shape. The pixie nose that had been flattened by its meeting with the wall twisted and contorted as innumerable bone shards reassembled themselves with horrifying little snaps. In a distant corner of his mind, Salim hoped the girl was still unconscious.

It lasted no more than a few seconds, and then it was gone as suddenly as it had come, the sickening, all-consuming power flowing back out of him. Salim gasped—had he breathed during the healing? There was no way to know—and then slid down onto his hip, one arm propping him up against the ground.

Next to him, Neila stirred. Her eyes fluttered open, and she turned, her gaze going to Salim's bloody, tear-stained face.

"What happened?"

It was a simple question, and an obvious one, yet to Salim it suddenly seemed the funniest thing in the world. Without bothering to wipe at his streaming eyes, he threw back his head and laughed.

"Nothing," he said, when he could finally get control of himself again. "Nothing you need to worry about."

Sitting up straight, he curled one black-robed arm around the girl, hugging her close despite the blood that spattered both of them and the wounds on his back and side that still burned with the last traces of demonic acid. With his other hand, he grabbed the familiar black amulet.

"Come on," he said. "We're going home."

And this time, they did.

Chapter Fourteen
Wounds and Scars

The scrubby hill where they appeared wasn't Anvanory Manor, but it was close enough. To the east, a few miles distant, a distinct squiggle of green and a patchwork of buildings with lanterns already lit against the encroaching evening identified itself as the south end of Lamasara. To the west, the land finally gave up any pretense at life and became the furrows and dunes of the true desert. Here, where the two travelers fell gratefully to the soft, sandy soil, a lone and twisted acacia tree held vigil as the last marker of habitability and a final warning to any who might seek to challenge the desert's authority. Amazingly, directly below the gnarled tree and shading the few hardy grasses that dared to thrust up their heads, another tree lay. Or rather, its corpse—a log just as fat as the tree that stood as its obvious successor, and equally naked of leaves.

It was to this fallen sentinel that Salim and Neila now crawled, scooting backward on their hands and sighing with exhaustion as they propped weary backs against its smooth, bulgy surface. Sand worked its way inside

Salim's robes and infiltrated his lacerations, but it was at least a familiar grit, and he paid it no attention. He looked over at Neila.

For a moment she continued to stare blankly off toward the horizon, as if to reassure herself that it was indeed her home, not just a hallucination from yet another bizarre plane of existence. Then she turned back and met Salim's gaze. The edge of her mouth twitched slightly. Slowly, it bloomed into a full-blown smile. She began to laugh.

The sound was infectious. Within seconds, both of them were howling, clutching their sides and pounding on the log in relief and exhaustion. And if that laughter was half sobs, what of it? They were both alive, and back where they were supposed to be, and just at the moment Salim didn't give a damn about anything else. It felt amazing.

At last the laughter died down, and the rest of the world reasserted itself unceremoniously. A deep gash along the side and back of Salim's ribs, pulled wide and ragged by his momentary merriment, sent a bolt of pain shooting through his torso and up into his brain. He grunted and grabbed at his flank, leaning over to one side in an instinctive attempt to push the broken seam in his skin back together.

Neila was instantly serious, her expression one of concern. "You're hurt."

Given the obvious nature of the statement, Salim contented himself with another grunt.

The girl reached out tentatively and felt the fabric where Salim was clutching at his robes. Her fingers came away wet and red.

"Why don't you heal yourself?"

The answer was automatic. "I'm not a healer."

Neila's hand went to her face, feeling at the unblemished skin of her nose.

"You healed me. I remember that."

Salim gritted his teeth, and this time it wasn't entirely from the pain. "That was different. I don't heal myself."

"Why?"

"Because it's *disgusting!*" The last word came out in a bark. "Some—*thing*—calling itself a goddess moving inside you, pouring its taint through your skin just to knit a few bones back together, and then expecting you to be thankful for it? It's an abomination."

Neila's brow furrowed, and the skeptical look she gave him made Salim feel suddenly like a child.

"You're telling me you won't heal yourself because you *don't like how it feels*? You'd rather bleed out on the sand than suffer an affront to your dignity?"

The strain of Salim's clenched teeth was starting to match the pain in his side.

"Lady, if the price for healing was letting a pack of lepers use your body until all were spent, would you take it?"

The deliberate crudity made her recoil, and for a moment Salim almost regretted it. It wasn't her fault she took such things for granted. But that greasy, unwashed feeling inside his skin—no, it wasn't worth it. Better the blood.

Neila set her jaw. "Very well then," she said. "We'll do this the hard way. Take off the robe."

Salim looked at her for a moment, but her face brooked no argument, and this time he couldn't think of one anyway. He slipped the robe from his shoulders and let its folds fall around his waist.

Neila's breath caught at the sight of his chest and stomach. Beneath the dangling amulet, the corded expanse of his sun-browned torso was a mass of old scars, crisscrossing his chest and stomach in no particular pattern. Some were thin lines, expertly closed by surgeons who knew their business. Others were monstrous, centipede-like things, the work of a few moments on a battlefield. Salim watched her, waiting for her reaction.

She gave none. Instead, she reached down to the hem of her blouse and began to tear a long, winding strip of the silk, working at an angle so that the tear continued several times around her body, baring the slightest line of flesh above the waistband of her breeches. When she had a strip longer than her arms could reach, she tore it off and waved a hand, motioning impatiently for Salim to turn around.

He did, and after a few more moments of rustling, he felt the soft touch of her hands as she began to daub delicately at the long furrows the demons' claws had made in his back. The silk stung, but her hands were cool, and she moved with unexpected confidence, never wavering. Stretching a hand over his shoulder and into his field of view, she snapped her fingers and pointed, and he handed her the waterskin from his belt. She uncorked it and let careful trickles run down his back, washing the wounds clean. The warm water burned like a brand.

For a time she worked in silence, and then she spoke. "I owe you my thanks. You saved me back there."

Salim grunted once more, noncommittally. Now that they were finally resting, a bone-deep weariness was settling over him. Neila ignored him and continued.

"You didn't have to," she said. "This morning, I would have told you I could handle myself, and treated you like little better than hired help. Yet you were right—I've added nothing to this trip, and nearly gotten us both killed. You would have been better on your own. I should have known that from the beginning, and the demons proved it."

"Wasn't your fault." As much as this revelation might have pleased Salim yesterday, he couldn't let it stand unchallenged. "You got the draw on the one that grabbed you, fair and true. It was your sword that failed. Steel's about as useful as a bouquet of flowers against a demon, and your blade had neither enchantments nor cold-forged iron."

She said nothing, but her hands paused on his back.

"Besides," he continued. "That little bastard in the market with the poisoned knife would have had me just as easily if you hadn't stepped in. I'd say we're even."

"If you say so," she said, but one hand rose up to the tendons where his shoulders met his neck and squeezed gently. Then it retreated, and was replaced by the sound of further fabric ripping. She moved closer, and delicate arms emerged from beneath his own on either side, carefully winding the cloth around his chest and torso to hold the bandages in place. Every time she leaned close to pass the wrapping across his front, her breath warmed the back of his neck, and the silk of her bodice brushed lightly across the skin between his shoulder blades.

"When you leaped off the cliff," she said. "I've never seen someone do something that foolish. Or was that magic as well?"

He shook his head. "No. Just luck, and a sense in my gut of where the demon ought to be."

"And yet you never hesitated."

In the distance, the sun was setting behind the dunes, turning the sandy waves into an ocean of fire.

Salim stared into it until his eyes watered, watching the air ripple where the land reached up to envelop the burning disk.

"Life is risk. You jump without looking, sometimes you win, and sometimes you lose. But if you hesitate, you lose every time.

"And this time you won," she said. "We won."

She finished tying off the last of the bandages, and patted his shoulder to turn him around. He did.

In the red light, her black hair was touched with flame, and her skin glowed like embers. The traveling shirt which likely cost as much as a day-laborer's hut had been torn half away, leaving a wide swath of creamy stomach exposed, perfectly smooth except for the dark cavern of her navel. In seeing her stomach bared, Salim was suddenly acutely aware of everything that wasn't— the small but rounded breasts pressing against the binding cloth that remained, casting their own shadow down onto the gentle peaks of her lower ribcage. Those ribs rose and fell quickly—too quickly for someone sitting and resting. His eyes went to her face.

She was staring at him, breathing hard, but not with exertion. For the first time in their acquaintance— perhaps the first time ever—she looked truly uncertain. One of those tiny hands came up and stretched out carefully, slowly, to touch his chest. He felt its weight there, pressing. She swallowed, and then her lips parted, and she spoke.

"So don't hesitate."

All at once, the full force of Salim's desire fell down around him like a cloak of sandstone, crushing him beneath it. His groin ached, and his hands itched to hold this girl—this *woman*—who had stood beside him in battle, who had refused to shrink away even in the face of those who would tear both flesh and soul. He wanted to lay her down right there, in the shadow of the log and the falling sun, and run his lips over every inch of her, to smell and taste her—to know her completely, inside and out.

And to let her know him. Know him for what he was.

As quickly as it came, the desire receded—not like a guttering fire, but like a door closing on a room with a hearth. The warmth was still there. But not for him.

She must have seen something in his eyes, for her own tentative smile faltered and grew brittle. He took the hand from his chest and held it in both of his.

"How old are you, Neila?"

A new flame, this one cold, sprang up behind her eyes, reddening her high cheeks.

"I'm twenty years old," she said sharply. "Many years a woman, and master of my own house and fortune."

Gods, but she was beautiful. Beautiful—and a child. "I'm too old for you, girl," he said. "Too old, and too scarred. Don't waste yourself."

Despite the gentleness of his voice, her head snapped backward as if slapped. Thin, perfect arms rose to cover her still-clothed breasts. When she spoke, her voice was ice.

"I don't understand you," she said, and Salim could hear tears in her words.

And you never will, he thought. Pulling back, he picked up his pack and plumped it like a pillow, then lay it down next to the log.

"Night will fall soon," he said, "and we've had a long day. Best get some rest."

Without waiting for a response, he wrapped his beleaguered and bloodstained robes around himself and lay back, propping his head on the rucksack.

For a few moments longer, Neila continued to stare at him, arms crossed, belly exposed, black hair wild. Though he didn't meet it, he could feel the force of that gaze—the anger, the shame, and most of all the burning confusion. Yet she did not speak. After a time she rose and crossed to the other side of the log, lying down out of sight. Eventually exhaustion overcame emotion, and he could hear her breathing slow and even out.

Lying in the sand, his hands woven together behind his head, Salim watched the rapidly darkening sky and waited for the first stars to show.

Chapter Fifteen
Rabbits in a Snare

Salim woke to a trail of ants crawling over his body, marching single-file from their nest in the shade beneath the log over to his waterskin, where an imperfect seal around the stopper let water bead slowly on its underside. As each ant reached the leak, it stretched forth its mandibles and carefully procured a single, tiny drop. Prizes held high, the ants then turned and marched back the way they had come, disappearing beneath the log, no doubt to bathe and refresh the fat queen who sat at the nest's middle. Salim briefly noted the similarities between the ants' situation and his own, then pushed the idea from his mind.

To his surprise, Neila was already awake and moving about. Even more astonishing, she appeared to have bathed, or at least employed some of their water to scrub the grime from her face and hands. Under other circumstances he might have been exasperated by such a waste of water in the desert, but given the awkwardness of the night before and their relative proximity to Lamasara and the river, he elected to keep his mouth shut. At least she'd cleaned her sword, he noted.

He spoke a brief word of greeting, and when he got only a nod in response, he followed her lead and went about collecting his gear in silence. It took only a few moments, and as he finished, Neila approached and sat down on the log, hands folded atop crossed knees as properly as if she sat in a receiving parlor. The fact that the missing strips from her shirt still bared her midriff to the sun like a temple dancer was more than countered by the stern set of her face.

"Shall we discuss the next steps in our mission, Mr. Ghadafar?"

Salim winced internally at the return of the honorific.

"Neila—"

"I assure you, Mr. Ghadafar, that anything which may have been said last night was entirely the result of trauma and overexertion. I thank you for your discretion in the matter, and am equally relieved that we will never need to speak of it again. Don't you agree?"

Salim sighed. If that was how she wanted to play it—fine.

"Of course, Lady."

"Excellent." Some of the tension drained out of her face, which he noted now had slight shadows beneath the eyes. Apparently she hadn't slept well either. When she spoke again, it was in more normal tones. "So what's the next move? Contacting the city authorities? Or one of the other churches?"

"Neither." Salim drew his sword halfway out of the sheath at his hip and glanced at the blade, checking to make sure the demons' acid hadn't etched it. Flawless steel gleamed in the morning sun, and he rammed it home with a snap. "This is a church matter, and best handled within the church."

"You mean you."

"Yes." He picked up the strap of the waterskin and slung it over one shoulder. "Khoyar's a powerful man, and the church more powerful still. The city authorities aren't going to casually accuse him on the word of two outsiders, and even the jihadist warriors of Sarenrae are going to be hesitant unless they can independently verify our claims."

"But we have evidence!"

"No," Salim said. "We have *beliefs*. We heard the protean speak, and I believe it. But our belief isn't going to be worth a pinch of camel shit if it means they have to go up against the church of Death Herself. That's why we also have this." He reached into a pocket and held up the emerald they'd borrowed from Buskin. "With this, we should be able to see through whatever illusions Khoyar's bound around your father's soul, and allow the proper authorities to do the same if it comes to that. But we'll never get the chance if we don't catch him by surprise. We need to take him out fast, release your father, then let Faldus himself exonerate us."

"Besides," he said, and now he was grinning humorlessly. "This is what I do. A bunch of guardsmen will just slow me down."

"Good thing we won't have to deal with them, then."

The emphasis she put on *we* made Salim want to scream—what happened to the girl who just the previous evening had acknowledged her own inexperience in these matters?—but he held his tongue. There was bloodshed in their immediate future, and potentially a lot of it, but he didn't see any point in arguing with her about the finer points of her own safety. And in truth, she'd held her own so far. Part of him was glad to have her with him, whether or not it made tactical sense.

"If it's surprise we're after," she continued, "we'd best get moving. There's no telling what Khoyar's been up to while we've been gone. For all we know, the protean's already contacted him, and he's arming himself as we speak."

Salim doubted it—he had the feeling the protean would rather see the poetic destruction of the arrogant priest who'd thought to employ it as an errand boy—but who could say anything for certain where the chaos worms were concerned?

Neila didn't wait for an answer. She turned and began hiking down the sand of their barren hill toward the scrublands leading into the river valley. As she did, Salim was suddenly faced with the bare expanse of her lower back. Twisting back and forth with the sway of her hips, a long, bubbled scar from the demon's acid now ran in a narrow river across her spine and down to a point just above the hem of her pants.

Seeing that imperfection sent a wave of emotion rushing back through Salim. In its rough red path, he saw her lying crumpled and tiny on the floor of the demon's cave; saw her biting back tears for her father as she demanded the right to accompany him into danger. He saw her outlined in the sunset, hands soft on his skin. All at once, he couldn't leave things as they lay.

"Neila, wait."

She stopped but didn't turn around. For a moment she stood there, scarred back straight and proud, face turned toward the city. Then she spoke.

"Salim," she said, "I appreciate everything you've done for me and my father, and I understand that you're about to risk your life once more on our behalf. But if you say one more word about last night, I swear to all the gods that I'll stick a sword through you myself."

She resumed walking, and after a moment Salim followed. He let out another sigh—quiet this time, so that she wouldn't hear—only to discover that something felt different.

It took him a second to realize he was grinning.

Over the course of their long walk back to civilization, Neila slowly managed to convince Salim that, while the element of surprise was crucial, it might be best for them to hedge their bets by at least notifying the authorities of Khoyar's betrayal before they confronted him, rather than afterward.

Salim wasn't entirely sure how he felt about the plan—working with anyone else always set his teeth on edge, let alone a passel of bureaucrats—but he had to admit that capturing or killing the priest before they'd tipped off the authorities made their story look suspiciously like an after-the-fact justification. Normally Salim wouldn't have worried about it, and simply moved on as soon as the job was finished, leaving the authorities to draw their own conclusions. But Neila still had to live here, and that complicated things. In the end, he agreed to stop by Anvanory Manor long enough for her to send a sealed letter by slow messenger—insurance with the authorities, in case something went wrong. If Salim knew the coin-counters and petty lordlings—and he was more familiar with their sort than he might have liked—when they were finally confronted with the aftermath of Salim's work, they'd be happy enough to take his word for it and chalk the whole thing up to internal conflict within the church, thus absolving themselves of the need to stir a finger.

A wronged public figure might squawk loud and long, but a corpse was something quiet and final, and with Faldus Anvanory to testify to Khoyar's guilt, Salim doubted that any of the other holy men powerful enough to raise the dead would want to touch the high priest's body.

And it would be a body, Salim suspected. Khoyar didn't strike him as the type to beg for mercy. He'd go to his final rest, and Pharasma would make her judgment. If his underlings were any sort of priests at all, they would have to respect that.

The sun was already high in the sky as Salim and Neila turned from the dusty road onto the crushed white stone of the long drive up to the manor house. They were no more than a few feet down it when a cry went up from the house, in several female voices. By the time they reached the front steps, the house was abuzz with activity, servants running hither and yon in preparation for whatever their mistress might desire, passing word that the young lady of the house had returned.

The majordomo met them at the front steps, cool and collected as ever. He bowed deep.

"The house is grateful for your return, Lady."

Neila's nod was quick and dismissive. "Thank you, Amir, but we won't be staying long. Is there any news from the church?"

"None, Mistress."

"Then at least our time hasn't atrophied further." She gestured toward the grand stairs. "Fetch me writing materials from the study. I need to send a letter at once."

"Of course." The little man with the puffed chest of a household despot bowed low, backed away his customary few steps, then turned and hurried up the staircase as quickly as his dignity would allow.

Neila sat down gratefully on one of the benches in the entry hall, resting legs tired from a long trek in the desert heat. Salim almost joined her, then caught sight of the passing servants, more of whom were finding reasons to pass near the entry chamber than could possibly be normal. One of the kitchen women—a huge, black-skinned matron with breasts the size of watermelons—went so far as to narrow her eyes and sniff disapprovingly. Salim felt a momentary surge of annoyance, and then realized that they weren't staring at him. Rather, their sidelong gazes were all fixed on their mistress.

With a start, he realized that she was still sitting there with her stomach exposed to just beneath her breasts, skin slick and glistening with sweat. And here was a stranger, standing far too close to her for propriety's sake. No wonder they were scandalized.

"You!" Salim pointed at random, to a young woman with a basket who was passing across the far edge of the room for what was at least the second time. "Bring your mistress a new shirt—hers has been damaged. Move quick!"

The girl leaped as if she had been stung, then nodded and scurried away. Neila suddenly seemed to realize the awkwardness of the situation as well, and Salim took several polite steps away from her.

The girl Salim had singled out returned only moments later, followed by the majordomo with paper and a small lap desk, as well as two women carrying an elaborate folding screen of wood and parchment. This last they set up around Neila, boxing her in with opaque designs of birds and sagebrush. Her tattered shirt and filthy breeches were thrown over the top, and a moment later she stepped out wearing a long gray skirt and a similar blouse of slightly more ornate make, light blue with gold knotwork embroidery around the neck and sleeves. She shooed the serving women away and accepted the desk from Amir, along with a pen and ink. She looked to Salim, eyebrows arched inquiringly, and he motioned for her to continue.

Pen nib scratched against paper for several moments, then Neila folded the paper crosswise several times, so that there were no longer any open edges. Without being asked, the chamberlain produced a stick of bright red wax and a long, sulfur-headed match, which he struck against his thumbnail. The taper blazed to life, and he set it to use dripping a bright puddle of wax onto the point where all the carefully folded edges came together. When she judged the pool sizable enough, Neila reached into her belt pouch and produced a signet ring, pressing its intricate crest into the wax. Then she handed the letter to Amir.

"I need you to deliver this directly to the head of the guard at Queen Zamere's palace—no one else. And I need you to do it personally. This is of vital importance." She looked to Salim. "How much time do we have?"

"The sooner we're done with it, the better."

"Fine." She turned back to the majordomo. "Go by whatever means you wish, but give yourself as much time as it would take to walk there slowly. To deliver this too early would be just as bad as delivering it too late. Understood?"

"Perfectly, my lady." Another bow.

"Good." She waved, and the servant removed himself from their presence, taking the crowd of gawkers with him. For a moment, Salim and Neila were alone again.

"Any reason to wait?" she asked. One hand went to the sword belt at her hip, adjusting it for a quicker draw.

There was a pregnant pause. Salim knew she was waiting for him to argue—to tell her that he'd be better off alone, and that she'd be safer here.

"No."

Her smile was half relieved, half grimly satisfied. "Then by all means," she said, "let's go see about a priest."

The carriage pulled up outside the cathedral, its team blowing hard at such exertion in the midday heat. Olar jumped down and opened the door, offering Neila a completely unnecessary hand down. Salim followed her out, gazing once more on the beautiful—and intimidating—facade of the church. For all its open doors and talk of welcome, the cathedral of Pharasma was one enormous reminder of the inevitability of death, regardless of race, gender, or age.

Or piety, Salim thought. Church members received no special favors from the goddess of death when their own time came. Less, really. It seemed that Khoyar needed a refresher on that particular fact.

Salim hadn't initially wanted to take the carriage, as shouting their presence to everyone within range rankled against his normal preference for stealth, but Neila made the point that arriving by any other means would no doubt seem suspicious. In this case, it was in their best interest to observe all the normal ostentations of rank until they were directly in Khoyar's presence. Announcing their arrival so thoroughly, especially when they came alone, would likely put him at ease.

Together they walked up the steps and into the pleasant stained-glass shade of the wide receiving hall, the sunlight slanting through a stylized image of the Lady of Graves and bathing the room in purples and blues. As expected, Hasam was waiting on his little wooden stool just inside the door—when a man worshiped the physical embodiment of death, little things like boredom ceased to be important.

"Master Salim! Lady Neila! Welcome! I hope your investigation is proving fruitful?"

"Not as much as we'd hope," Salim replied. "We need to speak to High Priest Khoyar, in private. It may be that he can assist us."

"Certainly, certainly! I'm sure he'll want to meet with you at once. Please, follow me."

In a fast shuffle that wasn't quite a run but still managed to kick up the edges of his acolyte's robes, Hasam led the two callers through the back hallways of the cathedral and up another spiral stairway. This time, however, they exited after ascending only a single high-ceilinged story, turning into a new tile-floored promenade lined with sconces. Each of these burned with low purple flames that sprang seemingly from the air above them—no doubt illusions, as even the most devout priests in Thuvia would be reluctant to introduce extra heat into their residences during the daytime. Soon they came to a set of tall wooden double doors banded with whorled strips of blackened iron. Hasam knocked enthusiastically.

"Enter."

Hasam pushed open the doors and scampered in, Neila and Salim following behind him at a more measured pace.

The chamber was large and relatively spartan, not much different from the receiving room in which Salim had first been introduced to Neila. Long tapestries covered the stone walls, embroidered with scenes of judgment, arguments between angels and devils over tiny, featureless souls. On the far wall stood the largest and simplest hanging, a beautifully rendered black-and-white artist's interpretation of the twisting Spire itself, rendered all in shadows and suggestive lines. In front of this stood an unadorned wooden writing desk stacked high with papers, behind which High Priest Khoyar Roshan sat with hands folded, pen laid crosswise across the document in front of him.

"Salim and the Lady Neila Anvanory, Master," the acolyte announced.

"So I can see, Hasam." The high priest's voice was dry, but not unkind. "Thank you for bringing them. You may return to your place, that they may find you easily if they require assistance."

Hasam bowed low and backed out, shutting the door firmly behind him. When he was gone, Khoyar pushed back his chair and stood up.

"A fine boy," he said. "Not the brightest torch, but the goddess demands only obedience." He circled around the table and stood in front of it, hands folded in front of his stomach. "How has your search been progressing? Time is growing short—as I'm sure you know better than I, Lady." He inclined his head.

Salim felt Neila stiffen beside him and stepped forward slightly, hoping to draw the priest's focus. It wouldn't do to have her run him through before they'd found Faldus's soul.

Or had they already? What was it that the protean had said—*can the hand that grasps let go?* He thought that might be an accurate assessment of any man with power, and something told him Khoyar was no different. Yet maybe there was more to the snake-man's words.

"Indeed it is, Lord Priest. Which is why we were hoping that you could assist us in deciphering a new riddle that's arisen."

"Oh?" One of Khoyar's eyebrows—waxed, Salim realized with disgust—rose in an expression of mild interest. To anyone else, it might have seemed the practiced, dispassionate expression of the veteran confessor. Yet Salim thought he saw a flicker of concern in that purse-lipped weasel face.

"'Oh' indeed. You see, we followed up on all the leads Faldus's corpse offered us—Lady Jbade, Master Qali—but found nothing to connect either of them to the crime. The house staff wouldn't have the ability. Even the fey of the forest beyond Anvanory Manor seem clean."

"How frustrating." Khoyar's tone was still level.

"Quite. And after wasting precious hours beating our heads against closed doors, it seemed prudent to fall back on the basics—visiting the scene of the crime."

"I thought you'd been at Anvanory Manor all this time."

Salim shook his head. "Not the scene of the murder, Khoyar. That's hardly our business." He began to move slowly forward across the room. "The church doesn't care about murder. I'm talking about the *real* crime— the soul's abduction."

Now Khoyar blanched. The hands in front of him, with their perfectly manicured nails and gaudy silver ring, tightened almost imperceptibly. "You visited the Boneyard? In the flesh?"

"Both of us," Salim agreed. "And we didn't stop there. Because when we got there, we discovered some things that didn't make sense. A *lot* of things that didn't make sense. Random things. Absurd things. Scattered across the path of the souls."

The priest's face was back under control again. The man was good. "I don't follow you."

"No?" Salim asked. "Surely a man of your faith—your *conviction*—knows enough about the planes to recognize a protean's handiwork when he sees it."

"If you call it such, then I believe you. I've never seen such a thing in person. So you believe that one of the chaos worms is responsible for the murder?"

"I do," Salim said. He stopped moving, now only a few arms' lengths from Khoyar. To his left, he felt Neila's presence as she joined him. He lowered his voice. "Which is why we need your help."

"Certainly," Khoyar said. He was once more completely himself. "What knowledge I lack on the creatures, I'm sure our priests can extract from the libraries, or from divine revelation, if it comes to that."

Salim let out a relieved breath and bobbed his head. "Good," he said. "That's extremely helpful. Because some of the things it said were pretty difficult to parse."

"You *spoke* to it? To the protean?" The horror in Khoyar's voice was real, but perhaps not for the reason an outside observer might presume.

"Of course, didn't I mention that?" Salim looked at Neila in mock surprise. "How else were we supposed to figure out why a fundamentally immortal creature would bother playing with petty human life-extension tricks? It doesn't make sense."

He turned back to Khoyar. "So we tracked it down, and we asked it some questions. It turned out to be rather agreeable, all things considered—almost as if it resented being treated as some human's errand boy. And when it started talking, a lot of things began to make sense. Of course the person running the ransom game wouldn't be off on some distant plane somewhere, biding his time. Someone who'd put that much energy into a con would want to be right up close, where he could keep an eye on things."

Salim heard a whisper of steel behind him as Neila drew her sword.

"So tell me, Khoyar: how long have you been afraid of dying?"

This was always Salim's favorite part: the sting. Even back when he'd been no more than a simple priest-hunter, this moment—the moment of realization, when the quarry knew for certain that the game was up—had been something he'd lived for. Undead and their ilk were a poor substitute for the simple, pants-fouling fear of a man caught in a snare he'd built through his own actions.

Khoyar didn't disappoint. His face went pale beneath his tan, and then bright spots returned to burn in his cheeks. His hands broke from their practiced lacing and became fists at his sides, yet he didn't step away.

"Am I to understand, Salim, that you believe *I* had something to do with Faldus Anvanory's murder?"

"Belief appears to be in short supply these days," Salim said, grinning. "I'd say it's more of a matter of assembled facts."

"Unbelievable." The high priest's voice was low and tense, yet he punctuated the word with a dry crackle of laughter. "You've come halfway across the world to solve a heinous murder and an affront to our shared goddess, and the first thing you do is take the word of a *protean* at face value. Gods!" He gave another brittle laugh and turned to Neila.

"My lady, I'm terribly sorry to have burdened you with this man's presence. It seems that reports of his much-vaunted abilities have grown in the telling. I assure you, I'll waste no more of your remaining time with such foolishness. Please accept my apologies."

Neila's thin-lipped stare could have been carved out of stone. Khoyar met her gaze for a moment, then turned back to Salim.

"To accuse me of both murder and heresy in the same breath is no small thing, Ghadafar. Yet since you clearly have no proof of your ridiculous claims—claims that I must point out again come at the suggestion of the *one creature* in all existence that can rival the Father of Lies himself in its love of capricious deception—I'm going to have to ask you to leave this church, with the added recommendation that you keep walking until you reach the shores of the Inner Sea."

"Of course, Your Reverence," Salim said, bowing in deference and simultaneously reaching into the folds of his robe. When his hand emerged, it was holding the emerald from Buskin's shop. "Just as soon as you let me examine that beautiful ring of yours."

This time the reaction was instantaneous. Khoyar snatched his right hand up to his chest as if it had been burned, the large silver ring—which Salim now saw was carved with a strangely crude Pharasmin spiral—glinting in the torchlight. His left hand rushed to cover it, but not before Salim brought the gem to his eye.

The world turned green, fractured into several identical pictures by the gem's facets. Yet each of them showed the same thing. In the split second before Khoyar's other hand came up, Salim saw the priest as clearly as noon on a sunny day, exactly how he'd appeared a moment before—with one exception. Rising from the hand where the ring should be was the spectral, screaming face of Faldus Anvanory.

"That's it!" Salim yelled, and drew his sword. Neila was already springing toward the priest, sword point rising toward his throat.

But the priest wasn't standing still, nor had his clerical position made him slow. He leaped backward around the corner of the desk, one hand reaching out to flip it easily into his attackers' path, filling the intervening airspace with flying paper. He shouted, and at first Salim thought the sound was a roar of denial. Then he realized that there was a word in there—a single word being repeated like a mantra.

"Now!" the priest screamed. "Now now now!"

The door they'd entered through slammed open, smashing into the stone wall. The pounding of steel-nailed boots filled the air, and Salim spun to see twin rows of crossbow-wielding guards filing in at a run, rushing to take up positions around the edges of the chamber. All had their bolts aimed at the pair of would-be judges and executioners.

The room wasn't big, but it was wide enough that moving any given direction to attack one of the guards would give all the others an easy shot, crosshatching them both with bolts. Even if their arrows weren't enchanted—and that was no safe assumption, in a damned *church*—it was an easy equation to solve. Salim froze, then slowly lowered his sword.

Neila had other ideas. For the first time since they'd entered the room, she spoke.

"You killed my father!" she shouted, and leaped across the overturned desk, straight for the priest.

Only Salim's quick hands saved her. One moment she was airborne, sword extended, face twisted in a mask of rage. The next he had hold of the collar of her shirt and was hauling back with all his might. She slammed down onto the stone floor, taking him with her, as crossbows thrummed and half a dozen bolts studded the wood of the fallen table.

"Stay down!" Salim shouted, but Neila was in no condition to press her attack. Landing flat on her back had driven the wind from her, and she now lay gasping, spine arching as she struggled for breath. Salim reached out and plucked the sword from her fingers, then pushed both of their weapons away from them and raised his hands.

"A wise move," Khoyar observed. The fear and anxiety that had been on his face a moment before was gone now, without a trace. Salim found himself wondering if any of it had been real. Certainly the man seemed unruffled by his brush with death.

Salim looked around him at the stern-faced men and women with the crossbows. All were priests, rather than true soldiers, but they held the bows competently enough, as any children who'd hunted in their families' fields might be expected to. At this range, a blind gnome with a bow of cattails and string couldn't be expected to miss. How the hell had Khoyar known to keep a dozen guards waiting outside his door? Had the protean warned him, or was he simply that paranoid?

Salim left those questions unasked, and tried a different one. "So what now, heretic? Will you order these priests to kill us, the way you killed Faldus Anvanory?"

Khoyar smiled. "Hardly, my son. No one is going to be sent to their final reward until there's been time to meditate on the matter, as is only proper. Provided, that is, that you don't try anything foolish." He gestured, and one of the guards stretched out a leg and toed the swords farther away from the two prisoners on the ground.

"As you can see," Khoyar continued, raising his head to address the men and women with the bows, "our suspicions have been confirmed. The fig, as they say, never falls far from the tree. These two have come here to reveal Faldus Anvanory's killer, and so they have." He cast a smug gaze toward Neila.

"Lady Neila Anvanory, I hereby accuse you of orchestrating the death of your father. May Pharasma have mercy on your soul."

"*What?!*" Neila's word was the scream of a wounded animal.

"Murdered," Khoyar continued, addressing the room once more, "by one's own child. If there's a sadder fate a father can suffer, I know it not. And for what? For what, brothers and sisters?" He looked around, made eye contact with several of them. "So that she might inherit the sun orchid elixir, and buy herself a few more years of youth—a mere blink of Pharasma's eye. What is a decade, or a century, compared to the eternity of the Beyond?"

"That's a lie!" Neila looked like she would tear the priest's throat out with her bare hands, but she stayed down. "You know I'm innocent! You said so yourself—your magic verified it!"

"Ah, yes." Khoyar was nodding, his manner sage. "But even magic can be deceived. Especially by one of these."

As he'd been talking, one of the high priest's hands had crept into his pocket. Now he held it up, revealing a strange little brooch in the shape of a lustrous black beetle.

"Look well, my friends. Use both your eyes and the goddess-granted second sight, and see just how easily evil can disguise itself—how a mere bauble can cloud even the vision of the angels."

Salim knew at once what the thing must be. He'd seen similar amulets and talismans before, on the creatures he'd hunted. A relatively simple charm, designed to occlude one's aura and soul, making it impossible for a priest's divinations to tell good from evil. An important tool for vampires and their ilk, lest they be called out by the first hedge-priest or friar to cross their path. Khoyar was implicating them by planting his own possessions. Brilliant.

The priest was still speaking, throwing himself into the speech. "As I grew more and more suspicious of Lady Anvanory's motives, in spite of the failure of my divinations, I made arrangements for one of her servants to covertly investigate her quarters for evidence of tools just such as this. And as soon as he brought me this corrupted, filthy item, my prayers and visions suddenly became crystal clear. I knew at once that Neila Anvanory had ordered the death of her father, and furthermore that she would attempt to pin the crime on *us*—the very church that sought to put things right, seeking justice even for a cowardly would-be immortal like Faldus Anvanory!"

"You bastard." Neila's voice was barely above a whisper now, but everyone in the room heard it clearly. "You know that's not mine. But it doesn't matter. The Lamasaran officials have already been contacted and told everything. They're undoubtedly on their way to arrest you as we speak."

Khoyar smiled. He was radiant, almost beatific. No wonder he'd made it so high up the chain of command—the man was born to preach.

"My poor, deluded child," he said sympathetically. "Who do you think turned you in?"

His hand dipped into his pocket again, and when it emerged the black beetle was gone, replaced by a carefully folded sheet of paper, its red wax seal with the Anvanory crest broken down the middle.

"It seems at least one of your staff suspected the truth all along, and was kind enough to inform me of the matter. Yet I wouldn't worry too much. For you see, I've taken the liberty of summoning the authorities myself." He looked toward the door and raised his voice. "Yusef, if you would?"

There was the sound of footsteps—softer this time, bare flesh on stone—and then a tall man strode into the room. He was bare-chested and bronzed from the sun, and as he entered Salim couldn't help but notice the grace with which each fluid step carried him forward. Billowy white pantaloons covered his legs, and thin strips of white linen wrapped his arms and shoulders in elaborate patterns, crisscrossing his back. Below a turban of similar white strips, his face was handsome but hard, a hooked nose giving him the look of a bird of prey. Matched scimitars hung at his belt, their curving pommels carved into golden suns.

A dervish—one of the blade dancers of Sarenrae, the sun goddess. If ever there were a church devoted to protecting the innocent and burning away wickedness, it was that of the Dawnflower.

"Thank the gods," Neila almost sobbed. "A Sarenite."

Yet when the newly arrived priest looked over at her, his eyes were hard.

"Thank you, Yusef," Khoyar was saying. "You've already heard the facts of the matter, in detail earlier and again just now. If you would be so kind as to read the young lady's aura, and tell us what you find within her heart?"

The newcomer nodded without speaking, then turned to Neila and sank effortlessly down on his haunches. Tears streaming down her face, disheveled and bruised, Neila still sat straight-backed and defiant. If Yusef the Dervish was an eagle, then surely he must recognize that this girl was a hawk.

For a moment, the priest's eyes softened. Then he blinked hard—once, twice. He pulled back, upper lip threatening to curl.

"Evil," he said, and stood. "Her heart is evil."

Neila cried out, and Salim joined his voice to hers, reaching one arm out to the dervish.

"Don't be fooled, Yusef," he warned, keeping his tone low and earnest. "Auras can be altered—a simple illusion. Khoyar's projecting his own evil onto her. Don't do this."

The Sarenite batted Salim's hand away with a casual swipe of his arm. He turned to Khoyar.

"Your suspicions have been verified. I'll carry word to my church, and to the governor's people as well."

Khoyar's smile was genuinely warm. "Thank you, Yusef. Your assistance is greatly appreciated in this time of tragedy."

This was going from bad to worse. A sudden inspiration struck Salim.

"Yusef, wait! The gem!" Salim pointed to the emerald, which had fallen to the floor during the commotion. "Use the gem! It'll cut through the illusions and show him for what he really is!"

Yusef paused, but Khoyar didn't miss a beat.

"That will be *quite* enough of your witchcraft, Mr. Ghadafar." His expression was pained. "It injures me greatly to see a respected affiliate of our church seduced into betraying his own by such base, *venereal* pleasures as this patricidal doxy has to offer—but then, you were never truly one of us."

The high priest took a single step forward, then drove his boot heel down hard. The emerald shattered to dust.

"Salim Ghadafar and Neila Anvanory, I hereby pronounce you guilty of the murder of Faldus Anvanory. May the Lady of Graves have mercy on your souls."

Neila moaned. Salim made one last, desperate attempt to make eye contact with the crusader called Yusef, but the sun-worshiper had already turned away.

Then something hard connected with the back of Salim's head, and everything went black.

Chapter Sixteen
Whispers in the Dark

Salim's first thought upon waking was that he had somehow gone blind. No matter how hard he blinked, the darkness behind his lids was indistinguishable from the darkness beyond them. He raised a hand to his face, almost touching his nose, but to no avail. Had the blow to the back of his skull—some crossbow's stock, most likely—been enough to knock the sight from his head?

Yet everything was not uniform. With agonizing slowness, his eyes gradually began to make out a faint glow coming from his left. He turned and crawled toward it, hands and knees grinding against dirty stone.

The light—no more luminous than a dying coal, yet blazing clear against the impenetrable darkness— resolved into a thin-lined rectangle. Salim reached up and felt at the edges, finding a lip where rough wood met the cold stone of the surrounding wall.

A door. This was a door, and the glow—too thin and soft to see anything by, but enough to at least orient himself—was from some light in the chamber beyond, creeping in through an imperfect seal in the doorjamb.

Slowly, so as not to knock his aching head on a low ceiling, Salim crouched and then stood, running his hands along the wooden surface before him. There was no knob, but he felt a metal plate with a keyhole and thick, rough iron bands that stretched across its length. No hinges on this side—that would be too easy—but it was a door nonetheless. When he was satisfied that he'd felt all there was to feel, Salim began to sidle sideways, his fingers sliding lightly along the stone of the wall, charting out the limits of his prison.

"Salim!"

His heart jumped, and he almost stumbled. The voice was close, almost right next to him, and clearly terrified.

"Salim, are you there?"

"Neila?" He dropped to his knees again, reaching out blindly in the direction he thought the voice had come from. There was a moment of fumbling, and then his outstretched fingers brushed cloth. A hand wrapped around his wrist, so tight it was painful.

"Salim! I can't see. I can't see anything."

"It's okay," he said, pulling himself awkwardly closer to her. "It's alright, it's just dark. Look at the light from the doorway. You're fine."

A small body pressed against his side. He could feel the mad thrum of her heart, her quickened breathing, but when she spoke again, her voice was calm.

"Where are we?" she asked. "How did we get here?"

Salim had a pretty good idea of both of those things, but instead he answered with a question. "What's the last thing you remember?"

"Khoyar." In the shelter of his armpit, her body tensed with rage. "That murdering bastard judging *us* guilty. Then someone said something else I couldn't quite hear, and then—nothing."

A sleeping spell. Hardly the most priestly of enchantments, but still a damn sight better than being clubbed in the back of the head with a chunk of wood.

"Where are we?" she asked again, and this time he answered.

"In a cell." Even without testing the other walls, he knew that much. He reached down with the arm not encircling Neila and touched the stone floor. It was cool. "Judging by the temperature, I'd say we're underground. Probably in the catacombs beneath the cathedral."

"The catacombs!" Her shiver might have been from the cold, but he doubted it. "Why would the church have jail cells beneath it?"

"It wouldn't," Salim said. "But a storeroom with a lock works just as well, when you're surrounded by stone on all sides." For all he knew, this was an auxiliary embalming chamber, or a place to store corpses still awaiting their turn beneath the knife. It might even *be* a holding cell, in which the Pharasmins could trap some of the undead they naturally ran across in the course of their work, studying them in order to train acolytes in their destruction. But Salim decided it would be better not to mention such facts to Neila.

"So he thinks he can just lock us up?" A familiar heat was back in Neila's disembodied voice, and Salim didn't need light to imagine her expression. "This will never stand. Even if Amir—that officious little *shit*—has thrown in with Khoyar, the rest of my household won't buy it. Someone will contact the authorities, and the guard will come for us."

The conviction in her voice was so strong that Salim hated to rob her of it. He squeezed her hand.

"I think we're on our own, Neila. The Church of Pharasma is no petty noble to be argued against. And whether or not he believes that you were responsible for your father's death, the dervish from the Sarenites thinks he saw evil in your heart. Never mind that Khoyar undoubtedly used magic to swap your auras, the same way he used that beetle medallion to cover up his own. The point is, there are now priests from the two most powerful religions in the city who say you're guilty, and I suspect that only Khoyar knows the truth."

"But surely at the trial—"

This time Salim couldn't help it. He laughed once, hard and without humor.

"With all due respect to your experiences abroad, Lady, you're a long way from home. I think you've overlooked some key details about how things work here for the common man. Or murderer."

"What—"

"There's not going to be any trial." His words were firm without being cruel. "Or rather, we already had it, up in that audience chamber. By now, word of our imminent execution—and the Church of Pharasma's generous offer to handle both execution and proper burial—is no doubt making its way to the queen's palace. And when it arrives, who will speak out against it? Your father's rivals? Some serving woman in your household, placing her character reference against the sworn testimony of one of the high priests of Pharasma?" Another chuckle. "No, Neila. The bureaucrats will be happy enough to let the church handle its own problems. And with you out of the picture, there will be no reason not to resell the sun orchid elixir again. What's more, unless someone from your family comes to claim your estate—an impressive feat, considering no notification will be sent—the city will reclaim Anvanory Manor and all of its holdings. Everyone wins." He grimaced into the darkness. "Except us."

Neila said nothing for a moment. Then: "So we're on our own."

"Yes."

"Then let's not waste any more time."

She had a point. Working together in the darkness—for though the lines around the door were now as clear as day, they still didn't provide enough light to see anything else—the prisoners took stock of both their possessions and their surroundings, feeling their way around the cold stone of the cell.

What they found was not encouraging. They were indeed in some kind of storeroom, though whatever had been kept in here once was long gone, leaving only dust. The walls were smooth stone, cut straight from the bedrock, and came to an end just above Salim's head with a ceiling of the same style. The entire room was no more than twelve feet across in either direction, and everywhere Salim knocked, his fist struck with the dull report of solidity—if there were other chambers neighboring this one, there was plenty of stone between them. The door was nearly as stout, and though Salim knew little enough about locks—personally, he was more fond of kicking doors down—the little he could feel of the keyhole and the blank plate surrounding it told him the church hadn't skimped on security.

Their supply situation was even worse. In tallying up what they'd been left with, it became clear that they'd both been searched with remarkable efficiency. Salim was momentarily surprised, then realized that men who prepared corpses for a living were probably quite used to checking over inert bodies, making sure that no one was accidentally buried with a potential contribution to the church coffers still in his pockets. Though they'd been left their clothes—certainly no one would want to be accused of impropriety at an execution—everything else that might be useful had been rooted out and removed. In addition to their weapons and belt pouches, the priests had taken Salim's magical amulet and both of their sets of shoes. They'd even removed the ribbon that had helped lace up the neck of Neila's dress. Perhaps they thought she'd try to garrote someone with it, or strangle herself and rob them of their justice. Somehow Salim doubted Khoyar was overly worried about the latter. But other than the two prisoners and the clothes on their backs, the cell was empty, without so much as a basin to relieve themselves in.

When they were done searching both the walls and themselves, the two inmates hunkered down next to each other, listening at the door. After several minutes of perfect silence, they gave up. Either there was some sort of magic blocking the sound or, more likely, Khoyar hadn't bothered to set a guard directly in front of the door. It was, in retrospect, a wise choice—any guard that could communicate with them might be convinced to hear them out, and they were bottled tight as it was.

At least by physical means. Neila reached out and touched Salim's shoulder.

"Salim," she asked, "can you use your magic to open this door? Or to tunnel out, or—or something?"

There was no way to know without finding out. He patted her hand once, then pulled away and dropped to his knees. Hands folded together, he put his forehead against them and began to pray.

As before in the cave, the posture of supplication felt stiff and unnatural. Yet if there'd ever been a better time for it, he couldn't remember what it was. Head down, eyes closed, he sent his mind out, and out . . .

And hit a wall. Not a denial, exactly—no sense of divine refusal. Instead, it was as if his head were surrounded by a cage, a glass box against which his mind beat itself like a frightened bird. After a second, he realized that the box was precisely the shape and feel of the room itself.

"No good," he said. "Khoyar's warded the room against magic. I can't do anything."

Neila sighed and slumped down against the stone of the far wall. Salim did the same at his end, and together they stared blindly across the darkness at each other.

"What I can't understand," she said at last, "is why Khoyar would risk so much. I mean, even if he got the elixir, he'd have to constantly disguise himself to keep people from noticing his renewed youth. And he of all people should have been assured a positive judgment by the Lady of Graves, and a corresponding reward in the afterlife. Why would he throw that away for a chance at a few more years?"

Salim shrugged, knowing she couldn't see it. "Fear of death is a powerful motivator. It can make a man sell out his friends, turn a wife against a husband or a child against its parent."

"But he *knows* what happens!" she insisted.

"There's a difference between knowing and *knowing*," Salim replied. "'Honor and fidelity are fleeting things, often cited but rarely seen.' In the end, everyone is betrayed. And everyone betrays. It's human nature."

"Do you really believe that?" Her voice was quiet, tentative.

Salim smiled without humor. "As I told Khoyar, belief's in short supply. Betrayal isn't something I believe. It's something I know."

"How?"

He paused. Even now, sitting in a makeshift jail cell awaiting execution by a high priest of the bitch-goddess herself—no shortage of irony there—Salim almost let the question pass. Almost held his tongue in front of an innocent girl who was about to die because he'd misjudged his own abilities, underestimated the preparations of his opponent. The sheer arrogance of that fact broke down what half-formed barriers were left, and suddenly the words were in his mouth.

"Because I've been the betrayer, of everything and everyone I ever loved. And been betrayed in return."

There was a period of silence, and then: "Who?"

"My wife."

Another pause, then Neila's voice, soft and careful. "What did she do?"

"She died."

Neila reached out and took Salim's hand. "I understand how you feel, but I don't think that's quite—"

"That wasn't her betrayal. Her betrayal came later, as a direct result of my own."

Neila faltered. "I don't—"

"Listen," Salim said, but he was no longer staring in Neila's direction. "She died. She meant more than anything to me—more than life, more than honor itself. She was my world. And then she died."

In the darkness before and behind his eyes, a picture was blooming.

"And I brought her back."

Chapter Seventeen
The Priest-Hunter's Tale

I was born in the slums on the north side of Azir, capital of Rahadoum. My father could have been any of several men—my mother did what she had to in order to get by—but she named me Salim after her own father, who by all accounts had been kind, fair, and a man of learning before the burning plague laid him low.

Outsiders never really understand what it is to grow up Rahadoumi. Even those atheists from other countries who come to join us are still burdened by their pasts. For them, atheism is all about rejection, their philosophy defined by what it is they're rebelling against. They can reject and rejoice, as the old mantra goes, and they're more than welcome, but their pasts still follow them wherever they go. They constantly reassure themselves and the world of their conviction because, deep down, some part of them still believes.

To be a child, though—that's something different. When you grow up in the Kingdom of Man, you do so knowing that your destiny is your own. The gods are real, certainly, and powerful—but so are the great whales off the island of Nuat, whose flukes can stave in a frigate. Stay out of their way, and you'll be safe enough. Being Rahadoumi isn't about attacking the gods or questioning their existence. It's about the freedom to live as you see fit, with no creatures from another world passing edicts on who or what you can be.

And what does a small boy running riot in the shantytowns of Azir want to be when he grows up? Why, a member of the Pure Legion, of course! Every day, one squadron or another would pass close to the crumbled tenements where we played, and the cry would go up, passing from scrap-wood fort to rooftop nest. Games would drop in the middle, fights would stop mid-blow, and all the children would scramble toward the alarm, waving our whittled wooden swords.

How majestic they were! Sometimes they were ahorse, other times on foot. Grim-faced men in shining breastplates and cloaks that billowed from bronze epaulets. Sometimes they would have a prisoner with them, some underground priest or prophet who'd evangelized to the wrong person and wound up outing himself. Those were always the most exciting times. We were always respectful of the legionnaires, as was due the protectors of the First Law, but such rules did not apply to the religious filth they transported.

Once, on a dare, I stood atop a garbage heap and threw a stone at an already bloodied priest of Sarenrae. It hit him between the eyes, and he cried out in pain. The captain of the squadron held up his hand to stop them, and walked over to where I stood. Ignoring the filth of the refuse pile that fouled his beautiful boots and greaves, he knelt down so that he could address me at eye level.

"Why did you throw that stone?" he asked.

"Because that man is a priest." I was both thrilled and scared, but I held my ground. Oh, I was a brave one, to be sure.

"And why is it wrong to be a priest?"

"Because priests are liars," I said. "Religion holds us down, makes us slothful."

The captain nodded, and I thought I had never seen someone more handsome. For a brief second, I wondered if maybe this man could be my father, for surely there was no one else in the world more worthy of the station.

"That's true," he said. "But there's more to it. Religion doesn't just cloud our minds. It asks us to deliberately deceive ourselves—to replace reason with its opposite, faith. And when men operate on faith, they can no longer be reasoned with, which makes them more dangerous than any sane man, whether good or evil. Do you understand?"

I nodded.

"A man without reason is no better than a mad dog, and mad dogs must be put down for the good of everyone. But we must always do so with compassion, and remember all the time *why* it must be done. For if we ever forget—if we let our anger toward gods and priests become its own sort of faith—then we become no better than them. Remember this."

Then he smiled, teeth white like the sun, and stood. A gauntleted hand fell on my shoulder.

"You've got a strong spirit, boy. Hold onto that."

Then he turned and led the soldiers and their quarry away. I stood there long after they'd turned the corner, part of me wanting to run after them, to tell the captain that I knew he must be my father, and wouldn't he please take me with them? I would fight, too. But of course I knew better. He was just a soldier, and rather than break the beautiful moment I'd been given, I stood on my trash pile and waited until the sun set behind the towers of the city proper.

When I was twenty years old, I joined the Pure Legion. My mother cried, her tears both of pride and out of fear that I'd be killed by some devil-worshiping priest, but she knew that I'd already stayed with her as long as I could. With my first pay purse, I brought her from the trash-roofed shed we'd called our home and set her in a small apartment in the city, above a weaver who I knew needed another hand at the loom. Then I joined the column of recruits winding their way into the desert, led by the recruitment officer and bound for the stronghold of Shepherd's Rock.

The training was hard, unlike anything I'd done before, but I was young and strong, my body hard from days hauling carts and boxes with the longshoremen, on the docks the men of other nations called Port Godless. In a few months, I learned fencing and spearwork, became a decent shot with a bow. I received a sword of my own, a beautiful tool worth more than everything else I owned combined. Yet I was quickly made to understand that for all their strength of arms, the most respected soldiers of the Pure Legion were those who were best able to sharpen their minds—to learn to think like priests, the better to sniff out their quarry and send them to the port or the gallows, depending on how much damage they'd done.

And I was good. Very good. My superiors singled me out early on for extra lessons, conducted after the regular soldiers—all good men and women—were released for the evening. They taught me to read, and took me to the Vault of Lies in the fortress's heart, so I could learn from the confiscated holy texts and better understand those I would hunt. And then, when they judged me ready, they sent me back to Azir, to put it all into practice.

I hunted. It was a wondrous thing, the hunt—more engaging than any of my childhood games. They hid, and I followed. They left clues, and I picked them up and pieced them together. They converted, and I redeemed. The only thing I loved more than the chase was the final confrontation, the point where we could look each other in the eye, and they knew for certain that they were lost. I was merciful where the law would allow it, swift where it would not. I gained my own command, and traded my well-worn blade from Shepherd's Rock for the ornate badge of an officer's sword. My men sometimes called me "The Hound," and joked that I could smell the priests' stink on the wind. Some days, I almost thought that I could.

It was at this point that I met Jannat. She was a legionnaire's dream, beautiful and fierce as a hunting kestrel, the daughter of my commanding officer. She wasn't a soldier herself, but she easily could have been had she wanted to. Her hair was long and as black as the night, her skin smooth and gold, and she could drink any man in my unit under the table. I watched her for a year, and she baited me mercilessly—would the Hound be hunting this evening? Would he like to be scratched behind the ears? But always it was with that sly smile.

Years later, in one of our quieter moments, she told me that she'd teased me because she knew I couldn't help but rise to the occasion, bettering my position. But at that time, I knew only that I loved her. At last, with the covert permission of her father, I took her to my favorite cliff looking out over the eastern sea and asked her to marry me. We made love for the first time beneath a cypress tree.

Those were good years. I was well off from my pay and bonuses, and neither of us was averse to making use of her family's generous endowments. We bought a little house overlooking the coast, not far from those cliffs where I'd proposed, and agreed that children would come in time, once I had climbed higher in the Pure Legion and no longer needed to travel as much. There were rumors that her father might retire soon, and that I might take his place as one of the heads of legion activities for all of Azir. Since the rumors came from her father himself, we were hopeful. In the meantime, we were happy together. I would hunt during the day, then return home to another world, a domestic paradise where she would sing to me, or let me watch her sit in front of the window for hours at a time, painting the sea and the sunset.

That all changed the day I returned home and found the front door open, its latch hanging broken.

We knew, all of us in the legion, that our war was not one-sided. For the most part, the small congregations of worshipers we chased down were content to run and hide. Yet there were always those few who sought to fight back, targeting the leadership of the Pure Legion, as if killing one man or a hundred could somehow shake the conviction of a hundred thousand, convince them to bow their heads and walk willingly into the theists' yokes. Seeing the door open, my mind went instantly to those stories. I drew my sword.

Inside, the house was a shambles. What furniture we had was knocked over, cabinets opened and looted, the stink and stain of spilled wine sprayed across the walls. Unwilling to call out on the chance that I might still catch the vandals by surprise, I stepped carefully over the shattered remains of my household and moved through the living room into the kitchen. And it was there that I found Jannat.

She'd died with a kitchen knife in her hand, its blade red with the blood of her attackers. But it hadn't been enough. High on her chest, a deep wound had welled out into a puddle on the floor, its river of red run dry and crusted. Her pale green dress had been slit open from collar to hem, baring her naked flesh to the air. And they'd done things to her.

I don't remember precisely what happened next, but I suppose I went a little mad. I can remember running through the rooms of our house, screaming challenges, but there was no one there to answer them. I scanned the nearby roads from the balcony, but there was no one who looked out of place. At last I returned to the kitchen and fell to my knees beside the body of my wife. With trembling hands, I pulled together the shreds of her dress, turned her cold cheek so she wouldn't have to look at the wound that killed her. Hands on her shoulders, I laid my head against her stomach, burying my face in her clothes and skin. And then I did a terrible thing. My great betrayal.

I *prayed*.

I had no idea who I was praying to, but even in my grief, I understood full well what I was doing. I didn't care. All that mattered was Jannat, and with the gelid blood of her heart sticking to my cheeks and running with my tears, matters of honor and justice were far away. I prayed, and in that prayer I promised everything. My life, my allegiance, my eternal soul—whatever was desired. Just to have my Jannat back. It would be worth it. I clutched her still form like a drowning man, and I sent my pleas—my *prayers*—out into the void with all the strength left in me.

And from the darkness, something answered.

There was a cough, and then a wracking, retching sound. Her body convulsed. I scrambled backward in surprise, half dragging her with me. I looked up.

Her head was off the ground, and she was staring at me with wide, terrified eyes. As I watched, the wound on her shoulder seemed to suck back into itself, scabbing over and then disappearing entirely. She began to shake, and then I was up cradling her head, pulling it into my chest as she wept.

"What?" she sobbed. "What just—?"

"Shh." I put a finger to her lips, and then bent my face down to rest in her hair, curling over her like a shield against the world.

"A miracle, love," I whispered. "A miracle."

But of course a miracle isn't a miracle when you're paid to hunt them for a living.

I tried to deny it myself at first, but she knew me too well, and she could see in my eyes what had happened. What I had done. In time, I came to accept it myself, thinking of it as my Moment of Weakness. Secretly, however, I regretted nothing. Jannat was alive, and that was all that mattered.

Yet at the same time, it wasn't. In bringing her back with my prayer, I'd made a lie of everything I lived for, everything we both believed. I still hunted priests, but my work suffered. Not because I sympathized with them—I didn't—but because a part of me was terrified that my own guilt stood out like a blazing brand on my forehead. With every preacher I confronted, I expected him to read my history in my face and proclaim it loud and long to the rest of my company. I grew furtive, nervous, and obsessed with locating those men who had been responsible for the attack, while simultaneously keeping it from my friends in the legion that such an attack had ever occurred.

At home, things were little better. Jannat was back, yes, and healthy, but it wasn't the same. In bringing her back, I'd made my choice, but she'd had no more say in her own resurrection than she had in her death. We tried to cover things up and move on as best we could, but the worm of shame had gotten into her heart, and refused to leave no matter how often I pointed out that *I* was the one who had been responsible. And some nights she would wake up screaming, remembering those last few seconds before she'd died, her attackers' hands upon her and the slow pump of her lifeblood onto the cool kitchen tile. I'd turn to comfort her, but she couldn't bear to be touched, and would stand at the darkened window until the memories passed.

All of this is to say why I wasn't surprised when it finally happened. Walking through the front door that evening, I felt the change in the house, and knew beyond any doubt that I'd just set foot in it for the last time.

They were waiting for me in the living room. Jannat, her father, and several men from my own unit. No one had drawn weapons, but neither were they resting easy. I ignored the legionnaires and looked at Jannat, where she sat at the low table, arms crossed across her breasts. Her eyes were red and puffy.

"I'm so sorry, Salim," she whispered. "I can't do this anymore."

"Jannat—"

"I think you've said enough to her, boy." That was her father. He was a mountain of a man, and though the hair above his slab-jowled face was white, he still wore the armor of the Pure Legion with practiced ease. His voice was low, but held the quiet air of command.

"I know what you did was out of love for my daughter, and I respect that. But you know what has to happen. You have the choice to conduct yourself with honor."

I nodded slowly. And then everything burst into motion.

Not a day goes by that I don't question why I drew. On good days, I tell myself that it wasn't my fault—that the goddess wouldn't let me turn myself in, or turn my blade on myself. On bad days, I fear a deeper truth— that at some level, I was scared to die. Despite all the men I'd fought, all the men I'd *killed*, I was too young to really understand death for what it was.

I drew, and I fought, and I ran. Behind me, three of my men—including Kelif, my best friend in the unit, a man I'd already secretly selected as the sword-father of my first child—lay on the floor of my house, screaming in puddles of their own blood. For my own inability to let go of the woman I loved, to acknowledge the fundamentally capricious and senseless nature of the universe, three good soldiers' wives would wear the ashes. And through it all, I saw Jannat's face, and heard her words. *I'm so sorry, Salim.*

They pursued me, and hard—treason among the Pure is the worst kind. But I had learned too many of the underground priests' tricks in my time, and before long I was across the border into Thuvia, and could breathe easier. Truth be told, I scarcely wanted to. What was the point of breathing, now? Without honor, without a purpose, without the woman I loved, breath was just a stalling tactic.

It was as I sat in a cheap room at an inn one night, somewhere along the Path of Salt, holding my knife and contemplating finishing what I'd been too cowardly to do before, that the angel first appeared.

"I wouldn't do that," a voice said.

I leaped up from my cot and spun around, coming reflexively into a crouch, the knife up and ready to stab.

On the other side of the bed, a figure floated in the air, its feet not touching the ground. It was pale and beautiful, neither man nor woman, and it filled the room with great black wings that sprang from its shoulders. It spoke again.

"That's somewhat better, if still inadvisable. But at least it shows spirit."

"Who are you?" I asked. "*What* are you?"

"A messenger," it said, and its voice was soothing, joyous. "Your divine liaison. You may call me Ceyanan."

"I don't understand."

The perfect lips twisted into a mock pout, but its eyes were still smiling. "Come now, Salim. Of course you do. Haven't you been waiting for this ever since you fled Azir?"

"I don't know what you're talking about." But somewhere in the back of my mind, a door opened, and I knew that it was right. The angel saw it in my face and nodded, ignoring my words.

"You made a deal, Salim. A promise. You called out asking for help, for your wife to be returned to you, and she was. You offered your soul and your allegiance, and my liege accepted. Now it's time to start honoring your side of the bargain."

It spoke the truth, and we both knew it. Yet it had overlooked one key fact: disgraced or not, when faced with slavery, a Rahadoumi always has a second option.

"My apologies," I said, bowing slightly. "But I'm afraid I'm going to have to renege on the bargain."

Then I drove the knife point-first into my neck.

The pain was . . . incredible. There were perhaps three hot bursts where I felt the blood pouring over my hands, flowing in rhythm with my heartbeat, and then the room faded and I felt nothing.

For an indeterminable length of time, I floated in darkness. There was no heat, no cold, no light or dark. Just an endless sea, rocking me. I scarcely knew who I was, and my last thought as I began to dissolve into nothing was: *so this is peace*.

Then the darkness exploded. My form was back, and now it was burning, every pore screaming with flame. Surely, I thought, if I weren't already dead, this would kill me. And then the pain was too extreme for thought, and I opened my eyes.

I was still in the room at the inn, lying awkwardly on the floor next to the bed. My knife was beside me, its blade red and crusted. I put a hand to my neck, but where there should have been a ragged hole, there was only smooth flesh. My mouth tasted of blood.

The angel was looking down at me, its expression one of concern.

"I would *not* recommend trying that again," it said.

"What—?" I started to ask, and then stopped, recognizing the horrible symmetry between my words and Jannat's, when she had first awoken on the kitchen floor. The angel answered anyway.

"Did you really think suicide was any way to cheat the goddess of death?"

I gaped. "Pharasma?"

"The Lady of Graves herself." The angel folded its legs up and floated lower, so that it could look me in the eye. "Who else would give you back your wife? You belong to Pharasma now, and if you think you can escape her through death, you're not nearly as bright as I'd hoped. The bargain was simple: Your wife got a second chance. We got you." It smiled. "You work for us now."

"And if I refuse?"

It waved the question aside with one long, perfect hand. "There'll be plenty of time for that later, if you insist. But first, hear me out."

Its big, black-pupiled eyes bored into mine. "There are creatures, Salim, that are worse than any priest. Things sprung ripe and rotting from the grave, living corpses that walk among the people and drink from their blood and tears. There are those who fear death so greatly that they transform themselves into twisted parodies of life, disrupting the natural flows of existence in their quest for power. These things are unnatural, and suffering follows in their wake. You, with your unique skills, are perfectly suited to helping us hunt down these monsters and drive them from society, to satisfy the church and protect the innocent, both atheist and religious."

I said nothing, only waited.

"Think about it, Salim. You've trained your whole life to be a weapon—the weapon of a nation that's now closed to you. Or do you think that you can somehow return to the way things were?"

I shook my head. There could be no going back. Even if I managed to sneak back into my homeland, there would be no redemption, no explanation for what I'd done. I'd be back in the slums, living underneath scrap board and hiding my face whenever a familiar figure passed by. There would be no reconciliation with my comrades in the Pure Legion. There would be no Jannat.

"No," the angel said, and the sympathy in its voice sounded genuine. "You can't go back. You're a man without a home, or a purpose. But you don't have to be."

The figure calling itself Ceyanan straightened, and those great black wings flared majestically.

"We're not just calling in what's owed to us by your bargain, Salim. We're offering you a chance at redemption. Not of the spirit—the Lady knows you don't care about that. I'm talking about a resumption of purpose, of *meaning*. Through us, you can continue to do what you were made for, and need bow to no priest or church, even that of the Lady of Graves herself. This is a covenant between you and her.

"Salim," it whispered, and its voice was triumphant, ecstatic. "You can *hunt* again."

The thought of serving a deity was repulsive. Yet what other option did I have? As it said, my choice had already been made, kneeling in the pool of blood on the kitchen floor.

I accepted.

Chapter Eighteen
Movements Underground

"A nd so began my servitude to the goddess of death,"
Salim finished. "With the angel Ceyanan as my
handler, I traveled far across the nations of the Inner
Sea—yes, and the Outer Planes as well—searching out
and destroying the creatures of the night who denied
Death. They offered me magic, divine spells to assist me
in my hunting, but aside from the amulet you've already
seen, I've rejected such gifts wherever possible. If it's my
destiny to act as Pharasma's hunting dog, I'll at least do
so as a man, not a puppet-conduit for divine filth."

For the first time during his story, Neila spoke up.

"But the angel—are you saying that you can't die?"

Her voice sounded hopeful, and it pained Salim to
kill that hope.

"It's true that the goddess won't let me rest," Salim
said. "I'm too useful, and I've not yet repaid my debt—if
I ever can. But it's not that simple. If anyone knows
about my curse and can figure out a way around it,
it'll be Khoyar. And even if they don't kill me, there are
other things. Maybe they'll blind and lame me, and set
me loose in the market with my tongue cut out. Maybe

they'll smash me under a rock, or keep me chained and barely alive in a stone sarcophagus for centuries. Regardless, it doesn't fix our current situation." He sighed. "I'm sorry, Neila."

There was a long silence, and then: "Did you ever go back? To Rahadoum?"

Salim suddenly felt very weary. "Once."

"And did you see Jannat?"

"Yes." The memory was so painful that he almost couldn't speak. "She had grown older, and remarried, yet even with white hair she was still beautiful. For a moment, she looked up, and I was sure that she recognized me. But then she turned away."

Through the darkness, Salim could feel Neila move uncertainly.

"Salim," she asked, and her voice had an odd, strained quality to it. "How old are you?"

He answered honestly. "One hundred and twenty-seven."

He heard the small noises of rustling cloth, and then her hand was on his face, caressing his stubbled cheek and spidering its way wonderingly over his features.

"You hide it well," she said.

Was that humor in her voice? Salim inclined his head mockingly. "You're too kind, Lady."

But Neila wasn't ready to give up the topic. "Back in the manor," she said, "you said you hadn't touched a woman since your wife died."

It was true. He acknowledged as much.

"Why?"

"Because—" he started, and then stopped. Why indeed? "Because I don't deserve to."

The hand on his brow now moved to his shoulder, trailing warmth across his arm and making its hairs stand on end beneath the robe. "You gave up everything you believed in for the woman you loved."

When he spoke, his words were hard and bitter. "It was stupid."

"Stupid is a hundred years of penance for a noble deed." She picked up one of his hands, and held it to the side of her neck, heating it against her skin. Then she slid it down until it was cupping the side of her breast. Salim jerked back, but her grip was firm.

"Neila, I—"

"Stupid." The word was sharp, but her voice was smooth and low. The hand holding Salim's palm to her chest slid up to his own, palm flat against his sternum. "We're set to be executed tomorrow, and you're still punishing yourself for things that happened before anyone except you was born."

"But—"

She was leaning so close now that he thought he could almost make out her face in the dark, half-lidded eyes catching the glow from the door and reflecting it back at him.

"If you can't die," she asked, "don't you think it's time you started living?"

He opened his mouth to argue, then stopped.

Perhaps the girl had a point.

Neila wrapped a hand around his neck and lay back, pulling him with her. Then all thought left him, and he was following her down, and down, and down.

They woke an indeterminate amount of time later, the darkness around them unchanged except for the faint smell of sweat and their lovemaking. Salim lay on his back, half on the splayed fabric of his robe, half on the cold stones of the cell floor. Neila was curled under his right arm, head on his shoulder and body pressed sweetly against his. Salim was staring into the blackness, mind drifting, when the shape next to him stirred and let out a sleepy grunt. Without lifting her head from the hollow of his collarbone, she stretched slowly and languorously, the smooth skin of her stomach and thighs sliding pleasantly against him. Then she shivered.

"It's cold in here," she murmured.

In response he reached for her, feeling the gooseflesh prickle up along her breast and back, but she pushed him gently away. There was a rustle as she gathered up her clothes from where they'd been discarded and began to slip back into them.

The rustling stopped abruptly.

"Salim." Neila's voice was tense. "Salim, get dressed. Now."

Salim had been a soldier too long to question that order. He rolled to his knees and immediately pulled on his robes, tying them securely. "What is it?"

"This."

In the darkness, she found his hand and unfolded it, pressing something small and straight into his palm.

"One of my hairpins," she said, her voice pitched low, as if it only now occurred to her that someone might be listening. "They removed them all from my hair, but this one must have fallen down inside my shirt, and the priests either didn't notice or were too proper to go digging."

Salim understood immediately what had excited her, and some of his own resurgence of hope abated. "This is good, Neila, but I'm no thief. My knowledge of locks is rudimentary at best."

"Then give it back," she said, and as quick as that the hairpin was back in her possession. She knee-walked over to the door, and Salim followed. The glow around the doorjamb was barely enough to illuminate the hairpin—just a thin, dark line against the light—but Neila began to bend and twist the pin with precision. Salim leaned against the wall on the other side of the jamb, giving her space.

"You can pick locks?" He tried to keep the incredulity out of his voice. He must have failed, because Neila's reply was both proud and sharp.

"A surprisingly useful skill for a young woman who wants to go out at night, or who wants a bit of spending money without a big explanation of *why* she wants it. Now be quiet and let me—ah! There we go."

There was a click, weighty and authoritative, from behind the metal panel with the keyhole. Neila grabbed Salim's hand and squeezed once.

"Ready?" she whispered.

He squeezed back, and she gave the door a push.

After so long in the dark, the light was blinding, and both prisoners' first response was to shrink back and shield their eyes. Salim fought the urge and barreled forward fast and low with arms outstretched, determined not to lose the element of surprise. His hands met the flat stone of a far wall after only a few paces, and he spun, forcing his eyes as wide open as he could, sending pain lancing deep into his brain.

The corridor was empty. As the shapes resolved themselves and the white sunburst of aching eyes broke into its component colors, he saw that they were indeed underground, somewhere in the Pharasmin catacombs. The brilliant nova of light turned out to be a softly glowing glass orb, welded into place in a wall sconce. He looked to Neila, who was blinking hard, reflexive tears coursing down her face.

"Beneath the church?" she asked.

He nodded.

"But you can find the way out." It was not a question.

Salim thought about it for a second, then nodded again. The hallway was too old and worn to be of the level they had visited earlier to view Faldus's body, but the fact that there was magical lighting down here—the globe right in front of him, and the similar glow visible farther down the corridor—implied that they were still in a relatively well-traveled section of the crypts. That probably meant they were close to the surface.

It also meant they were more likely to encounter someone. Salim popped his knuckles. Despite his pleasant interlude with Neila, he was still far from pleased with the situation, and would welcome the chance to express his displeasure physically on any guards they ran across.

"Come on," he said. "Walk softly, and keep to the shadows where you can. Let me go ahead a little."

Moving with a grace he'd had little cause to use in their adventure thus far, Salim slid almost silently down the hallway, his bare feet an asset against the dusty stone of the floor. Ten feet behind him, Neila followed in his tracks, her own step light as a dancer.

Several times they passed other doors and branchings in the corridor, lit by more of the globes. At each of these Salim stopped and stooped long enough to study the trails in the dust, then stood and moved on. It was obvious to anyone who bothered to look which of the turns and offshoots received the most traffic, and Salim made each turn to follow the most traveled path. It was no different than following a stream to the sea.

At one point they came to a passage where a section of wall had caved in and not yet been repaired, strewing rubble across half the width of the hall. The two escapees stepped over the stones easily enough, but there Salim stopped. He bent, studied the scree for a moment, then selected a jagged chunk of masonry twice the size of his fist and straightened, hefting the rock. It was at least fifteen pounds—more than sufficient to crush a skull, if used properly.

Neila eyed the stone warily. "What's that for?"

"In case we meet anyone on our way out." He tossed the rock lightly and caught it again.

The girl looked uncomfortable. "Salim, most of the priests here probably believe the allegations about us. It's not their fault Khoyar's lying to them."

"Nor is it ours, but they'd lead us to the gallows just the same."

She shook her head. "It doesn't matter. We can't just kill them."

Salim kept his voice reasonable. "Of all the people you can kill, death priests are probably the least inconvenienced. And it might only put them to sleep, the way they so kindly did for us." He smiled and touched the swollen, egg-sized knot at the back of his head. But Neila would have none of it.

"Salim. Please."

He sighed. "Well enough. We won't kill anyone unless we have to."

"Thank you." Her face brightened, and she surprised him by rising to her tiptoes and planting a quick kiss on his cheek. In the light of the corridor, such physical affection felt awkward, as if the two figures that had moved together in the dark had been different people. "Now let's get out of here."

They continued. Though the corridor remained flat, they could tell that they were approaching more traveled areas by the conditions of the walls, the trails in the dust, and the increasing prevalence of the globes. Salim slowed their pace, motioning for Neila to stay well behind him each time they came to a corner or branching. At last they reached a T-shaped intersection that appeared to be the best-maintained yet, complete with a mural of a robed skeleton surrounded by roses and spirals. Salim craned his neck around the corner, then ducked back and flattened himself against the wall, motioning for Neila to hold her position. He lifted one finger, then motioned to the right with his head. Her eyes widened immediately in understanding, and she crouched back into the shadows.

Careful not to move too quickly and draw attention, Salim leaned his head out just far enough to get one eye around the sharp-edged stone of the corner.

Beyond it, the room opened up into a landing similar to the one they'd passed through before when visiting Faldus, with the grand spiral staircase dominating one end as it extended both up and down. Just in front of it stood the man Salim had seen, a Pharasmin brother he didn't recognize, his dark robes bunched awkwardly underneath a breastplate marked with Pharasma's spiral. A sword—probably never used before, if the man had been raised to the church since boyhood—hung at his belt, but the crossbow he held had the plain look of a farmer's tool, and rested easy in the man's hands. He stood with the straight back and glazed eyes of a man used to long vigils and arduous penance, if not actual combat.

Salim withdrew and looked to Neila. He mimed a crossbow, then raised both the chunk of stone and one eyebrow. She pursed her lips and shook her head.

Damn, Salim thought. As if this wasn't going to be difficult enough. But he'd already given his word, so they'd do this the hard way.

He nodded and lowered the stone to show he understood, then motioned for her to stay where she was. He took a deep breath, held it, and slipped around the corner.

The guard was looking in his direction, but Salim understood the difference between looking and seeing. The man had probably been staring down the passageway for hours without so much as a puff of dust to change the view, and in that sort of situation the mind quickly grows complacent, seeing only what it expects to see. Salim was already halfway across the room when the guard's eyes snapped into focus, and three-quarters by the time the crossbow came up from its resting position and drew a bead on the charging figure.

Thock! Running flat-out and bent almost double to present a smaller target, Salim swung his chunk of masonry in an underhand arc just as the priest squeezed the crossbow's trigger. Stone connected with wood, and the crossbow was driven out of alignment, its string snapping home ineffectually and sending the bolt spinning end over end into the darkness. Both stone and crossbow flew from the men's fingers, hands vibrated into near-nervelessness by the impact, and Salim slammed his newly free fist roughly into the priest's mouth, bloodying his knuckles on the man's teeth even as they gagged him.

The priest's shriek of alarm came out as a gurgle, and untrained fingers scrabbled for the sword at his belt. Salim responded by yanking the belt around so that the guard's sword hung in the small of his back—the idiot hadn't even bothered with a tie-down to keep it in proper drawing position—then swung around himself and pressed hard against the priest's back, trapping the sword between them. The arm that wasn't busy clogging the man's prayer-hole snaked around his neck from behind and locked in place, squeezing the priest's windpipe between bicep and forearm.

The guard wasn't totally without heart—Salim had to give him that. Three times the man's fists came up over his shoulders, slamming down on the back of Salim's head in precisely the right spot to send lightning from the already bruised skull screaming through Salim's brain, closing his eyes and turning his stomach. Yet in the end, it was a foregone conclusion. With each blow, the guard grew weaker, until at last he slumped in Salim's arms.

Salim waited a moment and then removed his fist from the man's mouth, listening. The rasping breath that emerged was weak, yet slow and measured. He lowered the man to the ground, then whispered Neila's name.

She appeared at once. She looked first to the man on the ground, then up at Salim.

"Is he . . . ?"

"He's fine." Salim forced himself not to touch the aching mass that was his skull. "He'll wake with a headache, but nothing like the one he gave me."

She flashed him a smile. "Thank you, Salim."

He waved a hand irritably and set to work divesting the downed guard of sword and scabbard. The crossbow lay a few feet from the unconscious man's hand, battered by Salim's chunk of rock but still functional. With a practiced grunt, he stood in the stirrup and hauled back on the string to lock it in place, then slid a bolt from the guard's quiver and dropped it into the slot. He held the weapon out to Neila. "Can you use this?"

She reached out an uncertain hand for the weighty weapon, cradling it awkwardly. "I can try. If I have to."

Salim moved behind her and reached his arms around, bringing the stock of the bow up to her shoulder and helping her sight down it. "Just point and squeeze. Be sure to make it count, as if it comes to that, there won't be time to reload."

The woman who had responded so handily with a sword—a more aristocratic art, to be sure—looked even less comfortable at that idea, but nodded. She lowered the bow and pointed to the guard's robes. "What about those? Could you put those on, pretend to be leading me to see Khoyar?"

But Salim was already shaking his head. "This is a small enough congregation, and they know my face— knew it the minute I walked through the doors. Best we're not seen at all. And if we are . . ." He nodded toward the crossbow in her hands. "No hesitation. These men may be priests, but they're also soldiers now, and no soldier is innocent. Understood?"

"Yes." Her lips were a thin white line, but Salim believed—or at least hoped—she would do what needed to be done if the time came.

Fortunately for both of them, she didn't have to. Though they went up the great spiraling stair as quiet and careful as mice in a larder, they didn't encounter any further guards. Once they came to a landing where another priest had been positioned, but this one had made the mistake of sitting down, and now dozed with his chin resting on his chest, crossbow lying loaded in his lap. There was a tense moment while Salim darted from the shadows of the lower stairs to the safety of the higher ones, and an even tenser one while Neila did the same, bare feet padding against the stone with a whisper that was still heart-stoppingly loud, yet the guard never stirred. A half-turn later, they were gone from view.

When they came out on the now familiar main floor, it became clear why the guards had been so lax. The sky through the narrow windows in the hallway was the deep blue-black of night's tail end. The guards had likely held their posts all night without relief—another amateur mistake, better suited to religious vigils than the battlefield. Before long, the men and women of the cathedral would wake for their morning prayers, but for now all took refuge in holy sleep—itself a little taste of death.

Their timing was perfect, but Salim still didn't dare take them out through the great receiving hall where he'd entered before. For all he knew, Hasam was still sitting on his stool by the doors, and if not him, then surely Khoyar positioned someone there to receive those midnight callers in need of the church's assistance. Instead, Salim led them down a series of new hallways, at each branch choosing the path with windows to the outside, or which seemed most likely to lead to such. At one point the rattle of pans indicated a kitchen where someone was already at work baking the new day's bread, and Salim turned them away quickly. At last, however, they came to what he'd been looking for: a nondescript side door, locked with a simple barred latch. He pulled it open, and they slipped through.

Outside, they found themselves in the predawn shadows on the southeastern side of the church. Here small gardens gave the Pharasmins a place to meditate and pray, while simultaneously supplementing their food supply. Beyond the rows and furrows was a simple fence of chest-high iron rails, an exposed length of street, and then the blissful cover of close-packed buildings. Salim looked to see that Neila was ready, then led them in a low, silent scurry across the freshly turned plots of sandy earth, boosting her over the fence before setting a foot against the rails and hauling himself over as well. Bare feet slapped cobblestones, and then they were around a corner and down a side street.

There they stopped, breathing hard with excitement rather than effort. Neila turned to Salim and threw her arms around him, burying her face in his shoulder. Her body spasmed with relieved, muffled laughter, and he allowed himself to lower his face to her hair and breathe in its scent.

"Excellencies! Mistress!"

The whisper was low but urgent. Both fugitives broke their embrace and whirled, the noblewoman bringing the crossbow halfway to her shoulder.

Farther down the alley, a tarp-covered cart neither of them had noticed sat half hidden in an alley. Next to it, a shadowy shape beckoned them excitedly. Neila recognized it first.

"Olar!"

The carriage driver grinned. Even as Salim and Neila ran across the street to meet him, he grabbed up the leads of the drowsing oxen and whipped them into wakefulness, backing the same little farm wagon Salim had ridden in earlier out of the alley. When it was clear, he lifted the tarp on a bed loaded loosely with barrels and other bric-a-brac and motioned for Salim and Neila to climb underneath, which they did gratefully. When they were safely stowed, he took the driver's seat and tutted to the oxen, sending them lumbering and jouncing down the road away from the church.

"What are you doing here?" Neila asked the question for both of them. In a space between barrels, she and Salim fit without so much as a suspicious lump. With the edge of the tarpaulin pulled down, they would be invisible, but for now they kept it lifted, creating a narrow space at the level of Olar's hips through which they could speak to him and see where they were going.

"I had hoped that one would be able to get you out," Olar said, not turning around but cocking his head sideways to indicate Salim. "After they took you, I was sent back to the manor to deliver the message of your guilt, and to let everyone know that Amir, as ranking member of the house staff, was temporarily in control of things." He leaned over the edge of the cart and spat loudly, showing what he thought of that particular proclamation. "The carriage was too conspicuous anyway, but as soon as I could find an excuse I slipped away with the cart." He patted the wood of the seat. "I've been waiting here since midafternoon."

"How did you know where to wait?" Salim asked.

Olar turned to Salim with a grin, eyes bright in the half-light. "How does a man know anything? Luck. Luck and the gods. This alley seemed as good as any."

"Where are we going?" Neila asked, and the servant's smile faded.

"You can't go back to the manor," he said. "Amir is well in the pocket of those lying priests, and most of the other staff don't know what to believe at this point. I doubt many of them actually believe you killed the master, but they also aren't about to stick their necks out."

"And you?" Salim asked.

Olar laughed. "My neck is tough as an old rooster's, and Mistress Anvanory's been good to me."

"So where *can* we go?" Neila pressed.

"Out of the city," the driver said. "I'm afraid the city guard will side with the church, and that means you're not safe here." He glanced down apologetically at Neila. "You're still an outsider, Lady. Without the benefit of your estate, your friends are few. I hope to get you to the harbor and see you onto a riverboat headed north. By the time they know you're gone, you'll be too far for them to bother with you. Perhaps you can cross into Osirion, or secure passage back to your home in Taldor. This one looks strong, and carries that sword easily—mayhap he can secure you passage, or at least keep you safe until you can access your father's funds elsewhere."

"So that's it." Neila's voice was bitter. "We run. Khoyar kills my father, steals my estate, and we run."

Olar's face was sad. "I'm truly sorry, Mistress. But I have no other ideas."

"I do." Salim's voice was deep and thoughtful as he turned to Neila. "But you're not going to like it."

"Does it involve giving in to Khoyar?"

"No."

"Then I like it better already."

"Fair enough," Salim said, and reached out a hand to tap the seat next to Olar. "Take us southeast, out of the city."

"With pleasure, excellency." Olar's grin returned, and he whipped the oxen into a lumbering trot. Together, the three of them rode southeast toward the forest, the river, and the ruddy glow of the rising sun.

Chapter Nineteen
Friends in Need

I can't believe I let you talk me into this."

Salim turned from where he was busy slashing his hands to ribbons attempting to thrash a path through a dense patch of brambles. He now wore both the guard's sword at his hip and the crossbow slung over his back on a strip of robe cloth, leaving both of Neila's hands free to maneuver through the underbrush.

"You need help," he said. "And if you'll recall, you're remarkably short on friends at the moment."

"That doesn't mean I need to go straight to my enemies!" Neila tottered on a slick-barked log and nearly fell, catching her balance at the last moment before she would have stepped straight into a patch of stinging nettles. This section of the forest was far from the most welcoming.

"On the contrary. The fey may hate you, but they hate you for different reasons. They're probably the only ones in the region who don't suspect you of killing your father by now. Or care, for that matter."

"And what makes you think they won't just kill us for trespassing?"

Salim held aside the final runners of brambles and let Neila pass gratefully into the clear space beyond. "I've got an idea," he said. "Just keep quiet and let me do the talking."

Neila sniffed loudly at that, but said nothing. She dabbed gingerly at the dirty scratches on her legs— the clothes she'd worn to confront Khoyar were hardly the sort of thing one wore to thrash about in the deep woods, and her skin was paying the price. She craned her head back to follow the boles of the great trees up and up until their branches finally spread out into the canopy proper, the leafy limbs as thick as barrels. There were a few patches of blue sky piercing that green roof and lighting the gloaming underneath, but only a few. This forest was old.

"I feel like we're wandering aimlessly," she said at last. "We've been walking for hours, but it seems like we've just been going in circles."

"That's precisely what we're doing." Salim used the sleeve of his robe to wipe sweat and sap from his face. Even in the relative cool of the trees' shade, midday in Thuvia was no time for marching.

Neila turned to him irritably. "And how exactly do you expect to *find* your new fairy friends?"

But Salim wasn't paying attention to her, and Neila fell silent as she saw him cock his head to the side, listening. His face was tense. Slowly, with fingers spread wide to show they held nothing, he raised his hands into the air.

"We don't have to," he said. "They've found us."

There was a sound of wood creaking, and Neila turned with a start.

A woman stepped out from between the trees, the bow in her hands bent fully and the arrow's fletching drawn back to her cheek. She was naked, or nearly so, yet though her skin was brown, it was not the smooth brown of Salim or other desert dwellers. Rather, it was covered in whorls and striations, raised in tiny ridges like the bark of a tree, and rose up to a head of hair that was as much trailing foliage as anything human. Around her narrow waist hung a belt of braided tree bark from which a full quiver depended. Yet though the fire-hardened point of the nocked arrow was pointed unwaveringly at Salim's chest, the woman was not what captured either human's attention.

For when the woman had stepped from the forest wall, a part of the forest had stepped with her. Easily twenty feet tall, the gnarled old tree was vaguely man-shaped, with massive clumps of unearthed roots forming the legs, and the lowest two branches curving and bending into arms. In the center of the bole, twice as high as Salim was tall, the knotted bark twisted into the vague outline of a face with two staring brown eyes, a broken branch for a nose, and a wide scar for a mouth. The scar was not smiling.

"You have a lot of nerve, humans." The woman's voice was low and husky, and not the least bit complimentary. "Did you think we'd forget what you did?"

"My apologies, Lady Dryad," Salim said. "I assure you we would not have come if it were not a matter of direst urgency for all concerned."

The bowstring didn't slacken. "You let Delini live, and for that we haven't hunted you. Yet now you come trespassing. That changes things."

"Yet that's why we've come," Salim said, talking a bit faster now. "To speak with Delini. We have a proposition that he'd very much like to hear."

The dryad stared at him unblinking, moss-green eyes hard. "We don't make deals with outsiders," she said. But this time the bow lowered, the string loosening until the arrow was merely nocked. She turned. "Follow me."

Salim made to do just that, but right then the great tree-man moved for the first time since entering the clearing, one giant step blocking the humans' path. Its mockery of a face turned toward Neila.

"You burned my trees." Its voice was a bass rumble, the groan of a dead tree as it sways before falling.

The noblewoman took a step back, and when she spoke, there was a quaver in her voice. "We—we planted new crops. Lots of them. And we care for them."

"Crops?" The word was the dry snapping of a branch. "Crops are slaves. My trees were free, and old—old as time. And you killed them."

Salim stepped in front of Neila, honestly not sure what he could do that would be of any use if the forest guardian decided to charge them. "Please, tree shepherd—that's why we're here. To make amends. At least hear us out."

It was the dryad who settled matters. She stepped up to the great tree's side and placed a hand on its root-leg, stroking it. "Peace, Egas," she said. "Delini will decide. The names of your flock will not be forgotten."

Egas the tree-man gave Neila one last baleful look, then turned. With a long-legged lumber, it led the dryad out of the clearing, and the humans followed.

They walked beneath the trees for the better part of an hour, crossing narrow gullies and bramble-infested thickets. The dryad melted through the latter with ease, while Egas strode over them in a few steps, leaving the humans to fumble their way through, the difficulty compounded by the desire to do as little injury to the plants as possible while Egas and the dryad were near. Salim suspected their course was specifically designed to put the humans through their paces, and the malicious chuckles that occasionally emanated from the nearby underbrush told him the other locals were enjoying it as well. Once he caught sight of a pixie darting ahead, buzzing between trees like a dragonfly, no doubt keeping tabs on their progress for Delini and the forest's leaders.

At last, however, the walkabout ended, and the two humans stumbled, scratched and stinging, into a wide clearing. The trees here were the largest they'd seen yet, and the canopy overhead was woven together so thickly as to become a roof, blocking even the sun. The floor between the boles was naked earth, and in the center was something neither of them had expected to see—a raging bonfire, with a young pig roasting on a spit at its edge. Aside from the fire, the whole clearing was lit by softly glowing lanterns hanging from branches, their lights colored from shining through membranes of dried autumn leaves.

The clearing was packed with fey. No one was hiding now—around the fire stood dryads and satyrs, while pixies and brownies perched on low branches or shoulders. Here and there, nymphs stood several inches taller than their companions, faces and breasts covered by light veils of gauzy moss that kept them from blinding the other celebrants while leaving nothing to the imagination. Gourds and woven reed cups held wine and food, but no one was drinking now. The fey stood still and stared at the newcomers, faces grim.

All but one, that is. From the far side of the clearing, where a throne woven from still-living shoots stood high on an old stump, a voice called out, and then Delini was springing forward nimbly on his backward-bending goat legs. He wore a sash of river lilies, and his head was crowned with blossoms.

"My lady," he said, stopping just out of reach and giving Neila a deep bow. "So you've decided to take me up on my offer after all. I'm honored." He placed one hand over his heart, the other over his groin. Neila ignored him.

"I see you're having a party," Salim said, gesturing casually toward the fire and the surrounding faces, as if the expressions there weren't carved out of stone.

"Always," Delini said, grinning. "'In the shadows of the eldest trees, the revels never end / and from their boughs the melodies like ripened fruit depend.'" He sketched another little bow. "I wrote that myself, but it's true just the same. And tonight we're celebrating something special."

"What's that?" Neila asked.

"A sacrifice." Delini's smile was no longer humorous. His sharp, goatish features suddenly made him look more like a fiend than a fairy. "Unless, that is, you can give me a satisfactory reason why you dare to enter my woods after killing my people."

Behind him, the fire crackled.

"I can go you one better," Salim said. "I've not come here to fight, but to make you an offer. We need your help."

There was a moment of shocked silence, and then a brownie sitting on a log erupted into hysterical laughter, which cut off only when a nearby dryad reached out and knocked him off his perch. Delini didn't turn, instead continuing to lock eyes with Salim.

"Findelas isn't the most eloquent of speakers," he said, gesturing over his shoulder at the brownie that was tottering unsteadily back onto the log. "Especially not when he's been drinking. But his point stands. Exactly what is it that you think you have to offer us?"

Salim didn't hesitate. "Your forest," he said evenly.

Delini frowned slightly. "You're hardly in a position to make threats, Master Priest."

"I'm not a priest," Salim said automatically. "And I don't make threats. My offer is exactly what I said it is: your forest. Help us, and Neila will sign over all the Anvanory lands that encroach upon your forest, fair and legal."

"*What?*"

Neila's voice was a squawk. Salim turned to her and stared hard.

"Do you want your lands or your father, Lady? Because right now, I don't think you can have both."

Neila set her jaw but said nothing, which Salim took for assent. When he continued, it was to Delini.

"There you go, then. If you help us reclaim her father's soul, they'll cede you the manor grounds. We'll have the contracts drawn up by one of the bankers of Abadar, and place the church on retainer, so that even if the city decides to challenge the deal later on, the church will intervene. You can replant the fields with whatever you want. What do you say?"

Delini looked thoughtful. "And in return? What do you get?"

Salim smiled, and in the flickering firelight he looked every bit as feral as the fey.

"In return, you give us a repeat performance of your firebombing of Anvanory Manor. Only this time, it's the cathedral of Pharasma."

Delini looked surprised, then mirrored the grin. "An interesting proposal."

"Don't listen to them, Delini."

The new voice was soft as a burbling creek. The crowd of half-human forms parted, and one of the nymphs stepped forward. Salim instinctively moved to shield Neila's eyes with his palm, narrowing his own eyes to slits. Through blurred lashes, he saw that this one had a dark poultice bandaged to the top of her head.

The one he had hit. Salim wasn't sure now if leaving her alive had been a good idea or a bad one.

"Don't trust them," the nymph said again, staring daggers at Salim. "They'll burn us out as soon as the job is done—just set a fire and let the wind do the work. You know they will."

Delini stretched out his arm and absentmindedly pulled the nymph close, reaching around for a quick grope.

"Easy, Yanora," he said, stroking her breast. "Normally I would agree with you, say we send the man home sore and the girl with a gift in her belly. But this one let me live when he didn't have to." He looked to Salim, measuring him. "I'd say he's hard, and tired, and as likely to cut your throat as bed you, if the situation warrants. But once he's given his word, he keeps it. That sound about right?"

Salim had heard worse. He nodded.

"And you?" Delini asked Neila. All lecherousness was gone from his manner now. "Will you abide by this covenant? We attack the cathedral for you, and in return—whether the attack is successful or not, whether you get what you want or not—you'll deed us the land beneath your manor?"

Neila looked like she'd just swallowed a worm, but her voice was strong. "I will."

"And you?" Delini called, turning to face the assembled fey. "Will you fight again to reclaim our forest?"

The answering roar was deafening. As if the question were a cue they'd all been waiting for, the clearing erupted into celebration. Wine was remembered or appeared from nowhere, and several of the smaller fey began to dance around the fire. Back near the wicker throne, a satyr and a dryad bent over the chair's arm and began putting it to good use. Delini sent the nymph under his arm on with a pat on the rear, then turned back to the two humans.

"There you have it, then," he said. "They're willing. I only hope your plan doesn't cost them too much."

"I understand," Salim said. "Now here's what I've planned. Once the sun—" He broke off as the satyr raised one horny-nailed hand.

"I said they're willing," Delini said. "I didn't say they were allowed. That's not my decision to make."

Neila glanced toward the violently rocking throne, then quickly back to the satyr. "I thought you were in charge."

"I am, more or less," the satyr admitted. "These woods and their residents are my responsibility. But we as a whole have responsibilities beyond ourselves. And before I can lead them away from those, I must seek permission." He turned and began to walk toward the far edge of the clearing. When Salim and Neila didn't immediately follow, he stopped and crossed his arms impatiently.

"Well?" he asked. "Are you coming?" He looked to Neila with a ghost of his old rakishness, then nodded toward the throne. "Or would you rather stay and enjoy the festivities?"

Neila colored slightly and walked quickly toward him. Salim followed.

The satyr led them in an arc that circumvented the majority of the celebration and then turned sharply into the woods, taking the humans between the trees at a quick walk. Salim and Neila had to hurry to keep up, though the satyr paused politely at fallen logs and other obstacles that they needed to scramble over. Delini himself cleared most such barriers with a single leap of his goatish legs, his gait more that of a deer than a true goat.

There was no honor guard this time, no nocked arrows. It seemed that the fey either trusted them or were confident in Delini's ability to handle them should the situation get tense. Either way, Salim was grateful—they'd already handled what he'd expected to be one of the most difficult parts, and the last thing they needed was some dryad with an axe to grind—though perhaps that was the wrong metaphor—getting startled and letting an arrow fly. If Delini thought he had the situation well in hand, then perhaps he was indeed formidable enough for their purposes.

They walked for perhaps fifteen minutes before Salim noticed the change. All around them, the trunks of the trees were growing thicker, expanding from giants of the forest to behemoths of nearly impossible girth, so thick that all three of their party holding hands would not have been able to stretch around them. The ancient trunks were covered with a coating of moss and crawling vines so thick that Salim had to tilt his head back and gaze up to find any flashes of naked bark. Where the ground should have been bare, shaded as completely as it was by the great trees, the forest floor was instead exploding with life, ferns and grasses growing incongruously up around the three travelers' waists as they moved, their leaves full and green in the arboreal twilight.

Yet these changes in the landscape were not what Salim noticed most. Instead, as they walked, he began to feel something new. It was difficult to describe—not a sound, exactly, but something like a deep hum that permeated the plants and air and vibrated his teeth. As it did, he felt his body coming awake—truly awake, in a way that he rarely experienced outside of combat or sex. The nerves in his skin reached out to feel every breath of air upon them. His groin ached, full and in need of release, and his stomach rumbled audibly.

"You feel it now." Delini looked over his shoulder and gave Salim a half-grin. "Really gets the old spring flowing, eh?" He turned to Neila, and the expression broadened into a leer. "You too, princess. There's no use denying it—I assure you it's perfectly natural."

Neila, already flushed, reddened further and said nothing, only crossing her arms across her chest, perhaps to hide the hardened nipples now straining against her bodice.

"What is it?" Salim asked.

"This," Delini said, and held aside a leafy branch to allow the two humans to pass.

They were in another clearing, but this one was as different from the meeting place they'd left as a deep forest from a village square. The ground—if indeed it was still there—was completely covered over by a writhing thatch of crawling vines. Strange, brilliantly colored plants and fungi that Salim had never seen before sprang up from the vines, or stood out sideways from the trunks of the surrounding trees in gravity-defying explosions of red, yellow, and purple. And in the center, above half a dozen weathered stone steps, hung a tear in the sky.

That was the best way Salim could describe it—a vertical rip in the air, its ragged edges peeled back and splayed open to make it perhaps ten feet high and three or four across. Bright green light radiated from it, and through the brilliance Salim could faintly see the outlines of another place—an open plain with the barest suggestion of mountains in the background. It was from this floating window that the hum was emanating, the song in Salim's bones.

Two satyrs with bows flanked the portal. Both came to attention as the newcomers entered, and Delini waved them casually back to their normal slouches. Salim paid none of them any attention.

"A breach," he whispered.

"A breach," Delini agreed solemnly. "Now you understand why these woods are so important, and why I can't just lead its guardians off to attack the cathedral."

"What's a breach?" Neila asked.

Surprisingly, it was Delini who answered, and without his usual swagger. "You know about the First World?"

Neila hesitated, then nodded. "Where the gnomes and fey come from. Originally, I mean."

The satyr made a face. "There's a bit more to it than that, but yes, it's where we all came from, back before time was time."

"The First World was the rough draft," Salim explained. "Before the gods created our world, when they were still dabbling with reality, they created the First World. When they were ready, they built the real world over it, like an artist painting over his sketchwork. Most of them abandoned the original in favor of the new, letting their half-formed creations run wild. But it's still there, behind everything. A world given entirely to nature and potential, unbound by the rules of our own."

"And that's a doorway to it?" Neila motioned toward the glowing portal.

"Not quite," Salim said. "A breach is more of a broken place—a spot where the image of our world has been rubbed too thin, revealing the world beneath."

Delini nodded. "Close enough. Even more than the river, the breach is what gives this forest life. But of course it's more important than just a few trees, or the creatures that live in them. Which is why our master set us to guard it."

"And who's your master?" Salim asked.

Delini shrugged. "That's a complicated question, but you'll meet him soon enough. Or her. Whatever." He stepped forward onto the springy carpet of vines, sinking in to just above his hooves. "Come on, we've dallied long enough."

At the top of the stone stairs, slick with lichen, he greeted the two guardian fey in a flowing, liquid tongue that Salim didn't recognize. Both bowed slightly in deference, their actions strangely stiff and grave for satyrs, and then Delini switched into common speech for the humans' benefit.

"I'll be taking them through," he said. "We're going to see Shyka. It may be minutes or days, but make sure that someone holds this post. I don't care how hung over they are. Understood?"

The fey nodded.

"And give me your bow." Delini snatched both weapon and quiver from one of the fey, who made no move of protest. He slung the bow over his shoulder, then tied the belt of the quiver around his waist. He looked back toward the humans waiting at the bottom of the steps. "Doesn't hurt to be prepared. Are you ready?"

Salim looked to Neila, who nodded, jaw set. "We're ready."

"Then why aren't you up here already?" Delini turned back to the satyr whose bow he'd stolen and winked. "Humans. If their thighs weren't so loose, they'd be no use at all. Ah, there we are now!" He reached out to Salim and Neila, who now stood on the step below him, and took their hands.

"Welcome to the homeland," he said.

Then he took a step backward into the glowing green radiance, pulling Salim and Neila with him.

Chapter Twenty
The First World

There was no sense of transition, none of the nauseating disorientation or freezing nothingness associated with Salim's amulet. One moment they were standing in the forest staring through a rip in the air, and the next they were on a wide, grassy plain, beneath a sky that was a clear and brilliant blue without any trace of a sun to light it. Behind them, the fey's clearing in the woods was a dark splotch suspended in the air, through which they could see the satyrs resuming their positions to either side of the portal.

Delini breathed deep, with evident satisfaction. "It's something else, isn't it?"

It was. The forest had been rich with smells—the sharp scent of the trees, the low and earthy scent of disturbed loam—but this was something entirely new. The air smelled as crisp and fresh as a winter morning, yet without the chill. The perfume of the grass was all out of proportion to what the humans recognized, and each breath felt laden with a barely restrained energy, an urge to grow and expand. It was as if the land itself were breathing out and into them, making Salim's head swim. He reached out a hand to steady Neila.

"What is it?" she asked. "This place feels . . . different."

"It's the First World," Delini said. "This is nature's domain, free of the taint of men and gods. Best abandon all preconceptions right now, Princess."

Neila looked ready to press the issue, but Salim had questions of his own. He turned in a slow circle, scanning their surroundings carefully. Aside from the portal, they were alone in the middle of an immense field that stretched to all horizons, the waving thigh-high grass unbroken by so much as a stunted tree. Only a distant line of mountains ahead of them, little more than blue shadows against the lighter blue of the sky, offered any point on which to set his bearings. "Where are we going?" he asked.

Delini gestured toward the peaks. "Shyka dwells in the House of Eternity, in those mountains."

Neila's response was shrill. "But that'll take weeks!"

The glance the satyr cast her was pure contempt. "What did I just tell you? The rules are different here. We'll be there soon enough."

Salim refused to be distracted by the bickering. "And this Shyka? What is he?"

"The boss. The one who set us to guarding the breach against anyone who might try to exploit its energy. One of the Eldest."

Salim nodded, but inside he felt a stone deposit itself in his stomach.

"And what's *that*?" Neila asked, clearly frustrated at being talked past.

"One of the little gods of the First World," Salim said. "Not true gods, but close enough. Fey lords of immense power."

"And we're going to ask one for help?"

"Yes."

Neila's face took on the same somber cast as Salim's own. One did not petition gods lightly. Even little ones.

"And now, if we're through with today's lesson," Delini said, "perhaps we can begin? There's no telling how far we've yet to go."

Wordlessly, Salim and Neila fell in behind him, and together the three set off toward the mountains, the portal that was their sole link to home quickly dwindling and disappearing into the featureless expanse of grass.

For all his mocking of Neila's ignorance, it quickly became apparent that Delini enjoyed the sound of his own voice more than lording his superior knowledge over the humans. Before long, he was conducting lessons of his own, explaining the nature of the First World as they walked, punctuating his diatribe with sweeping, grandiose arm gestures.

Though Delini himself was a product of the Thuvian wilderness, and had never so much as glimpsed the First World until the appearance of the breach several years ago, he was full of ideas and opinions about the place. In his view, the First World was superior to the planes of the multiverse, Heaven and Hell and Axis and all the others, because it was bereft of any underlying moral or organizational strictures. Instead, the First World was ruled by possibility and potential, a place where nature and evolution were granted an unlimited canvas and the freedom that came with a flexible interpretation of natural laws. Anything could happen here, and because it could, it did.

Salim had heard bits of the story before, but there was a difference between a scholar's speculations and experiencing something in the flesh. As he and Neila quickly discovered, the satyr was right about the unusual flexibility of natural laws here. Time seemed different, and distance was distorted in ways that were difficult to discern, save that as they walked, the mountains grew in size far faster than they had any right to, in fits and starts, looming high on the horizon before any of them were even winded. It was as if the landscape were a sheet that had been folded to bring two points together, with the intervening sections conveniently removed.

Around them, the landscape changed as well. When they'd arrived, there'd been nothing but fields, flat as a calm ocean of yellow-green grass. Now the field was still there, but its shape changed, bowing up into hills or down into valleys, and new features seemed to pop up out of nowhere—forests that appeared full-formed off to their left, or high mesas around which dark shapes fluttered and dove.

There were stranger things, too. Once the land twisted to reveal a massive black sphere in the distance, seemingly floating above the sea of grass without moving. Straining his eyes, Salim was just barely able to make out a jumble of pockmarks on its surface that turned out to be a mismatched assortment of holes and doors, gates leading into the obsidian orb from every angle. Another time Neila glanced back over her shoulder and gave a little shriek, drawing all their attention to the full-sized mountain that had appeared on their backtrail, so close that there was no way they could have overlooked it. As they stood there, transfixed, the mountain began to move before their eyes, sliding across their tracks and into the fields beyond as smoothly as a sailing ship.

Of the land's residents, however, they saw little. Judging by the way Delini occasionally squinted into the distance and then adjusted their course, Salim suspected that wasn't entirely coincidental. At one point they paused to rest at the top of a low hill, and Neila pointed out a strange phenomenon off to their left, much closer than the others. It looked like a river, but only a small section of it, perhaps thirty feet long. The segment of stream, sharp-edged at either end, seemed to stretch several feet above the top of the grass, pouring onto new ground and then curling up behind itself as it slithered across the landscape.

"What's that?" she asked.

Delini looked, then ducked reflexively, motioning for them to lower their profiles.

"Grodair," he said. "Giant fish-person. Takes its own stream with it wherever it goes."

Neila smiled at the idea, so like something out of a child's fairy tale. "Are they dangerous?"

"That depends," the satyr replied. "Can you breathe underwater? If so, then I'm sure they're perfectly nice. If not—well, once it realized what it had done wrong, it would likely apologize profusely, but it would be too late to make a difference to you. Still want to go make friends?"

Neila said nothing in response, just joined Salim in hunkering down at grass level until the portion of stream disappeared beyond the too-near horizon.

Only once did they truly have to hide. By that time the field had at last given way to the foothills of the mountains, and gnarled, lichen-covered trees held court between boulders the size of houses, cut through with tiny, perfect streams small enough to hop over or cross on makeshift bridges of upthrust stepping stones. They were near one such rivulet when Salim suddenly noticed a new sound above the water's babble: a high, fluting chorus, less like a bird call than a set of mismatched panpipes played by the wind. He turned to mention it to Delini, but the satyr's eyes were already big.

"Skrik nettles," he said, grabbing their hands and yanking them over to where two enormous stones leaned against each other to create a low, narrow opening. There he promptly dropped to his belly and wriggled into the dark hollow, tugging and motioning frantically for them to follow him in. Soon all three were lying in the hole, pressed well back into the shadows and likely invisible to anyone passing by.

"What's a skrik nettle?" Neila whispered.

In response, the satyr slapped a hand over her mouth and left it there. He looked to Salim, as if considering doing the same to him, then clearly thought better of it.

The fluting was louder now, its smooth vowels creating strange, discordant compositions that were somehow too pure and clear to be unpleasant. Then the source rounded one of the big rocks and came into full view.

The skrik nettles were enormous jellyfish creatures, translucent and eight feet across at the dome of protoplasm that formed each body. Perhaps a dozen of them floated in the air at easily twice Salim's height, moving serenely without any apparent mechanism of flight. Below the iridescent bubbles of their bodies, long tentacles stretched to the ground, ringed by an incongruous fringe of feathers where they met the main dome. At its end, each tentacle was tipped with a birdlike beak. It was from these beaks that the fluting came, twittering and hooting to each other—sometimes even at other beaks attached to the same creature—as they trailed along the ground, writhing and investigating the grass and dirt.

They looked absurd, but Salim had grown up near the ocean and seen men scarred and crippled by the poison of jellyfish no more than a few feet long. He looked questioningly to Delini, and the satyr gave a grim little nod. All of them shrank farther back into the shade of the stones, which suddenly seemed far too exposed.

And it might have been, had things gone differently. The skrik nettles were in no hurry, sliding through the air with their tentacles just barely touching the ground, piping beaks hunting into nooks and crannies for anything attempting Delini's tactic. One of them drifted close enough that a single tentacle peeked under their stones, twitching in the dirt with horrible, blind intensity. Salim wondered if the thing could smell them.

Up ahead, something broke cover. A creature like a cross between an alligator and a piglet, no larger than a small dog, crashed out of the brush and raced forward in a low-slung, back-twisting run, desperate to escape the floating menace.

The tentacle that had been questing toward the three travelers was instantly withdrawn as the pack converged. From their vantage, Salim and the others could see clearly how the skrik nettles broke ranks and swarmed, surrounding the squealing animal. Tentacles flicked out and stroked pebbled hide, and Salim knew that the creature was finished.

Yet the reptilian piglet didn't drop. Instead, it did the opposite. With its tiny clawed feet kicking wildly in terror, the creature began to drift *up*, out of contact with the ground. Cut free of its moorings, the little beast pitched and yawed, tumbling somersaults in the air as its bladder and bowels let go in panic.

The tentacles continued to lash out, stroking and caressing. The animal rose faster, first ten feet, then twenty. As it rose, so too did the skrik nettles, an aerial entourage that matched the creature's steady ascension into the cloudless sky. They passed from the cave-dwellers' view, and soon even the sounds of the tiny creature's cries and the skrik nettles' fluting—now bearing an unmistakably triumphant tone—became faint and indistinct. Delini waited for several breaths after they lost track of the sound, then scrambled out from beneath the stones and took off in the direction they'd been traveling before, moving at a slow run and keeping to the shadow of overhangs and tree branches whenever he could. Salim and Neila were quick to follow, and the satyr kept his pace slack until they caught up, then began to run in earnest.

"What just happened?" Neila asked, breathless. "Where did they go?"

"It's how they hunt," Delini replied, ducking low beneath a branch. "We've got a few minutes while they climb for altitude—they'll be too focused on their prey to notice us, and once they start to feed they'll hopefully be distracted for a bit longer. But I want to be far away when that happens."

"Feed?" Neila echoed, horrified. "How do they—"

Without turning, Delini made a fist in the air and brought it down, adding a descending whistle. He ended it with a sudden spread of his fingers and a little popping noise. Neila gagged, and then all attention was turned to escape.

They ran for perhaps ten minutes before returning to their strangely effective walk. Around them, the landscape had changed once more, trending uphill and turning into the mountains proper. The valley they had been running in became a steep-walled cleft, and the grasses and trees gave way to fields of scree and boulders. In some places the rubble was new, knife-edged, while in others the sides were rounded and softened by thick mats of lichen, spanning every color from deep purple to a shocking, vibrant green. These the travelers clambered through as best they could, feeling exposed but seeing few creatures, and none of any size. Above them, rookeries of unknown birds occasionally cawed and trilled at each other. Something like a rabbit, its body stretched snakelike beyond any reasonable length, slithered between two burrow entrances in the rocks.

Salim was on the verge of asking exactly how much farther the satyr expected them to travel when they found the staircase. It began innocently enough, cut into the rock at the top of a small slope of shale. The steps were only wide enough for them to travel single file, and Delini took the lead, stepping from the scree field to the first of the stairs with a small sigh of relief.

"This is it," the satyr said, putting a touch of pomp in his voice. "The stairway to the House of Eternity. Not far now."

But of course it was. They climbed for hours, twisting and winding as the last of the low valleys gave way to bleak rock. The path they followed was immaculate, the right angles of the steps bereft of any sign of erosion, as if they had been chiseled just yesterday by some giant's hammer. The stairs wound their way up through narrow passes and along exposed cliff faces, up chimneys so tight and steep that the stairs almost became a ladder, with all three of them using the side walls as handholds, lest they overbalance and fall backward into open space. At times the path was joined by other staircases writhing their way in from other trail heads far below, yet so well crafted was the path that there was never a question as to which way the staircase led. Others joined, but always the course continued upward.

At last they came to what could only be their destination. Here the river of stairs that had been collecting for miles finally came to a head and gave out onto a narrow courtyard of natural stone. At its far end, a palace rose.

It was primarily a construction of spires, either carved from the native rock or growing from it like some strange, organic being. The towers, more than a dozen of them, were of varying heights, but all were tall and slender, tapering near their points into tips so long and needle-thin that Salim guessed any natural stone would have cracked and fallen in the breeze. The sides of the spires were as smooth as ceramic from a potter's kiln, broken only by tall, open windows set at seemingly random intervals, all lit from within by golden light.

At the spires' collective base, a castle emerged from the mountainside, its shape following that of the gray slope. Its grand arched windows were similarly lit, yet here the phenomenon took on a more sinister cast. For though it seemed to Salim that he should be able to see into the nearest of them, everything beyond the thick stone sills was lost to the gentle radiance.

Delini crossed the courtyard to the enormous metal double doors that stood at its end, their swirling faces embroidered at the edges with a continuous line of tiny figures marching single file. As he walked, there came a metallic booming, then silence as the portal split down the middle and swung inward.

Despite the obvious invitation, the satyr stopped a good twenty feet away and bowed his head, hands folded. The simple sincerity of the gesture was so different from his usual capering and grandstanding that the back of Salim's neck prickled into gooseflesh.

"It's Delini, Lord, with two humans come to beg your aid."

For a moment, there was no sound at all save for the sighing of the wind through the smooth obelisks of stone. Then:

"Enter."

The voice was mild, genderless, and seemingly everywhere at once. Salim looked to Neila and saw her glancing around as well, clearly unnerved. Ahead, Delini was already striding forward, and the two humans moved swiftly to keep up.

They found themselves in a palatial receiving chamber, its high ceiling arching like the great hall of a king or emperor, yet bereft of a throne or the hangings and tabards mortal lords were so fond of. Instead, the walls themselves were art, carved in the same motif as the doors behind them. Around the room's edges and up and down the walls, a twisting serpent of foot-tall engraved humanoids marched in an orderly procession, sometimes seeming to be walking, others sprinting with swords or trumpets held high. Despite its convoluted weavings, Salim got the impression that the train of figures made a single continuous loop, never repeating a figure. Above the parade, the arched ceiling was embossed with four titanic figures in flowing robes, their shapes twisting and swirling clockwise as they stretched and reached for the dome's apex, a circular window of crystal that blazed like the sun, illuminating the entire room. Inside the robes, the bodies of the figures were thin and lithe—two male, two female—yet the cowled heads were faceless, the stone blank and smooth beneath strange runic halos.

"Welcome, travelers. You have come far."

Salim looked back down. When they'd entered, the room had been empty. Now a woman stood before them, golden hair cut short and body draped in a gray gown not dissimilar from those of the carved figures above. Delini straightened into an almost military posture, and Salim found himself doing the same. The satyr opened his mouth to speak, but Salim beat him to it.

"My name is Salim. This is Lady Neila Anvanory, formerly of the Taldan aristocracy, currently of Thuvia."

"I know who you are," the woman said, pleasantly enough. "And also why you have come. Why else do you think you'd have been allowed to climb my stairs? I am Shyka the Many."

"Greetings, Lady Shyka," Neila said, dropping into a curtsy deep enough for royalty. "We—"

But the lady was no longer there. Salim didn't remember blinking, yet he must have, for he never saw the transition. One moment the woman was there, listening to Neila speak, and the next she was gone. In her place, a dark-skinned man maybe ten years older than Neila stood in an identical posture of polite interest, his gray robes undisturbed. Neila's jaw dropped and hung.

"—were wondering why I'm called 'the Many,'" he finished for her, grinning broadly. "No reason to hide your curiosity, child—I could read it in your face. And I believe the answer should be self-evident."

"Illusion," Salim said.

Shyka and Delini both shot him scandalized looks.

"Hardly," the young man said, only now he was no longer the black man, either, but rather an emaciated patriarch several inches taller than Salim himself, with a long silver beard and an elaborate topknot. "You really should know better, Salim. This is the First World. What use is illusion when reality itself is malleable? Anyone with a little imagination can bend it to his or her will— you saw it yourself on your way here. Or did you think the landscape folded of its own volition?"

Salim hadn't truly considered the matter until just now. As he did, Delini jumped in.

"Shyka is one of the Eldest," he said, puffing out his lightly furred chest. "Worlds are born and die at his whim, and all elements bow before him."

"Including my favorite," Shyka added.

The old man waited expectantly, hands folded. After a moment, Neila obliged him.

"Which is what?" she asked.

"Time." The whisper came from every direction, and as it did a hand fell on Salim's shoulder. Shyka was now behind all three of them, back in the original guise of the blonde woman.

"Shyka the Many is a name," the Eldest explained. "But it is also a title. The Eldest live long—too long for even you to rightly conceive of, Salim—but we are not immortal unless we choose it. Over the ages that have been and have yet to come, there have been many Shykas, all of them masters of perceived causality, the shimmering ribbon that you understand as time."

"You're talking about chronomancy." Salim felt cold sweat ooze from beneath his arms, between his toes. He'd dealt with necromancers, both hunted them for the church and allied with them against greater evils, but chronomancy was a heresy far more dangerous than simply defying death. Time magic defied reality itself—all of it. Across the myriad planes, only the steady progression of cause and effect was a constant. To break that was to invite insanity.

Shyka was nodding. "A crude term, but fair enough. The Shykas of history have all been and will be adept at the manipulation of time. Yet as honored as we are by our position among the Eldest, you can imagine how the temporal limitations of a dynasty—ruling from *this* date to *that*, in consecutive order—might seem unbearable to someone capable of viewing the birth and death of your universe. So sometime in the distant past—or perhaps future—we came to an arrangement."

The woman was now a new figure, this one a seemingly elven beauty with light green skin and pupilless eyes the color of the deepest ocean trench.

"We decided to intersperse our reigns. Instead of ruling in sequence, we trade from moment to moment, sharing completely—our minds, our goals, our existence—so that all may experience the full range of eternity."

The young black man again. "Reality flickers like the shadows of a magic lantern play," he said, "giving us a collection of scenes rather than a single long passage. Yet it is a small price for a picture of the whole." Again the brilliant smile. "So you see, we are all Shyka. And we are all the Many."

Neila was gaping, and even Delini looked a little shocked at the sudden disclosure. The Eldest's voice— each of them, though they spoke as one—was hypnotic, and it took an effort of will for Salim to shake off the desire to be lectured and remember why they were here.

"Your nature is fascinating," he said. "Yet it's not for your mastery of time that we've sought you out, as I gather you already know."

Shyka inclined his head. "Of course. You seek the use of my breach guardians in assaulting your goddess's desert dollhouse." His tone was wry, and Salim remembered that there was little love lost between the fey of the First World and those gods that had abandoned them when the Material Plane was still young.

"Yes. I require only a distraction, not dissimilar to their attack on Anvanory Manor. If all goes according to plan, few should be harmed. They'll be returned to their post within a day."

"A day." Shyka's blonde, short-haired incarnation turned her eyes upon the satyr. "Delini, do your people know whom they serve?"

"A few, Mistress." The satyr bowed deep and held it. "Those who needed convincing. But many suspect, and are honored accordingly."

"And you, Delini. Do you know?"

The satyr looked up, confused and a little troubled. "My lord?"

"Did it occur to you, my lecherous child, that to Shyka the Many, one of your days might be so short as to be completely beneath notice? That it might have no more value than an individual speck of dust on your hooves?"

"Master," the satyr said hastily, "I sought only to—"

"You sought to impress the humans with the power and majesty of your connections," the Eldest continued, "thereby increasing your own status in their eyes. Respect by association. You do not need my permission to assist these humans any more than you needed it to attack the woman's manor, for which you did not consult me. I gave you the responsibility of guarding the breach because I believed you could handle it without supervision. And now I find you imposing upon my hospitality for the purpose of putting on airs."

Delini didn't bother bowing deeper. Instead he threw himself on the floor, prostrating himself completely and placing his arms over his head in a posture of ultimate supplication, his goatish tail poking into the air.

"Please, Master—Mistress—I—"

"Peace, Delini." Shyka's voice was smooth again, the guillotine steel that had crept into it blowing away like a cloud. The Eldest bent gracefully and placed a hand on her servant's head. "You have brought me a chance to meet a pair of most interesting individuals, and for that I absolve you of your impertinence, provided you learn from this. And since you come on the pretense of asking permission, I shall grant it: you and your band shall help Salim and Neila, after which you will return to your forest, which you will now hold in the eyes of the local government as well as in reality."

"And if you ever seek me out again without sufficient reason," Shyka's old man form said, "you will return to the valley floor swiftly, and without benefit of the staircase. Do I make myself clear?"

"Perfectly, Lord." Even facedown on the floor, Delini was already regaining his composure, though Salim thought he heard a slight quaver that hadn't been there before.

"If you'll excuse any impropriety," Neila asked, "why do you have him guarding the breach near my home? Or do you guard them all?"

Salim was amazed that the girl could so calmly dig for information after their guide had clearly come close to losing his head for wasting an imperceptible amount of the fey lord's time, but the smile through Shyka's beard was indulgent.

"No one could guard them all, child. The First World extends behind the entirety of the Material Plane, from the woods behind your manor to the farthest reaches of the night sky. There are thousands of breaches on thousands of worlds, and no one can count them all. Some seek to close them for the scars they create, their gross and static imposition upon the unbounded purity of the First World. Others seek to exploit them, either siphoning energy from one world to the other, or else waiting to bilk travelers of their baubles, such as the Crone in the Cart and her vagabond Witchmarket. For my part, I simply wait, and watch."

"Watch for what?" Salim asked.

Shyka smiled and shook his head. "That, Salim, would be cheating. Mortal or not, you must live your life forward. Suffice it to say that for someone interested in the vagaries of time, your nation of Thuvia is somewhat intriguing. But for now, I watch."

"Fair enough," Salim said, unsure whether or not he was relieved by the answer. "In that case, unless you have further matters to discuss, we will happily repay your graciousness by not intruding on it further. Delini? Neila?"

The noblewoman was already bowing, and the satyr did likewise, simultaneously getting his feet back under him and somehow making the whole thing look graceful.

"Indeed," Shyka said, back in her original form. "I wish you luck, and will take steps to ensure you have safe passage back to the breach." She waved a hand in casual dismissal. The three petitioners turned and started for the door.

"Oh, Salim? A moment more, if you would."

He stopped and turned. The woman-Shyka was standing with one hand on her chin and a finger to her lips, studying him.

Something was wrong. Not with Shyka, who was still exactly the same as when they'd first entered, but with the rest of the scene. The air looked strange.

With a start, Salim realized that Neila and Delini hadn't turned with him—were in fact both still frozen in the motion of walking away, their postures impossibly still. Neither chest moved. Just below Delini's beard, a tiny bead of sweat had fallen and been stalled in midair.

Salim broke off his examination and took a step toward the Eldest, hand going to his sword.

"Release them," he growled. The air—as dead and still as a crypt, with the dust hanging motionless in space—burned in his lungs. He took another step.

"Please." The fey lord waved wearily for Salim to cease. "They're perfectly fine. As far as they're concerned, this isn't even happening. I've simply taken you outside the continuum for a moment so that we might converse in private."

It was true that neither of the frozen figures looked like they were in pain. Salim quit advancing, but kept his posture stiff and ready, left hand remaining on the hilt of his sword. Shyka ignored this minor rebellion and advanced. Hand still on her chin, expression pensive, she circled slowly around Salim like a woman studying a horse she intended to buy.

"You must understand that the others are of only mild interest. There are innumerable spoiled nobles and randy satyrs in their little nation alone. But you—you, Salim, are something special." As she moved around behind him, she trailed a hand lightly across the back of his shoulders, the motion at once sensual and dangerously proprietary.

"A servant of a goddess, yet one who has no faith of his own. A priest-hunter who serves alongside the clergy. An immortal who disdains eternity." She completed her circuit and stopped just in front of his right shoulder, peering up at him with shockingly green eyes. "You are a paradox, Salim. A study in contrasts."

"What do you want?" he asked.

"On the contrary, Salim." She waved a delicate finger. "The question is: what do *you* want?"

Around the two of them, the castle dissolved into a gray haze the color of Shyka's robes, taking Neila and the satyr with it. Though Salim's body told him that his feet remained firmly planted on something solid, he and Shyka appeared to be floating in a sea of mist that stretched out of sight in every direction. Slowly, shapes began to swim into view through the fog.

"Time is the true illusion, Salim," Shyka murmured, now in the solid baritone of the young black man. "The idea that what's been done cannot be undone. Of the lies mortals tell themselves in order to make sense of their surroundings, this is the greatest."

The mists thinned, receded to the edges of the walls. They were in Salim's house in Rahadoum, as it had been the day everything had gone awry. There was Jannat, sprawled on the floor, dress askew and blood congealing in the dark pool around her. Everything was still. Silent.

Then he entered the room. From a point somewhere to the side, in the dining area, Salim watched as a younger Salim, resplendent in the glittering armor and cloak of a Pure Legion officer, rushed to his wife's side, going to his knees and staining the immaculate breeches, blood wicking its way up through the fabric. He saw himself stand and rage, rushing from view with sword drawn. Though the mist muffled all sound save for his own breathing—that of the real him, not this long-lost echo—he could imagine the crashes, the screaming as he frantically searched the house for someone responsible, something that could be killed, punished. After a time he returned and knelt by his wife's side once more, hanging his head.

And then the memory changed. With gentle fingers, the figure on the ground reached out and closed his wife's eyes. He kissed her forehead, her cheek, her bloody lips. And then he stood, back straight and face set, and left the room.

"Nothing is fixed, Salim." Shyka's voice was a whisper, reverent as a man in church. "Nothing is permanent. Time is a stream. And a stream can be diverted."

The room disappeared. In its place, Salim was assaulted by a fusillade of images, each lasting no more than a heartbeat. Salim standing proud as he accepted command of legion forces in Azir. Salim on a shore where waves surged between rocks large enough to support trees, a new woman beneath his arm. Salim dandling a boy on his knee, then showing an older child the basic sword forms.

Salim on his deathbed, hand closed around a gray-haired woman's as he closed his eyes.

He shut his own now, blocking out the sight. "Why are you showing me this?"

"There are many worlds," Shyka said softly. "Many branches of the stream. You chose yours in haste, but I am master of the stream entire. I can give you the choice again. The chance your goddess never allowed you."

Salim opened his eyes once more and met Shyka's, earnest and brown.

"I can give it back," the Eldest said.

Salim reeled. To take back his prayer, his *betrayal*, so that he and his wife might live and die as the world had intended—hadn't he wished for that every day since his flight from Azir? In truth, hadn't he known his error the moment Jannat opened her eyes? Yet he had been blinded by love, by his own desperate need, and he had faltered. If he could undo his mistake, let his wife find what peace she could in the atheist fields of the Boneyard, and join her himself in his time . . .

In his mind, he saw again the image of him on his deathbed, the gray-haired woman at his side. Yet as he watched, she turned, and her face changed, losing the weight of years and becoming that of Neila Anvanory.

He looked over at Shyka, who still gazed at him expectantly.

Suddenly he was filled with rage. His hand shot out and grabbed the fey lord's arm, squeezing hard. The Eldest's eyes widened in surprise.

"Take us back to Neila and Delini," he commanded.

"Salim," Shyka said soothingly, a little affronted, "I assure you that I truly have the power to—"

"You always do," Salim spat. "Your kind has the power, so you use it, playing with those less powerful for your own amusement. Gods, Eldest—it doesn't matter." He squeezed tighter, fingers digging into Shyka's arm hard enough to turn brown skin pale. "I made the mistake once of trying to undo what had already been done. It cost me my honor, my wife, and my soul. I won't make it again."

Even in his anger, Salim knew that it was himself he was talking to, letting his rage act as a buffer against that desperate longing to erase the sins of his past. Yet as the emotions churned inside his chest, Neila's face floated into view again, unbidden. There was no way he could abandon her to Khoyar's schemes after coming this far. He'd failed to protect his wife, but Neila still had a chance.

To his surprise, Salim discovered that the fey lord was smiling broadly. He released the Eldest's arm.

"Fascinating," Shyka said. "To make the decision so easily. Truly marvelous."

The fey lord brought his hands together in a clapping gesture, and the mists flew apart, leaving them back in the receiving hall of Shyka's castle. Delini and Neila were still there. At the sound of the Eldest's hands, they broke free of their stasis, taking a few more steps before looking around in puzzlement, spotting Salim and the Eldest farther behind them than they should have been.

"What just happened?" Neila asked.

"Nothing, child—nothing." Shyka was back in her blonde incarnation. "I simply called Salim away for a moment to discuss something—a matter of no particular importance. And now, I believe it's time for you three to be off."

Neila looked toward Salim, expression concerned, yet he strode past her before she could ask the question on her lips, leading them briskly from the great hall.

"Salim?"

The swordsman whirled, almost drawing steel at the fey lord's playful tone. Behind them, the Eldest was grinning.

"Don't forget: Regardless of the things we discussed, I'm still lending you the assistance of my servants. Which means there's a debt between us."

Without answering, Salim spun on his heel and shoved open the big metal doors, stalking out into the bright, omnipresent light of the First World. Behind him, he heard Neila and Delini scramble to keep up, followed by the hollow boom of the doors closing.

Gods, he thought. They were all the same. And now he was indebted to two of them.

Jaw clenched, he moved quickly back toward the portal, and home.

Chapter Twenty-One
In the House of Death

The journey back to the breach was uneventful, just as Shyka had promised. Several times during their trek, Neila looked over at Salim inquiringly, but after his first noncommittal grunt she didn't bother asking him about his private conversation with the Eldest. Salim appreciated the discretion.

They found the breach again easily enough, though Salim couldn't have said exactly how, given that the fields which had originally surrounded it were now a miniature orchard, with trees no higher than Salim's waist bearing an explosion of strange fruits, no two of them quite alike. Neila seemed delighted and prepared to investigate, but Salim and the satyr pulled her along in their wake, marching through the tear in reality without so much as a last look around at the warped pastoral paradise of the First World.

On the other side of the portal, Delini greeted its guardians. The two satyrs had been relieved of duty, and a gaggle of bleary-eyed pixies sat on mossy patches along the stone steps. One of them tossed Delini a salute as he came through, though he didn't bother to stand.

"How long have we been gone?" Delini asked.

"Through the night," the commanding pixie answered, gesturing at the weak light filtering through the canopy and following it with a little hiccup. "You missed all the fun."

"On the contrary," Delini said. "The fun's just getting started. Hold your post—I'll send a runner to let you know what's happening."

"Not a problem," the fairy said, and settled back on his elbows.

With no further discussion, Delini led the humans at a brisk trot back through the trees, which gradually lost their unnatural fecundity to become simply the heart of a Thuvian river-wood. After a short time, the nearly invisible deer trail they followed broke through into the clearing of the fey's original gathering.

The celebration that had been beginning when they left had clearly lasted all through the night, a bacchanal that must have rivaled the temple orgies of the lust goddess Calistria. Berry wine and fermented tree sap stained the earth where goblets had been knocked over, and those fey who remained in the clearing were sprawled in twos and threes in leafy bowers and beds of soft loam, some even perched precariously in the branches of trees, their sleeping forms held there by luck alone. Delini strode over to the nearest group—two satyrs and a pixie, all bundled together in the same long streamers of beard moss—and toed them roughly awake.

"Up!" he cried, cheerful as a circus barker. "Up, my beaming brethren! Today's the day, and now's the time, and anyone who doesn't bestir his ass will find it stirred for him!" He winked at Neila.

The fey woke, scrubbing at bleary eyes or emerging from the trunks of hollow trees with wide yawns. Delini let them wake and turned to Salim and Neila.

"They'll be ready," he said. "Leave that to me. Now what's this plan of yours?"

As it turned out, Salim's plan was remarkably simple. Now that the Pharasmins were undoubtedly alerted to their escape, they wouldn't find the priests nearly as complacent. The temple would be heavily guarded, and likely by warriors who knew what they were doing. There would be magical wards and alarms. All of which meant that it would be much more difficult to slip in undetected.

"That's where your fey come in," Salim said. "If you can give me a repeat performance of your little firebombing of Anvanory Manor, there'll be such chaos that the priests won't be able to focus on anything but the immediate threat. While you're attacking from one side, I—" he faltered as he saw Neila's expression, "I mean *we* can slip in through the back. Once we're in, we find wherever they've stashed my sword, locate Khoyar and the soul-ring, and finish this. Remember, you're not trying to take the cathedral, just keep them occupied until you see us signal our success. Then you get out of there before you lose any more people. Understood?"

Delini nodded, but Neila was looking at Salim strangely.

"A decent plan," she said, "but why would we waste time looking for your sword, instead of going straight for Khoyar?"

Salim opened his mouth to respond, then stopped. The honest truth was that it had never occurred to him that they might not locate his sword first. His sword—which in one of his more poetic moments he had named the Melted Blade—was the only thing he still retained from his old life in Rahadoum. The first time he had used the goddesses' magic, it was to protect him from flame, and afterward he had held the basket hilt of that sword in a mountainside forge until the brass of the hilt ran like wax around his fingers, obscuring the markings that identified it as an officer's sword of the Pure Legion. But the way Neila was looking at him made him uncomfortable. He floundered for words and came away with nothing.

"It's important," he said, feeling foolish.

"Important enough to risk our lives? To risk finding Khoyar before he destroys my father's soul?" Her voice was gentle, but underneath the velvet was stone.

Salim wanted to say yes, of course it was. His sword had been with him longer than she could imagine—had been his right hand in the hunt before her father had been a damp patch in her grandmother's nightclothes. But instead he slowly nodded his head. She smiled without malice.

"When?" Delini asked.

Salim lifted his head and looked around the clearing. For all their drunken stupor, the fey were moving with purpose, quickly and efficiently.

"Soon," he said. "Very soon."

They were ready by early evening. Most of the day had gone to preparations, larger fey brewing the flammable pitch missiles that had been so effective in setting portions of the manor house ablaze, while smaller fairies fluttered and sprinted through the forest, gathering troops and spreading information. At one point Neila strong-armed one of the satyrs, a one-horned old goat named Eschus, into leading them back out to where the ox cart was still concealed at the forest's edge.

Olar had been waiting, dozing on the driver's bench, and stood anxiously when they arrived. The man was adamant about participating when Neila explained the plan, but was eventually convinced that it was more important for him to remain at the manor, to keep an eye on things and not raise undue suspicion. At last he had acquiesced, turning the cart and whipping the bulls hard for home, but not before pulling a long, thin bundle from beneath his perch and handing it to Salim.

Salim pulled apart the loose sacking and hefted the sword. It was heavy, longer than Neila's and double-edged, made for hacking through armor rather than the polite dueling of the nobility. "Where did you get this?" he asked.

Olar smiled. "One of the master's many trophies. In the confusion of the fey attack, it went missing. Thought you might be able to use it."

"Indeed." Salim held it out at arm's length, sighting down the blade, then took a tentative swing.

"Thank you, Olar," Neila said. She reached forward and took the servant's hand with both of her own. "For everything."

The old man grinned again, surprised and a little embarrassed, then twitched the reins and set the cart in motion.

Now Salim and Neila crouched in their position, an alley due west of the cathedral. Down the crooked street and above the roof of the stocky shop that hid them from view, the three soaring spires of the church rose dark and foreboding against the evening sky. Next to Salim, Neila fidgeted nervously inside the drab shawl that hid her face and hair.

"Soon," he whispered, and touched her arm. At their feet was the canvas sack that held both of their swords, concealed so as to avoid any possibility of suspicion.

For an instant, the old resentment rose. If he'd been alone, there'd be no need to reassure anyone, no one to watch out for once the fighting started, or to become a liability in a pinch. No one to become collateral damage if things went poorly.

Yet that wasn't fair, and even in the anxious pre-battle stillness, Salim couldn't quite make himself believe it. The girl had proven herself as well as any legionnaire—more, if he wanted to be fair. She'd saved his life in the markets of Axis, and held herself together in the face of some of the strangest things a mortal could bear witness to. She was smart, she was fast, and she was stubborn—all things which he knew could be said about him, in his better moments. And if it made him uneasy to take her into combat, to see that delicate skin go before the sword, then that was his problem, his weakness. The girl had earned her place. He squeezed her arm again, and she stopped shuffling and smiled up at him.

A new light, as bright as the sun but from the wrong direction, suddenly flared into being over one of the cathedral's towers. Brilliant white, the cloud of ghostly orbs whirled and swarmed through each other like fist-sized fireflies, leaving golden comet-tails behind them. From east of the church, a howling clamor rose.

"That's it. Come on." Salim shook out the sack and handed Neila the slim sword they'd taken from the guardsman, buckling Olar's heavier weapon around his own waist. The weight was off, tugging hard against his hip without a counterbalance, but comforting nonetheless. He took hold of Neila's shoulders.

"Ready?"

She nodded.

Tensing his arms, Salim opened himself to the goddess.

The sick thing was that it got easier every time, his disgust carrying the uncomfortable knowledge that, given time, he might even grow to like it. As it was, it was all Salim could do to keep his hands steady as he let Pharasma's filth—death magic and birth magic, the slick of placenta and musk of the grave—slide through him, into him. He called, not with words but with his need, and the Lady of Graves answered.

Neila disappeared. Only the sensation of flesh under his hands and the girl's soft gasp of surprise gave lie to the illusion. She shifted, and he gripped harder.

"Don't move," he said. One of his hands crabbed awkwardly down an arm that wasn't there until he found her hand, which he placed on his belt. "If we get separated, you won't be able to find me. If there's a fight, I'll go visible, and you press yourself up against the nearest wall and stay there until I'm done or I ask for your help." He put special emphasis on *ask*—he didn't want her getting in the way or wasting such powerful magic unless absolutely necessary. "Otherwise, you keep hold of me. Understood?"

There was a pause, and he could imagine her nodding. Then, "Understood."

"Good," Salim said, then stopped stalling and let the goddess's magic, which still writhed beneath his skin, finish what it had come to do.

There was a brief burst of light as his corneas became transparent, then adjusted to the new situation. Salim rarely used such intense magic, and felt the momentary disorientation and nausea as his brain tried to process the absence of his arms and legs—all those parts that should be visible. He closed his eyes for a moment and breathed, letting the vertigo settle. Invisibility was like fumbling in the dark—you couldn't see where your hands and feet were, even out of your peripheral vision. You had to feel them, to trust your kinetic memory.

Neila tugged on his belt. "Salim?"

"I'm still here," he said. "Let's go."

Together they moved out of the alley and ran across the wide street that split like a river around the cathedral, angling toward the window Salim had chosen earlier. From the other side of the temple, the shouts and screams had doubled and tripled, joined by the smashing of glass and the muffled reports of explosions. Salim could easily imagine the scene—fey bursting from hiding and flooding through the city streets in an angry mob, whooping and waving their blazing brands as they converged on the church. In the face of that yammering horde, who could be expected to worry about watching the back door?

With the goddess's magic shielding them, the infiltrators didn't bother scaling the low fence around the churchyard, instead passing straight through the little side gate and then running, silent and unseen, toward the target window. It was small compared to the massive stained-glass creations that were even now shattering under the fey's onslaught, but it was open to allow the desert breeze access.

At its foot, Salim stretched up and poked his head inside. The long hallway was empty save for the echoes of panicked shouts and running footfalls, no doubt headed for the eastern side. He withdrew and used his hands to make a step for Neila, communicating its location by touch. Then he straightened, grabbed the sill, and muscled himself over the shoulder-high barrier, tumbling inside without a sound.

In the corridor, there was a moment of silent scrambling, and then his hands found Neila's and placed them once more on the back of his belt. So far, so good. Keeping their shoulders to the wall in case someone came charging down the corridor, Salim moved quickly and instinctively, trusting to a lifetime—or several of them—of experience with Pharasma's churches to give him the cathedral's basic layout.

His instincts led them true. Within minutes they had passed into more populated chambers, moving slowly and carefully as all around them brothers and sisters in dark robes stampeded like frightened horses down the halls, attempting to secure the cathedral against a siege it had never been intended to weather. After all, what sort of maniacs attacked the clerics of birth and death? At one point the intruders passed an archway opening onto the main entry hall, where several monks strained to lift an enormous wooden bar into place, sealing the main doors. Salim turned right, leading them down a corridor they both recognized.

"Khoyar will go for height," he had told Neila, as they waited in the alley, "the better to view the situation and direct his people. His chambers are in the tallest of the spires. That's where he'll be."

It was a gamble. If Khoyar were a military man, he might think twice about such a position—exposed, isolated—and instead opt for something more central as his command post, trusting to sentries and runners to observe enemy movements. Yet Salim didn't think Khoyar would do that. To do so would require trust—in his subordinates' observations, and in their unsupervised presence in his quarters—as well as a certain understanding of his own vulnerability. Salim didn't think the man had either. So he and Neila moved quickly through the church, angling for the now familiar spiral staircase.

And stopped short, reflexively pulling themselves up against the wall. There was a man on the staircase.

It was Hasam. The excitable little acolyte's usual expression had been replaced by fear and a grim, if shaky, determination. He stood on the third stair up from the floor, a long spear held horizontally so that its ends almost touched the walls on either side, barring the way.

Salim swore softly. The stairway was wide enough for them to slip past without touching the man, but there was no way they could slip under or over the spear without brushing it or making some telltale noise. There was no help for it. He reached for his sword.

Neila's hand covered his, stopping the draw. A voice in his ear whispered, "No. Let me."

Salim resisted for a moment, then let his hand drop. Tugging softly at his belt, Neila led him smoothly forward, until they stood less than an arm's length from the sweating priest.

"Hasam."

The little man squeaked and thrust the spear forward, forcing Salim to leap backward to avoid being skewered. Neila stayed with him, moving them even closer to the bug-eyed priest.

"Hasam," she said again, only the voice wasn't hers. This one was husky, commanding. "Why do you work against my will, child?"

The priest goggled, head whipping from side to side in search of the speaker. He paused as the words sunk in, then breathed, "Goddess?"

"Khoyar has betrayed my faith, Hasam." The voice was a rich purr. "He has led this church astray. And now his judgment has come."

Hasam sank to his knees, the spear forgotten. On his wide-cheeked face was the rapturous terror unique to prophets and madmen. "My lady," he whispered, "what would you have me do?"

Neila didn't hesitate. "Do you serve faithfully, Hasam? Do you live in the shadow of the Spire, and seek judgment in your course?"

"Yes, yes!"

"Then go." The voice was hard, final. "Leave here. Hide yourself away in the catacombs, among those who have passed beyond. When Khoyar's judgment is complete, you will return and speak of my words. You will rise to lead this church, in faith."

"Thank you, Goddess." There were tears streaming down Hasam's face, curving around the trembling smile. "Thank you."

"Now go."

Hasam went, fleeing down the staircase into the crypts, stumbling over his robes without bothering to lift them. In seconds he was gone, the sound of his gasps and careening trajectory receding into the ground.

"That was lucky," Salim said. "He might have screamed for help."

"No, he wouldn't." Neila's voice was calm and back in its normal register. "What does any priest want more than divine revelation? And a little mandated self-aggrandizement doesn't hurt."

"True. Let's just hope Pharasma doesn't mind being impersonated."

Her unseen figure, soft and lithe, pressed itself into his back.

"Who's the one setting fire to her church?" she whispered, breath warm in his ear. "And since when do you care about upsetting the Lady of Graves?"

Salim grinned. He was really starting to like this girl. "What if he realizes he's been tricked and tells someone?"

"Then we'll have to move quickly, won't we?" She grabbed his hand and began pulling him up the stairs.

They climbed. With only the small windows in the tower walls, Khoyar hadn't bothered to set any more guards. Within minutes they were at the landing leading into the high priest's chambers. Through the door, Salim could hear the voices of several people, mostly men.

He gripped Neila's hand, and she gripped back in answer. Then he let it drop and drew his sword, using his free hand to test the door latch.

It was unlocked. He took one last breath, then let the door swing open, moving in and pulling the ghost of Neila along in his wake.

Khoyar was there, conversing heatedly with several other priests. Two Salim recognized by the stoles on their robes—a thin young woman a few years older than Neila, wearing the robes of the church's high priest of birth, and an older man with thin gray hair and sad eyes whose embroidery identified him as the high priest of prophecy. In theory, both positions were of equal status to Khoyar's as the high priest of death, but in Salim's experience one priest often rose above the others to take charge, as Khoyar clearly had here. The two supposed peers stood in an unconsciously servile line on the window side of the room, flanked by two men in the plain robes of rank-and-file priests, while Khoyar paced back and forth, haranguing them with sweeping hand gestures.

None of the five noticed the door open. Salim didn't bother stopping to listen to Khoyar's lecture. Instead he slipped silently around behind the high priest and embraced him, one arm curving around Khoyar's stomach, the other bringing the blade of his sword to the man's throat. He saw the other priests' jaws drop open as the shroud of invisibility fell away.

"Hello, Khoyar."

Salim had to give the man credit. The priest faltered for only a second, and when he moved it was without the slightest regard for the blade under his chin. Faster than Salim would have imagined, Khoyar dropped, jerking his head backward to avoid the sword and ducking violently out of Salim's grasp. He threw himself sideways, away from both Salim and the group, and came up in a crouch. His hand shot out in Salim's direction.

Only Salim's reflexes saved him. While his mind was still marveling at the high priest's response, instincts that had seen him through a hundred battles were already hurling him down and forward as the light in the room seemed to draw into Khoyar's palm, coalescing around it in an almost physical sphere. At the priest's shout, it exploded outward in a line of brilliant fire that stabbed over Salim's right shoulder, barely missing his head. Salim felt the heat against his ear like a cattle brand and smelled burning hair.

Then he was within reach of Khoyar once more. Grabbing the still outstretched arm—the one meant to burn a hole through his chest—Salim let his momentum carry him slightly past the priest, twisting so that the arm locked out straight and backward. Then he lifted his sword arm up, bent it, and brought it down.

Khoyar screamed as his elbow shattered. His ruined arm went limp, now bent in a direction no god had ever intended. Unsatisfied, Salim swung around behind Khoyar a second time, not letting go of the man's arm, feeling the bones grate against each other as he twisted the limb up and flat against the priest's back. This time the sword that snaked around to Khoyar's throat dug deep enough to draw a trickle of blood.

One of the unmarked priests found his courage. Clutching at the silver spiral of Pharasma hanging from a chain around his neck, he raised his free hand and pointed it toward Salim, the fingers closing partway as if grasping an invisible ball.

Salim felt his body stiffen, his limbs going numb and rigid under the assault of the spell, unable to so much as turn his head to follow the spellcaster's movements. His chest constricted, the numbness spreading up his arms and legs and into his torso.

And then he was free again. Across the room, the priest casting the spell yowled and clutched at his arm, his robes darkening with blood where the suddenly visible Neila had snicked through tendons with the point of her sword. She menaced them with the bloodstained blade, and all four fell back, allowing her to herd them into a tight knot in the corner.

In Salim's painful hold, Khoyar had ceased his screaming, and now only moaned through gritted teeth, staying as still as possible to avoid jostling his ravaged arm. When he could draw a full, ragged breath, he spoke, his words aimed at Salim.

"So you're here," he said, voice wavering. "Now what?"

Salim gave the arm a little jiggle, and Khoyar hissed in pain.

"Now," Salim said, raising his voice so that the priests huddled in the corner could hear it clearly, "we're going to tell these people the truth. About how you lost your faith and betrayed the church, murdering Faldus Anvanory for his dose of sun orchid elixir.

How you attempted to pin the crime on his grieving daughter."

"I—" Khoyar began, but the word cut off in a howl as Salim tugged on the arm, making a tutting noise with his tongue.

"No," Salim said, "don't start yet. It's important that we do this properly, don't you agree?" He lifted his head and looked toward the priests. "You. As there's only one dose of the elixir, I can't imagine that any of you are in on Khoyar's heresy. At least one of you must be capable of using magic to tell lies from truth. Who is it?"

There was some staring and shuffling of feet, and then the sad-eyed priest of prophecy stepped forward, careful not to get too close to the point of Neila's threatening sword. "I am capable of such divinations," he said.

"Good. Use them." Salim looked to Neila, whose sword had shifted to point at the speaking priest. "It's okay, Neila. I suspect these people will want to know the truth about their former leader as much as we want them to hear it."

Beyond her, the two attendant priests looked awkward, but the young birth-priest's face was hard and determined. She inclined her head slightly.

The man who'd stepped forward lifted the sign of Pharasma in both hands, whispering to the smooth silver of the spiral as one thumb traced its curve from the outside in. He kissed it and pressed it to his forehead, then let it drop. "I am ready."

"Ready to hear how Khoyar summoned a monster of pure chaos to murder an innocent man and hold his soul for ransom? How he forsook the church in an attempt to cheat his own goddess of her due? It's a hell of a story, really."

But of course that was enough. The prophetic priest's face went slack as Pharasma's own magic confirmed Salim's accusations. He turned those wet hound's eyes on his former compatriot. "Khoyar," he said. "Oh, Khoyar—how could you?"

But Khoyar wasn't paying the old man any attention. He squirmed around in an attempt to face Salim, and Salim allowed him the motion, releasing his grip and rising from his own crouch only to put a boot in Khoyar's chest, driving him to the floor. Salim's sword pricked the hollow of the man's chin, but Khoyar ignored it, sprawled back on his good elbow and glaring up at Salim.

"What do you know of it?" he spat. "How could you possibly understand what it is to grow old, to face death as not just a possibility, but an inevitability?"

Some of Salim's surprise must have registered on his face, for Khoyar laughed hoarsely, baring his teeth.

"Oh yes, Salim Ghadafar—I know all about you. I know that you already sold out your own faith—or lack of it—once in exchange for immortality. And to do what?" He attempted to gesture at Neila with his broken arm and grimaced, settling for a shrug. "To hunt skeletons and seduce stupid girls? I would have led this church for a thousand years—risen in the ranks, brought Pharasma's worship to countless souls—but you've wasted your time. The goddess's greatest gift, and you've wasted it. You who believe in nothing." He gave a laugh that was half cough. "Who are you to speak of heresy?"

"Khoyar," the old priest said again, sadly, but no one was listening to him.

Without moving his sword, Salim reached down to Khoyar's good hand and slid the ring—the silver circle that the gem had revealed as Faldus Anvanory's prison—off the priest's finger. Khoyar made no move to stop him. Salim palmed the ring but stayed bent, looking deep into the man's eyes.

"You truly know nothing," Salim said, his voice not angry now, but quiet. "Only someone who's never tasted immortality could think my life is a gift. You of all people should know this."

Then he cut Khoyar's throat.

Neila flinched and looked away as the blood sprayed and gradually slowed, but the other priests had no such compunctions. They watched, faces set, as their former leader kicked once and was still.

Suddenly very tired, Salim went to one knee in the spreading pool and closed Khoyar's eyes for the last time. Then he bent further and whispered in the man's ear.

From somewhere far below them came the crashing of glass, and Salim became aware once again of the sounds of rampant destruction drifting up from lower floors. He wiped his sword clean on the priest's robes, then sheathed it and drew the stained stole of office from around Khoyar's neck. He stood and addressed the room.

"I have carried out the goddess's judgment," he intoned, "as I was sent to. If you doubt me, cast your own auguries, but I have no further business here. I trust that you will set things right with Lady Anvanory and the Lamasaran authorities." He held up the ring. "I also expect that you will work to free Faldus Anvanory's soul from this object, so that he may be properly resurrected, as per his original contract with your church. Am I understood?"

The two high priests nodded, and the other clerics followed their lead.

"Then in the name of Pharasma, the Lady of Graves, I leave this church in your care." He tossed the bloody stole to the priest who'd cast the divinatory magic, and the man caught it easily.

"Fly that from one of the eastern windows, and the fey will cease their attack." Salim looked hard at each of the high priests in turn. "You will not allow retaliation against the fey. They may have damaged your church, but they've saved its soul. I advise you to view its repairs as penance."

"Of course," the young birth-priest said, bowing.

"Then go."

They left, filing out down the tower's narrow stairway. When they were gone, Salim moved over to the wide eastern windows and looked out, past the flickering lights of the fey torches and the steadier lights of the city's first evening lanterns, toward the distant river.

Still holding her bloodied sword, Neila moved up beside him and took his hand. She was quiet for a moment, taking in the skyline. Then she spoke.

"What did you say to him?" she asked. "At the end."

Salim didn't turn. Outside, the sun had almost set behind them, bathing the world in blood and gold.

"I told him that death was the goddess's only true gift," he said. "And that he should make the most of it."

Then they were quiet again, and stood and watched as the long shadows of the cathedral reached out to swallow the city.

Chapter Twenty-Two
Everything Forever

S alim leaned back in his chair and sipped at the cold tea. At his side, the scabbard of his sword—*his* sword, its disfigured hilt gleaming in the sun—clanked against the thin metal struts of the chair, its familiar weight as comforting as a child's stuffed toy. It was matched by the unnaturally cold circle of the amulet against his bare chest, beneath his robes.

Across the long yard and gardens of Anvanory Manor, Olar—now dressed in the official robes of the Anvanorys' new majordomo—shouted good-naturedly at several men attempting to muscle an enormous trunk on top of a stack that was already threatening to overwhelm the flatbed cart. Near them, the kitchen door swung in an unending oscillation as a constant stream of serving women ran back and forth, calling requests to the porters. In the distance, empty fields waved with the breeze, bereft of men and plows.

Despite all the commotion, the little paved veranda where they sat was quiet, its round table and two chairs positioned to give the best view of the greenery down at the river's edge. Neila held her own teacup in both hands, sipping slowly as they watched the trees shiver and whisper, their leaves quaking against the cloudless blue sky.

"I still would have thought he'd come back," she said.

Salim nodded his agreement.

"I mean, after all that—to spend your life working toward a goal, and achieve it, only to let it go so casually." She took a drink. "It doesn't make sense."

"It does if you realize your goal wasn't worth having," Salim said. In truth, he'd been equally surprised by Faldus's reaction. Upon being released from his imprisonment by the Pharasmin priests, the late Lord Anvanory had been overjoyed, effusive in his thanks—and then promptly refused resurrection, offering only a few loving words for his daughter before departing for the Boneyard and points beyond.

"What most people fear about death," Salim continued, "isn't really death. It's the unknown, the uncertainty. While Faldus was alive, those things terrified him. Once he was dead, there was nothing left to be afraid of. Faldus has seen what death has to offer, swum through the astral void and seen Pharasma's Spire twist up from the heart of everything." He paused. "He understands that it's a reward, not a punishment."

Neila said nothing, but the set of her lips still held a twist of uncertainty. Salim changed the subject. "Where will you go?"

She shrugged. "The paperwork is complete. Once I leave, the land is Delini's. With my inheritance—unquestioned, this time—I'm a very rich woman. I suppose I could go back to Taldor and renew our old acquaintances there. Perhaps find someone to teach me a little magic of my own." She smirked and wiggled her fingers. "Wizard magic. No churches."

"A sound decision." Salim tried to smile back at her, but must have made a poor show of it, for her own wavered and dropped. Her eyes flicked to the object they'd both been ignoring. In the center of the table, a squared-off glass vial no bigger than an inkwell squatted, its transparent core filled with amber liquid. There was no label. Only the lead seal on the stopper bore any markings at all: an impression, as from a signet ring, in the delicate shape of a sun orchid blossom.

"And that?" Salim asked, gently.

Neila refused to look at the bottle again. Instead she reached across the table, removing Salim's teacup and taking his hand. "We've been a good team, haven't we, Salim?"

Please, his mind whispered. Please don't. But he said only, "We have."

"I've been useful. I've saved your life twice now, and held my own against things no one else in this whole city has imagined, let alone seen."

Salim's chest was tight, tighter than it had been when the priest had held him with magic in Khoyar's tower. "You've done wonderfully, Neila. Truly. There's fire in you, girl. You'll do well."

She gripped his hand hard. "This doesn't have to end here, Salim." Her eyes were bright with tears, but also with excitement. "It doesn't have to end at all. The elixir is mine now." She smiled, the expression so warm and radiant that he might have wept.

"You don't have to be alone anymore."

As she said it, he realized that it was true. All of it. She would come with him, eagerly, readily, wherever his burden carried him. She would stand beside him, would laugh with him, would watch his back when things got ugly. And when she grew too old for their adventures, she would drink the elixir and return to the flower of her youth, using her investments here to purchase another potion. An unending cycle.

She saw his recognition and drove the dagger home.

"We can be together, Salim. Always."

In response, he stood and moved around the table to where she sat, still holding her hand. He looked down at her, at the incongruous blue eyes wet with emotion.

He loved her. There was no question. In just a few days, she'd gotten under his skin, made him alternately furious and protective—made him feel what no one since Jannat, his wife from a lifetime ago, had been able to. And just like with Jannat, he had to make a choice.

He leaned down and kissed her hard, her mouth soft against his, the fingers of his free hand wrapping themselves in the long, dark hair.

Once he had been offered a choice, and he had taken it, robbing the woman he loved of the death that was hers by right. Now he was offered another: to take this girl—this beautiful, firebrand young woman—from the life that was hers, and make her a part of his own strange existence.

He broke the kiss and tilted her chin up with two fingers, caressing her cheek.

"The fact that you can say that," he said gently, "is proof that you don't yet understand."

Then he straightened, turned, and walked away.

Behind him, the girl said nothing, only stared at his retreating form and then, long after he had turned onto the road and disappeared, at the little vial on the table.

Considering.

Epilogue

Salim followed the road. At his feet, the desert wind kicked up little flurries of dust, turning the black of his robes a dirty beige. Eventually the dust would cover the road completely, and men would have to come to carve its route anew. And then, one day, the men would be gone, and the desert would reclaim the road as if it had never been. It was the way of things.

He felt the blood, half-expected, and made no effort to wipe at it, only stopped and turned.

The angel hung in the air behind him, its black wings sharp against the distant dunes.

"Hello, Salim." Its smile was beatific. "I've come with commendations. You've done a marvelous job."

In response, Salim spat, the blood and saliva barely missing the angel's pointed toes. It landed in the road and disappeared beneath the shifting dust. When he spoke, his words were dry and cracked.

"I'd prefer some answers."

"Oh?" The angel arched an eyebrow in polite interest, and Salim's grip tightened on his sword hilt until his fingers were half numb.

"This was a setup from the beginning, wasn't it?" It took all the self-control in Salim's body to keep his voice from shaking. "You knew from the beginning who was responsible, and why. Yet you sent me anyway."

The angel's expression was less saintly now, dangerously close to smug. "And what makes you say that?"

"It's obvious!" Salim roared, then wrestled himself back to a more conversational volume. "Pharasma kept answering Khoyar's prayers, giving him the spells he needed, all while he was performing the greatest heresy in her church. Don't tell me she didn't know what he was doing. She granted his requests. She knew. So why didn't her other priests' divinations about the murder expose him? Why didn't you *do* anything?"

"But Salim," the angel said, folding its hands patiently. "We did do something. We sent you."

As quickly as it had come, the anger in Salim collapsed, giving way to exhaustion. He let go of his sword, arms hanging at his sides like lead weights. "I don't understand."

"Of course you do," the angel chided. "Who better to hunt a priest? But that's not what you mean. You want to know why Pharasma didn't simply kill Khoyar where he stood as soon as he turned from her. And the answer is faith."

"Faith?"

Ceyanan reached out a hand and brushed a lock of hair back from Salim's forehead.

"Faith, Salim. Khoyar always had a choice, right up until the end. At any point, he could have repented, rediscovered his faith, and been—if not absolved—at least part of the natural order once again. By letting things play out to the very end, the goddess gave him every possible chance at redemption. And as her agent, you represented that freedom, that choice."

The angel withdrew its hand. "It's a shame, really. Free will is the greatest gift of the gods. Yet give mortals enough rope, and most will eventually hang themselves."

Salim grimaced. "Myself included?"

The angel laughed.

"Oh no, Salim," it said. "You're the rope."

Then the angel faded away and was gone, leaving only another flurry of dust in the rapidly building storm. Salim was alone once more.

Sighing, he turned and continued down the road.

About the Author

James Lafond Sutter is an award-winning game designer, author, and musician, as well as the Fiction Editor for Paizo Publishing. In addition to *Death's Heretic*, he has written extensively for the Pathfinder's Journal in Pathfinder Adventure Path, and his short fiction has also appeared in such venues as *Black Gate*, *Apex Magazine*, *Catastrophia* (PS Publishing) and the #1 Amazon best-seller *Machine of Death*. His RPG credits include such books as *City of Strangers*, *Misfit Monsters Redeemed*, *The Inner Sea World Guide*, and the *Pathfinder RPG GameMastery Guide*, and his Planet Stories anthology *Before They Were Giants* pairs the first published stories of science fiction and fantasy greats such as Larry Niven, Cory Doctorow, China Miéville, and William Gibson with new interviews and writing advice from the authors themselves.

James lives in the Ministry of Awesome, a house in Seattle consisting of five roommates and a fully functional death ray. For more information, visit **jameslsutter.com**.

Acknowledgments

This book would not have been possible without a number of people: Paizo Publisher Erik Mona, for saying "this guy should write a novel!" before he knew that "this guy" was me. Christopher Paul Carey, for his invaluable edits and literary camaraderie. The rest of the Paizo team, for backing my play. My family, for fostering the delusion that "author" was a viable career choice. The Wabi kids in general and the Ministry boys in specific, for their sanity checks and constant enthusiasm. And of course Margo, whose love and support never wavered, even when finishing the novel meant spending whole weekends in my bathrobe.

I owe you all more than I can say.

Glossary

All Pathfinder Tales novels are set in the rich and vibrant world of the Pathfinder campaign setting. Below are explanations of a number of key terms used in this book. For more information on the world of Golarion and the strange monsters, people, and deities that make it their home, see the *Pathfinder Roleplaying Game Core Rulebook*, *The Inner Sea World Guide*, or any of the books in the Pathfinder Campaign Setting series, or visit **paizo.com**.

Abadar: God of merchants, law, and cities.

Abadaran: Of or related to Abadar or his worshipers.

Abaddon: Evil plane devoted to destruction and home to daemons.

Absalom: Major island city of the Inner Sea.

Abyss: A plane of evil and chaos ruled by demons.

Adamantine Crucible: Massive factory where the mechanical armies of Axis are constructed.

Avistan: Continent north of the Inner Sea.

Axiomites: Sentient mathematical abstractions given humanoid form. Native to Axis.

Axis, the Eternal City: A plane of absolute order, entirely urban in nature.

Azir: Capital of Rahadoum.

Boneyard: Pharasma's realm, where all souls go to be judged after death.

Brownies: Small fairies.

Calistria: Also known as the Savored Sting; the goddess of trickery, lust, and revenge.

Calistrian: Of or related to Calistria or her worshipers.

Cassomir: Port city in Taldor.

Cerulean Void: The Maelstrom.

Cheliax: Devil-worshiping nation in Avistan.

Daemons: Evil denizens of Abaddon who exist to devour mortal souls.

Dawnflower: Sarenrae.

Demons: Denizens of the Abyss who seek only to maim, ruin, and feed.

Devils: Fiendish occupants of Hell who seek to corrupt mortals in order to claim their souls.

Dryads: Fey women who bond with trees.

Egorian: Capital of the devil-worshiping nation of Cheliax on the continent of Avistan.

Eldest: Fey lords of the First World.

Elves: Race of long-lived, beautiful humanoids. Identifiable by their pointed ears, lithe bodies, and pupils so large their eyes appear to be one color.

Elysium: Outer plane where good-natured, freedom-loving souls go when they die.

Erages: Village in the elven nation of Kyonin.

Erastil: Stag-headed god of farming, hunting, and family, also known as Old Deadeye.

Ethereal Plane: Plane of mists and nothingness just beyond the material world.

Fey: Fairies, magical creatures of the natural world.

First Law: The law by which religion is outlawed in Rahadoum.

First Vault: Vast storehouse on Axis where Abadar keeps a perfect master copy of everything in existence.

First World: The precursor to the Material Plane, from which fey and gnomes originated.

Garund: Continent south of the Inner Sea, renowned for its deserts and jungles.

Ghouls: Undead creatures that eat corpses and reproduce by infecting living creatures.

Gnomes: Small humanoids with strange mindsets, originally from the First World.

Golarion: The planet on which Thuvia and the rest of the Inner Sea region resides.

Graveyard of Souls: Vast graveyard where many atheist souls go when they die.

Great Beyond: The planes of the afterlife.

Griffon: Magical half-eagle, half-lion creature.

Half-Elves: The children of unions between elves and humans. Taller, longer-lived, and generally more graceful and attractive than the average human, yet not nearly so much so as their full elven kin.

Half-Orcs: Bred from humans and orcs, members of this race have green or gray skin, brutish appearances, and short tempers, and are mistrusted by many societies.

Halflings: Race of humanoids known for their tiny stature, deft hands, and mischievous personalities.

Hell: A plane of absolute law and evil, where evil souls go after they die to be tormented and transformed by the native devils.

Imentesh: Protean of the diplomat caste.

Inner Sea: The central sea between Avistan and Garund. Abuts Thuvia along the nation's northern border.

Iomedae: Crusader goddess of valor and justice.

Katapesh: Merchant nation southeast of Thuvia.

Keketar: Protean of the ruling priest caste.

Kelesh: Empire far to the east of Thuvia.

Keleshite: Of or related to the Empire of Kelesh.

Kingdom of Man: Rahadoum.

Kyonin: Nation of elves, far north of Thuvia.

Lady of Graves: The goddess Pharasma.

Lamasara: Prominent river city in Thuvia.

Maelstrom: Plane of absolute chaos, whose form is constantly shifting.

Manaket: City on Rahadoum's northern coast.

Material Plane: The fundamental plane of existence on which Golarion resides, and to which humans are native. The "normal" world.

Mwangi: Of or related to Garund's central jungle region, known as the Mwangi Expanse.

Nagas: Magical serpents with humanoid heads.

Nemret Noktoria: Underground city of ghouls.

Nirvana: One of the planes where good-natured souls go when they die.

Norgorber: God of assassins, secrets, and murder.

Nymphs: Fey women whose beauty can literally blind those who look at them.

Oppara: Coastal capital of Taldor.

Osirian: Of or pertaining to Osirion.

Osirion: Nation sharing Thuvia's eastern border.

Outer Planes/Outer Sphere: The various realms of the afterlife, where most gods reside.

Path of Salt: Trade route on Garund's northern coast.

Pharasma: The goddess of birth, death, and prophecy, who judges mortal souls after their deaths and sends them on to the appropriate afterlife; also known as the Lady of Graves.

Pharasma's Boneyard: Pharasma's realm.

Pharasma's Spire: The plane on which Pharasma's realm may be found.

Pharasmin: Of or related to the goddess Pharasma or her worshipers.

Pixies: Small fairies with the ability to fly.

Protean: Insane serpentine resident of the Maelstrom. A creature of pure chaos.

Pure Legion: Elite military enforcers of Rahadoum's government-mandated atheism.

Rahadoum: Atheist nation where religion is outlawed. Abuts Thuvia's western border.

Rahadoumi: Of or related to Rahadoum.

River of Souls: Unending procession of recently deceased souls traveling from the Material Plane to Pharasma's Boneyard for judgment.

River Styx: River that runs through many different Outer Planes.

Sarenite: Or or related to the goddess Sarenrae or her worshipers.

Sarenrae: Warrior goddess of the sun, healing, and redemption, also known as the Dawnflower.

Satyrs: Male fey with horns and the legs of goats.

Shepherd's Rock: Stronghold and training center for Rahadoum's Pure Legion.

Sothis: Capital of Osirion.

Sun Orchid Elixir: An extremely rare potion produced only in Thuvia, capable of temporarily reversing the effects of aging and prolonging one's life.

Taldan: Of or related to Taldor.

Taldane: The common trade language of Golarion's Inner Sea region.

Taldor: A decadent nation northeast of Thuvia.

Thuvia: Desert nation on the Inner Sea, famous for the production of the magical sun orchid elixir.

Thuvian: Of or related to Thuvia.

Yanmass: City in northern Taldor.

F or half-elven Pathfinder Varian Jeggare and his devil-
blooded bodyguard Radovan, things are rarely as they
seem. Yet not even the notorious crime-solving duo are
prepared for what they find when a search for a missing
Pathfinder takes them into the gothic and mist-shrouded
mountains of Ustalav.

Beset on all sides by noble intrigue, curse-afflicted
villagers, suspicious monks, and the deadly creatures of the
night, Varian and Radovan must use sword and spell to track
the strange rumors to their source and uncover a secret of
unimaginable proportions, aided in their quest by a pack
of sinister werewolves and a mysterious, mute priestess.
But it'll take more than merely solving the mystery to finish
this job. For shadowy figures have taken note of the pair's
investigations, and the forces of darkness are set on making
sure neither man gets out of Ustalav alive . . .

From fan-favorite author Dave Gross, author of *Black
Wolf* and *Lord of Stormweather*, comes a new fantastical
mystery set in the award-winning world of the Pathfinder
Roleplaying Game.

Prince of Wolves print edition: $9.99
ISBN: 978-1-60125-287-6

Prince of Wolves ebook edition:
ISBN: 978-1-60125-331-6

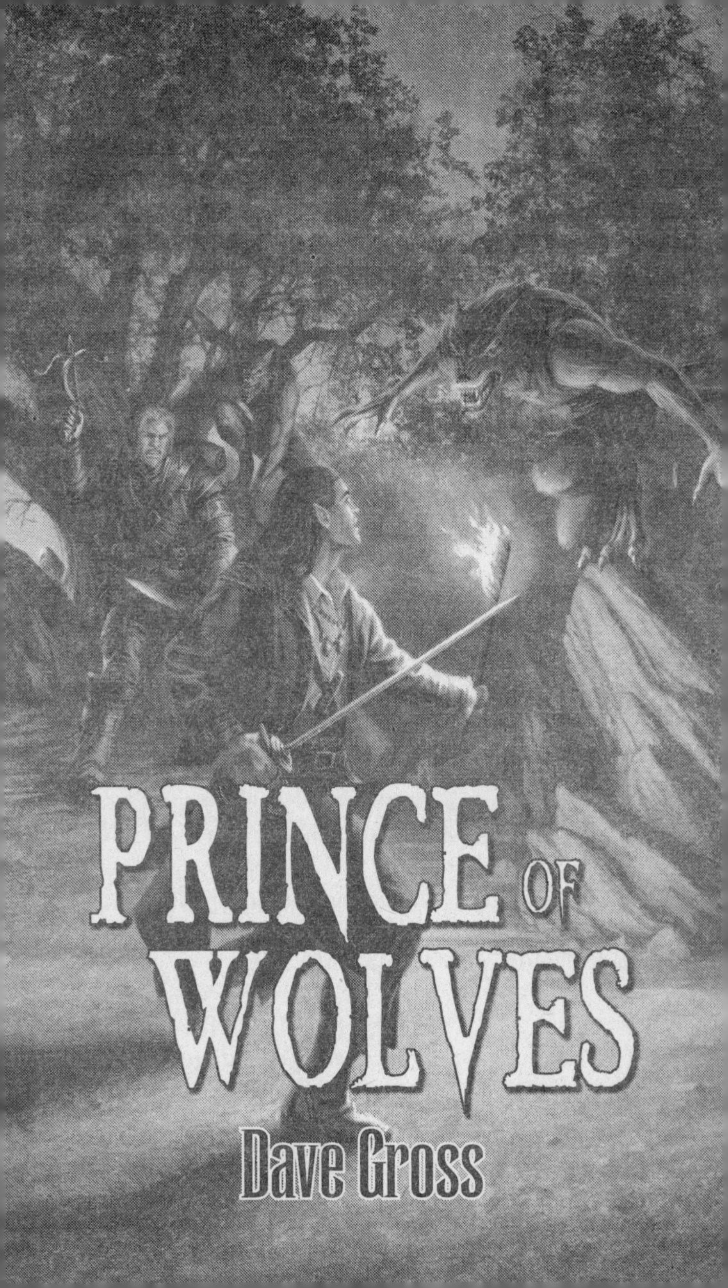
PRINCE OF
WOLVES
Dave Gross

In a village of the frozen north, a child is born possessed by a strange and alien spirit, only to be cast out by her tribe and taken in by the mysterious winter witches of Irrisen, a land locked in permanent magical winter. Farther south, a young mapmaker with a penchant for forgery discovers that his sham treasure maps have begun striking gold.

This is the story of Ellasif, a barbarian shield maiden who will stop at nothing to recover her missing sister, and Declan, the ne'er-do-well young spellcaster-turned-forger who wants only to prove himself to the woman he loves. Together they'll face monsters, magic, and the fury of Ellasif's own cold-hearted warriors in their quest to rescue the lost child. Yet when they finally reach the ice-walled city of Whitethrone, where trolls hold court and wolves roam the streets in human guise, will it be too late to save the girl from the forces of darkness?

From *New York Times* best-selling author Elaine Cunningham comes a fantastic new adventure of swords and sorcery, set in the award-winning world of the Pathfinder Roleplaying Game.

Winter Witch print edition: $9.99
ISBN: 978-1-60125-286-9

Winter Witch ebook edition:
ISBN: 978-1-60125-332-3

Winter Witch

Elaine Cunningham

The race is on to free Lord Stelan from the grip of a wasting curse, and only his old mercenary companion, the Forsaken elf Elyana, has the wisdom—and the swordcraft—to uncover the identity of his tormenter and free her old friend before the illness takes its course.

When the villain turns out to be another of their former companions, Elyana sets out with a team of adventurers including Stelan's own son on a dangerous expedition across the revolution-wracked nation of Galt and the treacherous Five Kings Mountains. There, pursued by a bloodthirsty militia and beset by terrible nightmare beasts, they discover the key to Stelan's salvation in a lost valley warped by weird magical energies. Will they be able to retrieve the artifact the dying lord so desperately needs? Or will the shadowy face of betrayal rise up from within their own ranks?

From Howard Andrew Jones, managing editor of the acclaimed sword and sorcery magazine *Black Gate*, comes a classic quest of loyalty and magic set in the award-winning world of the Pathfinder Roleplaying Game.

Plague of Shadows print edition: $9.99
ISBN: 978-1-60125-291-3

Plague of Shadows ebook edition:
ISBN: 978-1-60125-333-0

Plague
of
Shadows

Howard Andrew Jones

In the foreboding north, the demonic hordes of the magic-twisted hellscape known as the Worldwound encroach upon the southern kingdoms of Golarion. Their latest escalation embroils a preternaturally handsome and coolly charismatic swindler named Gad, who decides to assemble a team of thieves, cutthroats, and con men to take the fight into the demon lands and strike directly at the fiendish leader responsible for the latest raids—the demon Yath, the Shimmering Putrescence. Can Gad hold his team together long enough to pull off the ultimate con, or will trouble from within his own organization lead to an untimely end for them all?

From gaming legend and popular fantasy author Robin D. Laws comes a fantastic new adventure of swords and sorcery, set in the award-winning world of the Pathfinder Roleplaying Game.

The Worldwound Gambit print edition: $9.99
ISBN: 978-1-60125-327-9

The Worldwound Gambit ebook edition:
ISBN: 978-1-60125-334-7

the WORLDWOUND Gambit

Robin D. Laws

On a mysterious errand for the Pathfinder Society, Count Varian Jeggare and his hellspawn bodyguard Radovan journey to the distant land of Tian Xia. When disaster forces him to take shelter in a warrior monastery, "Brother" Jeggare finds himself competing with the disciples of the Dragon Temple as he unravels a royal mystery. Meanwhile, Radovan—trapped in the body of a devil and held hostage by the legendary Quivering Palm attack—must serve a twisted master by defeating the land's deadliest champions and learning the secret of slaying an immortal foe. Together with an unlikely army of beasts and spirits, the two companions must take the lead in an ancient conflict that will carry them through an exotic land all the way to the Gates of Heaven and Hell and a final confrontation with the nefarious Master of Devils.

From fan-favorite author Dave Gross comes a new fantastical adventure set in the award-winning world of the Pathfinder Roleplaying Game.

Master of Devils print edition: $9.99
ISBN: 978-1-60125-357-6

Master of Devils ebook edition:
ISBN: 978-1-60125-358-3

Master of Devils

Dave Gross

To an experienced thief like Krunzle the Quick, the merchant nation of Druma is full of treasures just waiting to be liberated. Yet when the fast-talking scoundrel gets caught stealing from one of the most powerful prophets of Kalistrade, the only option is to undertake a dangerous mission to recover the merchant-lord's runaway daughter—and the magical artifact she took with her. Armed with an arsenal of decidedly unhelpful magical items and chaperoned by an intelligent snake necklace happy to choke him into submission, Krunzle must venture far from the cities of the capitalist utopia and into a series of adventures that will make him a rich man—or a corpse.

From veteran author Hugh Matthews comes a rollicking tale of captive trolls, dwarven revolutionaries, and serpentine magic, set in the award-winning world of the Pathfinder Roleplaying Game.

Song of the Serpent print edition: $9.99
ISBN: 978-1-60125-388-0

Song of the Serpent ebook edition:
ISBN: 978-1-60125-389-7

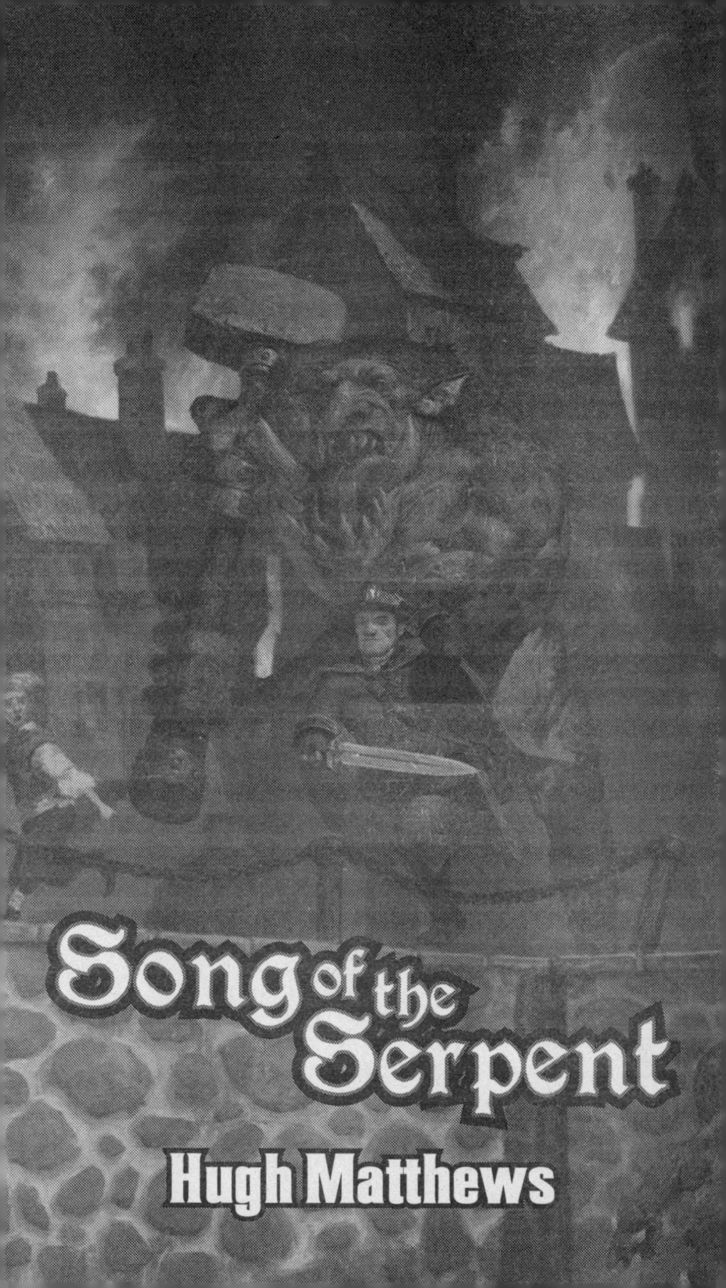
Song of the Serpent
Hugh Matthews

NOVELS!

Tired of carting around a bag full of books? Take your ebook reader or smart phone over to **paizo.com** to download all the Pathfinder Tales novels from authors like Dave Gross and *New York Times* best seller Elaine Cunningham in both ePub and PDF formats, thus saving valuable bookshelf space and 30% off the cover price!

PATHFINDER'S JOURNALS!

Love the fiction in the Adventure Paths, but don't want to haul six books with you on the subway? Download compiled versions of each fully illustrated journal and read it on whatever device you choose!

FREE WEB FICTION!

Tired of paying for fiction at all? Drop by **paizo.com** every week for your next installment of free weekly web fiction as Paizo serializes new Pathfinder short stories from your favorite high-profile fantasy authors. Read 'em for free, or download 'em for cheap and read them anytime, anywhere!

ALL AVAILABLE NOW AT PAIZO.COM!